TERRELL CHAFIN

Awakening

For my wife, Charlie.
She's why I still get up in the morning and go to sleep each night looking forward to another day.

Contents

VI Thursday

I

Saturday

1

Say "High" to the Mushrooms

Rage and Tim found the mushrooms while scouting for dog crap. That may be a more noble statement than the activity warranted. The neighbors had been complaining for days about the smell and Tim and Rage were just looking to see how much effort they would need to expend if they decided to take on the task of shit removal. Tim knew his effort would increase in direct proportion to how much Rage helped, so it was his fervent hope that somehow Rage would see it as too much effort, leaving the whole dog shit removal project to his chump roommate, Tim. Tim could deal with that. It would be quicker. Rage's dog Fatty was a good dog and for the most part did his business in one general area. Unfortunately, Rage and his friends fed the dog anything that their munchies fueled binges inspired them to pursue and sometimes the poor dog just couldn't help himself. So, they were looking in places typically unsullied with Fatty's leftovers.

Rage saw them first, "Dude, check it out."

Tim saw a three-foot circle of fuzzy back mushrooms, ranging in size from tiny ones an inch high and a quarter inch around, to a couple that were eight inches high, and three or maybe even four inches across. The bigger ones had little red and blue markings. He also saw Rage slowly reaching for them, the way a baby might reach a hand out to explore a new toy - or food. He grabbed Rage's arm to keep him from touching them. "Rage, don't touch them. You don't know what they are. They look like they might be poisonous."

Rage answered, "Nah, I know mushrooms, man. I don't know what these are exactly." He paused thoughtfully. "But they don't look like any poison ones I've ever seen."

Tim asked, "So, you've seen poisonous ones?"

Rage didn't respond.

The mushrooms looked like fragile uncircumcised black penises... the kind with red and blue flecks. They had a delicate look about them, like a strong wind could tear their outer membranes. Tim shook his head, "They don't look like any mushrooms I've ever seen before, poisonous or not."

"Hey Dude, not my problem you've led such a sheltered existence. These look fine." With that Rage reached down and picked up a two-inch specimen. He gave it a sniff, and despite his stated confidence that they were safe, took a rather tiny bite and let the morsel of mushroom swirl around in his mouth. He explored it with his tongue for a few seconds before swallowing it, closing his eyes for a moment and tossing the rest into his mouth, smiling.

Rage coughed a little, "Bitter. Tastes like shit. Always a good sign."

Tim shook his head, "What was the point of that? We could have checked it out on the Internet to see what it was."

"Man, you are such a fucking geek. You live in some kind of geeky, baby bubble. How do you think pioneers discovered what was edible and what was nasty?"

"I'm guessing they waited to see who died after sampling unidentified flora."

"Flora? Fuck dude, speak English."

Tim said, "Wait here. I'm going up to the house to get my laptop. I want to check out those mushrooms. Don't eat any more while I'm gone."

Tim headed through the wooded yard up to the house while Rage plopped down in a lawn chair and leaned back, examining the world below and waiting for his new mushrooms to kick in.

Rage's house was situated at the end of a cul-de-sac in an area of Los Angeles known as Mt. Washington and the yard meandered about a hundred yards down a hillside and into a wooded wash. The location where they found the mushrooms was next to where Rage's lawn furniture—an old Formica table and five chairs made from old wine barrels—sat. The barrel chairs had at one time served in the kitchen when Rage was a kid. Over the years, the chairs had made it out to Rage's favorite "getting high" spot. It was about ten yards from a thirty-foot cliff. This area afforded them a great view, one that on the fourth of July let them see no less than seven separate municipal firework displays, ranging from La Canada to the northwest through Pasadena, all the way to, if you could believe Rage—and you really couldn't—Temple City. It was also shielded from the neighbors on the sides by at least a dozen assorted Cypress, Juniper, and Eucalyptus trees and from those down the hill by its distance from the cliff. Rage called it his happy place.

Inside the house, Tim grabbed his laptop off the kitchen table. He glanced around the kitchen, wondering if the cheap rent was worth the filth and drama of living with a perennial fifteen-year-old. He opened the laptop, flipped it on, and carried it by the screen, letting it hang beside him like a kid's teddy bear while it powered up as he headed back out to keep Rage from eating more mushrooms.

When he got to Rage's happy place, he found Rage sprawled in his favorite chair. His eyes were closed, his mouth hung open, his arms were outstretched, and his head lolled back over the edge of the chair. He looked like a crucified skateboarder. Fatty was asleep at his side. After checking Rage to make sure he was breathing, Tim sat down in a barrel chair and searched the Internet for sites about mushrooms. He explored several mushroom sites until he found one that had pictures. He scrolled through several pages and looked through what turned out to be pictures of several hundred different mushrooms. While there was some variety of shapes and sizes, it was clear there were often clusters of forty or fifty that would seem to be closely related.

What he didn't find were any that bore more than a slight resemblance to the mushrooms they had found in the yard. He noted that a number of the hallucinogenic mushrooms did in fact have red and or blue spots. Reading the little descriptions that accompanied the pictures, he could see why these particular shades of red and blue were often associated with so much old school psychedelic art; it was actually an homage to the mushrooms more than to the hallucinogenic effects.

There was one other thing he learned from the site. Some of the same markings were also found on poisonous mushrooms. It made sense, particularly given that the hallucinogenic ones were technically poisonous too. They were just not deadly. He assumed the seriously poisonous ones where probably also hallucinogenic, merely providing more of a one-way trip.

He shook Rage by the shoulder and said, "Rage, we need to take you to the emergency room."

Rage woke up with a start. "Dude, what the..."

Tim asked, "You okay? You know I think those mushrooms may be poisonous."

Rage nodded slowly, "Everything is."

"I mean, those markings are on lots of different mushrooms. All are either hallucinogenic or poisonous."

Rage stared down the hill, blinking. Smiling, he said "My money's on hallucinogenic."

Tim shook his head, "They could be both. Let's head down the hill and make sure you didn't just get poisoned."

Rage shook his head, "I just told you I did. You know, man, everything is poisonous. You want to live forever? Just sit in one place, drink water, and eat rice. You need to just let some shit happen. I may be dying, but I'm pretty sure I already was. On a scale from one to ten, I'd say I'm feeling pretty goddamn good right now."

The whole time he spoke, Rage never turned to look at Tim. He kept his gaze steady down the hill. Tim had known him for about six months, ever since he had answered an ad for a roommate on the bulletin board at school. The room turned out to be huge, cheap, and about a ten-minute bike ride from campus. Sitting in one of Rage's barrel chairs, you could look down into town and see the Occidental College campus below.

Rage wasn't a student at Oxy, and that was one of the reasons this had seemed like such a good place to live. Rage wasn't a student anywhere. In fact, he wasn't really anything anywhere; Rage had no job and had never had one. He lived off a meager inheritance in the house he grew up in. He rented out a room—sometimes two—to make sure he had a little party money. Tim liked the idea of living with someone who wasn't always on the same schedule. His theory had been that he could step out of the madness of cramming and finals, (not to mention the routine weekend bacchanalia of campus) into the relative sanity of civilian life. Of course, once he got to know Rage a little better, he realized not just why the rent was so low, but that sanity could be considered a relative term.

Rage mumbled, "Hey, look at that."

Tim asked, "What?"

"What what?"

"You said, 'Hey, look at that'."

Rage nodded slowly, "Exactly."

Tim waited him out.

Finally, Rage said, "So...is that real?"

Tim looked out in the direction that seemed to be the center of Rage's attention. He said, "I don't see it. Is what real?"

Rage nodded his head slowly, blinking. He stood and took a couple of steps toward the edge of the cliff. He turned and grinned goofily at Tim, "Dude, I think it is!"

Tim started to say, "Is what?" but wasn't able to get it out before Rage ran to the edge of the cliff, and a few steps beyond. Tim ran to the edge of the cliff and looked down to see if Rage was hurt – or worse. Fatty beat him to the cliff and ran from one side of the yard to the other, barking over the edge from various spots, looking for his master. Finally, having the sense to not jump off a thirty-foot ledge, a sense that Rage apparently lacked, the dog sprinted down a path that ran the long way around and down into the wash below.

Looking down over the edge, Tim couldn't see any sign of Rage. All he could see were trees, grass, and rocks. And mushrooms. The whole hillside beneath him was covered with thousands of tiny mushrooms - the kind with red and blue flecks.

2

Animal, Vegetable, or Mineral?

"Animal, vegetable, or mineral?"

Pippi sat on the edge of her bed with her legs crossed, in a fashion her father grew up calling "Indian style." She stared at her father, who sat at her desk and said, "I don't understand."

Pippi's dad, remembering that the current term was "cross-legged," explained, "It's how you start the game. The first question helps you home in on where your second question should begin. You start by asking if the item is animal, vegetable, or mineral."

She shook her head, "But I don't understand what that has to do with anything. I'm thinking of a thing, not any of those things."

Alan McNealy smiled. His daughter had a very direct way of looking at life. She jumped from idea to idea, from game to game, and once she mastered something or got tired of it, it was time for a new thing. The only thing she never seemed to tire of was the whole Pippi phase. Ever since Patty was five and first saw a Pippi Longstocking movie—God help him for showing it to her—she had insisted upon being called Pippi. She wore her hair in pigtails of a Pippi Longstocking style and wore clothes she thought made her resemble the strange little Swedish freak. But it was still Patty's bright little smile that shown out from underneath the whole orange pigtailed, overly striped caricature that his daughter had become, so he could abide by almost all of it as it made her happy. But he drew the line at calling her

Pippi. "Patty, the reason we say animal, vegetable, or mineral, is that it pretty much divides up all matter."

"Not mine. My thing isn't any of them."

Alan shrugged, "Okay then. I guess it must be some kind of alien. Anyway, is it bigger than a bread box?"

Pippi looked at her dad like he was an alien. "What's a bread box?"

"It's just something you say. I'm trying to get an idea of how big your thing is."

"Well... how big is a bread box?"

Alan couldn't really say. He'd never seen a breadbox as they had gone out of vogue before he was born. He always pretty much assumed it was a little bigger than a loaf of bread but wasn't looking for that kind of accuracy with the question. He held his hands up, about two feet apart, trying to simulate the size of a bread box. "Let's say it is as big as this."

"Well dad, there are different kinds of bread you know. Some might need a bigger box. But I'll let you off the hook. My thing is much smaller than a bread box." Before Alan could respond, she smiled and said, "Except when it's much, much bigger."

Alan glared at his daughter. "So, you're saying your thing that is neither animal, vegetable, nor mineral is also both bigger and smaller than a bread box?"

She flicked her eyebrows up and down in a manner that she thought was evocative of the problem-solving abilities of the true Pippi Longstocking, but that, to her father, looked more like a bad Groucho Marx impression. "That is correct, sir."

Alan shook his head, exasperated. "I give up. What is it?"

She laughed, "It's a mushroom, silly!"

He furrowed his brow and almost scowled. "You know, when we play this game, you have to answer the questions honestly or it really isn't fair."

Pippi's smile faded, and she raised her voice. "I was being honest."

"Mushrooms are vegetables."

She shook her head, "No they aren't. And I can prove it." Then, she jumped off the bed, ran over to where Alan sat, slipped onto his lap, and began typing on her laptop.

She pulled up Wikipedia, did a quick search and pointed. "See there, it says that mushrooms are not vegetable because they don't have chlorophyll. And look here. This part says that the part that lives underground, the mycelia, are all linked up and are the largest living organisms. So, even though the mushrooms we eat are smaller than a bread box, the whole thing is the biggest living thing."

Alan read the article over his daughter's shoulder. He wanted to say she should be careful citing Wikipedia as a source, but realized he had to give her credit. Later he would remind her to check her facts with more credible sources, but he was always glad to see her stretch and use her mind. "Good job, I guess you got me there."

Pippi's smile returned. "Want to play again?"

Alan was still reading the article about fungus displayed on Pippi's screen. "No thanks. You're too smart for me. I need to study up a bit before our next round."

Pippi hopped off Alan's lap and started to run out of her room calling, "Suit yourself. I'm available whenever you want another schooling."

Alan grinned as he called after her. "Hey, you said mushroom. But you were really describing fungus. So, you may have lost on a technicality."

She glanced back at her dad, giving him a pitying look as she made her exit. "Oh, give me a break. I'm just a kid."

Alan kept reading the article, wondering how it was that so many people were willing to put so much effort into keeping up a community-based encyclopedia. He was finding it increasingly the case that his students would include Wikipedia citations in their papers. Although this was becoming an excepted practice, he still found it disturbing that college students grew increasingly comfortable presenting group-think as fact. He often found provable errors in their source material and found that the disclosure of said errors was just as routinely met with a shrug.

Oddly enough, as he looked over the article on fungus, the most glaring error in the article escaped him. It noted that an outcropping of Armillaria solidipes growing in Oregon's Malheur National Forest was the world's largest organism in the world, covering more than 2200 acres.

That wasn't true.

The largest organism on the planet wasn't the giant fungus in Oregon, but the much larger and much older fungus that was, for all intents and purposes, its parent. The largest, and for that matter, oldest living being was the continent-wide fungus that spanned most of North America. Although it was much more apparent and more discernible in the green zones of the Pacific Northwest and the eastern seaboard, it ran much deeper and ran through Mexico and into Central America where it had long ago been amputated by the Panama Canal.

Of course, this wasn't true either. Not anymore. For this fungus, once cut in half by the hubris of Theodore Roosevelt had been declining by dribs and drabs over the past century. During that time countless toxins released into the air, earth, and water had diminished it piece by piece. In the past few months, a tipping point was reached —one that could only have been predicted by a mere ninety-nine percent of the world's scientists. Now, in addition to the changes in water and soil quality, changes in weather patterns had diminished the core of the fungus to the point where instead of a continent-wide mass of interconnectedness, there were now mere pockets of life, many no larger than small cities. And these pockets were still shrinking.

Sadly, even though the plight of the fungus was directly attributable to mankind, they remained oblivious to its fate. Given that the scientific community didn't know of either the rise or the fall of the North American fungus, it was no wonder the amateur "factologists" that updated Wikipedia didn't. And that was why Alan still didn't.

Of course, most of this was lost on the fungus. The finer points, at least. But it was, nonetheless, deeply disturbed by the parts it did understand.

3

Mother

It was dark. Real dark. She couldn't remember it ever having been this dark before. There was no light coming up from the earth, and the view, normally clear and vast, was only of dirt. At least it felt like dirt. It didn't feel like earth. Earth was light. Earth was rich. Earth was alive and was home to all. It was everything to her.

This was dirt.

But that wasn't the worst thing.

She was alone.

For as long as she could remember—if remember was the right word— she had never experienced loneliness. She was by her very nature, never alone. She lacked the ability to really put her loneliness into perspective. Now, there was a singularity to her inner dialog that was unnerving. Once again... if that had been possible.

To a casual observer, if such a thing truly existed, she would have seemed to be surrounded by others. And she was. But it would be like saying to someone from a large family that sitting in a room with another person was like being in a crowd. There was no comparison between being engulfed by love and merely existing among a few neighbors.

Since the last moon, she had been cut off from the light. The earth had lost its richness; she had withered to a tiny fraction of what she had once been, and a darkness had surrounded her. Without the warmth of her family and children, without the light of the earth surrounding her, she was alone. She was beginning to feel the strain, and it was taking its toll.

It had been months since the light had started to fade. Now she was fumbling in the dark, trying to grow. It wasn't as though she was starving. She found food. Plenty. But she couldn't grow fast enough to make up for all she had lost. The idea of size, or of boundaries would be lost on her, but before the light faded, she had been vast, feeling the glow of trillions of lights. Now she was merely a minuscule fraction of her former self. And she was ravenous.

She required company. No, not company. She required union. She wasn't so much a being as an assemblage of beings. The her who was her was her in the same way that thousands of individual brush strokes could be seen as a great painting. There was no individual thing that was the Mona Lisa. Instead, there were hundreds of strands of fabric woven together to form a canvas, and on that canvas were thousands of distinct brush lines and points, some completely obscured by those that came later, others built up not on canvas but on earlier bits of paint. Each was placed by a man who saw not the painting he was creating, or even the model that sat for him, but some image in his head that even the model couldn't obscure. Some lines of paint were made subtly skewed because of the drink the painter used to dull the regret that refused to let his vision completely fade to black. The drink was easily the work of dozens of men, each with their own demons and each with no fewer obscured intentions than the painter. Yet all these distinct, disparate elements, to the naked eye can be, and usually are seen as a single thing.

And so, it was with her. The her who was her, the central self-awareness that lay sprawled in the earth underneath Los Angeles, was really a few million threads that wound together into a sort of democratically elected her. But damn it, she wasn't herself these days. Without a few trillion more strands, she couldn't find her balance. She needed the soothing effect of growth. She needed the smoothing effect of sprawl. She needed children. She needed lovers.

She needed to feed.

Using the clean spring water that bubbled up under her new home at the base of the hill and neighborhood known as Mt. Washington as a safe place to grow, she burst forth from the earth. Thousands of tiny tendrils broke ground and softened the area, opening into a green valley, ready to begin the long steady expansion that would be her redoing.

4

Mr. Navarro Doesn't Sleep

Emile Navarro could barely remember the fall. But he could remember every single thing leading up to it. And he could remember the last twenty years. Lying in the dirt has a certain sobering effect. It gives one the ability to truly focus on the present. That was something he'd failed to do when he was alive. But dead...now that was different.

He thought about his loneliness, and he thought about every mistake he'd ever made, every wrong turn he'd taken. He thought about Innocencia. She had been the young love of his life. He remembered the way she had smelled. Her skin had always carried the faint scent of roses. Her kisses were like a thick, cherry flavored honey – soft and sticky. He remembered the taste of her breasts, roses with a hint of sweat. Not that horrible old lady sweat he remembered from Dora. No, it was that fragrant sweat of youth.

No place was the scent greater or the distinction between youth and age, life and death, stronger than the sweet spot between her legs. Not that he'd had much to do with it. They'd only made love the one time. She had only been fifteen and in those days... Well, damn it, that was just another damn thing to regret. But he'd seen her naked twice more and another time he'd brushed the back of his hand against that spot.

When he was alive, he'd thought about the smell of her and the sight of her every day. For fifty years and through almost as many years of marriage, he'd remembered the smell of Innocencia and compared and contrasted it to just about everything else. And he had found everything else wanting.

It was funny how it was the smells and tastes of Innocencia he found the most memorable. Twenty years in the dirt had taken its toll on what had once been his body. If he had been presented with the fifteen-year-old Innocencia today, it would be wasted on him. He was almost exclusively bones. Certainly, he had no nose or tongue. He did, however, still have one eye. So, if push came to shove, maybe he could see her. But he couldn't touch her as there was no real meat on his bones. It would have been torture. But dwelling on her in his mind's eye for the past twenty years hadn't been much better.

In life he had also spent an inordinate amount of time dwelling on the past. It was just that then he had had a present and future to in some ways compete with his memories. Sadly, nothing much ever changed the trajectory of his life. He had for the most part lived his last fifty years waiting for a do over. Wondering what he would do the next time he was seventeen and lying naked with Innocencia. How he would cradle her in his arms and make whatever promises would open her legs and keep her from hating him. For the life of him, or whatever expression someone in his state should use, he couldn't remember what he had done wrong.

Mr. Navarro wanted a do over. He wanted his seventy years back...not to mention that last twenty lying in the damn dirt under his damn house. He tried to move his right arm. He focused all his being—what there was of it—on the act of moving his arm, flexing his elbow, or wiggling a finger. This was something he had done for as long as he had been buried back here. At first it had been easier. Well, not as easy as you might think, and certainly not easy enough to have had much of an effect. He had been dead for Christ's sake. Even moving your finger was an almost herculean task for a dead man. But, by the same token, so he would have assumed was thinking. Yet here he lay. Twenty years in the dirt, thinking and planning. Reliving and regretting. Even now, with a skull packed with more dirt than brain, he lay thinking. And...trying...to...move...his...damn...finger.

Nothing. Not today.

One thing that disturbed his thoughts was that he wasn't sure precisely where the body of the girl was. He had buried her behind the house. What was that, forty years ago? She had been somewhere behind the house, between it and the slope. He had often wondered if her body was near his. He wondered what, if anything, she was thinking. He was just lonely enough to wonder if by some miracle, perhaps one of her bones was touching one of his. Really, however, there was no point in it. Not only would they not know it, but if she did, she would surely hate him.

He could understand if she did. She was another one of those things he had been regretting for quite some time. Maybe even before he died. Damn it though, it wasn't something he had decided to do anyway. It had just pretty much happened. She had knocked on *his* door. She was standing there on his stoop, carrying a clip board wanting him to sign a petition or some such thing. She had been wearing cut-off jeans (why did they have to wear them so damn short back then) and a tight tee shirt, tied so that her belly was bare. She was one of those hippie girls who were running all over the hills back then and she had no bra, so right there, you could pretty much see every damn thing.

He took all that in in an instant, but it was her face that had rendered him speechless. For just a second, she was Innocencia. He smiled and invited her in so he could get a better look. Perhaps to take a sniff where she wouldn't be so close to the flower bed. He invited her in under the guise of his needing to find his checkbook. He remembered being thankful Dora liked to spend Sundays down at the damn church.

He found himself in a completely illogical state. He was old enough to be her father. Truth be told he was old enough to be her grandfather. And yet, when he looked at her, what he saw certainly seemed more his peer than what he saw when he looked at Dora. He was a man in his fifties, married to a woman in her late forties. But inside, where things really mattered, he felt like the sort of man that this girl could - what did the kids call it back then - relate to.

A part of him knew his wife, a woman he had promised to love and cherish, was just down the hill, hobnobbing with the local priest and his other admirers. But that part of him wasn't the part that was running the show.

18

The dominant voice was the one that made him smile at pretty girls. It was the part that knew sometimes girls responded to a little flirting, just like they knew sometimes an old man might write a bigger check to a pretty little canvasser that was flashing a little too much tit. It was the part that ignored the lessons of a lifetime and still believed something could be gained from failing to acknowledge common wisdom. Looking back, which was pretty much all he did now, one could argue that it was the part of him that knew that sometimes pretty, young girls underestimated their fragile place in an ecosystem created and cultivated by men.

Whatever the reasoning, the girl did come in and he had returned to the front room with his checkbook, intending to let her linger as long as he could. But when she looked up at him, he saw Innocencia in her eyes again. He saw the same longing that had been burned into his memory by a lifetime of regret and he leaned down and without another thought, kissed her. For a moment – was it just a moment? – he was transported through time. The taste of a young girl's lips was something one never forgot. The sweetness and the...freshness. Yes, it was a freshness, untouched by the disappointments of life and the inevitable decay that would be the death of us all. In that instant he was young himself, in a timeless state, looking forward again and not aware of the decay that had already almost consumed him.

Then he tasted the cigarettes on the girl's breath. It broke the spell, and he opened his eyes and pulled away. Her eyes were wide with fear, and he realized he had been holding her tightly and that she was trying to pull away. When he understood her fear, he realized she had misunderstood him and so he tried to calm her so she would realize he hadn't really done anything wrong, just that she had misunderstood. But she started to scream. In an instant he realized she would bring the neighbors if she didn't shut up, so he held his hand over her mouth. The look in her eyes went from fear to panic and still trying to scream her way out of the room, she bit his hand. He pulled his hand away as though he had been shocked or burnt and the instant he did she screamed again and tried to knee him in the groin. Because of his height advantage she came up short, merely kneeing him in the thigh.

But her intent was clear and instinctively, he hit her in the mouth with his unbitten hand.

She crumpled, and the grandfatherly old man in him popped out long enough to cradle her as she began to fall. He helped her to the ground, lowering her body, wondering what had come over him. He'd never hit a woman before.

He checked her breathing. She was fine. Once he knew she was alright, he considered his options. He realized she couldn't just lay there on the floor. If, God forbid, Dora came home early, he'd never be able to explain what happened. At the time, he was hard pressed to explain it to himself.

He decided to take her out onto the back patio. That would be a good place for her to revive. It wasn't someplace she had been before, so she wouldn't associate it with the scene in the hallway. Better yet, it wasn't visible from inside the house, so if Dora came home, or for that matter if some damn Jehovah's Witness looked in the front window, the girl would be hidden.

He leaned over her and managed to get hold of her, his right hand around her waist and his left hand behind her back, through the space between her arm and her torso. Although she was a little bitty thing, she was still heavy enough that he found it a little hard to manage her all the way to the back of the house. He found himself alternating between leaning her on his left shoulder and his right. His left arm kept brushing the side of her breast and as he got her through the sliding doors at the back of the house, he felt himself getting a bit of an erection.

He sat her down on a chaise lounge in the back yard and took a moment to catch his breath and calm himself down. Watching the girl, making sure she was breathing, it was hard not to watch her breasts rising and falling. Her little damn hippie tee-shirt guaranteed her nipples kept a steady beat. Something in him, the voice that so often took his mind to places one wasn't really supposed to go, convinced him to lean in and lift her shirt up. Just a little bit. She was sleeping and he couldn't see the harm.

Once he pulled her shirt up, he noticed the freshness again. She had a pinkness that could only be found in the young. From his current point of reference, she may as well have been from another species. He leaned over her to catch her scent. He was thinking about loosening her shorts when she opened her eyes. For an instant she was too confused to react. She blinked a few times, coming back into the moment, assessing the scene when she started to scream.

He hit her harder this time. He still considered removing her shorts, but decided it was too risky, and besides, he really wasn't that kind of a man. Instead, knowing there was no way she would ever understand that he wasn't really a bad man, and certainly not the sort she must by now assume him to be, he picked up a brick and used it make sure she wouldn't wake up. Looking into her lifeless eyes, he calmed down a bit.

Once he was sure that she wouldn't wake up again, he went ahead and pulled down her shorts. She had worn no panties. He guessed a lot of hippies didn't. The shorts caught on her shoes, and as he removed them, he noticed she had little embroidered puppies on her socks. Cute. He smelled her feet and looked up at the now nude girl that lay bleeding on the floor of his patio. Once again, he was caught by the sense that somehow he and she though occupying the same physical plane, had somehow been almost transparent to each other.

He took a few moments to examine her body, both scrutinizing and enjoying every pink blotch, birth mark and ingrown hair. He took care that he could smell her, examining her from no more than seven or eight inches. He took care not to touch her. He wasn't some kind of pervert. This had just been an accident. He was just admiring her as one might admire a butterfly. A wonderfully fragrant butterfly.

Now he lies in the dirt, deep under the earth, thinking about the smells of the girl. He had wanted to keep her around to marvel at but knew she wouldn't keep. Within a few hours, she would reek of decay, and besides his Dora wouldn't be gone all day. No, reluctantly, he had placed her body in a shallow hole that he dug on the back side of the hill. He wondered again if she was somewhere near him. He somehow knew this question would haunt him forever. And that he'd never know.

Sometimes, he wished he could cry.

5

Down the Hill

Looking over the edge of the overhang, Tim couldn't see any sign of Rage. The mushroom coated landscape of rocks, trees, and grass was steep enough he found it hard to believe that if Rage wasn't caught up in the first hundred feet or so, he must be dead at the bottom. Fatty started barking and began running around the right side of the property, heading into the woods. Tim surmised that the dog was heading for the path that Rage had told him about several months earlier. Rage had claimed that it had been an old Native American path, but of course, Tim had his doubts. Rage seemed to be perpetually stuck in post adolescence, and all his stories seemed to gravitate toward girls, drugs, pirates, Native Americans (which Rage still called Indians) and "the man." He had even tried to convince Tim on one occasion there were ruins at the base of the hill.

Tim followed Fatty at a distance down the trail that wound down the side of the hill, through the woods and back to the base of the cliff. As Tim made his way to the bottom, he alternated between shouting out Rage's name, and listening to hear if there was a response. Until he was near the bottom of the hill, he couldn't hear anything over the sound of Fatty's barking. Then, as he turned the last corner, Fatty's barking turned to a whimper.

At the bottom of the hill, Tim stood surrounded by a green outcropping of trees, bushes, and mushrooms. He surveyed the area looking for signs of Rage or, God forbid, Rage's body. He followed the sound of Fatty's whining as he wound his way through the brush.

He'd never been down here before. Rage had wanted to include this spot on the grand tour the week after Tim moved in. According to Rage, when he'd been a child, the path had meandered down the hill, but the hill had been much more gradual, and the path had wrapped around the hill rather than running alongside the slope. During that time, Rage's parents' house hadn't had quite the prime hillside location it now enjoyed. There were two other houses perched between them and the slope. When Rage was ten, two weeks of heavy rain undermined a section of the hill and the two houses lost their footing and came down, along with a significant amount of the hill itself. When he learned the history of this part of the hill, Tim had opted to skip this part of the tour. This was the sort of story he had wished he'd known before he'd signed a one-year lease.

The clearing at the bottom of the hill wasn't what he'd expected. It had the trees, rocks, and mushrooms, of course. But here, wedged so close to the cliff face that he'd never seen it on the few occasions he'd had the nerve to step to the ledge and look down from above, was the wreckage of the two houses that had fallen to their demise. They were badly damaged and decomposed, but still, unmistakably houses from the same subdivision as Rage's.

One house had ended up, for the most part, right side up. It sat with its foundation hugging the cliff, leaning forward at about a thirty-degree angle. It had been a pink, ranch style three bedroom with an antique brick skirt and if you squinted just right, or perhaps were just high enough, it could almost pass as a normal house. The real sticking point that blew even a stoned and perhaps overly forgiving view was that jutting out of the left side of the roof was a large section of what was at one time the green house next door. That house had apparently landed upside down, somehow wedged itself into the roof of the former neighbor and snapped in half. The green house was essentially upside down and draped over left side of the pink house. The whole tableau was overgrown with weeds, grass, bushes, and more than a few trees, which was apparently why Tim hadn't seen it from the top of the hill. Both houses had their doors and windows, such as they were, hastily boarded over.

Rage was propped up on the pink house's porch and Fatty was licking his face. Rage was clearly not dead, but he did seem to have assumed a funny shape. Rage squealed, "Dude, I think I broke my fucking leg."

Tim nodded. That was what had seemed so strange about Rage's shape. His left calf was bent at an alarming angle. He thought to himself that perhaps any angle in the center of a calf should be considered alarming. "You're lucky if you just broke your leg. You could have killed yourself."

Rage was blinking and looking at his hands. He said, "Nah. I made that jump a bunch of times when I was a kid." He paused for a couple of seconds and added, "There just didn't use to be so many rocks."

As Tim approached Rage, he could see through the spaces between the boards that covered the otherwise open doorway behind him. Gazing into the house, he could see into the entryway and living room. It was the same floor plan as Rage's house. It was like peering into some twisted alternate universe. A filthy one. "So, you knew this was down here?"

Rage shook his head, still blinking and looking at his hand, opening and closing his fingers, "No, man. That's why I hurried. The place is crawling with them." He giggled and poked at what Tim could now see was an open wound in Rage's broken leg.

Tim asked, "You mean there are more than these two?"

Rage laughed, "Hell yeah. There's fucking millions." He paused, "So you see them, too? Far out." He continued to play with his leg. He pushed his finger into the bloody gash, then pulled this finger, dripping with blood up to just inches in front of his face. He blinked and smiled, drawing imaginary circles in the air with his bloody finger.

"Of course I see them. Is this what you meant by there being ruins down here?"

Rage slowly stopped grinning and his whole face scrunched up in a highly stoned, over-the-top expression of concentration. He glanced up at Tim, making eye contact for the first time since he had laid eyes on the mushrooms. He looked confused. Tim slapped his hand against the side of the entryway where Rage sat and added, speaking slowly, "I can't believe they are still here."

Rage shook his head, doing a mental reset, "You mean the Navarro's house? Shit man, of course I knew it was here. It's been here at least twenty years. It used to have a whole lot more dirt and shit covering it up. And before that, it used to be up the hill. You would have known it too if you weren't such a pussy. I tried to get you down here a bunch of times." He looked back down at the ground that surrounded the house, then back at his finger. "I thought you were talking about the lights."

"Lights?"

"Yeah, they're everywhere."

Tim nodded. The mushrooms were hallucinogenic. "I see. You saw lights."

"Yeah, you don't?"

"Of course I don't. But then again, I didn't eat an unidentified hallucinogenic mushroom. And then, I didn't jump off a cliff."

Rage said, "Yeah well, don't say you didn't have the chance." He tried to get up. He whimpered a little and dropped back down.

Leaning over to try to help Rage up, Tim said, "You probably have a concussion too. That may account for at least some of the lights."

Rage waved him off. "Give me a minute, I need to get my shit together here." He pointed in the front door of the pink house. "Why don't you just take a little look around. I mean, now that you are finally down here, you should check out the old place. I mean, we couldn't get inside before."

Tim peered through the open spaces in the door. Rather than trying to pry them open, which wouldn't have taken a whole lot of effort, he instead walked around the pink house, examining it through the different partially blocked windows and doors. There really was only one door, given that the back of the house was embedded in the foot of the hill. It looked like the back of the house where he assumed the kitchen would have been, was under the landslide, or had been crushed by it. To the casual observer, it looked to be the former.

Rage narrated Tim's exploration. "When I was a kid, we used to pull off the boards and hide out in Navarro's house. Every year or so someone would board the place up again. Probably some insurance asshole. Didn't matter.

We would just rip them off and reclaim the space. It was a great place to get high."

"But you stopped."

Rage said, "Yeah, well, I'd like to think we matured."

Tim laughed, "You can think that, but you didn't."

Rage shrugged, "Guess I just don't need to hide out anymore."

Rage stood, still with a whimper, but this time, instead of sitting back down, he hopped in a tight circle on his good leg.

Tim grabbed his arm, pulled it over his shoulder and started leading him toward the path back up the hill. "Let's get you out of here and up to the hospital."

As they hobbled up the path, Rage quietly slipped a couple of small mushrooms from his pocket and turning as if to cough, popped them in his mouth. He slowly chewed them as they ascended into his domain, marveling at the lights.

6

Navarro Gets a Raise

The thing was, Mr. Navarro was in an almost constant state of now. Oh sure, he spent a lot of time ruminating on his past. But that was predominantly because now was so boring - and of course, there was no future. Given that all he could do was lay in the dirt, motionless and in the dark, he could only spend so much time focusing on the now before he was dragged away into the past by memories and regret. But he was always aware of the present. What he wasn't aware of at all times was time itself. More to the point, the passing of time. He had no point of reference. As he thought about things or wondered about the cold or heat, things no longer held sway over his physical being but still weighed heavily on his old man's mind, he had no real point of reference as to how long he had been thinking about it.

So, the fact he had been feeling something for some time, couldn't be exactly spelled out. It could have been a few hours, or days. Perhaps it was weeks, but that really didn't matter. What mattered was that for that last few hours, days or whatever, he had been feeling as though some thing was touching him. There was a change from below. That presupposed he was right all these years when he had assumed he was lying face up. He laughed a soundless, dusty laugh at the idea he could have been wrong. It probably wouldn't have mattered as he had only lived for a few hours once he had been here. When the hill had given way, he had been half-way down it, attempting to lay down tarps to avoid what turned out to be unavoidable and inevitable.

So when the hill came down, it came down on top of him. He had always assumed the house came too. He had heard rescue workers above him. They had yelled for him, but the earth had been packed so tightly that his jaw had been completely immobile. He had yelped as best he could, but the weight of the earth on his throat made even the slight movement necessary to form and project a sound impossible. He had laid there alternating between sobbing and trying to be heard until the pain in his lungs gave way to exhaustion which gave way to sleep.

The sleep had given way to death. In practical terms it had given way to another type of dreaming. On some level he still believed he could be dreaming. This dream, aside from the fact it involved him being dead but conscious, was far more realistic than the dreams he had had before the fall. Now he lay in one place, thinking or dreaming about the world he was trapped in and ruminating over the mistakes he'd made before, back when he had still had the power to make them.

What he felt now was a warmth in his bones. Not warmth in the sense that the earth was somehow heating up due to the weather. It was as though something was touching them or holding them. It felt like thousands of long thin fingers encircling his bones. It started with his left foot and had slowly moved up his leg. When it reached his hip bones, it had continued both up his spine and down his right leg. While his right leg was being wrapped, the strain that reached up his spine encircled both arms and finally enveloped his skull in a soft wet mass. He tried to move a finger or smile because this was the first time in what felt like an eternity that anyone or anything had interacted with him in any way. But he couldn't move. Only the tangle that encircled him could move. And now that he was aware of it, he realized whatever he was caught up in was in a constant state of motion. Excruciatingly slow and seemingly random motion, but given the patience born of the past few decades of stasis, he had the ability to pay proper attention to the fact that motion it was.

This process may have happened over a period of days or even weeks, but what had started out as gradual had accelerated over time. He could feel his wrapping was being wrapped. There were layers upon layers that were being built upon. At first he feared he was being eaten, or absorbed. He wondered if that were to happen, what would become of him. Clearly most if not all his flesh had been eaten by insects and decay. But here he was. His brain and all his organs save for his single remaining eye had long since become a part of the food chain. Yet here he was. If his bones—assuming that was what he was now—were consumed where would he be? Would he be part of whatever organism consumed him, or would he just be some at long last completely disembodied assembly of thoughts and regrets? But he began to believe whatever was happening to him was good. He felt more at peace than ever before. He felt somehow loved. He felt like he wasn't alone anymore. He wondered if this was finally the Heaven that Dora had so often harped on about.

Just like he couldn't tell how long it had taken to enshroud him, he couldn't have said how long it took until he felt himself begin to be moved. A pressure had built up behind and under him. It hadn't been uncomfortable; it had in fact been comforting, like a mother's hand on your back, letting you know whatever it was that mothers instinctively knew that somehow their spawn instinctively needed to know. As the pressure grew, he felt himself slowly being pushed up through the earth.

Having been transformed from stasis to being part of the world again, Mr. Navarro was now better able to relate to things around him. He became aware he was moving through the earth, not of his own power, but was being pushed along by the fabric that had engulfed him. As he got closer to the earth's surface, he began to sense light. He wondered how that could be, given his one remaining eye certainly wasn't hooked up to, well, anything. But nonetheless, he could see that his new outer layer sent little shoots of itself up to soften the earth and then pushed him up through the newly broken soil.

The proximity to a world where the sun rises and sets somehow brought with it his long-lost awareness of time. After a few hours, he felt his right arm thrust up into the air. He tried to move it and found that for the first time in twenty years, he could. He took control of his left arm and pushed it up and out of the dirt. He used his now functional appendages to pull himself completely out of the earth.

As he left the hole through which he had been thrust (or was it reborn?) he sat on the grass he had disturbed and blinked his eye. He couldn't for the life of him—should that phrase still be applicable—fathom how his eye worked, but he knew the light from the sun was overwhelming. He wouldn't realize for several minutes he wasn't outside and what he perceived as sunlight was in fact deep shadow.

Once he was able to look around without wincing, he saw he was in a house. In fact, it looked remarkably like his house. As he stood and gazed around the space, he realized that it in fact was his house. He was standing in his and Dora's bedroom. He couldn't understand how his house could be there, given that it had undoubtedly come down the hill on him many years prior. Then he noted the state of the room. Not just that it was crumbling in disrepair, but that it seemed to be seriously off kilter, pitched toward the front of the house and there were gaping holes in the roof. There was grass growing on the floor, and there were dandelions and sunflowers growing up and around the broken-down bed and turned over dressing table.

He blinked. Not really. He just imagined he did. It was what one did when encountering such a sight and in his mind's eye, he did it. When he peered around, he noted the world he had left had been waiting patiently for his return. He smiled.

The smile felt odd. He felt a tightness in the muscles around his face. He considered for a moment that there were no muscles there. His eye was beginning to adjust to the light, and he held up a hand to examine it. He moved the finger he had concentrated on moving ever since his death. It moved. He wiggled his hand and could see, but not really feel, that the whole hand worked as it should. It didn't look entirely like a hand though. The "skin" was grayish white with a number of dark spots and was covered with tiny tendrils, some gray, but others had red and blue flecks. It looked like his hand was draped with something pulled out of a compost heap.

Glancing down at Dora's broken-down dressing table, he searched the grassy floor for a piece of the mirror that had adorned it twenty years ago. He dropped down to the ground and began rooting through the debris, noting there was little visual distinction between the things his hands had become and the filth through which they rummaged. He found a section of mirror wedged behind the dresser, but not before it sliced off a bloodless chunk of his hand that included two fingers. Navarro dropped the mirror and picked up detached section of his hand and examined it more closely, holding it up to his face. He could see tiny white strands of fungus reaching out from the wound as though they were looking for the body they missed. He examined his hand and saw that it, too, had fine hairlike tendrils that moved like little snakes searching for something. He held the two pieces of his hand together and watched the strands weave together and begin to mend the hand. He tried to move the fingers but found they were not functioning. Closely examining the hand again, he could see the tendrils that had initially pulled the hand back together were still hard at work. He decided he would either regain the use of the two severed fingers, or he would still consider the reanimation of the other eight as an improvement over the past twenty years.

Navarro used his unbroken hand to pick up the mirror again, this time more carefully, and used it to examine his face. He looked in the mirror. The face that stared back at him with its one bulging eye was only a terrible attempt at a human face. A failed attempt Navarro noted. It confirmed what Navarro had begun to believe. He had been recreated out of fungus. Studying his face, he could see alternating layers of the tiny tendrils, larger ones and sheets of what appeared to be mold. He poked his cheek with his finger and slowly pushed it through the membrane and deep into his skull. As he withdrew the finger, it was covered with a thick, wet, dripping coating of green mold. Without even thinking, he scanned the floor and spotted a wad of rotting vegetation that was teaming with what appeared to be red and blue lights. He absentmindedly scooped up the muck and used it to patch the hole in his face.

Staring into the mirror, Navarro evaluated the repair job he had just made to his cheek. He could see that tiny tendrils were busy at work exploring the newly placed debris while the face in the mirror stared back at him in wide-eyed fascination. He thought it looked like the him in the mirror—if that was in fact him—was trying to scream.

7

Fatty Hears a Bone

As Tim helped Rage navigate the trail up the hill to Rage's house, Fatty found himself conflicted, something that dogs don't take too well to. He was torn between two primal canine directives. The better part of him, or at least the part that a life among the two-legged had enforced, pulled him toward his master. He was afraid for Rage, knowing he was hurt and wanting to clear the way to help. He ran in circles around Tim and Rage, spinning around to make sure Tim was following. But he was also a dog. He was a hunter, and a scavenger. He had the canine mix of playfulness and foolishness, lacking the wisdom to understand the long-term implications of any action.

Running around the beat-up old house while Rage had sat alternating between howling in pain and gasping in awe, Fatty had smelled some wonderful things in the old house. Of course, what smells wonderful to a dog isn't necessarily something a human would recognize as such. But Fatty smelled the overwhelmingly appetizing aroma of rotting things. And he smelled bones. Lots of bones.

Now, as Tim and Rage were reaching the top of the hill, at a time where if a dog could rationalize, he might say to himself the danger had passed, Fatty sprinted back down the hill to nose around the house a little deeper.

When he got to the doorway, he paused, sniffing the air to get a better idea of where the scent was coming from. That's when he heard the sound. It was the rattle of bones. At first he thought some other dog or animal must have found the dead animal and was tearing it apart. He got down on his belly and crawled under the boards that barred the entrance, entering the house to see if he could claim some of the find, but stopped a few feet into the house. He realized, in a way that only a dog can, there wasn't any other animal in the house. He was alone. But he could still hear the bones. They sounded like they were in the back of the house. And they were coming toward him.

As he backed out the front door, he had a sense that wasn't all that common to dogs, but one that his master might have understood. The hair on the back of his neck—and for that matter all the way down his back—stood on end and stayed that way for more than the thirty seconds he took to sprint out of the house and up the hill and catch up with Rage and Tim. If dogs understood the concept and necessity of guile, he would have been pretending to worry about his master as he ran up the hill and wouldn't have kept running past him, through the dog door and into his crate.

8

So...What Exactly Makes Pippi Tick

Pippi was not your average ten-year-old girl. First off, her name was Pippi. Secondly, that wasn't her name. Maybe that only counts as one thing, but to Pippi's way of thinking, it was almost three things.

What she knew was that sometimes when she was in a room full of adults, she was the only one who seemed to get what was really going on. Okay, typical stuff for a ten-year-old to think. But for Pippi, she found that when other kids thought the same thing, they were usually off too.

That was another thing that made Pippi feel special. If special was the right word. She figured everyone sometimes felt that the rest of the world was all squirrelly. But she seemed to be the only one who realized she, too, might suffer from the same condition. It made her a little reticent to just jump into things. She saw things as both wonderfully exciting and potentially stupid.

Unlike most of her friends, she was reluctant to call anything stupid. She knew when most other folks did it they were missing something. Something that was perhaps clear to others - at least to Pippi. She didn't want to appear to be too eager to either jump into something fun or dismiss it as stupid.

So, that made Pippi not your average ten-year-old girl. It also meant when she took her dog, Bruno, for a romp in the hills, she was traveling with the only soul that truly seemed to get her. Kids were kind of stupid—not that she would say it out loud—but somehow they kind of knew she thought it.

Running down the wash with Bruno, she could jump and kick stuff and not worry about not being cool. Bruno didn't know from cool as far as she could tell and if he did, he was a good enough friend to act just as goofy as she did. On this fine morning she ran behind Bruno as he tore out for some as yet unknown adventure.

Halfway down the wash, Bruno went a little crazy, barking, snapping, and growling in a way that could only indicate the presence of his apparent arch-enemy, Fatty. Fatty was a good dog. So was Bruno. But together they seemed to always be getting into some kind of trouble. They were both little dogs, and neither was much of a fighter or threat to anyone but themselves, but they just acted like buttheads when the other one was around.

Wanting to avoid the sort of stupid antics between Bruno and Fatty, Pippi decided to head back up out of the wash. She called Bruno so they could explore elsewhere.

9

Rage Sees the Light

Sitting in the emergency room, Tim thought Rage looked like a little kid. He sat in his chair with his body hunched over, somehow trying to wrap himself around his wounded leg. He scanned the room wide eyed as though he needed to be on guard in case someone might attack him at any moment. In the months he had known Rage, he didn't recall ever having the feeling that Rage knew fear.

Fortunately, in spite of what appeared to be a pretty good crowd, it was a fairly low severity morning in the ER, so they only had to wait a half hour before Rage was called back to an examining room. The attendant, a short, heavyset, seemingly disinterested African American woman who could to Tim's mind best be described as spherical—although her name tag described her as Leticia—motioned for Tim to wait in the lobby while she took Rage back to be treated. Tim thought if he squinted, it would look like Rage was rolling her in front of him. Tim returned to his seat and turned his attention to the cartoons playing on the waiting room's television.

**

Leticia apparently chose to let her name tag take care of not just the introductions, but in fact, all the pleasantries. From the time she called out "Sutherland. Reginald Sutherland," she failed to utter another recognizable, non-grunted syllable until Rage had been led to a small curtained off area. Once there, she said, "Up on the table" and attempted to help him onto the

37

examining table. The help was minimal and forced, consisting mainly of shoving him toward said table. Rage, who had essentially hopped through the emergency room, bumped his leg against the table and squealed, "Jesus Christ, lady. Take it easy on me... I already broke my leg."

Leticia, used to a certain level of patient abuse, sometimes deserved, sometimes not, didn't react, but merely made sure to help ease Rage's leg up onto the table. Once there, she bumped it once for good measure and gave him a cool icy stare that was meant to suggest he had stumbled into a battle he couldn't win and that a quick surrender might help him avoid serious bloodshed.

He yelped, "Fuck. Don't you people have some kind of plan for shit like this? How about doing something like bringing me something for the pain."

She smiled, thinking "you people?" And she had gone out of her way to get this little white piece of shit on the damn fast track. It was starting to look like he might be in for a bit of a wait. She put on her best 'can I be of service' smile. It was a look that up until this point, neither Rage nor Tim had been exposed to. "I'm sorry, sir. Only the doctor can do that. I'm sure he'll give you a little something once he's looked at your leg." To emphasize the word leg, her smile faded back into her don't fuck with Leticia stare and she brought her hand down and gave his knee a firm squeeze right above the break.

Some level of insight Rage had never before experienced made him aware that calling her a bitch at this point might have frightening repercussions. He winced and quietly grabbed his leg.

As soon as the once again smiling Leticia closed the curtain behind herself, Rage checked his pockets to see how his mushrooms were holding up. He smiled, noting he must have at least a dozen more. He figured that over the past couple of hours he'd eaten six or seven. Although his leg was hurting like a bitch, he had to acknowledge that overall, he felt damn good. He felt kind of warm and fuzzy. Like when he was a kid, sitting on the couch under a blanket with his mom. Just...comfortable and content.

Earlier, sitting in the emergency room, he had found that when he looked around, all the people seemed somehow familiar. And some of them had little halos of light. The lights were brightest on the older ones, but he had seen a baby that had them too. The baby had had snow white hair and the lights reflected off it eerily. He found he wanted to touch all the people, but the ones with the lights he felt particularly drawn to. As he thought about it, the only way he could describe the feeling was that he loved them all. He shook his head and thought *fag*.

Although the lights had been visible outside and back in the waiting room, the only lights he could see in the examining room were the ones that swirled in and around his wound. Earlier they had dripped out of him along with his blood. Now they twisted and throbbed, glowing all around the wound. When he poked the wound with a couple of fingers, he could scoop up a small bit of the light and bring it up for a closer look. The lights, the same deep blue ones he had seen all day, when examined from inches away, were rich with specs of other colors. After a minute or two, the lights would fade away to nothing.

He wiped his hands in the blood and light that dripped from his leg and cupped them over his eyes. In essence, he created a tiny planetarium in his hands, and looking at the lights, they seemed to go on forever - like stars. It was like a tiny, little, infinite universe in the palms of his hands. He shook his head, giggling as they slowly faded out.

He popped another mushroom in his mouth and was quietly munching, rooting around in his leg for another handful of lights when a tall, dark man wearing green scrubs and black canvas high-tops parted the curtains and joined him in the examining room. He smiled and said, "Good evening, Mr Sutherland. I'm Dr. Patel. I understand you've broken your leg. Let's take a look at it, shall we?"

Rage looked up and noted there were no lights circulating the doctor. He shrugged, "You're the doctor. Speaking of which, that b...lady that brought me in here said that you could give me something for the pain."

Dr. Patel nodded, "Yes, well...first let's see what we're up against." He noted that his patient looked like he may have imbibed a bit already. He thought it best to do a little investigation before adding to what might already be a pharmacological swamp.

39

While examining the break in Rage's calf, the doctor casually asked, "So, did you take anything for the pain before you got here?"

Rage, looking as innocent as he could muster, shook his head, "Nope. Just came right here. You know... like it was an emergency."

The doctor nodded, "Yes, of course." He stepped around the table to get a look at the leg from the other side, "And, have you had anything to drink today?"

Rage smiled and nodded. These people, always trying to be so coy. "Yes. I had some water. But that was before I fell off a cliff and broke my leg."

Dr. Patel smiled, "Yes, yes... of course. But, before I prescribe any pain medication, I need to establish anything you may have already imbibed that could interfere with its effectiveness...or cause a more serious reaction. I need to ask, have you taken any type of drug earlier in the day?"

Rage found himself in inner turmoil. On the one hand, he knew the doctor wasn't on his side here when it came to the whole painkillers are for more than painkilling thing. However, the mushroom he had just eaten was making it hard not to love the hell out of good old Dr. Patel. He kind of wanted to hug him. He shook his head and said, "No sir. My roommate and I were working in the backyard when I fell off the cliff behind my house. We were, you know, pulling weeds and cleaning up dog shit. I mean, canine excrement. It was first thing in the morning. Too early for a drink, and I don't have any reason to take drugs. You ever hear the term straight edge? It's the only way to live, man. Anyway, I'm usually healthy as a horse." He glanced down at his leg theatrically, then back up at Dr. Patel. "Still am... except for that one thing."

Dr. Patel nodded and said, "Yes, well, I'm just going to get everything I need to set that leg...and I'll order you something for the pain as well. If you will excuse me."

Once the doctor was out of the room, Rage popped another mushroom and sat thinking about how much better he would feel when he combined this mushroom contentedness with the tingly euphoria of what he hoped would be some wonderful codeine hybrid. When he woke up this morning, he hadn't had a clue as to what a kick ass day had been in store for him. First a whole hill full of mushrooms just fall into his lap, and now here he sat waiting for just what the doctor was ordering. There was no telling how much better this day was going to get. He peered down at the lights circling his wounded leg. *Life is good.*

10

Lisa

Her name was Lisa. Lisa Whitely. She tried to focus on that fact a little every so often. She could say every few hours, but that hadn't been true in years. She had no idea how long she had been here, but sometimes it felt like it had been forever. But that was just sometimes. Certainly it seemed like this life had been longer than her real one.

It was in her first one that she had been Lisa, but for now, that fact seemed to merely be one of the few anchors she had to hang on to. She said it over and over in her mind. Lisa Whitely. My name is Lisa. More and more, over time, it sounded funny to her, like a word that had been used so often and in vain that it no longer held meaning.

Over time, she found herself drifting into and out of other realities. Perhaps "realities" wasn't the right word, but the longer she was dead, the less control over her vocabulary she had. She flowed into and out of her physical body, sometimes being bound to it and other times reliving parts of her life or of lives that had no meaning for her. Sometimes she was the child who had been Lisa Whitely, and other times she was without form, surrounding yet surrounded by people from someone named Lisa Whitely's former life. There was a woman, sometimes very young and sometimes much older. She sometimes recognized the woman as her mother. Lisa Whitely's mother. Once she even experienced that woman as the same type of formless being that Lisa sometimes became herself.

Those forays out of her grave were the good times, sprinkled with other moments that she didn't have the vocabulary to express. She sometimes smiled in her mind's image of herself thinking that sometimes she felt like when she had dropped acid, only thousands of times more intense and drawing upon a much wiser mind to alter. But over the years, between her moments of ecstasy and visits with those who she presumed to be loved ones from Lisa Whitely's past life, she found herself here: lying in the dirt where she had died.

That sounded funny. She had died here. She thought about the word. "Died" didn't properly convey what had happened here. She had been murdered here. That was the proper description of what had happened. That crazy old man had beaten her to death. As her blood had poured out onto the pavement, she had found herself floating around the scene, watching helplessly as the old pervert stripped off her clothes and examined her body as she lay dying. She had seen her legs twitching as he gently separated them to get a better look. She could feel his hands as he had touched her, first to pose her for his little examination and later as he had pulled her by her arms to the little grave he had prepared for her. A grave. It was where she laid now.

She had felt the concrete scraping her backside as the old son of a bitch dragged her through his yard and she remembered the moment of relief when her ass hit the lawn and left the gravel-strewn pavement. When she was lowered into her grave, she could feel the warmth from where the sun had been shining on the dirt.

Throughout this whole scene she had found herself swirling all around, taking in the sights and smells, yet somehow gathering, coalescing back into her body. By the time she lay face up in her final resting place, she felt completely reunited with her body. The old man took no care as he deposited her in the grave and she was acutely aware her left arm was pinned behind her back. She tried to squirm and straighten her arm out, but the time to get comfortable had passed. As she felt the warmth of the sun and the dirt began to cover her body, she was suddenly aware the warmth she felt was the last of it. Soon the surrounding earth would cool. Then she would cool.

Then she would be cold forever.

Lisa Whitely. She had been cold for decades. Her mind had been slipping in and out of her grave, but her body had been planted in this grave and her past life had ended on a warm sunny Sunday in 1969. She had approached the old man's door looking for money for some cause that in retrospect hadn't been worth her time, let alone her young life. His expression when he saw her should have sent her running back down the hill. But she had been young and had somehow believed she was invincible. In fact, if she thought about it enough, and God knew she had over the years, she really hadn't even seen the old man as real. He was, like most older people, just a background character in the Lisa story. Alive, she had barely given him any thought at all, certainly not the attention he had been due. Now, when she thought about him and replayed the scene, she explored every detail.

For a few moments, fifty years ago, when the old guy had been spreading her legs and smelling her, she had felt an odd sense of relief when she realized he hadn't planned on raping her. But it hadn't taken long to get over it. During the hour she had spent on his patio, she had moved steadily from the shock of his actions and confusion at her out-of-body state, through her moment of relief, ultimately settling on anger. As the light hitting her skin was being replaced by the earth, she tried to savor her last sensation of the sun. But as the dirt hit her face, she fought her urge to take one last look up at the sky. Instead, she focused her gaze on the face of her killer. She wanted to remember that fucker's face.

11

Rage Goes AWOL

Tim sat in the waiting room of the ER, wondering just how long it took to set a broken leg. There was only so long one could watch cartoons before realizing unless you were stoned, cartoons were just for kids. Therefore, he noted two problems with the room. One, he wasn't stoned. Never had been. Never would be. Two, there were no kids in the room, unless you counted that there was a couple with a baby. The baby didn't really care much for the cartoons though; it had been alternating between crying and coughing ever since the couple had brought the baby in.

He checked his watch, did a little math and realized that he had been sitting watching Sponge Bob Square Pants for over an hour. He decided to step outside and get some quiet. On the way out, he checked the vending machines near the lobby, hoping to find something worth eating. It was past lunchtime, and he hadn't eaten anything all day. He worried about his blood sugar as allowing a drop could have serious repercussions when it came to studying later in the day.

While scanning a vending machine that was primarily stocked by companies that he was hard pressed to believe were still in business, he noticed the baby that had been crying for the past hour had finally shut up. He smiled at the quiet while wondering if it was healthier to skip a meal or eat a sandwich purchased from an emergency room vending machine.

The silence was broken when he heard a woman scream, "My baby! He's not breathing!"

He stepped back into the waiting room in time to see the woman with the little white-haired baby running to the attendant who was busy running around her desk to get to them. Tim wondered if the baby's head was really as red as it looked, or if it was just in contrast to the whiteness of his hair.

***

When Dr. Patel returned to the examining room, he was pulling a wheeled cart. It was covered with an array of items that seemed to run the gamut from medical props to paraphernalia for construction. Fortunately, Rage also recognized two little paper cups that could only mean one thing. He was about to get some kick ass hospital grade pain killers.

The doctor asked, "I know you filled out the form when you came in, but better safe than sorry. Have you ever had an allergic reaction to any codeine-based medication?"

Rage feigned a concerned expression, pretended to think about it and then answered, "No. I don't have any allergies as far as I know."

Patel nodded, "Good, good." He handed Rage the first little paper cup with two fat white pills in it and the other filled with water to wash it down. He waited for Rage to swallow before he picked up a syringe off the table and added, "Unless you have an objection, I would like to give you a local in the area of the break. We need to root around a bit before putting on the cast and it will make it significantly less unpleasant."

Rage nodded and gave a royal wave to proceed. He was never one to turn down any type of chemical agent or enhancer. As far as he was concerned, the whole point of science was to create higher highs, brighter colors, and just basically better living though chemistry.

It took about forty minutes to examine his wound, tend to the break, and apply the cast. Once completed, Dr. Patel told Rage that Nurse Leticia would get him his crutches, take him for x-rays, give him instructions as to take care of his cast and help him out. He added, "And before you leave, she will also take a blood sample."

Rage raised his eyebrows, "Blood sample? I broke my fucking leg. Why would you need a blood sample?"

"Because you've been injured and came in here with an open wound. We've treated you with antibiotics, but a blood test is a great diagnostic tool."

Rage shook his head, "But my diagnosis was a broken leg. Diagnosed!" He knocked lightly on his new cast, not sure how strong it was, "Treated! Simple as that."

Dr. Patel started to once again explain why there was no argument on the point when he heard Nurse Leticia call out, "Code blue! Doctor Patel, we have a code blue!"

As Dr. Patel turned to leave, he said, "Wait here, Nurse Leticia will be here in a few minutes," and quickly made his way out of Rage's examination room.

Rage didn't want to wait for Nurse Leticia. He didn't want to stick around for a blood test. He wasn't sure just how the doctor would react to the mushrooms in his system, not to mention what had to be trace elements of the variety of uppers, downers, painkillers, and ecstasy that were surely there for easy discovery. He wasn't sure if Dr. Patel would give a rat's ass about the voluminous quantities of whatever residue weed might have left in his system. But he did have a pretty good idea that the hospital management would feel the need to narc him out. He came in many colors and wore many hats, but when it came down to it, the man was still the man.

Rage checked the cart to make sure it held no additional pharmacological delights, then slipped off the table, hopping mostly but testing his new cast by lightly trying to put a little weight on it. It only took a second to realize the cast wasn't there to allow him to walk, only to keep the leg in place. He would have to hop out of this place.

Hopping out of the examining room, he could see people gathered around a metal cart. The little enclave was buzzing with energy as they all focused on a tiny baby that lay motionless on the top of the cart. The baby was bathed in blue and purple as it was completely engulfed in the lights that had been enticing Rage all morning. He paused for a moment to watch. The doctors, nurses, and whatever the hell you called the other people orbiting the child, were way too busy to notice him hopping in place ten feet away.

As he watched the child, he realized that every fiber of his being was loving it. No, it wasn't necessarily love he was feeling. He was feeling a barely controllable urge to run over and grab the child. He wanted to rub his hands over the baby's head and cradle it in his arms. He tilted his head as he contemplated that in fact, he really wanted to smother the little thing with kisses. Jesus, he was turning into a fag.

He turned to leave but found that the baby was too much to pass up. He had to get a closer look. He found that if he carefully slid his newly bound leg carefully in front of him, he could slowly shuffle instead of hop. It wasn't as quick as hopping, but it wasn't nearly as conspicuous. As he approached the baby, he found himself wondering about his desire to touch the baby. As he shuffled toward the baby, his stomach growled and for a moment he feared that the noise would draw attention, but his need to bury his face in the baby's strangely lit hair was too great and he continued his slow pace.

When rage was only a few feet away, the baby coughed and started to cry. Instantly the moment was lost. The lights began to dim, and Rage stood staring at the baby, surprised to think that he had just been starting to wonder what the baby would taste like. He wondered what they mixed with the hospital grade codeine that could cause such a side effect. He decided he would have to get more when the coast was clear.

As the baby became more and more obscured, by not just the people attending but by the increasing number of devices that were being brought to bear, he decided it was time to book. He turned toward the back of the hospital (the way he came in was blocked by emergency workers) and started to weave/hop his way to what he hoped would be a back door. On the way, he scored a half dozen little cups of pills which, after swallowing a couple, he assumed he could identify through a little empirical testing. Better yet, he found a single crutch leaning against the desk of a temporarily unoccupied nurses' station. He was able to get the hang of using the crutch in a couple of steps and could glide his way out of the hospital in only a few minutes.

Tim had driven him here, but getting Tim out of the ER would be risky. Besides, if his father had taught him anything, it was take care of number one. The lesson had been absorbed well. Rage rarely thought of anyone else's needs before his own. He certainly wasn't concerned about Tim waiting for

48

him in the waiting room. Tim was a big boy, at least he tried to act like one. Rage figured Tim would figure out a way home or else he should get a refund from that overpriced college he was always going on about.

Rage hobbled through the back parking lot looking for his car. Tim had driven them here in Rage's car and still had the keys, but Rage always kept a spare key inside the wheel well. He got the key, threw the crutch in the back and hopped around to crawl into the driver's seat. Once there, he took a few minutes to gather himself in such a way as to feel ready to drive. He was high as hell, but that had never stopped him before. For a moment or two he considered that with only one operational leg, a manual transmission could be a challenge. However, he tested and decided he could work all three pedals with his right leg.

Rage's car was a strange looking alleged sports utility vehicle that was primarily marketed toward the sort of city dwelling post adolescents who somehow fancied their predilection for skateboarding to be a sign of some inherent capacity for sports. It was what could be called "extreme." So extreme, in fact, that manufacturers of such a vehicle saw the need to label it as such with decorative decals. They also appreciated the fact that those who craved such vehicles would better recognize the vehicle's extremeness by ensuring they properly misspelling it as Xtreme! Rage had opted for the double-Xtreme trim package, so in addition to rollbars that did nothing but point out to other motorists that the vehicle for some reason needed roll bars, it was also highly decorated with red, green, purple, and orange Xtreme patterns that marred its black paint job.

Just before he turned the key, he was overwhelmed with a sudden wave of nausea. It was as if his whole body instantly came to the decision to puke, having concluded that Rage was in no condition to be consulted. He was just able to get his head turned as his mouth opened on its own and his stomach began the process of draining itself. If someone had been watching from some other part of the parking lot, they would have wondered if someone had been throwing a bucket of multi-colored soup out the window of Rage's strange even more multi-colored SUV. He doused the car to his left and managed to even hit the car on the other side with a good bit of collateral damage.

He sat for a couple of minutes, during which he threw up a couple more times. He looked down at the seat next to him and found that the mere sight of the little white pill cups made him start to retch. Without even thinking about it, he found himself grabbing the pills and throwing them out into the mess he had just created. He regretted it the second he finished doing it. He sat staring out the window, sadly contemplating the little white ones—surely codeine—slowly sinking into a pool of his now blue and red tinged vomit. He wanted to cry as he absentmindedly sat eating the rest of the mushrooms that he had been carrying in his pocket.

After using some leftover Taco Bell napkins to wipe up the puke that he'd managed to get on the door of the SUV, Rage turned the key and started the arduous journey back home. He really needed to get to his happy place.

***

Tim sat in the waiting room contemplating the fact that Sponge Bob Square Pants can really take it out of you. After they took the screaming baby back to the examining area, Tim found himself back in his seat, transported to some weird little postmodern cheaply animated world where the jokes weren't funny, unless you were laughing at them. It felt like he had been pacing around the waiting room for seven or eight hours, but according to the clock on the wall, it had only been two and a half hours since Rage went back to be treated. He decided when the attendant came back, he would ask about Rage. Shortly after the thought occurred to him, the attendant did come back and sat down at her station.

Tim went to the desk and asked the round woman, "I know you folks are busy, but can you tell me how much longer for my roommate?"

Nurse Leticia looked up from her computer screen, ensuring to project with her eyes the extent to which he was messing with her mind. She contemplated messing with the boy's head by making him squirm about the "you folks" near faux pas, but instead just said, as slowly as possible, "Your...room...mate?"

Tim nodded, "Yes, my roommate. Rage, ah, Reginald Sutherland? He has a broken leg."

She stared at Tim and slowly nodded as she said, "Oh yes, your roommate." She began to move her head from side to side, adding, "Let me tell you something, young man, your friend must have thought that for some reason the rules don't apply to him. He ran out of here without finishing his treatment. I guess that boy thought he wouldn't have to pay if he wasn't here to pick up the check."

Tim interrupted, "Are you saying he isn't in there?"

She glared at him wide-eyed, "Well I guess I just am not being clear enough for your college boy tastes. Hell yes I'm saying he's gone. He's gone and I'll be damned if he isn't going to be receiving a bill for these rendered services."

Tim shook his head and turned to leave. If he was the sort to mutter such things as "fucking Rage," he would have been muttering "fucking Rage".

As Tim stormed toward the door, Leticia stood and added, "And for his own damn good he better come back in here and get that leg x-rayed."

Tim headed out of the emergency room and into the parking lot. Halfway to where he had parked Rage's car, he could see that it was gone. He muttered, "fucking Rage," under his breath as he continued to the space. Standing in the empty parking space he could see that someone— and he had to assume it was Rage—had puked all over the next car. He wasn't sure, as the sheer volume of the vomit could easily have been a group effort as it was hard to imagine all this coming out of just one stomach.

He checked his pocket to ensure he still had Rage's keys, then shook his head and made his way out of the parking lot. The hospital was a little more than three miles from the house. This being Los Angeles, public transportation really wasn't going to get him anywhere. He either had to call someone for a ride or start walking. Given that he'd left the house without his phone, walking would have to do. This being spring break, the only person in town who could have come for him was Rage. He started walking.

12

A Guy Named Don is Good to Find

He didn't know how long he had lain there. How long it had been since he moved was something he didn't care to think about. Wasn't that the whole point? He saw nothing, and he heard nothing. He was at rest. Don Hardman was decked out on his favorite floating lounge chair. He wore a pair of swim trunks and an old beauty mask that he'd found in his first wife's things after she died. He'd looked for it specifically, because somehow he had coveted it when she'd been alive. It wasn't a sick or out of the ordinary kind of coveting. He just knew when she'd worn it, she had really been able to relax. He remembered thinking what a blessing it was that for all intents and purposes it was a blindfold, because if she could have seen how ridiculous she looked, she would have found it difficult to let herself give in to its power. But he envied her ability to relax when she wore it.

He was past worrying about looking ridiculous. Five years retired, he no longer played to anyone else's tune. He was his own man. He had always been so, at least had seen himself as such. But as his societal ties had fallen away, he had realized the subtle effects his first marriage and the firm hand of management had had on both his self-image and his self-esteem. He had always been a believer in doing what was right. He took the long road. No shortcuts. He had played by the rules and had done okay for himself - a solid career, first in the Marines, and later as an Assistant District Attorney for the County of Los Angeles. He had had two successful marriages, the first to

Betty Trumaine, God rest her soul, who had given him two sons. Don and Betty were both in their fifties when she had passed away and those sons were grown and long gone by then.

After she passed, he felt his first twinges of freedom. He'd never lived alone before and took a very slow liking to it. The freedom he liked, but fending for himself in what he considered the womanly arts was a taste he failed to acquire. He puttered around, alternating between the wonder of getting to eat what he wanted when he wanted it and wondering how one actually went about procuring said anything. He lived like this for a little over a year before Dora, the widow who had once lived next door, started checking on him to make sure he was getting on all right.

At first he had found it a little off-putting. He was a man who took pride in his ability to take it. He didn't show need, and if he had been the sort who could admit to himself that he lacked for something, he was not the sort who would have allowed himself to share that admission with another. Still, it was nice to have a woman knocking around the house. As noted, his skills in the kitchen weren't really on par with his skills at the dinner table, and Dora had a pretty mean way with a frying pan. Of course, at first, after thirty years with the same woman, he had been a bit concerned about the state of his skills in the bedroom, but Dora proved to be just the sort of sparring partner he hadn't known he'd needed. Dora's first marriage had been a rocky one, and it turns out Don was just what she'd needed as well. Together, they burned hot for each other and had been doing so for well over a decade.

Looking back on the last few years, at this stretch with Dora, he saw it as one of his life's brightest spots. In a life of control and discipline, Dora gave him fifteen years of spontaneity and if not passion, then something as close to it as a man like Don could ever understand. Looking back on his earlier life, when he and Betty used to socialize with the Navarros, he would never have imagined there was such a streak of life hidden under the surface of the woman who had once been known as Dora Navarro. It was like discovering upon unfolding a beige cloth napkin that it was held together by a slender scarlet thread.

Back in the day, his worldview was that there was a plan and everyone's part in the plan was to just keep moving forward, asking as few questions as possible. You worked toward goals and sometimes you achieved them and sometimes you didn't. But if you didn't, at least take a shot, you could expect nothing. Today, his philosophy could be summed up pretty much the same, but with a good dose of "what the fuck" thrown in for good measure. Dora had proven to be a happy wild card, one that wasn't part of the plan and one that had added more to his life than could be had by adding up the parts of all his hard work and sticktoitiveness. She had fallen into his lap, both literally and figuratively, and he hadn't had a damn thing to do with it.

What Don liked about this time of the afternoon was that as it was the lull between lunch hour and what for most was still quitting time, there was little traffic and as such he could easily forget he was in the city. He could lay on his floating pool chair, eyes covered and let the sun bake his body. He wore a pair of blue swim trunks. Back when Dora had first taught him about the joy of doing nothing and really enjoying the simple paradise that was the fruit of his life's work, they had both worn a little less. However, at seventy, Dora had claimed her naked-in-the-backyard days were over. That was when Don bought a pair of swim trunks and established his current routine. Now, wearing his trunks and beauty mask, he just enjoyed the feel of the sun on his skin and the peace, quiet, and timelessness of the afternoon.

Don's peace was suddenly shattered by the sound of screeching tires and the crunching of metal. Peeling back his beauty mask, he turned around in time to see over his roof a shower of leaves billowing from a tree in front of the Sutherland house and getting caught by the breeze.

It was a constant source of wonder to Don Hardman that the Sutherland boy didn't kill himself. Not a suicide kind of thing, just that that boy never seemed to be really hooked up right and living alone the way he did, lacking any common sense and having an insatiable taste for the drink and such, it just seemed a gruesome death was somehow on the horizon. Over the years, Don and Dora had tried to keep a bit of any eye out. He, Betty, and Dora had all been close to the boy's parents, had watched the boy grow up and now he felt an obligation to see to it he didn't blow up the house.

It was Don who had taken care of the arrangements when Bob and Nancy

Sutherland, Reggie's parents, had been killed in an automobile accident. Bob had been an associate at one of the few downtown law firms Don had no truck with. Don, being a former assistant district attorney, had no use for the type of firms that dealt with criminal defense, and Bob Sutherland was on track to be a partner in a corporate only practice. Don's conservative roots made it hard for him to consider white-collar criminals as true criminals and as such, those who defended them didn't qualify as true scumbags. Bob Sutherland defended businessmen who sometimes played a little too aggressively, and as far as Don was concerned, that was a good site more respectable than defending drug lords and rapists.

Bob was good people in Don's book. So was Nancy. That was why when Bob had asked him to help handle their affairs, he was happy to do it. Bob must have considered Don okay as well, considering he was not a family attorney, but an assistant DA. Bob had done the bulk of the work himself, mainly looking for someone to administer the Sutherland estate in the event that it ever became necessary - someone who actually knew the boy. Given that Don was a neighbor and had known the family for years, it made sense.

When Bob and Nancy had been killed, Don took care of all the arrangements. He also went a step beyond. Noting that the boy was only a few months from being eighteen and therefor of age, Don had himself appointed temporary guardian so that what was already quite a disruption in the young man's life wouldn't include being uprooted from his home and placed in some temporary foster care. As he would be a free and clear adult in less than six months, Don helped ensure Reggie could keep his home and he and Dora would periodically look in on him. Dora brought him food for a while, but once the boy got used to his independence, it became clear he preferred fast food to Dora's casseroles and salads. When the boy reached legal age, Dora stopped dropping in and Don's legal involvement was limited to administering the estate. Once it was established that Reggie wasn't going to take an interest in paying bills and keeping up the property, Don helped set up a trust to keep Reggie taken care of financially and the property handled from a maintenance perspective. This wasn't just because of his fondness for Bob and Nancy, but out of a concern for his own property's value, should

Reggie continue to shirk his responsibilities as a budding adult.

Over the years Don had begun to feel a little like some old peeping Tom. No, that wasn't quite right. He wasn't a peeping Tom so much as a good old-fashioned snoop. He had a couple of spots in his yard where he could get a good look into the Sutherland back yard. He also had found a few spots on county land, back behind their respective houses where he could get a better look. He didn't do it out of some need to know what was going on. He'd been young once and certainly had done his share of fun and stupid things. No, he did it because on more than one occasion he had been able to prevent a fire, prevent a landslide inducing flood or call a paramedic.

He shook his head thinking about the kind of man that boy had grown into. And in addition to that, he wondered about the type of friends he attracted. Don had lived through the sixties, so he knew a thing or two about drugs and the company they keep. That boy—strike that—man often had a lot of friends who were either always stoned, getting stoned, or providing others the means to do so themselves. On most mornings after those parties— and the sounds that filtered to his kitchen made it clear when they were happening—he would wind his way through the bushes and peruse the Sutherland property for bodies. It sounded a little melodramatic when he said it out loud, but over the last decade he'd found four people so dead to the world he'd called paramedics. In all but one of those cases, the paramedics had thanked him and told him he may have just saved a life. On all those occasions, he'd gotten some serious verbal abuse from Reggie. So be it. When he finally met his maker, he didn't want it to be in the company of those he could have saved but had failed to do so because he didn't want to upset the spoiled punk that lived next door.

Dora was out in the garden, tending to her roses when she too heard the sound of what Don referred to as the Sutherland boy's idiot mobile barreling around the corner and into its driveway. Don said, and she agreed, he could never understand what made that boy tick. Don also said that how anyone could have picked that monstrosity as a vehicle would just get added to the list of life's unanswered mysteries. Red and green with purple highlights, it had all manner of what Don and Dora took to be drug references stenciled on what little there was of its frame. Don believed it was supposed to suggest its driver was an avid sportsman. To Don, and he had to assume to anyone who was of sound mind, it signaled the driver was a damn fool.

Dora just peered up over the roses in time to see Reggie—which he apparently hated to be called—run over the curb and smack into the old maple tree that sat on the boy's property just between his driveway and Dora's garden. The impact knocked loose hundreds of leaves showering the Hardman house and Dora and her garden. As Don ran around the side of the house, Dora looked at the leaves, thinking she could rake them into rows and that they would eventually make nice mulch.

Don arrived in time to see Reggie back up about eight feet, backing up over his trash can, only to take a second pass at avoiding the maple tree, this time just clearing it before plowing into a sixty-foot cedar and knocking a blast of a few million needles from the old cedar, this time giving both Don and Dora a good dusting.

The boy stumbled out of his idiot mobile, and Don could see he was wearing a cast and engaging the services of a crutch before hobbling off. It was clear he hadn't seemed concerned about his car, either tree, or for that matter the fact he had just doused his neighbors with debris. Don called out, "Afternoon, Reggie."

Rage looked over at the old guy who lived next door, Mr. Hardman. The grooves that a lifetime of living here had set in place allowed him to get ready to verbally shuck and jive and blow smoke up the old man's ass before he even turned around. But as he did turn, he saw the old man and his wife were bathed in light. They looked like they were wearing giant capes. Their capes—or were they royal robes—were wrapped around them, covering their heads as well as the ground at their feet. He blinked, unable to say anything, just trying to adjust his eyes to the brightness of the light.

Don said, "Looks like you've got yourself a broken leg there. Have you been in an accident?" It only made sense the way the boy drove. Not to mention the fact he was probably always high on something. He only prayed that the fool hadn't killed someone.

Rage shook his head, "I fell." He normally would have finished that off with a perfunctory coughing of his favorite Mr. Hardman alternative, "Mr. Hardon," but right now, looking at Mr. Hardman, he couldn't help thinking the old guy was okay. Truth be told, he even had a momentary desire to run over and hug him. To thank him for all the times he'd butted into Rage's business and helped out, and for helping him get through the financial mess when his parents had died. Instead of telling the old guy to fuck the hell off, he managed to add, "It's no big deal... see ya."

Don watched as the boy headed into his house. He wondered why he thought of Reggie as a boy. My God, the boy had to be thirty by now. But he didn't think he'd ever seen him in long pants or anything but a tee-shirt. He seemed to live on pizza and burgers, and aside from the heavy quantities of beer that clearly were consumed on the premises, he also saw evidence of large quantities of the kind of super sweet sodas and Slurpees usually reserved for children. He dressed as a child, he ate as a child, and to Don's knowledge, had never worked a day in his life. *What the hell*, he thought. *If it looks like a duck...*

He turned to Dora, "You know, dear, that boy is headed for a fall."

Dora shrugged, "Sweetheart, you know as well as I do, we all are."

Don nodded and shrugged. "I guess that's why we need to make the most of every day the Good Lord gives us." He studied Rage's newly dented vehicle, then scanned up and down the street to see if anyone was watching before taking Dora's hand and adding, "Care for a swim then, my dear?"

Dora giggled as they headed back through the gate.

13

Navarro Pulls it Off

Mr. Navarro found that no matter how hard the reflection of him tried, it couldn't scream. As it happened, it turned out he really didn't feel the need to anyway. His mouth had opened, and he had tried to close his eye, but in spite of the fact that in his mind's eye it was all happening, in fact he had no eyelids and of course no speech apparatus. He was just a bunch of bones, held together by some sort of fungus. He held up his left arm and examined it. He couldn't see bone. He saw that the fungus that covered him was arranged in alternating layers. Some layers looked like thin sheets of whitish gray rubber. Others were strands of intertwined tendrils, not that dissimilar from how he imagined his muscles may have looked when he was alive. These were white and gray, with the occasional black, red, or blue streak.

After spending a long time carefully examining his fingers, hands, and arms, he spent even more time testing the rest of his body. He realized that although he could feel a wholeness in his being, his skin really didn't feel like anything. If he touched his arm with a finger, neither the arm nor the finger had any sensation.

He finally stood and took a few careful steps. Once again, he felt the wonderful sensation of once again being mobile but couldn't feel the earth on his feet or any pain as he stepped on the rocks and broken glass that lay in the refuse scattered throughout his old house.

As he continued to examine and be amazed by his newly formed body, he noted that not only did he have fungus muscles in all the right places, he even had his genitalia again. He contemplated his penis and scrotum for a minute. He shook his head, wondering how such a small piece of his person, relatively speaking of course, could have wreaked such havoc on his life. Virtually every mistake he had made, at least the ones that had haunted him for the past twenty years, and for that matter, most of the seventy before that, had been as a result of not being able to control this one thing. Knowing that physical pain didn't seem possible in his new configuration, although he wasn't sure it would have mattered, he grabbed the thing at its base and pulled it off. He dug out everything in the neighborhood of where his package had been, deeming the whole area as useless and nothing but a hangout for a bunch of troublemakers.

His wounded groin oozed a thick white fluid for the next few minutes. He stuffed some red and blue debris into the hole and held it firmly in place as he began to explore the rest of the old Navarro spread. He pushed the bedroom door aside and stepped out into the hallway. Parts of the house were now unreachable as the Fonda home had apparently taken a nosedive into the part of the house where the kitchen and a second bedroom had been. As he moved through the hallway, carefully gaining some bodily mastery, he pushed open what doors remained, checking each room before finally arriving in what had been his and Dora's living room. He stood in the center of the living room, slowly turning and taking a few minutes to survey the place. Sitting in the corner, turned upside down was his old chair. He struggled with it, discovering that his muscles weren't nearly as functionally impressive as they appeared. He was, though, eventually able to push it over and turn it upright.

He sat in his old chair. "His throne" was what Dora had called it. From the throne he surveyed his kingdom. It was pretty sad, really. His former domain had been reduced to a third of his old house, filled with dirt, weeds, and fungus. Now here he sat, a dead man perched on his filthy, dilapidated throne. The worst thing of all, there was no television. Truth be told, when he had sat here in life, it was the television, and a hell of a lot of vodka sours that kept him numb. Without the distraction all he had ever thought about was the scent of Innocencia.

For a number of years, early in his marriage to Dora, he had felt he could somehow overcome his yearnings for the long extinct moments with Innocencia. Dora was almost twenty years his junior and not much older than Innocencia had been when she had bewitched him. Back then, Emile Navarro had still had prospects, or at least the illusion thereof, and the seventeen-year-old Dora had fallen for his charms. For a time, Dora's youth kept Navarro entranced and able to forget the pull of the memories of Innocencia. Of course, just as seventeen is a far cry from thirteen, twenty-five is another thing all together. By the time Dora reached her thirties, Navarro had begun to look for his olfactory fixes elsewhere. He sought out the company of prostitutes. It didn't take him all that long to realize a couple of equally disturbing facts. First off, whether it was real or all in his head, there was no way a prostitute could offer up the fresh unspoiled scent that he craved. Second, and this one was a killer, he could see in the eyes of those he approached that the fifty something year old Navarro no longer had the charm that had seen him through his youth. His promise was gone—gone just as Dora's youth was gone—and he then realized it had been wasted. Wasted on a few fleeting moments with Innocencia and more than a decade with Dora. All he could have was paid for and the knowledge that it was with someone who considered all but his money as somehow repulsive sealed his fate. He had been done with getting what he needed in this life. He would spend the next twenty years sitting in his chair trying to forget what he had missed and another twenty in the ground regretting it without the benefit of television or vodka sours.

The self-awareness that had been haunting him the past twenty years had been present before, but he had been able to drown it out with some semblance of sex, alcohol and televised entertainment. Now, without his old distractions, his little kingly chamber didn't feel much kinglier than had his unmarked grave. He decided this time, in this new life, he wasn't going to sit in this room waiting for another shot. He wouldn't spend another lifetime waiting for someone to come to find him. Damn it, he was going out. Now!

Stepping outside the house, Navarro surveyed the surrounding area, looking for less claustrophobic environs. It was funny how being buried for twenty years could make one pine for wide open spaces. He had the presence of mind to understand a being such as himself, a rotting skeleton covered in fungus, might cause a stir ambling down the road, so he decided to stay to the bushes. As he approached the base of the hill, looking to hug the hill he stared down at his hands and saw he wasn't quite so solid as he had believed.

The tendrils that wound around his arms were beginning to wilt. Even though he couldn't feel his new flesh, he quickly realized the sun was taking its toll on the delicate membrane that formed his new skin and sinew. He ducked into the bushes and scrambled for deeper cover.

As he worked his way up the hill, he could feel a weighty sluggishness in his motions. Looking down at his feet, he could see he was accumulating debris as he moved through the decomposing underbrush. Leaves, sticks, and filth in general were glomming onto his feet and legs. It looked as though his legs had more than doubled in size and his feet were even larger.

It took him almost an hour to make it halfway up the hill. By then he found he could barely walk. He assumed it was a combination of the additional weight he was carrying in his legs not to mention the more frightening loss of fungus happening all over his body. The sun was clearly taking its toll even though he had avoided direct sunlight for most of the trip.

Looking for a place to rest, he discovered a green patch that gave way to a small mushroom covered hole. It was like a grass and mushroom covered crack in the soil that upon further inspection opened into a small cave. Crawling through the slanted opening, pushing away the grass and tendrils that lined the moist entrance to the cave, he couldn't shake the image he was crawling into a womb.

14

Rage Gets His Home Ec On

Rage walked into his house feeling anything but at home. Nothing felt right. Fatty greeted him in his usual way - licking his face and trying to somehow signal his human master he hadn't been fed today. Rage waved him off. He felt like shit and didn't have time for Fatty's bullshit. His leg hurt and his guts hurt. He could have sworn he had puked so hard he'd at least pulled a muscle if not broken something. He even wondered if it was possible to have coughed up something that wasn't supposed to get coughed up - an organ or something. He was no scientist or anything and certainly didn't have a very complete knowledge of the inner workings of the human body, but by God, he knew when something was wrong. He went into the kitchen and opened the refrigerator. He needed to get something in his stomach to ease the burning. He didn't think this was the time for a beer—a thought he rarely would have entertained—so he grabbed a bright red sports drink and chugged half of it. The sugar felt good but drove home the fact he needed something solid.

He rummaged through the refrigerator while Fatty tried to do the same. There wasn't much in the way of food. He mainly kept beer and sodas in there as he mainly lived on fast food, but he had some stuff for sandwiches. Looking at the assortment of items in the drawer where he kept his meat and cheese, the only thing that looked even remotely appetizing was a baggie that had some old moldy turkey in it. The ham, cheese, and salami were all still good, but it turned his stomach just looking at it. Fatty licked his chops and barked a suggestion that ham and cheese were a proper snack. Rage put the lunch meats back and grabbed the baggie of old turkey and opened it over the sink. It was dripping with red and blue juices and the smell of it gave him the dry heaves. He figured that after the puke fest he'd put on at the hospital, dry heaves were about the only ones he was capable of. Fatty nudged him and tried to remind him some of the finest things in life are a few days past their prime.

Rage stood there staring at the sink when his right hand, almost of its own volition, reached down into his right pocket and started rooting around. He looked down, curious, and remembered the mushrooms. He had none left but realized thinking about them was helping to settle his stomach. He thought about it and realized mushrooms could be for more than getting high. *After all*, he thought, *don't some people eat mushrooms as food?*

Rage was starting to get the hang of the crutch and grabbing it he headed out to the back yard with Fatty running alongside, barking about the crime of letting food go to waste. Rage scooped up as many mushrooms as he could hold in his pockets and left hand. Hobbling back toward the kitchen, he lost a few mushrooms due to his greedy attempt to bring back more than he could carry.

Fatty looked at a large mushroom and gave it a good smelling. He decided it might be worth a shot. It was no rotten turkey, but then again, not everything could be. He took the mushroom into his mouth whole and bit down. The bitterness struck him as something that neither man nor beast should ever consume. He did something that goes against the grain of every dog that ever took breath. He spit out food. Then he ran into the kitchen to warn his master that the mushrooms tasted like crap - well, not like crap - more like something that doesn't taste good. When Fatty got to the kitchen, his master had placed the mushrooms on the kitchen counter and was rummaging through one of the cupboards. Fatty started barking a warning.

Rage took a frying pan out of the cupboard and without turning to address the dog said, "Fatty, shut the fuck up." Fatty didn't. Rage was no cook, and even if he had been, he wasn't what you would call an herbivore in any sense, so anything other than meat and cheese would have fallen outside the universe of ingredients with which he was familiar. He had no idea what one did to cook mushrooms. It did occur to him to at least wash them, so he managed to rinse them before throwing them in the pan. He cooked them, whole, with a little salt and pepper, over medium heat for a little less than ten minutes. While cooking them, he noted that they exuded from their spots drops of red and blue juices and that as they mixed in the pan, it created a thin purple sauce. However, as he continued to cook them, the liquid either evaporated or was absorbed by the mushrooms. He couldn't tell which. Fatty barked warnings the whole time.

Rage stood in the kitchen, eating the mushrooms with his fingers. He smiled at the realization that they were pretty damn good. Apparently he was a guy who knew how to cook mushrooms. They were so good that he thought about cooking another batch but realized he was stuffed. He tossed a couple of his cooked mushrooms to Fatty, hoping that would shut him up.

It did. Fatty sniffed the mushrooms, making sure to confirm they were indeed the same things cooked that they had been raw. Then he looked up and tilted his head, affecting the age-old position dogs take when reminded that their masters lack the power of reason. Then he lowered his head and made for the backyard. It looked like he was going to have to drum up his own lunch today.

Rage thought about taking a nap. It had been a rough day. When he went into his bedroom, he felt closed in. He'd never been claustrophobic before and had always assumed people who claimed to be were just being fags, but he now wondered if this was what it was like. If it was, then being claustrophobic sucked. It seemed the walls were too close. Maybe, thinking more about it, it wasn't that the walls were too close, but that there were walls at all. He felt like being outside. He grabbed a joint from his dresser, a beer from the fridge, and headed out to his happy place.

Sitting in his favorite chair, he leaned back, got high, and relaxed. He smiled as the lights swayed and danced around the canyon at his feet. He was getting used to the fact they were all around and was starting to understand that they weren't just where he could see them. They were obviously all around all the time, just stronger in some things at some times. At least this was obvious to someone who had been eating hallucinogenic mushrooms all day. Rage had always believed, and had often unsuccessfully tried to explain to others, that hallucinogens didn't make you see things that weren't there. They helped wipe away all your societal filters and allowed you to see what was really there. They opened your mind and your eyes to reality. That, and of course, they also fucked you up real good.

So now, he could see there was some kind of red and blue energy emanating from things. It was beautiful, and it made him wonder if somehow we were all linked by the light. People, animals, objects, everything seemed to have some of the light. It seemed pretty cool. He figured it was why he kept loving everyone he saw today – he somehow was feeling his connection to everyone and everything. He drained his beer and closed his eyes. He could still see the lights and realized he could also still feel their warmth. The light was encircling him, coursing through his veins, both in and around him. He was smiling as he lost consciousness.

15

Navarro Goes Down

When Navarro arrived at the cave, he could barely stand. Crawling into the cave, he had felt a deep relief. His pace had become burdened, both from the heat and, he assumed, from the debris that had accumulated around his legs and feet. When he had arrived at the cave, his lower extremities had more than doubled in size, covered with a thick coating of rotting leaves, grass, sticks, and twigs. He had squeezed through the opening of the cave and found that it opened up to a fungus covered chamber about eight feet by ten. As he sat down in the far corner, as far away from the heat of the day as possible, long thin tendrils from the floor of the cave where he sat began to slowly explore his body. He felt no fear when the strands of mycelia picked over his body, removing the accumulated residue from his climb up the hill. He calmly watched the extraction and then watched with increasing interest as the same slender tendrils used some of the gathered materials to patch his body. After watching the fungus work on him for a time, Navarro reached down, scooped up a handful of rotting leaves and shoved it into a gap in his chest. He watched as tiny fungus shoots wound around the new material and continued to repair his body. In a little over an hour, he was as good as new - or at least as good as the newly refurbished Navarro.

One might think twenty or so years of lying in stasis would teach a thing or two about patience. Perhaps if one had spent a couple of decades laying face up in the dirt, thinking about the past and knowing there was no future save for more of the same, then the idea of sitting around in a cave all day, waiting for nightfall would not present itself as an interminable experience. This should have been something Navarro could do without the least bit of effort.

The problem was, for the past twenty years, he had been without hope. He had lived in the past, wondering how he should have done things, and more importantly, how he shouldn't have. He had been without hope and the expectation of things to come. But now, a whole new world of possibilities had opened for him. He was suddenly, not just for the first time since he died, but for many years before, filled with hope. He was like a kid the night before Christmas. He knew all he had to do was wait until the sun went down and once that happened, he would be free to...to...to do something. He didn't know what he was able to do, but the knowledge that he could move around was making it difficult not to do so. He wanted to feel something. So far, physically feeling something was eluding him. Perhaps this fungus coating would never let him feel things, but emotionally he felt good. He didn't feel the sense of isolation he had while buried under the house. As the afternoon stretched on, left to his natural inclination to ruminate on the past, it occurred to him he felt more at home in this skin than he believed he had in his original equipment. He felt content with himself.

Of course, that contentedness didn't naturally extend to his surroundings. Every few minutes he would stand up and pace his little cave, enjoying if not the actual feeling of motion, then at least the experience of seeing the motion and knowing he was no longer trapped in the dirt. But he was still trapped. He couldn't leave the cave. At the end of each of his little pacing episodes he would stand at the cave's entrance, careful to stay out of the direct sun, and longingly survey the area. Looking past his old home he could see a few more trees and then a drop off. He knew from when he was alive that there was a street below with houses. And those houses had yards that crept up his hill. Beyond those houses was another drop off and another level of yards and homes even further down the hill. He believed the reason his and the Fonda's homes had never been fully excavated was due to some fear that any level of the hill, if properly disturbed, could collapse causing some kind of domino effect. He agreed, but had to think that somehow those houses at the bottom of the hill were responsible for the failure to rescue him...that the people who lived down the hill and the protection of their homes had been responsible for his death.

He wondered if Dora was alive. After all, maybe Dora had been in the house when it fell. It seemed to have done alright in the fall. Maybe she had fared as well. Or, perhaps she had been buried, but not as deep as him. Maybe she had been saved from the wreckage. For that matter, as far as he could remember, she may not have even been on the hill that day. She had spent a lot of time gallivanting down at the church. Yes, as he thought about it, he figured she would have somehow escaped his fate. She had always been luckier than him. Most people were. People seemed to like her more, although God only knew why.

As he stood surveying the world and wondering about Dora, he realized it didn't really matter if she was alive. First of all, she had been damn near fifty when the hill gave way. Now, if she was still alive, she could be in her seventies. He shuddered just thinking about it. She was no ray of sunshine twenty years younger, and he couldn't imagine that she had improved all that much. He wasn't sure if he had so much as touched her for the last twenty years of their lives together, and he couldn't see why her proximity would matter to him now. Second, he guessed that technically he was some kind of damn monster now. So, she probably wouldn't be any happier to see him than he her. And third, he had had the foresight to rip off his damn private parts. So, even if he wanted to touch the old bag, and she had wanted to touch him, there really wouldn't have been any point to it. Lastly, the only thing he could think of that Dora had ever really been good at was cooking. He didn't believe he had any need or capacity for food in his current state. To Navarro's old way of thinking, when it came to women, if you couldn't enjoy smelling or rutting with them, they had better be good cooks. Otherwise, it was just a bunch of pointless blather.

By the middle of the afternoon, the boredom took its toll. Navarro decided it was time to go outside again. He noted that the "skin" on his arms and chest had toughened considerably, and he decided he could venture down to the tree line on the other side of his house. He remembered there used to be a good deal of brush that ran down the hill and he wanted to see if the houses were still there. He needed to witness the houses whose owners had subjected him to being buried alive. He decided if he hurried down to the house, he could limit his time in the sun and he could then cool off inside and make the tree line on his second effort.

He stepped out onto the grass at the foot of the cave and took in an imaginary breath of fresh air. He began to scramble down the hill toward his house when he lost his footing and fell headlong into a large rock outcropping. If he had been able to hear, the sound of breaking bone would have given him cause for alarm. As it was, it wasn't until he tried to stand that he discovered he couldn't. He cursed his luck. This ability so recently gained had already begun to be taken for granted. Glancing down, he discovered his left femur was broken and his leg wouldn't support him. He could see the break through a large tear in the fungus that had formed his new leg. Although he couldn't stand, he found he could crawl. Even dragging his useless leg behind him, it only took fifteen or twenty minutes for him to crawl to the house. Not being able to feel with his fungus flesh, he didn't realize until he pulled his way into the old Navarro home's entry way that his leg had torn off under its own weight and laid halfway between the house and the cave.

He sat, leaning up against the front door for several minutes, contemplating his missing leg. He wasn't sure its value or why he cared at this point, but even if the leg was new, the bones had been his for the past ninety plus years and something in him refused to just let it go. He decided he and the fungus could repair his leg. He got down on his belly after formulating his plan and began a combat crawl back to the place where his leg lay.

He realized he must have been somehow losing strength due to the heat, because it took him at least twice as long to get back to the leg as had the original journey. Once he got there, he slung the leg over his shoulder onto his back and slowly turned himself around for the trip back to the house.

Looking back the way he had come, it was clear he had been losing fungus along the way. He could see the fungus had been scraped off as he had crawled. There was a thick trail made up of white, blue, and red tendrils as well as torn sheets of gray fungus that lay drying in the sun. A few of the tendrils writhed and twisted in the grass as they lost their battle with the heat.

He spent the next half hour attempting to make it to the house but continued to shed his coating of fungus. Finally, he was lying face down a few yards from his old house, unable to move, now only a skeleton, partially covered with fungus. He realized that in the heat of the day the last remaining fungus would shrivel and flake away over the next few hours.

He thought, *Son of a bitch!*

16

Tim Takes the High Road

Tim was beat by the time he made it home from the hospital. He had stopped at a local restaurant near campus to have lunch and while there had run into a couple of classmates that, after hearing about his morning, took pity on him and offered him a ride home. Not having to walk the last couple miles up hill was a good thing. However, the company left something to be desired.

The driver, a guy Tim was pretty sure was named Ben, insisted on lighting up a joint as soon as they got in the car. Under normal circumstances, Tim avoided drugs at all costs. This had been a lifetime habit and one he was even more adamant about having spent the last six months witnessing the burnt-out lifestyle of Rage. But Tim had also learned under the tutelage of Rage that sharing his distaste for the stuff would have no effect on its users, save to make them mock him. And in this case, perhaps put him back on the street for the long walk home.

As they made their way to Rage's place, he dutifully held the fat joint Ben passed his way to his lips and looked away as he pretended to inhale. He then passed it back to the front seat from which he hoped it would never return. He tried to hold his breath for as much of the trip as possible, but it was at least a fifteen-minute ride, so he just tried to avoid breathing deeply. At one point he realized he was also sitting with his fingers crossed. He hoped his finger crossing strategy would pay off, because Ben got turned around a few times and ended up taking almost forty minutes to get Tim home.

As they pulled into the big circular driveway that sat in front of Rage's place, Ben said, "Hey, man. I know this place. This guy throws a hell of a party."

Tim nodded, thinking that it only made sense this pothead would know Rage. "Yes, yes he does."

The guy in the passenger seat, who Tim could only be sure wasn't the guy whose name he thought was Ben said, "So, you room with Rage? That's cool."

"Yeah, it's great. Either of you want to move in? I'm pretty sure there's about to be a vacancy."

Ben laughed, "No, hey, that's cool. I'd never graduate if I lived in this party hole." As he said the words "party hole" his voice went up an octave and he formed some strange sign with his right forearm and hand that Tim had to assume was some sort of sign language for those who could only enjoy life when destroying brain cells faster than the body could produce them.

As Tim exited the car, he took as big a cleansing breath as he could, hoping to ensure his lungs were free of any remaining contaminants from the long and winding ride. "Well, if either of you change your mind, let me know. I'm probably going to move out."

"Too bad, man. This is one hell of a sweet oasis."

"Yes, well. Thanks for the ride, Ben."

Ben smiled and furrowed his brow just enough as he was driving away to make Tim wonder what Ben's name really was.

While still standing in the driveway, Tim noticed Rage's car was covered with pine needles resting with its bumper slightly violating the space of the tall cedar tree that sat watch in the front yard. Tim thought that perhaps the tree had saved the front door from a similar fate. He was examining the damage when he heard his name.

"Good afternoon, Tim."

Tim turned in time to see the next-door neighbor standing beside him. He smiled at her. He realized his smile felt a little..."funny." He answered, "Hi Mrs. Hardman."

Dora said, "Please, Tim. You know it's just Dora."

He nodded, noting that, too, felt a little funny. "I'm sorry. Dora." He had trouble addressing his elders by their first name. It felt disrespectful, and on some level made him feel as though he was somehow held more accountable for his opinions.

Dora shook her head, "Reggie looked in a bad way when he got home today. He said he fell and broke his leg. Were you hurt too, are you okay?"

Tim didn't know whether to nod or shake his head. "I'm fine. Rage...Reggie had quite a fall." He didn't see any reason to note that Rage had jumped. "He fell down the back of the hill and broke his leg. At least I assume that's all he broke; I haven't seen him since I took him to the emergency room."

Dora said, "He looked like that was probably all that was broken when he came through here." She looked up at the tree, then down at the car. "Of course, he looked like he may not have been feeling all that well."

"Well, I have to assume they gave him some real strong pain killers at the hospital."

Dora nodded, looking concerned, "I'd guess that is a pretty good assumption."

Tim asked, "Mrs... Dora, have you lived up on the hill for a long time?"

"A very long time, Tim."

"When Rage fell off the cliff, he ended up sitting next to a couple of old houses that Rage said slid down the hill around twenty years ago."

Dora still smiled as she nodded, but inside a part of her stiffened. She didn't like to think about her time in the old house where she and Emile had spent so many years. "Yes, there were two homes that were lost when a water main broke during some unusually heavy rains."

Tim asked, "Yes, but why wouldn't they have removed them? I mean, after all this time, you would think they should have been torn down."

Dora continued nodding. "I would have thought so, yes. But you know, I guess I just don't spend any time thinking about that mess down there. That's all in the past."

"Well, I guess. It just seems dangerous."

Dora smiled, "Not if you leave it alone. Just let it be. Just forget about it. That's what I do."

74

Tim shrugged, looking at the mess Rage had made. "Well, I guess I better check to see if Rage has everything under control inside."

Dora wished him good luck and headed back to her roses.

Inside, Tim found the remnants of Rage's rare cooking experiment—a dirty pan in the sink and some mushrooms on the floor—and checked every other room in the house before stepping out to the back yard. He saw Rage lounging in his chair and went out to check on him.

Rage was snoring when Tim got there. If it had been anyone else but Rage, he would have woken him and talked him into coming into the house. It was getting dark. But even though he had only known Rage for a few months, he had learned by now he viewed his happy place as almost sanctuary. If Tim woke him up, he'd give him shit for doing so, and then go back to sleep just to prove he hadn't passed out but had meant to sleep there. No, if Rage was uncomfortable, he'd wake up and move. He was a big boy - sort of. Tim thought Rage might be closer to Tim's dad's age rather than his own, truth be told. Let him take care of himself for a change.

Tim had studying to do and had already wasted the whole day on Rage's mushroom adventure. Tomorrow was Sunday. He could study tonight and all day tomorrow to catch up. Then on Monday, he'd check the boards at school and see if there were any promising, less dramatic living situations that he might want to check out.

Unfortunately, when Tim sat down to get to studying, he realized his attention span wasn't quite...working. He'd never been stoned and was pretty certain he wasn't now. But he decided he may have, nonetheless, been deprived of clean oxygen for a time and that perhaps it had taken a bit of a toll on his brain cell situation. It wasn't even dark outside when he decided to turn in for the night. His last thoughts before drifting off to the deepest sleep he had ever had, was how good Taco Bell would have been - right then.

17

Fatty Finds a Bone!

Fatty spent most of Saturday doing what he did most days. He ate, licked himself, and tried to catch any cats or squirrels that entered his field of vision. He liked to make rounds several times a day, just to keep the yard free of invaders. Sometimes, when the yard was particularly uneventful, like this particular Saturday, he took his show on the road, clearing out a neighbor's yard or the wash behind his own.

About six o'clock, a concept that was well beyond his world view, Fatty found himself crouched about a third of the way down the hill, waiting for a possum to take just one more step.

The possum was waiting for the dog to move, feeling that it had perhaps waited too long to begin its feigning of death. Instead, it decided to believe that the dog hadn't seen it. Sometimes that kind of faith could pay off.

In a sense, the faith did pay off. Fatty hadn't seen it. But he had smelled it. His eyes weren't what they once had been, but his nose gave him fits. If he'd known what it meant, and he had the power of speech, he could have told you he could smell in 3D. He, of course, being a dog, would have been exaggerating slightly - as is their way. But he did have the ability to do a pretty decent job of gauging distance and direction based on smell.

Fatty had the possum locked in long enough to go for it. The animal was farther away than he would have preferred, but he thought, *Hey, that's why it's called hunting instead of shopping.* No he didn't. He was a dog. But he did pounce four feet to the place where the possum was just beginning to regret its decision to stay there and not act more dead.

As Fatty landed, his front paws pinned the possum who was in turn just attempting to turn and waddle away. Fatty's momentum caused them both to start rolling down the hill. The whole way, Fatty attempted to somehow grip the possum while the possum tried to somehow be a whole lot bigger and faster. Neither animal was successful.

They rolled about halfway to the bottom of the wash and stopped short, landing next to a small outcropping of rocks that marked the entrance to a small cave. The possum squirted down between the rocks, only momentarily celebrating its victory, before forgetting this incident ever happened due to its inability to form lasting memories.

Fatty spent a minute rooting around the edge of the rocks, pining for his missing prey. But that didn't last long, as he soon found himself overcome by the smell coming from the little cave. It was a wonderful mélange of two of his favorite smells. He smelled bones, and he smelled human. He, of course, like all domesticated dogs, loved the smell of human. It was the smell of food, pets, toys, treats, and just your basic all round sucker. But bones had a special place in a dog's olfactory palette that went back much farther in their evolutionary makeup than did human companionship. And in this day and age, where so many denied their dogs any bones, it was an all too rare item.

Fatty stood at the base of the cave, contemplating the wonder of the rich, dense odor, before stepping in. Immediately upon entering the cave, two things crossed his mind—quite a lot to handle for a dog's mind. He realized the little cave was littler than he had thought, really only about the size of one of the small rooms in his master's house, the ones where his master and other humans constantly were in dispute over who owned the big white drinking bowls. More importantly, this cave had no bones in it - it just reeked of them.

He circled the tiny cave. He repeated this nine or ten times—dogs don't really get bored—and finally pinpointed the direction the bones had come from, and more importantly, which direction they had left by. He sniffed his way out of the cave, over the rocks—there was something about the rocks, but he couldn't remember—and down the hill. He was almost to the old smashed up house when he found the bones.

The bones were all stuck together in an arrangement he had never seen before. He'd seen them individually wrapped in plastic, and on occasion he'd encountered a sliced off section of a bone sitting in his bowl. But here, stretched out in front of him was a collection consisting of more bones than he'd ever seen before, probably in his whole life, stuck together at the ends. The shape kind of reminded him of something, but lacking anything that even vaguely approached abstract reasoning, he wasted no time trying to figure out what that something was. Instead, he grabbed a bone from the pile. Because the bones were all stuck together, when he tugged on the first bone—a nice long one—the whole thing moved.

For just a second, Fatty stopped and the bones stopped moving. He pulled again, the bones jiggled again, and he stopped again. Then he began the age-old practice of shaking the head and separating the bones. He didn't know why he did it. No dog did. But somehow, when they ate food, they shook it - even when there was no reason to shake it. Because he didn't know why he shook it, he didn't realize it had worked when the leg bone pulled free from the skeleton. When he did so, the bones got flipped over and he saw that one of the bones was looking at him.

**

Mr. Navarro had been staring into the grass for what had to be hours when he became troubled by the fact his head seemed to be moving. It was a sort of herky-jerky sensation where his skull rocked back and forth briefly, then fell to rest before rocking the other way. After another few seconds he found himself clumsily flipped over onto his back, just in time to see a dog with a bone in its mouth. He thought *Oh God, don't let that be one of mine!* The dog stepped up to look him in the eye. The dog stood face to face with him, their eyes no farther apart than a few inches.

**

Fatty watched the eye. At least, it looked like an eye. But it never blinked or moved. If he stepped to the left, the eye didn't move. He stepped closer and smelled the eye. He thought about eating it. He'd found eyes before, and they were usually pretty good. He dropped the bone and leaned forward, giving the eye a lick. He gripped the eye between his teeth and toyed with it a bit, giving it a slight tug and pressing down on it with his teeth, testing it before he bit into it. It tasted a little funny. Under normal circumstances, a funny tasting eye would have definitely been something to enjoy, but surrounded by this many delicious bones, he decided he would eat the eye some other time. He let the eye pop back into place and picked up his bone. He took another close up look at the eye and turned to eat his bone at the foot of the pile of bones. That way he could protect his newfound bone stash.

***

Mr. Navarro watched as the dog began to toy with his eye. As the dog started to pull at the eye, the pressure of his teeth caused a distortion of his vision. For a half a second, it was like looking into a fun-house mirror - everything was very tall and thin. He couldn't believe that the last thing he would ever see on this earth was the inside of a dog's mouth. It occurred to him he had no way of knowing if that would, in fact, be the last thing he would see. For all he knew, he was in the eye. Perhaps the last thing he would see was in the dog's belly. He wondered if he would relish the return of the light when the dog shit him out. He was completely in a panic when his vision suddenly returned to normal and he saw the dog pick up his leg, give him one more good look, and step away from the eye. *Thank God!*

After a few minutes watching the dog chew on and begin to consume what appeared to be a bone from his broken leg, he reassessed the situation. *Son of a bitch!*

18

Navarro is Reborn

What Mr. Navarro had failed to realize while watching Fatty eat his leg bone was that Fatty was in fact his glorious benefactor. As the sun began to go down, Fatty realized it had perhaps been hours since he had had a nap. The thought of leaving his bone pile unguarded caused him quite a bit of concern. There were other dogs in the neighborhood. They couldn't be trusted - especially that damned white one with the red ribbons on its head. The thought of the McNealy's Maltese, Bruno, caused Fatty to growl under his breath. But, no, it wasn't just that damn Bruno that couldn't be trusted. They were all a bunch of dishonorable thieves. He could spend the better part of the day pissing all over these bones, and in fact had, and they still would steal them when his back was turned.

No, he needed to bury these bones or there would be no way to protect them. With him being late for nap, he decided that putting the bones in the hole he found would be almost as good as burying them. Then, he could sleep in the hole and protect them. He could bury the ones he didn't eat once he woke up. He decided to forgo eating the strange round bone with the eye in it. There was just something about the way he felt when he looked in the eye, almost like it was looking at him, that he just couldn't get comfortable with.

It only took him a few minutes, just three trips, to cart the bones up to the hole, because they were still mostly stuck together. He had tried to leave the one with the eye behind but couldn't shake it loose from the big long one that he recognized as having the most marrow, so he begrudgingly placed the whole assembly in his new bone pile and laid down to guard it.

***

Once again, all this was good for Navarro, but if he had had the capacity to scream, this trip up the hill would have been a great time to do so. He watched the god damn dog drag what had until that moment been his one remaining good leg up the hill. It then came for his left arm and half of his rib cage. The last trip was his hips, backbone the remainder of his ribs, left arm and, of course, his skull. Until the last trip he could see little bones—bones he couldn't for the life of him identify—falling away. The damn dog was permanently destroying him. If there had been a reason for his having been left conscious in the dirt for the past twenty years, it certainly couldn't have been this.

He lay in a pile in the darkened cave and watched the dog gnawing on one of his rib bones. He thought to himself, *I'm gonna kill that dog.* And then, as if it was the sort of thing he had thought every day of his ninety plus years, he added *And then I'm gonna eat it.*

While thinking this over and over and showing no concern for the fact he had no idea if he could eat anything, much less a dog, he noticed movement on the floor of the cave. There were little tendrils coming up out of the ground. He took for granted the speed with which they moved. He'd seen them before. Their movement seemed almost animal-like. He watched expectantly as they began to wrap themselves around his scattered bones and begin to reform his muscles. As soon as the first tendrils touched him, he was reminded of the warmth he had felt earlier when he had discovered his new body. He remembered the feeling of satisfaction, of not feeling the need that had always engulfed him. It had been so brief, and the feeling's absence was so much his norm for nearly the past century, he had forgotten it as he had lay melting in the sun. Now it hit him with full force. This was what life was supposed to feel like. The fungus was him and he was part of the fungus. The fungus understood and accepted him.

As he watched the tendrils begin to weave themselves around his leg and drag it to him, he saw that it was being attached upside down. The foot was about to be affixed to his hip. Mentally he shook his head - of course he couldn't, as his neck muscles hadn't yet regenerated. *No, not like that. The leg goes the other way.*

He felt a wave of peace wash over him as the leg, riding on a thousand tiny mushroom tips, turned itself around and was repositioned in just the manner he envisioned. He began to test the process, deciding which pieces should be assembled next. For the most part it worked. Where it didn't, he felt as if the answer to why was being inserted into his thoughts. As he tried to collect a rib bone that had pulled away while the accursed dog had been dragging him into the cave, he was suddenly aware the dark was the only effective place to get this job done. The bone lay near the sun, and he had an overwhelming sense that the sun was for resting and the dark was where all work was done.

While Fatty lay sleeping, dreaming about a wealth of bones, Mr. Navarro began to crawl around the back of his cave. He knew the dark was for working and he wouldn't attempt to go after the dog until the sun went down. He was missing a leg and a number of ribs, but on the whole, he was feeling better than he had in a lifetime. He sat back in his cave, one eyeing the sleeping dog and wishing he had another leg.

19

Dora Ruminates

Dora sat at the patio table in the backyard drinking a cup of coffee, while Don pulled weeds in the garden, and Pippi's dog, Bruno, attempted to help with the digging. She couldn't get her mind off her conversation with Tim. Tim had asked about the houses at the bottom of the hill. She hadn't thought about them in years and didn't care to now. Her years with Don were the best of her adult life and even living on the same block for forty years, she felt no overlap. Of course, that was probably made easier by the fact her old house, once just two doors down, was for all intents and purposes, no more. The cul-de-sac bore no actual resemblance to how it had been when she and Emile had lived there.

In her former life, she had married young to a man who wasn't really a man. Emile Navarro was forever a boy. Not in the sense that he was forever young, but in the sense he never matured. He had been much older than she was and had, for a time, seemed somehow sophisticated. He had money, and a good job, and had worked long and hard to court her. He had managed a shoe store. Funny how to the seventeen-year-old Dora that had seemed like the pinnacle of success.

It didn't take long once she was married to see she had made a huge mistake. Emile never grew and the image she had fallen in love with didn't define the man—it was merely a paper-thin veneer. Under the surface, Emile Navarro was an unhappy, selfish man who never appreciated what he had. He always thought someone was trying to put one over on him. He always treated her like she was trying to waste his money. He drank too much and ranted late into the night about having been sold a bill of goods and having wasted his life. He wasn't bad. He just wasn't good. He didn't live, he just occupied space. And in said space, he festered, growing more bitter and convinced that everyone and everything was somehow against him.

Dora had been raised to believe that divorce was a mortal sin and that the hell she was in was far preferable to an eternal one in the next life. She tended to Emile when she could bear it and spent long hours working on charitable activities at church when she couldn't.

The day the hill gave way, she had been down at St. Fiacre's, sorting donated clothes and sharing a little harmless gossip with a couple of other refugees. Driving up the hill toward home, already knowing her house was gone, but not knowing Emile's fate, she made a point of not praying. When she first got in her car, instinctively, she crossed herself and touched the crucifix that hung from her rear-view mirror. But the moment she heard herself say the words "Oh my Jesus, forgive us our sins," she paused. A thought passed through her mind so quickly, and she didn't dare entertain it for a second, so she hoped the Lord hadn't heard her. In that instant she knew she couldn't pray that Emile had died, but by the same token, she feared that praying for his safety might somehow bear fruit. She drove silently all the way to the spot where their home had stood.

Emile was nowhere to be found. At the time she couldn't say it, let alone think it, but now every time she thought about it, which, thank the good Lord, wasn't all that often, she could only say "Thank God."

Dora had spent almost two years living with her sister in Glendale once she found herself to be a homeless widow. During that time Don's wife Betty died. Having been Betty's and Don's neighbor and friend for a good many years, Dora found herself going back up the hill to help. Don's boys, and more importantly, their wives, lived far enough away that it was clear to her Don needed a little tending to.

Dora dropped in once or twice a week to make sure Don was eating and for that matter getting out of bed. Betty was gone almost a year before Don asked if he might take her out for a bite. He said she had fed him so well that he had ended up putting on a few pounds, but that he knew a restaurant where the food wasn't so good, and would she care to join him on what he hoped would be a less than spectacular start to a more austere diet.

Don had lied about the quality of the food, or at least the restaurant. It had been wonderful. They spent the evening talking about things unrelated to life on the hill. Neither of them spoke of Betty or the hole she had left in Don's life. They talked about when they were kids, about Don's kids, and about their interests, hobbies, and places they both wanted to see.

When they got back to Don's place, without any big announcement or fanfare, they both just fell into Don's bed and made it theirs. Dora had spent the first ten years of her married life with Emile, reading all sorts of magazines looking for a way to spice up their sex life, hoping to spark more passion both in her husband and herself. It hadn't worked. But it had left her with a head full of rather ambitious ideas about what one could and couldn't do in bed with a partner. All these years she had been like an artist with no outlet for her craft. That first night, she made Don her canvas and although neither of them had the strength to get through even a fraction of her repertoire, without further discussion, both drifted off to sleep knowing they had the rest of their lives to practice their art.

Dora had been lost in thought as Don joined her at the table. He leaned over and kissed her neck, giving her a bit of a start. He smiled and asked, "What's going on in there, sweetie?"

She shook her head, "Nothing all that pressing. I was just thinking about what a great life we've got here." She paused and then suppressed a grin, looked away, and added, "And, just now I was thinking back to our first night together."

Don laughed, "My God woman, you're quite the trollop. But, twice in one day? What do you think I am - sixty again?"

Dora shrugged and stood, taking Don by the hand, "I wasn't making an overture, just reminiscing. But now that you seem to be taking it as a challenge, come with me, I think I still may have a few tricks up my sleeve."

20

Lisa Gets Into the Mix

Lisa didn't spend all that much time in her body anymore. Mostly she was flitting around through time and space. She slid easily through scenes from her life, great moments and sad ones. The profound and the mundane. Passing through them, she would often repeat a hard part of her life hundreds of times over. It wasn't like opening a wound or wallowing in pity. It was more like studying and understanding. As she found herself learning more and more about herself, she was able to dig deeper into other more esoteric aspects of her life.

Even though her life had been cut short at nineteen years, it was amazing the number of moments she had experienced and the way they tied together to create her unique history. The more she studied her past, the more amazed how much there was of it, and how little she had understood it when she had lived it all the first time.

These moments she relived were more like living them than watching them. She was in herself, but more aware. Lisa felt what she had felt, and she saw what she had seen. She could taste the food, got stoned on the weed, and she cried real tears. When she and her boyfriend, Franco, had sex in his parents' bed, it was better each time she relived it. There were times when she wished she had had a longer life with more variety of experiences, a larger percent of which would not be spent in childhood, but in the fifty years she had spent reliving nineteen, she realized she had just begun to scratch the surface.

And that only covered the times she traveled back in time. Other times she was with people she had known, but in settings she hadn't lived. Or she found herself in a gaseous, nebulous state somehow mixing in and being interspersed with other, similarly disembodied beings. They passed easily through each other, somehow laughing, though without a means to do so. These moments were closer to ecstasy than anything she had ever felt in life.

No, her post life experience was full and varied. One could say her dance card was full and as a result, she spent little time in her body. That, of course, was a bit of an overstatement. She was always there but reached out constantly. She would take her little trips, both forward, outward, and back in time, but would always come back, remind herself she was Lisa Whitely and that she had been murdered by a crazy old fuck named Emile Navarro. Then, after calming down from a few minutes of her angry stewing, she would suddenly find herself on another trip.

The time she spent in her body was the worst of it. The time she spent laying there and looking up had diminished significantly over the years. After her murder, she had been confined to her body almost exclusively. Slowly over time, she had begun to take little journeys back to life. It had started by remembering her murder but had spun backward over time like a web of interconnected moments. The murder led to the canvasing job that had led her there. The canvasing job had been the suggestion of Franco. She had met Franco at a party. The party had been setup by friends from church. At any given point, any of these connections had multiple paths that led to them, and she spent more and more time reliving those points, sometimes moving backward through them and sometimes forward.

Now, the only time she spent in her body, except as a sort of landing pad between jumps, was when something happened to it. Occasionally there was a little earth movement, or there was that time a coyote ripped off her foot. Maybe twenty years ago there had been a major event in her body's journey, when the hill had collapsed. Her little grave had been washed down the hill and she, of course, with it. Okay, she had been buried at the top of the hill and now she was buried at the bottom. Perhaps that wasn't a major event, but looked at in the proper context, how many times did a dead body take a physical trip of that size? Whenever something physical like that was happening to her body, or what was left of it, she found herself pulled back to it.

That was happening now. Moments ago, she had been sitting in a dirty diaper wondering how she could have avoided it. She was crawling toward her teddy bear when she felt herself pulled back into her grave. She thought, *I'm Lisa Whitely and I was murdered by a crazy old fuck named Emile Navarro* and wondered why she had been pulled back so soon. Then she felt herself moving. The movement wasn't like the traveling she did through space. No, her bones were being pulled through the dirt. She sensed the motion but couldn't feel the hundreds of tiny tendrils that wrapped her bones and pulled them through the dirt and deposited her in a small cave.

Lisa had no eyes, but she had eye holes. More importantly, she had an active spirit that, though it hadn't yet given up this shell, was no longer completely trapped in it. She stared up, eye holes wide and saw that fucker, Emile Navarro. He was staring at her. She thought he looked different than she remembered. His skin was funny. It was mottled with white and gray. She might have been able to convince herself it was because he was so old— he had to be ancient—but he also had red and blue flecks covering his neck and running in streaks down his chest.

***

Navarro looked at the bones that had been brought to his cave. He watched them for a while, thinking that somehow, he was to get a companion. He didn't know whose bones he was looking at and had no idea the bones were watching him back. So he certainly had no idea they were also hating him. For a while he split his attention between the bones and the dog. He knew the sun would be going down soon, and that until it did, he was too weak to kill the dog. Thinking about killing and eating the dog made him laugh. He didn't know if he could eat it, but it had eaten part of him, and he was determined to find a way to eat it back. He silently laughed at the idea.

***

Lisa watched as Emile Navarro mimed laughing. How could he still be alive? He was old when he had murdered her. How did he not get caught? How had he not died from natural causes? For Christ's sake, the number of times she had relived her brief encounter with him had afforded her ample opportunity to study him. He had been a rheumy, out of shape alcoholic. Hell, he looked like death fifty years ago.

***

While looking from the doomed little dog back to the bones, wondering why they were just lying there, he thought about his missing leg and smiled. The dog was sleeping with its head resting on one of Navarro's partially eaten ribs. Navarro started to calculate in his head just how many bones the dog had eaten. Then he crawled toward the new bones and touched them. They had, for the most part, just laid in a pile. He arranged them in such a way he could figure out exactly which ones could be used to create another leg and replace two ribs.

***

Inside Lisa's mind, she was screaming. Even though she couldn't feel his fingers, her mental skin was crawling. That fucker was touching her, pulling her apart, and examining her again. She tried to flee, to get back to reliving her potty training, but she was trapped in the now.

***

Navarro placed the leg and foot bones in a row on the floor of the cave and crawled into position, holding the end of the leg against his hip bone. He thought this was his leg now and mentally asked it to attach. He saw tendrils begin weaving a sheath to cover the end of the bones and begin attaching the new leg. Over a period of perhaps twenty minutes, layer upon layer of fungus attached, wound around and reattached, recreating Lisa's left leg but now using it to complete Mr. Navarro.

***

Through the whole process Lisa found herself being simultaneously horrified and somehow soothed. She watched in horror as her killer, or whatever had become of him, for he was certainly a changed man, took a part of her and used it to complete himself. The man who had ended her life was somehow able to extend his own, by taking from her again. She wanted

89

to scream.

But much like the duality she had been living for the past fifty years, where she was able to live and relive her life, experiencing it from multiple perspectives, she was now able to live this experience from multiple perspectives. She was still present in her leg. She could feel what was happening from that perspective as well. There, rather than horror, she felt awe. She felt a gathering of brokenness, and a collective healing. She felt Navarro's need and some odd frightening sense of satisfaction at the prospect of helping him. She fought those feelings as best she could, using every fiber of her being to refocus on the hate. She wasn't ready to allow herself to see beyond the monster.

***

After a time, Navarro stood and tested the new leg. The leg was almost two inches shorter than his right one. He found himself walking with a limp. He walked as close to the mouth of the cave as he dared. He was about two feet from the now sleeping dog. He scanned around the cave, wondering if he could fashion a weapon. He glanced back at the pile of bones laying in the corner and smiled.

***

Lisa didn't like the look of that smile. She had seen a fleshier variation fifty years ago, and a thousand times since.

Mr. Navarro went to the pile and pulled out the other leg bone. He thought it would make a nice club. Lisa watched as the old man carried her other leg high over his head like a club, or more to the point, like some old silent movie representation of how one might choke up on a baseball bat. She watched him creep up to the mouth of the cave and ready himself for a mighty swing. He was going to try and hit the dog that was sleeping in the doorway.

Because she wasn't able to hear, she didn't hear what woke up the dog. But just as Navarro brought down his club—her leg!—she saw the dog woke up with a start, and without even looking over his shoulder to see Mr. Navarro, looked hard to his right and ran away at full speed before Navarro was able to make contact. She laughed. *Fuck you, Navarro.*

***

Navarro jerked up at the thought. He heard his name. In all the years since he had died, he had thought a great many things. He had felt cheated by life, disappointed in what had been dealt him. He had wondered what it would have been like to have been born more likable and to have gotten more out of his youth. But he had never referred to himself by name.

He had felt the presence of the fungus that wrapped him and somehow felt that there was some shared awareness. Clearly the fungus was responding to his thoughts. But that felt like support or some symbiotic, cooperative union. What was with the "Fuck you?" Navarro's self-awareness had never been acute enough to have included self-loathing, merely self-pity.

He turned to stare at the bones and wondered if it could have been them – or it. He stepped over and bent down over the skull on the floor, trying to look deep and get some sense that it was his critic.

***

Lisa thought this must be the version of déjà vu they play in hell. Navarro was examining her again. Only now, instead of a dirty old man examining and sniffing at her pussy, an old rotting corpse was examining her bones. *Fuck you, Navarro. Eat shit and die.*

21

Navarro Feeds

After the dog ran away, Mr. Navarro waited a couple of hours before he ventured outside. During that time, he walked around his tiny cave, getting used to his new body. At first, he viewed it as a "getting to know you" session with the new leg, but it only took him a few minutes to realize, for all intents and purposes, he was occupying an entirely new body.

On his first trip out into the world after being reborn, he had impatiently started running around the neighborhood and what had it gotten him? Eaten and left for food, that's what. Now he had taken the time to learn how it felt to walk around in this body. In some ways it felt like putting on an old comfortable shoe. Just like one allegedly never forgot how to ride a bike, he found that pointing, shrugging, turning around, taking a step - all these things just seemed to happen at his bidding. But he could sense there was a certain jerky, choppy quality to his movement. He believed if someone watched him walking around and reaching down to grab something, they would have thought he looked a little bit like stop animation from the nineteen sixties.

One thing he had noted from his practice, and perhaps something he should have learned earlier in the day when he fell, was that he was a little bit shaky on his feet. He wasn't sure if it was due to the fact his bones were old and brittle or that his new fungus flesh was weak. He decided it was probably a combination of the two. He knew he was going to have to take it easy out in the world. He didn't want to overdo it. He couldn't break down again out in the open. There wouldn't always be a greedy, ravenous dog to drag him to the safety of his cave.

During the time he spent waiting for twilight to turn to night, he noted that his thinking wasn't altogether right. He heard voices. Not in the sense he heard distinct voices in his head or he heard external voices. Of course, he couldn't really hear anything - another potential danger out in the world. No, it had started with his awareness that he could use the new bones for a new leg. In his mind, he had heard himself think *I wish I had a new leg*. There had been an odd feeling about it. It felt different than any other thought he had had before, alive or dead. He had had thoughts that seemingly came out of the blue before. Who hadn't? This was sort of like that. Only here he felt that although what he heard or felt was in his own voice, it seemed to originate separate from his own internal workings.

His internal monologue was getting decidedly more confused as the evening wore on. The first time he noticed it again, he thought *It is good we are here*. Once again, he was thinking it, but...why? He also seemed to alternate between joy - which made sense, he was alive again and mobile - and sadness. The sadness felt like loneliness, but much more profound than he'd ever experienced in life.

He seemed to flit around between different emotions very quickly. Elation, anger, hunger, and loneliness seemed to wash over him like waves breaking on the shore; one after the other, none clearly signaling the one that would follow. Earlier, he was about to kill the dog when he had been washed over with an overwhelming sense of self-loathing. How else to explain the "Fuck you, Navarro?"

As he contemplated all of this, he became increasingly aware he wasn't trapped anymore. The moment he had been reborn, he experienced freedom from his former physical bonds. He could move and was free to step away from his grave. But what he was just becoming aware of was that he didn't feel alone anymore either. He wasn't trapped in his own mind. He wasn't alone with his thoughts.

He hadn't chosen to rest in this cave. He had been brought here by the accursed dog against his will. He had spent the whole day being re-reborn and waiting for the night so he could reclaim his freedom. When he finally did step out into the night, he felt like an alien taking his first steps on a new planet. It was a planet full of potential, and although familiar, one that would require a complete new set of approaches. He decided he wanted to give the old house a good looking over. Perhaps Dora was still buried there. Although she wasn't always the wife he had wanted, at least alive, perhaps in her current state, she might finally be of some use. Perhaps she could be used for additional spare parts, truly becoming bone of his bone. He could drag her bones up to his cave and see if the fungus would work its magic on her. That sounded a little odd in his head. "The fungus working its magic" had a bit of an unreal sound to it. Even to a reanimated corpse, there were limits to one's capacity to suspend disbelief.

Mr. Navarro nosed around the house for twenty minutes or so. During that time, a time which bore no fruit in his search for Dora, he felt a steady sense of unease. He needed to be outside the house, not trapped in his old habitat, but out in the world, feeling it and taking part. He didn't know how he could really participate, but he felt the need to reach out and touch things. In life, he had waited for his chance to experience all the things he consistently found out of his reach. He had wondered what was going on in the world and always assumed someday it would somehow find him. He had, in life, regretted his missed opportunities. But, during his decades in the dirt, he had regretted that he hadn't taken advantage. Now, he was going to reach out and take whatever there was, to experience whatever there was that someone in his condition could experience.

Stepping out of the house, he headed for the tree line, wondering how close he could get to the houses below without drawing attention. He hadn't bothered to check the mirror again to see what his refurbished face looked like. But he assumed if his head looked in any way as inhumanly put together as did his body, he must certainly resemble some sort of monster. No sir, he wasn't about to look in the mirror. He wasn't ready to test those waters.

It didn't take long, however, for him to face a similar barometer. As he stepped under a streetlight that lit a path down the hill, he saw a skunk that had seen him and had decided to make some sort of stand. If Navarro had had a sense of hearing, he would have heard the skunk growling and hissing, something he wouldn't have believed anyway, it not being a common action for a skunk. The skunk bared its teeth and lunged toward Navarro. The skunk had no intention of attacking the substantially larger creature. It only intended to scare it away.

It didn't work.

Navarro watched the animal and attempted to smile at it. He thought, *You, I am going to eat.* His smile widened. He thought it would be good practice as he needed to work his way up to that god damn cannibal dog. But more than that, there was a sense that came over him that he wanted to eat the skunk. To absorb it. He wasn't even sure he was capable of eating anything. But on some level, part of him knew this was something he had to do. It was, he assumed, very similar to the way a young animal knows it is supposed to fly or that it can hunt. It does it because it is in its nature.

Navarro took a small step toward the skunk, smiling and reaching down with his left hand. As the skunk lunged toward him, he smashed it as hard as he could with the leg bone he had been hiding behind him in his right hand. He bashed the creature five or six times before holding it up and examining its corpse. Twenty years without a win made this victory almost overwhelming in its visceral effect. It wasn't just filling the void of the last twenty years, but at least the twenty or thirty before that. He had settled for everything that happened to him in life, never reaching out beyond himself for anything, letting things either fall in his lap or watching them roll by. He would not spend a moment regretting having failed here. This skunk, small as it may be, represented the biggest challenge he had stepped up to in over half a century. He smiled thinking about it because he was going to do it again. Even if he'd had adrenaline glands, he didn't think he would have felt so overcome with life.

He felt an overwhelming need to eat the creature. He bent down and placed the skunk on a rock. He took another rock and used it to beat the skunk until he had managed to tear it into ten or twelve smaller, bloody pieces. Not knowing how it could work or whether it would, he followed instinct and put one of the smallest pieces, a hind leg into his mouth. He began to chew it when he felt a hunger that seemed to permeate his whole body. His legs, arms, and the flesh on the back of his neck all screamed out for food. Without understanding how the skunk flesh might possibly benefit him, he swallowed it.

He felt an overwhelming sense of rightness about the swallowing. He had no idea where it went - didn't care. He wanted more. He picked up the head and rather than attempt to chew it, opened his mouth almost impossibly wide and threw it down his throat. He was both surprised and yet completely accepting of the fact he had a throat. He guessed he always had, up to a point, had one. He doubted he could have swallowed something that large with his old one. Without the need to chew, Navarro was able to consume the rest of the still warm skunk carcass in less than a minute. Without giving it much of a thought, he wiped the blood off the rock and wiped it across his lips.

Navarro continued to work his way down the hill and carefully watched for danger. He was afraid to get caught from behind by a dog or perhaps something worse. He remembered there had once been coyotes that roamed the hillsides. Without the benefit of hearing, he feared something might sneak up on him. He turned around every few seconds, taking care to watch for any motion out of the corner of his eye.

He felt stronger than he had earlier. At first, he chalked it up to his getting used to his body, but the more he watched out for potential predators, the more he became aware that he was also keeping an eye out for small prey. He felt satisfied by the meat he had consumed. But he had a hunger for more. He wondered where that dog lived.

II

Sunday

22

Rage Rises

Tim woke up, and for a few moments, forgot the day he had just spent carting around and caring for his giant juvenile delinquent landlord. The moments were few. By the time his feet hit the floor he had stopped wondering why he had dreamed about tacos and was already shaking his head and remembering their stupid mushroom adventures from the day before. He was able to wipe from his mind the fact he, himself, had been high when he went to bed.

Tim had intended to study from the time he got home until around midnight, but instead had given up not long after dark. During those few hours he had stepped out on the patio a few times to check on Rage. The first time he made it out was just to make sure he was breathing. Once he saw Rage had not only survived his broken leg, but had seen fit to sit in the backyard, get stoned, and knock back a few beers, Tim realized the man was either impervious to destruction or drawn to it. Either way, on the subsequent checks, Tim merely stepped out onto the patio to make sure he could still see Rage.

Now, with a clearer head than he had enjoyed last night, he decided to wake Rage, make up for lost study time, and take care of his inexplicable need for some Mexican inspired junk food—but not necessarily in that order. He grabbed a burrito out of the freezer, popped it in the microwave, and put on the coffee while the burrito came into its own. Once he had his burrito in hand, he headed into the backyard to see if Rage was still alive. As soon as he stepped onto the patio, he dropped his burrito and ran to the spot where he had left Rage.

Rage, Rage's chair, and in point of fact half of what constituted Rage's happy place had been somehow encased in a coating of mushrooms and a white tuberous material. It was what appeared to be an almost solid mass made up of white tendrils that wound and wound around Rage's chair until it became solid. Interspersed with the whole material were hundreds of tiny mushrooms. It almost looked as though he were covered with a light gray soft serve ice cream—studded with red and blue mushroom sprinkles. As Tim reached the spot, he reached out and found that the material was soft, and he was able to tear it away pretty easily. Rage was about two feet into the mass of fungus and once Tim reached him, he felt his neck, confirming he could feel him breathing.

He started yelling at Rage to wake up. It took less than a minute to uncover Rage's head. There was a long thick shaft of fungus that ran down his throat and similar, though smaller tendrils were tangled in his hair and tunneling into his nostrils and ears. As he pulled away the last sheet of fungus from Rage's face, Rage woke up coughing, sputtering out "I am not a fag." For a moment, Tim thought Rage looked like his head was sticking out of a giant marshmallow - the kind with blue and red flecks.

Rage looked down and started laughing. "Shit, I thought I was dreaming this." He spread his arms wide and broke the top half of the fungus cocoon, stood, and kicked his way out of the rest.

Tim said, "Dreamed what?"

Rage shrugged, "I remember thinking I was somehow being eaten by the mushrooms that were growing down in the wash. I even imagined I could feel it wiggling around inside me."

"They were inside you. I pulled them out of your mouth and nose."

Rage shivered slightly at the thought of what the mushrooms were doing in his mouth. Then he nodded, letting the known world shift and rearrange itself for him for a few seconds. He finally responded, "Radical!"

Tim shook his head, "Radical? I don't think that's so radical. Fungus in our back yard was trying to eat you."

Without looking at Tim, Rage said, "I gotta say, if being eaten alive by a fucking plant doesn't meet your definition of radical, then I don't know what the good folks down at the college are charging you, but you should get your money back."

As he said this, Rage looked out over the wash and beyond. He could see the town of Eagle Rock down below and the college in the distance. He loved this place. He was in the city but could sit up here in the woods and breath in what he liked to believe was good clean air. He could smell the pine rather than the exhaust from below. But he could still get a pizza delivered and go to a club if he wanted to party with a crowd.

Tim asked, "So, are you feeling okay? I think that thing was starting to cut off your breathing."

Rage glanced down at his domain, then considered the fungus that lay at his feet. He nodded, "Fuck yeah. I feel great."

He did too. Rage had gone to sleep last night feeling a warm sense of well-being that had eluded him since long before his parents had died. If he was honest with himself, something he was normally incapable of, he hadn't felt that sense of safety and comfort when they were alive either. He had been a below average student, hadn't applied himself much in school except finding ways to get out of it. He had always looked for ways to party, long before he was old enough to even know what it meant.

He never pulled his own weight or had a job. His parents were the ones who financed his world, and as he got older, cleaned up his messes. He took them for granted and didn't go much deeper than looking to them for a place to crash and some beer money. Now he stood here, contemplating the world they had left him in. He was, for the first time, aware he hadn't been much of a son to them. He wondered, again for the first time, if they had been ashamed of the way he never applied himself. But, through all this new self-awareness, he kept smiling. Today, the sense of warmth and belonging he felt, somehow told him his parents had known his limitations and loved him anyway. In fact, the sense of love that was engulfing him made him think they loved him more because of his failings as a son. He required more of what they, as parents, had wanted to give.

He began to wonder if he could find where they had been buried. It had been what, twelve or thirteen years? He knew it was down the hill at Forest Lawn. Hell, he could see the cemetery from in front of his house. But that was a pretty big place, and he hadn't ever been back after the funeral. He decided it was high time he did. He stood here assessing his domain and his place in the world and for the first time in his thirty years of life, really understood that he loved his parents. He wasn't sure if he had when they had been alive, but by God, he sure as hell did now. As long as it had taken for him to realize it, he didn't want them to have to wait another hour to hear it.

He absentmindedly put his hand down his pants and dug free a strand of fungus that had anchored itself by wrapping tightly around his scrotum and then extending into his asshole. As he pulled in out, he could feel a tingly sensation - kind of nice, he thought. He flicked the broken explorer to the ground while thinking about how damn good it felt to be alive. He turned to head into the house.

Tim cried out, "Hey, what about your crutch?"

Rage looked down at the cast on his leg, then at the crutch that was propped up against his chair. He tested the leg a few times then shrugged and said, "Don't need it." They started toward the house, while he only slightly favored his unbroken leg.

Tim asked, "Where are you going."

Rage answered without breaking stride, "To see my mom."

23

Navarro Reflects

Navarro sat in his house, oblivious to everything outside his new world. He was sitting in the hole in his old bedroom. It was the hole he had been pulled out of by the fungus, the fungus he now viewed as having adopted him. Tendrils, thousands of them, pulled and tugged at the debris he had picked up on his night's foray into the world. While the fungus digested the rotting material he had brought back for this benefactor, he was ruminating on the night he had had and trying to digest things in his own way. So much life had happened in such a small space after such a long respite.

After his first kill of the evening, he discovered he was quite the hunter. Over the course of the night, he had managed to kill three cats, a rat, one raccoon, and a little brown dog. Each had been somehow easier than the last. Each had been made easy to catch because apparently, he was good bait. He somehow seemed to frighten the animals but fascinate them as well. He had to laugh thinking what a sight he must be, and what the little creatures must have tried to make of him.

In each case, he had found his body craved the animals, and he found each a little easier to eat than the last. Except for the raccoon, he had been able to swallow most of them whole. All he had had to do was get his jaw wide enough to get them over the threshold. After that, his gullet seemed to take over. The raccoon, however, had changed his whole notion of how eating worked.

After he killed the raccoon, which was considerably larger than the other animals, he was getting ready to start tearing it apart, when he caught himself thinking that he should just "let it melt." It wasn't the first time his strange new inner voices said something he didn't know he was thinking, but it was the first time he couldn't even follow the thought. This gave him pause. He could understand having misunderstood motives, but actually speaking to himself in a code he didn't understand pretty much sealed the possibility that there was more at play here than himself.

He held the raccoon, staring at it, wondering what melting meant when, without a further thought, he watched his arms hold it to his abdomen. Then he watched as tendrils began to encircle the animal. Over a period of about ninety seconds, he felt the weight of the animal seemingly lessen in his arms as the tendrils began to bear the weight of the corpse and draw it to him. Once the animal was firmly attached to him, he could feel the warm sense of satisfaction that eating each of the other animals had given him. He let go of the corpse and turned his attention to other things.

Now, thinking about it, he wondered about each creature he had eaten. He wondered about where they were now. Not the meat, or the bones, but the them that had occupied the meat and bones. He, himself, had lain for twenty years in the dirt, just bones, a few hardened bits of fat and an eye. And yet, through it all, the him who had been there when the earth had first closed in around him, was still there.

What of the animals he had killed last evening? They had been alive and then they weren't. How was that different from him twenty years ago? Were the bones he had consumed, quietly hating him, seething with an impotent rage?

He peered down at his belly. He reached down with two hands and dug a hole in the fungus that formed his abdomen. By now, having watched his body react to minor cuts and abrasions, not to mention having watched it being rebuilt the day before, he was fairly confident any minor damage he did would be temporary.

Navarro dug deeper through the fungus that was the meat of his midsection until he found a bone that wasn't his own, or at least hadn't been until last night. He pulled it out and examined it, assuming it came from the raccoon, since it was his final kill of the evening and wasn't too far in from where he had placed the animal. He contemplated the bone, turning it and viewing it from different angles and wondered if the raccoon was inside, looking at him.

He wondered at the fact the raccoon that may be looking at him had in the course of its life eaten hundreds, if not thousands, of other animals. He wondered if they had stared at the raccoon from their fish bones or frogs' legs or insect wings. He wondered about the possibility they were watching him now from whatever molecular level they now occupied in the raccoon bone. He wondered at the idea all of creation that came before today was somehow touched by, connected to, or contained within the raccoon's bone.

Navarro held the bone in his left hand, not breaking his gaze, but digging around in his middle for more bones. What he found was that they had accumulated around his backbone. In fact, it seemed less that they were accumulating there than that they were somehow being collected there. As he tried to remove one, he noted that it felt pretty snugly placed among a number of smaller bones.

He placed the raccoon bone, containing sparks of life that he believed might be traced back to the first life, back at the base of the hole he had dug in himself and watched as small tendrils began to drag the bone toward the assembly of other bones. He noted that even as this was happening, other tendrils began the process of repairing the hole he had dug in himself.

Navarro smiled as he contemplated that he was all here together...and not alone.

He thought about the human bones he had left piled in the corner of his cave and wondered just what marvels they had seen.

24

Tim & Rage Have Left the Building

Living with Rage had turned out to not be quite the disconnected-from-others experience Tim had originally been seeking. Although he was free to come and go and wasn't surrounded at home by students on the same roller coaster of emotions and schedules as himself, it turns out he still found that he was trapped in some strange cyclical dance with his housemate. In spite of the fact that Rage had, to Tim's knowledge, never really held any sort of job, he apparently still had what to some degree we all have - a hard-wired assumption that the weekend was a special time that all are somehow entitled to exploit as a means of escape. It didn't really matter that what Rage escaped into was really just a more over the top version of what he escaped from. But no matter how dissimilar the goals and day-to-day activities experienced by Rage and Tim, they always seemed to be on a similar emotional trajectory. There was a steady, unstated psychological path that seemed to lead steadily from Monday through Friday.

Tim's reaction to reaching the weekend goal was significantly less extreme than Rage's. One advantage for an eighteen-year-old living with someone Rage's age was that he was always in proximity to beer. For Tim, two beers on Friday night and sometimes one or two more on Saturday was a clear sign he was living the adult life he had long looked forward to.

Rage's handling of Friday also included one or two beers, but only in the sense that one needs to pass through one or two on the way to eight or ten. Fridays for Rage also included a good deal of Jack Daniels, mixed with Mountain Dew or Hawaiian Punch. In addition to his daily dose of what until recently had been "medicinal" marijuana, courtesy of a doctor for hire found in the back pages of the LA Weekly, he also liked to augment the weekend with some amphetamine fueled sex, the funding of which was the real point of Tim's rent money.

The symbiotic link between Tim's and Rage's respective needs to party was always broken by sometime on Sunday. Although it wasn't unheard of for Tim to sneak away from the madness on Saturday, which he had attempted to do yesterday, Sunday was definitively where they parted ways. Whereas Rage invariably saw Sunday as an equal player on the weekend team, using every minute of his other magic day where he hoped to find additional playmates, it was a day Tim used to get centered and regroup for his work week. Today was no exception.

Although he was a little pissed about having wasted his Saturday on one of Rage's crazy adventures, not to mention more than a little freaked out about finding Rage in what could only be described as some sort of mushroom cocoon this morning, he had his own issues to deal with. He was behind on his studying and needed to get out of the drama dome and get back on track. He decided to spend the day, much like other Sundays, split between his favorite coffee shop and the library. Later though, he would also hit the bulletin boards on campus and check for some other living arrangements.

Leaving the house, he threw his backpack in the back seat and pulled out of the driveway. Heading down the hill, he could see the cross from one of the chapels at Forest Lawn, the gargantuan cemetery that separated the south side of Eagle Rock from Glendale. As he did on every Sunday, he made a mental note that one of these Sundays he was going to check out one of the local churches. Just not this Sunday. He hadn't been to church since moving to Los Angeles and he figured it would be there when he decided it was time to get back into his old habits.

At the bottom of the hill, he saw Rage's car parked at the seven-11. It was hard not to notice that odd, little, highly impractical tribute to what he assumed was meant to be skateboarding and Mountain Dew. He decided

Rage was either stocking up for his trip to the cemetery or picking up a six-pack to kick start day two of his weekly homage to the other five days. He turned right on Eagle Rock Blvd and headed for the library.

***

Rage hobbled out of the Seven-11 sporting a bag full of munchies, some beer, and a couple of six packs of extremely sugary sports drinks. Although he normally lived on a combination of crappy food and seriously over sugared beverages, today he felt like a hummingbird in his desire to get some of the sweetest stuff in the store. He felt like some serious sugar water was in order. He threw everything in the back bed of his truck—God how he loved this radical beast—and pulled out the reddest bottle of anything he'd ever seen, popped the top, and chugged half of it. He noted it tasted a lot like Hawaiian Punch, only really sweet. He wondered why he'd never tried it before. He downed the rest of the bottle, tossed the empty on the pavement, and then took another bottle for the road.

He drove past the cemetery almost every day, but he had some serious exploring to do just to find the entrance. *What the hell,* he thought. It wasn't like he had to be anywhere. It was the damn weekend.

Once on the grounds of Forrest Lawn, it took Rage quite a while to find his parents. Rage was both surprised and delighted to find that they had a doorman. Without that dude, the expedition could have taken days. The place was fucking gigantic. The guy sat in a little booth and if you told him who you were looking for, he would give you a little map to help you find them. That took them a few minutes, because for the life of him, Rage couldn't remember his parents' names. He stopped short of calling them Mom and Dad, but once the guard started reading off the names of the not insignificant number of Sutherlands interred at the great cemetery, Rage caught one that brought it all back. Even with the map, Rage found the place exceedingly hard to navigate, and he took over an hour before he finally found his parents.

It wasn't as moving as he had expected it to be. He had approached the graves expecting to feel something more significant than merely the relief he hadn't gotten lost again. He had been sure that once found, he would feel some connection to them and to the spot.

He didn't.

It wasn't that he wasn't still overcome with the sense of belonging and connectedness he had felt earlier. He was. He was feeling at peace and a kind of love that he guessed saints and other old dead dudes were always rambling on about. He realized that whatever disappointments he had caused his parents fell well within his limits as a person and that his own earlier discontent with them wasn't what defined their relationship. Deep within him he recognized he was sounding a lot like a fag.

The problem with the cemetery was that it really didn't make him feel closer to his parents. It just reminded him of their being gone and made him feel farther away from them than ever before. It somehow made him miss them. He hadn't done that before. Not really. When they had died, he had been deep in the endless feud in which they had been engaged since he was ten. Shortly after that, he was digging his newfound freedom. He guessed he had cried or something at the time—like some sort of...he didn't know what...maybe a fag?—but it now crossed his mind that he had never really mourned them. They, the people, had in his mind just been fulfilling their roles, Mom and Dad. In his memory, until he got to the cemetery, they could have just been cardboard cutouts, simple placeholders thought up by a lazy novelist.

He thought that getting high might help, but there were too many people in the cemetery, including the occasional vehicle, that to Rage's eye, may not have been a real police car, but was probably full of the kind of assholes that liked to think it was.

For several hours he sat on his parents' graves, alternating between the two. He drank a six pack and munched from a sack of mushrooms he had brought from home. He laughed at the way it sounded in his head. "Brought from home." It was really a sack from the seven-11, and as for the mushrooms, he just kept finding them in his clothes. He found a couple under his shirt in the crevice just above his belt line. There had been a good half dozen in his underwear, but they smelled okay. And it always seemed there were a good half dozen in his pants pockets. He just kept harvesting them and then tossing them in the sack. No matter how many he ate, the sack seemed to keep getting fuller.

He drank the beer out of habit, but he had a powerful thirst for sugar as well. He alternated between the beer and the sports drink. He wondered if this warm feeling he had was from the mushrooms. He remembered taking other mushrooms in the past and feeling some kind of connection with nature. This felt like that, but much bigger. Much more all-inclusive. He didn't just feel like he was at one with nature, he felt like it was at one with him. Just like he could see the light that seemed to surround all living things, he felt the light around him and felt that the light was seeking him out.

When he had woken up this morning, deep within the fungus cocoon, for just a second, it had seemed perfect. He was at one with the fungus in more than just some spiritual, psycho mumbo jumbo way - they were really, actually connected. When Tim broke him out, he was a little pissed and a little shocked. The separation was so sudden and the loss, for a moment, had seemed very real. Now he was pretty sure he was still just as connected as he had been before Tim ripped the fungus away. All things were held together by the light. All living things. He decided the reason he couldn't feel the connection with the graves was that aside from the grass and weeds growing on them and the bugs burrowing underneath, there was no life here.

He stared down at his parents' graves and knew that in life they had been just as connected, even if he hadn't understood it at the time. He stood and poured some of his beer onto each grave. He remembered their connection. He willed himself to feel it now. Then he poured a bottle of Budweiser over each grave. Then he took a handful of mushrooms and crumbled them over each grave as well.

He said what he thought was a prayer, "Sutherlands out."

25

Pippi & Dora See a What

Each afternoon around four o'clock, Don and Dora Hardman made it a habit to go for a walk around the neighborhood. It was something Don wished he had learned to do before he retired; it gave him such joy now. Until Dora dragged him out for the first time, he couldn't have named any neighbor that lived more than three houses away in any direction. Now he could not just name every individual that lived within a mile, but, based on the information gleaned from their nightly walks, could also write a nice little biography for each of them.

Sometimes their walks took as little as a half hour. Other evenings, they might not make it back until bedtime. One thing would lead to another, between stopping to visit or being asked to help with a chore. Dora said it was all a part of being a neighbor. Don assumed she had been doing it long before they got together. In fact, he believed her relationships all over the hill were part of how she had managed to cope with all those years living with Emile Navarro.

Emile had been one queer duck as far as Don was concerned. Although he and his first wife Betty had socialized more with Emile and Dora than anyone else on the block, it was all due to the persistence of both Betty and Dora. Neither he nor Betty had had much of anything positive to say about Emile, but Betty had always felt a kinship to Dora. He laughed and shook his head at the thought, wondering what Betty would say about his current kinship to her old friend.

"What are you laughing at, Don?" Dora asked.

Don looked over at his wife, "Nothing. Just laughing about how things always seem to turn out right when you have anything to say about it."

She gazed at him, her expression suggesting she understood more than she did. "You mean how I made sure our walk was a short one tonight?"

They were just rounding the corner, turning into the cul-de-sac they shared with Reggie Sutherland. Don asked "You made sure? How do you figure that?"

"Well, I applied just the right amount of pressure to make sure you avoided turning north on Nordica, knowing you wouldn't be able to resist stopping to check for new berries on the Inesco's fence."

Don said "That's right. Their berries are just about where I like them. Why would you try to avoid that? Trying to get me alone again?"

Dora scolded Don, "Now you be quiet about that, there are little ears about. Besides, I believe you've had your allotment of those type of sweets already."

Don mugged looking over each shoulder before asking, "Little ears?"

Dora shook her head, "Pippi is coming by before supper. She is bringing a friend to go swimming."

Don shook his head. Dora and that little Pippi girl were like two peas in a pod, and he sometimes wondered if either of them even noticed the sixty years or so that separated them.

As they passed by Rage's truck, they saw Pippi sitting on their front porch. She sat with her legs crossed, her posture suggesting she was attempting to look alert, or as Don saw it, not unlike a prairie dog. When she saw the Hardman's coming, she waved. It wasn't a cool, "Oh, hi there, I didn't see you coming" kind of wave, but a little kid's "hi, hi, hi," whole body shaking kind of wave. It reminded Don of the way the girl's dog, Bruno, acted when confronted with bacon. Don thought even though the girl might be ten, she sometimes seemed like she was four.

Pippi was smiling in an equally over the top kind of way and called out, "Hi, Mr. Hardman. Hi, Dora."

Dora smiled back, "Hello, Pippi. Have you been here long? I hope we didn't keep you waiting."

"Nope. I just got here a couple of minutes ago."

"Where is Joyce?"

Pippi's smile faded, and she furrowed her brow. "She couldn't make it. I came alone. Is that okay?"

"Of course, honey. You are always welcome here."

"Can we still go swimming? I mean, I know I'm supposed to bring a buddy, but is it okay with just the two of us?"

Dora couldn't help wondering why Pippi seemed to relate more to her than to her little friends, or why she seemed to have so many problems keeping them. But she liked spending time with Pippi, and never minded when the girl came by alone, which was good, because she came alone more often than not. "I'll just put on my swimsuit. Why don't you and Don go and check the garden while I get changed?"

Pippi led Don around the side of the house, trekking to the spot in the back yard where Don had raked the maple leaves and pine needles that Rage had unleashed yesterday. The debris was piled on the west side of Dora's vegetable garden, which butted up against the fence the Hardman's shared with Rage.

Pippi noted, "That's a whole bunch of leaves you got there."

Don nodded, "Yup. The work of that idiot..." he caught himself and shut up.

She asked, "Where'd all the pine needles come from though?"

"They came from the Sutherland's yard. Reggie had a parking incident."

"Why do you call Rage Reggie?"

"Well, I guess I call him that because it's his name. Or more to the point, his name is Reginald, but Reggie is the proper nickname for Reginald."

"But he doesn't like to be called Reggie. I think people should be able to choose the name that suits them best. I mean, I don't feel like a Patty. I feel like a Pippi. That name fits, so that's my name." She nodded, confirming the idea to herself, as much as to Don.

Don answered, "Well, you make an interesting point. I'll have to think it over a bit. You know, old habits are hard to break."

"I know. My Dad still calls me Patty. I still like the way it sounds when he says it, so I don't make a fuss."

Don was considering making a joke about picking a new name for himself. Young people didn't usually understand his jokes, they just thought he was weird. So instead, he grabbed a shovel and started to pile earth from the garden over the leaves and needles that would form the basis of a new compost pile. As he tossed the first shovel full of dirt onto the leaves, he shrugged, "Tom-aaa-toe, tom-ah-toe, Reggie, Rage. A rose by any other name. That boy gave me a pile of leaves and we might as well put it to some use."

Pippi shook her head, "What can you do with a pile of leaves?"

"Turn it into good, rich soil."

"How do you do that?"

Don tossed another pile of dirt from the garden onto the pile. "By letting it mix with soil and then waiting for nature to do the rest. As the leaves break down, they release nitrogen and that is the perfect plant food. I just need to keep turning this pile over every few days and letting the water, oxygen, bugs and whatnot take it from there."

She asked, "You mean you want it to rot? What good is that?"

He said, "Life my dear. New life comes from old life. Our new plants are fed by the richness that comes from the decomposition of – well, of old former life."

Don stepped around the pile and took a shovel full of dirt from along the fence. Pippi called out, "Mushrooms!"

Don kept shoveling and nodding, "Yes, mushrooms help too."

"No, I mean look - there are mushrooms along the fence." She skipped around the compost heap to get a better look.

Don looked down at an outgrowth of perhaps a dozen mushrooms, pushing through a crack in the fence. They were dark gray, almost black, and had little red and blue flecks. He put his hand out to block Pippi, trying to avoid actually touching her, because...well... because that's what you do with little girls. "Careful there. Don't touch them, they look poisonous. You don't want to get them on your hands."

Pippi stopped and looked up at Don, "How can you tell they are poison?"

Don thought to himself, because they look a lot like the sort of mushrooms that twenty years in the District Attorney's office told him kids might eat to get high. Those mushrooms always seemed to have some crazy colored markings. They might not kill you, but they might as well, considering the lives they destroy. He answered Pippi, "Because of the colors. Many poisonous mushrooms have markings like those. But don't ever eat a mushroom you find. Even without the colors, they could be deadly."

Pippi said, "I thought that mushrooms were good."

Don nodded, "Mushrooms from the store? I guess some would say they're good. I've never been one for vegetables, except for tomatoes. But leave picking them to the professionals."

Pippi knew it was rude to correct adults, except her father, so she bit her tongue and let Don continue to think mushrooms and tomatoes were vegetables rather than fungus and fruit. Instead, she bent over the mushrooms, carefully avoiding getting close, nodding as though she believed what Mr. Hardman was saying.

Dora emerged from the sliding back door and joined Pippi and Don at the garden. Although she had changed into her swimsuit, she wore it under a pair of coveralls, rather than her usual pool wrap. As she stepped up behind Pippi she said, "I couldn't help noticing you two were engrossed in the garden, so I thought maybe we could pull weeds a bit, to warm up for our swim."

"Mr. Hardman found some cool poison mushrooms."

Dora raised an eyebrow, "Well then, perhaps we should work on the other side of the garden, while Don disposes of them."

Don half smiled and half grumbled as he headed to his shed to get a trash bag for his new assignment.

Pippi told Dora, "They are really pretty ones. And look, they go all the way along the fence." She went to where the mushrooms poked through the fence and walked to the end of the fence, documenting the extent of the outcropping, looking for additional cracks.

The fence that separated the Hardman and Sutherland yards was made of cinder block and ran from a spot about eight feet from the front of each of their homes all the way back to where the slope of the hill would no longer support a fence. All in all, it was about eighty feet. Where the houses met, it was six feet high, but every fifteen or twenty feet it lost a row of blocks, so that by the time the slope started, just past the Hardman's pool, the fence was only three feet tall.

When Pippi reached the point where she could easily see over the fence, she gasped in awe. Then she called out, "Dora, come look."

Dora joined her and saw what the girl had seen. There were hundreds, if not thousands, of mushrooms on the other side of the fence. They blanketed the back part of Rage's yard, spreading down the hill behind the Hardmans' yard, covering the ground, rocks, and the first couple of feet of the trees.

Pippi said, "It's like the whole hill is covered in a purple blanket."

Dora took hold of Pippi's arm, holding her in place. She called out, "Don. Come and take a look at this."

Don trudged from his shed, dragging a thirty-gallon black garbage bag and his shovel. He wondered what kind of nonsense these girls were up to as he stepped up to the fence.

Dora said, "Don, what do you make of this?"

He shook his head, "I think I'm going to need a bigger bag."

26

Rage Lays Down in the Dirt

When Rage got home from the cemetery, he headed back to his happy place. Earlier, he had stopped using his crutch. He had gotten to the point where he didn't need it. The longer he went without it, the more he wondered if the doctor might have messed up the diagnosis. It made sense. He was always suspicious of those who learned from studying, rather than from doing.

As he approached his throne, he whistled for Fatty, popped into his chair, and opened a sport drink. He stuck his hand down his pants and pulled a mushroom out of the fertile little spot which had for most of his life been the source of most of his happiness but was now proving to be even better. He ate the mushroom and then whistled again for Fatty. He muttered to himself, "What's better than perfection? Perfection with your dog at your side."

Fatty came skidding to a stop next to Rage and Rage leaned over to give him a pat on the back. When he looked down at the dog, for a second, he thought the dog had some kind of glow stick in its mouth. But then he realized it was some kind of bone and that it was positively screaming with light. He reached down and took the bone from Fatty. The dog pretended to fight a little before letting go of the bone, but in his little dog mind he contemplated not pretending before letting go.

Rage examined the bone, holding it up to the light, applying pressure here and sniffing there. It was as if it were covered with millions of tiny glowing bugs. The lights seemed to swarm the bone, not just swirling around its surface, but orbiting it as well. He broke the bone over his cast and looked quickly at the center. Color spilled out of the hole in the bone and like some form of fiery liquid, poured out onto his cast and onto the ground. The lights on his cast quickly disappeared, but the ones that hit the grass melted into the earth, glowing longer and brighter in some areas and pooling up and then dissipating in others. As he turned his gaze toward the ground, without really thinking about it, he started rubbing the bone on his arms and neck. He felt the need to get the lights onto his bare skin.

As interesting as he had found the bone and the lights, when he looked at the ground, he was mesmerized by it. He realized he had never really looked at it before. Not like this. He watched the liquid lights dissipate, only to be followed by ants, and other bugs. He was suddenly in awe of what he had spent his whole life walking on. It was teaming with life. Not just the bugs and shit. He suddenly understood what all those geeks were always talking about. It was where everything he had ever eaten had come from. Good things, the kind of food that didn't come directly from the earth, ate things that did. Pizza and Taco Bell could trace their origins in the very earth that Rage walked on and pissed on, every day of his life. And it wasn't just what came from it, it was what went into it. Whatever died was placed into the earth where it was consumed by the bugs and ultimately made part of the earth. It was beautiful. He started to cry.

He dropped out of his chair and sat caressing the dirt and the grass. He held up a handful of dirt, smelled it, rubbed his face in it and let it fall over him. He laid down flat and rolled in the grass. Fatty, who did this on an almost hourly basis, wondered what had happened to make his master finally come to his senses. Fatty rolled around too, making it a point to roll in the stinkiest spots.

Rage pulled off his shirt and took a few more rolls in the grass before standing up and heading into the trees at the edge of the hill. He could see the earth under the trees was richer, having been fed a steady stream of decaying cedar needles for a half century. Before lying down in the mulch, Rage pulled off his pants, wanting to really feel the earth. Moving the thirty feet to the edge of the hill, he stared down at his cast. Now, standing in the pine mulch, naked except for his cast, he realized having it was more trouble than it was worth.

Rage picked through some rocks his parents had once placed as a property border and found the sharpest one he could find. He took it back to the cedar outcropping, then sat down in the needles and began to use the rock to remove his cast. It was slow going until he remembered the jagged bone he had taken from Fatty. He used the bone like a dagger to hack away at his cast, alternating between the bone to pierce it and the rock to smash it. The pine needles poked his bare skin, but he found it pleasant in an odd sort of way. It was real. It only took a few minutes, using the rock and bone. Once the cast was off, he didn't bother to stand up and test his leg. He didn't want to get off the ground. He used the rock and bone to dig into the earth. He wanted to crawl into it. Once he had a spot cleared out enough that he could lay in it, he crawled in and pulled the dirt back over him. He laid in the hole with just his head sticking out.

Fatty rolled around in the dirt right next to him. Being a creature of habit, the dog chose to forgo burying himself, satisfied to merely get the smell of the earth on him.

Laying in his little grave, Rage could feel the warmth on his skin. He could feel life all around him, he could feel the way the sun warmed the earth on top. He could feel little bits of earth movement here and there on his skin where either bugs were slogging their way around him or gravity was helping the newly turned earth settle. He could feel thousands of tiny points on his skin where the pine needles were caressing him.

His whole body was in play, seemingly being touched and caressed by the earth. But Rage was still the boy he'd always been, and part of that boy reacted more viscerally than others. His new awareness enhanced the old one rather than replacing it. All this stimulation had given him some pretty serious wood. He managed to move his right hand into position and jerked off. He could barely move, but it didn't matter much. This was one of the few areas where Rage truly excelled. Besides, his whole body was cocked and loaded for some kind of release. He came into the dirt and as he lay twitching in his little dirt grave, he closed his eyes and floated. The earth, the mother of all life, cradled him as he settled into his post coital slumber. As he floated off, he remembered some girl telling him some old dudes used to call coming "the little death." As he lost consciousness, he was hoping it was an understatement.

27

Dora Almost Says a Bad Word

Dora stood with her arm around Pippi as Don surveyed the hill. She asked, "What do you make of it?"

Don said, "Mushrooms."

She smiled, "Yes, Don. I guess I noticed that too. But have you ever seen such a thing? They're so odd looking. And there must be thousands."

Don nodded, but aware of the young Pippi's presence didn't want to call attention to what he really thought. These things really weren't something he'd seen before. But they didn't look all that dissimilar to the kind of hallucinogenic mushrooms he'd seen during his days as a prosecutor. Given their proximity to the college, a hotbed of activity when it came to stupid experimentation, he suspected a correlation. Probably some kid was getting high in the wash below and spoors from his stash got into the air. God knew that mushrooms could come up in a day and spread like wildfire.

"My guess is someone down below was experimenting. You know, growing some... exotic mushrooms, and the spoors got away from them."

Pippi asked, "Why would they want to grow such funny looking mushrooms? Do you think they're to eat?"

Don answered, "No I do not. You should never eat any mushrooms that you didn't buy at the store. There are just too many that will kill you as quick as a bullet. As to why folks would grow something for no other reason than to look at, I guess I'll leave that to Dora here to explain. It sure has always eluded me."

Dora smiled, "Yes, I guess life is just full of mysteries for Don Hardman. But I don't really see why anyone would grow these things for show. I think they are quite ugly." Dora shook her head, but try as she might, she couldn't shake the fact they bore a striking resemblance to little penises. Little erect penises - with red and blue flecks. But the color made her imagine they looked like the penises one might find on a corpse rather than a living specimen.

Pippi leaned over to get a better look. "I don't know, I think they look kind of neat. The little red and blue spots almost look like they are glowing."

Dora thought the spots were certainly unusual, but the whole corpse penis image was now the only thing she could see when she looked down at the outcropping of mushrooms at her feet.

Pippi shivered, "But I don't like the shape of the mushrooms. That kind of gives me the creeps."

Don nodded. He thought, *That's good, little girl. You just keep thinking like that.*

Don said, "Well, however these things got here, I think it's time we got rid of them."

Dora asked, "How?"

Don answered, "Weed killer. I've got a sprayer in the shed."

Pippi chirped, "But mushrooms aren't weeds."

Don responded, "Doesn't matter, it works on most any unwanted plants."

She smiled and shook her head, amazed at how many grownups didn't know about fungus and its place in the universe. "But mushrooms and fungus aren't plants. They don't have chlorophyll, so you see, they aren't really considered plants."

Don nodded, thinking that was just about the damnedest bit of nonsense he'd ever heard. People were always coming up with silly crap like that, messing up the way things worked by looking too closely at them. He said, "Well, fortunately for us, the good folks down at the chemical plant that made my weed killer, weren't any smarter about this stuff than I am. When they made industrial strength Weed-Away they didn't know any better, so neither does it. It will be able to kill that fungus by accident - sort of a case of mistaken identity. So, I think we're in luck."

Pippi furrowed her brow, wondering if Mr. Hardman was making some kind of joke at her expense. Dora patted her on the shoulder and said, "Come on, let's get a better look at this before Don wipes out the whole species - not to mention poisons us all in the process."

She turned to Don who was heading for the shed, "We're just going to take a little walk down the hill and see how far this goes. Don't get too carried away with your spraying until we get back."

Don kept it businesslike, "You've got ten minutes. And then the killing begins."

Dora and Pippi edged down the tree-lined path that led from the Hardman backyard into the wash. Dora focused on the overall color of the wash rather than its individual components. The red, blue, and dark gray fused into a dark purple frosting that swirled over and through the dark, almost red earth, and the green grass and brush. The whole area was rustling in the breeze, adding a shimmering glaze as the setting sun reflected off the odd bits. The colors in the wash were vivid and somehow took the edge off Dora's unsettling concern for the vast sea of, God help her, little corpse penises that were waving in the breeze at her feet.

At each turn of the path, Pippi would punctuate the change of view with variations of "cool" and "wow." As they neared the bottom of the wash, she said, "There must be a million of them, don't you think?"

Dora didn't answer. She felt a new sense of uneasiness as they reached the bottom. Tim had mentioned her old house yesterday. It didn't make sense to her, and she had managed to let it go. But now, Tim's mention of her old house was again heavy on her mind. She had told him to just not think about it, that that is what she had done for all these years. For the most part. Suddenly, seeing the pink of her former home poking out of the hill, not fifty feet away, she found ignoring it to be particularly challenging.

The house stuck out of the base of the hill. It was pitched forward and maybe three quarters of its face was exposed. She also saw parts of the old Fonda house exposed above and somehow mixed in with part of her old house. It looked like a part of the hill, maybe fifty feet above the houses had broken free and slid down to the base of the wash, exposing the houses. The houses and spots on the hill above were so covered with mushrooms they almost appeared to be throbbing.

Pippi asked in awe, "What's that?" She pointed at her new discovery.

Dora said, "A house."

"But I've been down here like a billion times and I've never seen it before."

Dora stared at the rubble and nodded, "I have." She paused. "A long time ago."

Pippi started to run to the house. Dora called out, "Pippi, don't go near it. It may be dangerous."

"Why would it be dangerous?"

Dora looked up and down and surveyed the setting. She answered, "Because that house has been buried for twenty years. For some reason it looks like there was a landslide that exposed it. Or them, I guess. There are two houses there."

Pippi stood and stared, "Two houses? Do you think there are more underneath?"

Dora shook her head, "No there are just two."

Pippi stared at Dora. She realized Dora didn't seem to be excited or surprised by two houses buried at the bottom of the hill, she asked "How do you know there are only two houses here."

Dora replied calmly, "Because twenty years ago, these two houses used to be at the top of the hill, just on the other side of the Sutherland house. They both came down during a horrible storm. Only two houses fell. One belonged to Ralph and Patience Fonda." As she said that, she paused remembering that the Fondas had both been home when the slide had happened. Their bodies must be in their house.

Pippi asked, "Who lived in the other house?"

Dora, realizing Emile must still be in the other house answered, "That was where Emile and Dora Navarro lived."

Pippi said, "What happened to the people, the Fondas and the Navarros."

Dora answered, "They were killed in the slide. The houses were buried under tons of earth and there was no way to save them. They must have all been crushed."

"That's terrible. And you knew all those people?"

"Yes, I did. I knew them all." Dora paused, looking at the houses, the mushrooms and the fading light. "Come on now, Pippi. Don only gave us ten minutes and I think we've been gone twenty."

"But what about the houses? Don't you want to get a better look?"

Dora thought the last thing she ever wanted to do was get a better look at her old house. She came as close to saying the F-word as she ever had – something along the lines of "F-word that." But instead said, "No ma'am. Those houses have been there for twenty years. They aren't going anywhere. And I don't want you coming back here later to get another peek. That hill may not be stable, and those houses could collapse in an instant."

Pippi nodded but wasn't sure that she would be able to resist coming back.

Walking up the hill, Dora couldn't look at the little mushrooms without feeling a chill run up her spine. The imagery had taken on a new meaning, and she found herself hurrying Pippi along the way.

They were halfway back up the hill when they heard Don trying to start the engine on his sprayer. He called out, "Where the hell have you two been?"

Dora didn't feel like yelling to him about their find, not the least of which because she was winded from climbing the hill. She plodded on silently until she and Pippi were close enough to carry on a normal conversation. She put her hand on Don's arm and waited for him to stop fussing with what appeared to be some sort of weed killing flamethrower.

Don looked up from trying to adjust the starter on his gas-powered sprayer. He saw the look on her face and asked, "What? What is it?"

She answered, "Down at the bottom of the wash. The houses aren't buried anymore."

Don looked puzzled. "Houses?"

"The Fonda and Navarro houses."

Don looked wide eyed at Dora, then down the hill, then at Pippi, coming back to Dora to ask, "What do you mean they aren't buried anymore?"

Dora looked like she was going to cry. "I don't know, Don. I just don't know. It just looks like part of the hill came down and exposed what was left of them."

Pippi nodded, smiling, "It's pretty cool alright.

Don didn't have the same set of concerns about the old house as Dora. She had no interest in thinking about the Emile Navarro portion of her life and letting the memory somehow undermine her happiness. He was more concerned about the fact he lived on a hillside and that a new landslide may have undermined their property. He said, "It's getting dark, and I won't be able to get parts for that damn sprayer until tomorrow morning. The mushrooms can wait, but I'd like to take a look at that slide."

Dora said, "I don't think I'm up for another trip back up that hill today."

Pippi said, "Can I go? I want to get a closer look."

Dora said, "You got as close a look as is safe. Don, don't you let her get too close to that house."

Don took that as his instructions to not say that the child couldn't come. He started down the hill, and let Pippi come or not, up to her. Pippi followed, skipping most of the way.

Don stood in the clearing at the bottom of the hill and examined the newly excavated section of the hill. He could see that Emile and Dora's old house looked strangely intact. Hell, for a second or two he could almost swear he had seen old Emile standing in the doorway. The Fondas' home hadn't fared so well. It was mostly smashed and partially merged into part of the Navarro home.

Don asked Pippi to stay back but wanted to get a closer look at the houses. He wanted to test them and see if they seemed they would hold. He feared that, given the amount of the hill that was sitting on top of the Navarro home, a cave in could cause another slide. The houses weren't directly under his home. They were really posing more of a threat to the Sutherland property, but there was no telling how much earth could still come down before the whole neighborhood would have to be abandoned.

Pippi watched from a distance while Don approached the old pink house and gave it a good kick. He knocked on the walls and stepped up onto what was once its front porch. Don leaned into the house, trying to see into its darkened recesses, but whatever windows weren't still buried under the mountain, were not able to funnel enough twilight to illuminate the ruins.

***

Navarro sat in the hallway just beyond his old living room and watched the man who he had finally placed as Don Hardman. Don was standing in his doorway, trying to see into the house. Navarro held himself very still—a skill he had apparently been perfecting for years—and waited for this intruder to leave. He had barely had time to scurry back into this little dark spot once he saw that Hardman was coming up to the house.

Navarro hadn't really recognized Hardman until he saw him standing in the doorway. When he had been watching Don from the window, all his attention had been on the little girl. Navarro had watched her longingly, knowing that although it would be lost on him, she must smell wonderful. He had been so lost in his thoughts, examining her features and imagining what she would have tasted like, that he almost didn't see Don approaching the house. He didn't want to think of what would happen if Don found him. He decided he was going to have to be more careful now that his hidey-hole had been found. He decided he would crawl deeper into the house once Hardman left the doorway, but once the coast was clear, he found himself unable to resist moving to the window and watching the little girl.

As he watched the old man and the little girl head up the hill, he couldn't help thinking that life was good. He grinned at the thought. Life... afterlife... either way. For the first time in as long as he could remember—and that was a very long time—he understood what it was like to have hope for the future. He felt he could let Innocencia go now. He had found her replacement.

28

Dora Ruminates Again

While Don and Pippi were still down the hill, Dora was having a quiet little melt down. That was probably too strong a word for it, but she couldn't think of anything else to call it. She remembered back when they would have called it freaking out, but she was holding it in as best she could and had no intention of letting Don, Pippi, or anyone else for that matter see what was going on in her head.

For a few minutes she had paced around the backyard, but the sight of the little mushrooms, her impression they looked like little corpse erections and the sudden awareness her long-dead husband's actual corpse might lay uncovered at the bottom of her hill, made that sight of the house unbearable for her. She headed into the kitchen, poured a little vodka into a wine glass and headed out to her rose garden. The rose garden was as far away from the hillside as she could get without leaving their property.

Dora stood in the garden and pretended she was taking a nice break from gardening with a nice refreshing glass of chardonnay. It didn't take long for her to realize the vodka wasn't her friend in this. Of course, it rarely is, and as so often is the case, her reaction was to assume that perhaps more vodka would be.

A few minutes later, when Tim drove into the Sutherland driveway, Dora was standing in the center of her rose garden, looking more like a statue than a gardener. Seeing Tim drive up, she blinked a few times and started moving around, attempting to look busy gardening and a little more nonchalant.

Tim saw Dora walking back and forth in her garden. For just a second, he thought she looked like one of those old mechanical figures that walk back and forth in front of those old fancy cuckoo clocks. Or maybe, like a duck in a shooting gallery. She was holding a glass of wine in one hand and walking first to the left, then to the right, taking a quick drink, then repeating.

He called out, "Good evening, Dora."

Dora continued her back and forth routine, but added a nod and mumbled something incoherently, adding a little wave as a flourish.

Tim approached slowly, wanting to make sure she wasn't having some kind of stroke or something. He did think strokes usually downed you rather than winding you up like this, but he was an engineering student, not pre-med, so wasn't all too sure about bodily matters. He asked, "Is everything all right, Mrs. Hardman?"

Dora nodded and smiled at Tim, blinked a few times, and asked, "What?"

Tim was just getting home from an all-day stint in the library. He had felt the need to get normal again and had stayed until he felt more like a student than some post-adolescent's sidekick. He also felt the need to get caught up with his studies so Monday's chem lab wouldn't catch him off guard. Dora looked a little freaked out, and he feared he may be stepping into yet another pit of drama.

He repeated himself, "Are you okay, Mrs Hardman?"

"It's Dora, dear, and yes, I'm okay." She drained the rest of her glass and added, "I guess I just had a bit of a shock, that's all."

He asked, "So then, everyone's all right?"

"All right? Of course. Pippi and Don are down the hill."

Tim thought her eyes looked pretty much glazed over. She continued, "But, everything is going to be fine. I mean, dead is dead, lost or found, right?"

Tim squinted and asked, "Dead? Is someone dead?"

Dora stared at Tim like he was addled, "Dead? No. I mean, just my damned husband."

Tim's eyes got wide, "Don's dead?"

"Not Don. Emile."

"Who's Emile?"

Dora tried to squeeze another drink out of her empty glass. Distractedly, she answered "First husband."

"And he died?"

"Apparently." She paused, "But I guess we are about to confirm it."

Before Tim could continue with his line of questioning, Dora turned and headed back into the house. He had picked up the odor of vodka and decided rather than a stroke, Dora was rambling due to a few too many cocktails. He figured her condition didn't warrant any further attention and chose to take a quick look in on Rage and get to bed early.

The house was dark. He checked Rage's room and even went out to the happy place. Rage wasn't to be found. He decided whenever Rage came home, he didn't want to get pulled back into his insanity. Tim made himself a sandwich, grabbed a soda, and headed to his room to eat and study in peace. Earlier, Tim had spent time trying to find another living situation, with no real luck. He would keep trying until he found an opening. He had heard that at or around halfway into each semester, several cheap rooming situations came available as marginal students took the hint and left school.

29

Navarro Licks his Lips

Once Don Hardman and the sweet little innocent had left the clearing in front of his home, Navarro started to pace. He was at first elated to see the child; it gave him a thrill to see the young thing and imagine what he would have loved to do with her, had he still been a living being - at least in the conventional sense. Now, however, his yearning was just as real, it's just that he wasn't sure what he was yearning for.

Stronger than the anxiety he felt over the ambiguous interest he felt in the child was the agitation he felt over the fact Don Hardman had found his house. He didn't know why, but it was clear from the way Hardman was nosing around that he was surprised by the house. That gave Navarro pause. He feared that Hardman was likely to come back and investigate further. He remembered Don Hardman as one of those annoying everything-by-the-book types. A real Boy Scout.

Smashing a few rodents with a bone was one thing, but an encounter with a grown man, Navarro wasn't sure he would prevail. Hardman would probably come back with a contractor, a structural engineer, some cops and an emissary from the fucking pope. Navarro peered around his home and realized it may no longer be safe. If he stayed here, he feared he could too easily be found.

He stood at the window and looked for any sense of movement on the path that had led Hardman and the girl both to him and away. The sun was barely down, but he felt stronger than he had yesterday. He had taken care of the fungus that held him together and with the additional bones had strengthened his frame. He decided to leave his house and chance a few minutes in the open.

Navarro stepped out in front of his house and scanned all around, lacking any senses, save for sight, he intended to avoid an ambush, whether by some coyote or Don Hardman and his goody-two-shoes posse. He spun around every few feet, watching in each direction for movement. He took a few minutes to get up to the cave where yesterday he had been re-reanimated.

Entering the cave, he felt a certain comfortable familiarity wash over him. It was somehow a better fit for the new Navarro than the old house. It was cooler, and the walls were covered with life-giving fungus. Just thinking the word fungus gave him a nice warm feeling. The whole room seemed to exist just for him - or perhaps he for it. When he sat down, tendrils embraced him - not just for nourishment. They also tended to him, performing minor repairs to his flesh. In this room, the quiet din that existed in his head spoke wordlessly of unity and family.

The only thing in the cave that didn't seem to exist entirely for his benefit was the pile of bones in the corner. Every time he looked at the bones, the symphony of voices that existed in his head and seemed to be related to the depth of fungus in, on, and around him, changed into a cacophony that wasn't so positive. Whereas the fungus seemed to be soothing him, the bones seemed to try to make him mad. Looking at them made him think of pain and hurting things.

Thinking about pain and hurting things reminded him that it was dark and a good time to do a little hunting. Considering that there might be human hunters on the prowl tonight he looked down at his leg bone club and decided it was lacking. It was effective against rodents, but even against the raccoon and the little dog he killed last night it had almost taken more strength than he possessed to take them down quickly. He needed something with more power.

By the time Navarro stepped out into the world for tonight's hunt, he had had a day to experiment. He had poked around in himself, discovering places where the bones from last night's victims had formed additional skeletal structures. He wasn't sure if victim was an adequate description. He realized that although on the surface, one less enlightened may see his actions as those of a hunter, or a killer, but in reality, he was really just rearranging the life forms. Navarro was coalescing creation into a more concise form.

Oh yes, and apparently, he was getting smarter. He certainly never had thoughts like these before. Whereas he used to think only about the mistakes he'd made and the opportunities he'd missed, now he thought about coalescing creation. He thought about right and wrong. Before, he used to rationalize that actions he had taken were often mitigated by circumstances beyond his control. Now he understood there was no wrong. All roads led to life abundant. All lives could continue, and he could be their enabler.

He considered heading back down the hill, when it occurred to him that even though his house was just below his cave, it had once inhabited a perch at the top of the hill. He decided to take a hike up the hill and prowl around his old stomping grounds.

When Navarro stepped out of his cave, his senses were heightened to being outside and defenseless. More accurately stated, his lack of senses were heightened. He turned round and round in an effort to not let anything sneak up on him. While continuing to monitor his surroundings, he rooted around in the small rock outcropping that partially masked its entrance. He found one that weighed about three pounds and had a rough edge. He found a patch of ivy at the base of the outcropping and using the jagged edge of his rock, cut out two long vines. He carried his finds, the ivy and rock back to his cave.

Sitting cross legged on the floor of his cave, Navarro carefully bound the rock to the leg bone club he had carried on last night's hunt. Navarro had never been much good with his hands, so winding the ivy around the rock so that it held it but wasn't cut by it took most of his concentration. He found himself distracted a couple times by an inner voice. *What are you doing, old man?* It confused him a little, because it had been his intent to form a weapon, but wondered if maybe he was questioning his own capabilities.

He guessed some things never changed. Apparently a lifetime of self doubt wasn't enough.

Navarro stood and tested the weight of his new mace. If he held it too high behind him, he found it was enough to cause him to lose his balance. He caught himself before he fell but would have to remember that in an emergency situation, he should keep the weapon below shoulder level to have his best chance of keeping his feet.

He looked down at the bones and for a second considered smashing the mace into them to see its power. He let the thought pass as this bone pile had served him well and he may need it again for spare parts. There was no telling what this new life had in store for him, and he might as well be prepared.

Navarro decided it was time to put his new weapon to the test. He felt the constant call to feed and as he stepped out of his cave, felt sure his prospects of a big night had greatly improved. He surveyed the area and although he had so far spent his time in the wash where his house had ended up, considered it wise to try another area. If Hardman did come back with help, he wasn't sure his mace would be enough for him to defend himself.

Navarro looked up the hill. A little over a hundred yards up the hill had once been the site of his home. But it was where Hardman lived. Navarro didn't want to get so near the houses that he would be seen by some goddamn yapping dog but was pretty sure the brush and trees that populated the wash and hillside would provide adequate cover for him to hunt and also survey the wash for intruders.

His theory that the new weapon would prove to be a time saver was proven within minutes. A raccoon and her three young were skittering along a break in the hill and for reasons that Navarro was only able to piece together after the altercation, didn't see him until he had already brought down his mace on one of the little ones. It was killed, if not completely flattened in one quick swing of the mace. He would have laughed at the simple efficiency of the thing if he hadn't had to react so quickly to the mama raccoon that turned and flew at him in a rage. She latched onto his leg, high on his thigh, and when he brushed her away with the base of his mace, she took a huge section of his fungus flesh with her. He kept his balance and was able to bring his mace down and behead her with the jagged edge of it in a single swing.

The other two young ones stood snarling at him, but when he turned to get a bead on them, they ran off it two separate directions. He smiled and thought that it didn't matter. They were defenseless now and something would get them. If it wasn't him, it would be something he would ultimately get himself. One way or another, they would be his. He reached down and picked up the flattened corpse of the young raccoon and held it into his wound, allowing tendrils to bind it and feeling an instant relief spread up and down his leg, radiating from his wound. He put the mama raccoon's head into the wound as well. For good measure, he scooped up a couple of handfuls of rotting leaves and used it to smooth over the rest of the missing tissue.

As Navarro was rubbing leaves and twigs onto his body, it occurred to him why the raccoons hadn't noticed him. Standing motionless while not out in the open, Navarro could pass for some kind of bush or shrubbery. As he moved through the world, he picked up enough debris to blend in. Of course, that only worked if he didn't appear to be a walking shrub.

While allowing his tendrils to absorb the rest of the mama raccoon, Navarro contemplated the sensation of the healing. When he first gained this body, he had no sense but sight. He couldn't feel his new skin. Now, he realized he was beginning to feel things, just in a different way. He felt warmth, not the kind that comes from the sun, but the kind that comes from life. He could feel the healing. He didn't feel the wound as pain, he felt it as the absence of presence. There had been a life force that, until it was missing, wasn't tangible. Replacing that hole with new flesh and letting it bond to him filled that void.

Navarro headed a little higher up the hill, surveying all that surrounded him and all that he could see down in the wash. It was his domain. He considered the fact all that he surveyed, both vegetable and animal, could over time become not just his, but him. He liked the idea, but wondered if it would be enough.

He climbed higher, to within a hundred feet of the properties at the top of the hill. That was when he saw the people standing at the top of the hill, looking down in his direction. He froze, hoping his theory regarding his ability to camouflage himself was sound.

Once he had a chance to steady his nerves, or whatever he had that passed for nerves, he was able to focus on the couple. One of them was Don Hardman. The old woman took him a little longer to place. But, after she gave Hardman a dismissive wave, Navarro recognized the subtlety of the gesture from half a lifetime as its recipient. Dora was alive.

30

Dora Sees a Ghost

Don and Dora rarely fought. In fact, if Don really worked at it, he couldn't remember any time in their nearly twenty years that either of them had had so much as a cross word for each other. That was why he was having such a hard time wondering what it was that made Dora act so strangely now. She had come up from the wash acting like she had seen a ghost, and Don guessed in a way he could understand that. After all, she hadn't seen her old house in decades, and it had to have come as a shock. When he had come back up the hill, he had found her in a fright.

The child had gone home at Don's suggestion and Dora had puttered around the house for an hour or two, acting more and more agitated. Don was pretty secure in his manhood and knew he and Dora had a good thing. They hadn't talked all that much about Dora's old life. In fact, it was a little strange to think about that life, since Don and his first wife had lived right alongside them all those years. Whatever it was like between Emile and Dora behind closed doors had for all intents and purposes died with Emile, as far as Don, and for that matter, Dora were concerned.

And that was why Don was starting to get upset with Dora. It was one thing when her former life was a secret she felt no need to share. It was her thing and only her thing. Now, somehow he felt the house itself had entered into her confidence. He wondered if she was somehow thinking about those old times and missing Emile. Don hated to admit it, and wouldn't out loud, but truth be told, her reaction to her find was starting to make Don jealous.

At around ten o'clock, he finally broke his silence. He asked, "So, are you going to go to bed without telling me what's bothering you?"

Dora said, "Bothering me?"

"Sweetie, in all the years I've known you, I've never seen you take a drink unless it was so someone else didn't have to drink alone. Tell me what's eating you."

Dora looked out the back window, toward where the yard turned dark and melded with the wild zone. Don had never been one to pry but had also never been one to let her suffer in silence. She studied him and said, "I don't know, Don. Seeing that house brought back memories."

Don swallowed. It was as he feared. She was thinking about Emile. He fished for more "What kind of memories? Good ones?"

Dora laughed. It was the sort of laugh that suggested to Don she had had more to drink than she had let on. "Good ones? From those days? I don't have any good memories of those days. In fact, the fact I can remember any of it at all is a bit of a shock. I've been in denial all these years."

"Denial? About what?"

Dora answered, "I guess denial might be the wrong word. What I meant to say is that I stopped thinking about that part of my life the second I knew it was over. I haven't thought about Emile or that house more than a minute or two in twenty years. Until this afternoon I had almost forgotten it was real."

Don thought he may be on the verge of ending the closest thing to an anxiety attack he had ever had. If she was saying the house had brought back nothing but bad memories, then in a kind of way —a selfish kind of way—he was starting to feel relief. He said, "I'm sorry this all happened. But, that time in your life is still over. That house just got uncovered by some freak slide. It didn't, you know, undo the last twenty years. Everything we have is still intact." He hoped that came out more reassuring to Dora than it had sounded in his head. He feared it may have come off like a question.

Dora smiled. "Of course, Don. It just hit me all of a sudden. There is nothing at the bottom of that hill that could ever interfere with what we have up here."

"You know, I believe I'll have a glass of wine, myself."

Dora got up from the dining room table and went to get a better look out the back window, "Bring me another too, Don, won't you." Then she added, "Oh, and mine is a vodka."

Don brought a vodka martini for Dora and a double Manhattan for himself and walked past Dora out to the patio. He set the drinks on the patio table, then headed back through the house to the kitchen, calling out after himself, "It's nicer outside, I'll bring us a snack and we can drink ourselves silly." Coincidentally as Dora was walking out to the patio, both she and Don simultaneously thought to themselves, *too late.*

Don took his drink out to the patio and peered down the hill. The mushrooms that covered the slope were almost luminescent, and their contrast with the other flora gave the appearance of otherworldliness. He cursed the fact he hadn't been able to spray the damn things today. There was no telling how out of hand they would be tomorrow. Mushrooms could spread in hours.

***

Dora joined him at the table. "Do you think the hill is safe?"

"I guess it is as safe as it ever was. Hills erode over time, but left to its natural course of events, it will take another fifty years before this property is affected."

Dora, in spite of being more intoxicated than she'd been in a great many years was starting to calm down. She was putting things in perspective, remembering her life with Emile was safely entombed in the past, even if the old house had excavated itself. She remembered that just as she was able to take control of the inside of their home, building a proper nest for her and Don- Don was able to take care of all the outside messes that the world threw at them. This was no different, just another batch of extraneous nonsense that in the grand scheme of things had no real bearing on their lives.

Don took Dora's empty glass and headed back into the house for refreshers. Dora scanned the hillside. She knew it shouldn't be visible from this spot, but looked down where she thought the house might be. It was an area covered in mushrooms. From here, it looked like the little recess at the bottom of the wash was where the greatest concentration of mushrooms was. They seemed to gradually dissipate as they reached up the sides of the wash and, from what little she could see, down the other side. It was like a giant fairy ring, with the bottom of the wash being the epicenter.

She let her eyes scan her own hill, starting at the bottom and working their way up toward where she stood. Something wasn't right, but she couldn't put her finger on it. She felt like she was being watched. She stood still watching for any sign of movement. There was a light breeze so here and there things were slightly swaying. But all of that movement had a connected, kind of orchestrated look. Each patch of motion was somehow in unison or just slightly leading to the next active spot. Her focus made it easy to see that the breeze was coming through the wash and up the hill toward where she stood.

Don was approaching through the yard when Dora noticed the movement of a couple of bushes perhaps a hundred feet down from where she stood. The movement was obviously disconnected from the breeze, and she assumed either a coyote or large dog must be moving through that area. It was too big a movement to be caused by anything smaller. She took half a step back just as Don arrived with their drinks.

Dora whispered, "I think there may be a coyote just down from us."

Don looked down the hill but his eyes were still tuned to the bright lights in the house. Staring into the blackness, he asked, "Where, I don't see anything?"

Dora pointed to the spot where the two bushes stood where she had seen the rustling a moment before.

If Dora hadn't known better, she could have sworn one of the bushes seemed to jump with a start at being pointed at. But just for a split second and then it again stood still. Just then, a breeze moved the other bush and all the tall grass and mushrooms that surrounded it. The hair on Dora's neck and arms stood up, and she gasped at the realization that she was sure that the bush was watching her.

Don said, "What, I don't see anything."

Dora couldn't take her eyes off the bush and was afraid to so much as speak. She felt like she was staring at one of those optical illusion paintings where if you squint just right, some meaningless pattern turns into a dolphin or a space ship. Try as she might, the bush was a bush, or maybe a tree trunk. But, if she squinted just right, for a half a second it looked a little like a man. In fact, something about the way it leaned to one side while whatever looked like a head leaned the other way, reminded her a little bit of how Emile used to look at you when he had a bone he couldn't let go of. She shivered at the thought.

"What is it? Did you see a coyote?"

Dora turned to Don and said, "Don't you see it, it's right where I'm pointing. I don't think it's a coyote, I think it's a..." and as Dora turned back to the spot, the bush was gone. She quickly surveyed the hillside, but whatever she had seen was truly gone.

"A what?"

Dora shook her head, "It may have been a man."

"A man? Did you recognize him?"

Dora shook a little, examined her glass and decided to not drink anymore tonight. "I'm not even sure it was a man." She thought to herself, that if it had been one, she knew who she feared it was. She made a mental note to double check the doors tonight.

31

Navarro Hears a What

Navarro wasn't sure what to make of seeing Don and Dora. He couldn't tell if Dora had seen him but couldn't imagine a scenario that was truly a danger to him. Obviously if she recognized him and tried to explain it, she wouldn't be taken seriously, and quite frankly would probably doubt it herself. But, if she thought she saw something she couldn't identify, well, he assumed Don was coming back to check the house because he might just assume there was some homeless person living in the wash. Navarro planned to avoid the house and stay down the hill in his cave - for now.

No, Dora wasn't his top concern for now. He had to hunt. Heading back down the hill he could feel his new strength. He knew there was more to his feeding than the pure visceral pleasure of the kill and feeding. He was becoming more. He was gaining from the lives he accumulated.

Halfway down the hill he saw a possum roll itself into a pale excuse for a corpse. He reached down and plucked it up, intending to smash it to the ground. He smiled. *Or I could swallow it alive.* He studied the small animal, still afraid to squirm. It must have believed if he thought it dead, he would let it go. He looked down at the small furry animal and realized it would be part of him forever and that in a way, he loved it. He held it to his bosom, holding it close and trying to make it understand that it needn't fear, that it, too, would live forever. Through Navarro.

As he hugged the animal to his chest, he felt its presence. Even though he couldn't feel his fungus skin the way one might feel their own skin, he felt the closeness of the animal and gazing down into its eyes, he saw it was being woven into him. For a few seconds he felt the animal's panic and felt it as his own. As he stared into the animal's eyes, he tried to concentrate on the part of him that was the possum. He tried to control its fear.

He could feel the possum's fear and he thought he could hear its voice interspersed among the cacophony inside his head. But he realized he heard something else. He heard crickets, and not inside his head. He heard real crickets. Peering around, he realized he was able to hear for the first time since being reanimated. As he watched the possum, he knew he was tapped into the possum, and was hearing what it heard.

He looked up from the possum and scanned all that was around him, now able to put sound with picture. He tried to control the visceral panic that still seemed to well up from his chest when he was hit with a new blast of terror. At the same time the possum's fear ratcheted up, he heard something approaching quietly from behind him. He wheeled around in time to see a coyote, ready to pounce.

Navarro held his bone club in both hands, batter style, ready for the animal to pounce. The coyote was much larger than anything he'd killed last night. It was also far more aggressive, not to mention, it was hunting him, not the other way around. A part of him, a very small part of him, flashed for a moment on the idea of pretending to be dead. He would have laughed out loud if not for the fact he and the coyote were busy trying to stare each other down and evaluate the situation.

They stood that way for thirty seconds or so, Navarro choking up on his bone mace while the coyote held his gaze, slowly rocking back and forth. Then Navarro heard another set of footsteps coming from his left side. He really was being hunted. He turned his head to the left to look in the direction of the second coyote, and the first coyote lunged. When Navarro turned his head, the possum's eyes, wide with terror, never left the coyote.

The coyote, flying through the space between them, was surprised by the accuracy of the swing, but only for an instant. The swing of Navarro's mace knocked it cold, and it crashed into the old corpse, Navarro, knocking him down. They slid down the hill several yards as the second coyote bore down on Navarro, not yet aware of its hunting partner's status.

Navarro got up to one knee as the second coyote lunged at him. Navarro, having lost his club, swung wildly, trying a roundhouse but barely connecting. He tried to get his left hand around the coyote's throat, a move he'd been waiting to use on an attacking canine for most of his adult life. Somehow, over the years of living near neighbors with large dogs, he'd always believed this was the move that would save him. Of course, until now it had never been tried. If he had tried it in his last life, it wouldn't have worked. Technically, it didn't work now, but that was to his advantage.

The gripped coyote bit into Navarro's arm, just below his elbow, and while falling to the ground, shook it trying to bring Navarro down with him. As it happened, the arm pulled off and the coyote stood staring at it for just a split second, wondering at the forearm in its mouth. That was all the time Navarro needed to grab a rock and bring it down on the coyote. Given that he had had to accomplish this with a single hand and in the blink of his eye, his accuracy wasn't what he had hoped for, but it had the desired effect. He had meant to try and smash the coyote's skull, but instead hit it just below the base of its skull. He had heard a crack, and the coyote had dropped to the ground, its head at a completely unnatural angle.

Navarro felt a cry of celebration raise up in his chest and looked down to see the possum staring wide-eyed at the coyote. He wondered at the coyote, and at the fact the possum had saved his newfound life. It had sensed its enemy and given him the ability to hear the coyote's approach. He could feel that the possum was elated from the battle, something he had no doubt avoided his whole life.

Navarro examined the two coyotes that lay at his feet. Both were breathing, one unconscious and the other with a broken neck. He decided there was no sense wasting good meat, bones—or ears—and considered the best way to use them. He wanted them alive, but where they could do no harm. Once he had it worked out in his head, he took the unconscious coyote and swung it over his right shoulder, letting the body drape over him with the bulk of the body in front of him, leaving just the head facing behind him, but at an angle where it wasn't flush with his body. He held it in place while the tendrils that he felt he could now control began weaving around the coyote, binding it to him.

The whole time the first coyote was being bound to Navarro, the second coyote, laying on its belly, with its head laying on its side, looked up at the spectacle of what was happening to the other coyote and whimpered. Navarro didn't know if that was from the pain of the animal's injuries, or out of terror. He hoped it was both. He looked at the coyote on the ground and focused on the fact it would have killed him for nothing. It wouldn't have eaten him, given he had no meat to offer save for the possum. No, this dumb animal would have killed him, just at the possibility of a meal. Navarro had just saved countless animals from this indiscriminate killer of a beast.

When Navarro picked up the second coyote, its head lolled around wildly while he threw it into roughly the same position as the first. As the head swung around, the coyote, left with control of only his mouth, tried to bite Navarro. Navarro laughed, admiring the sheer futile tenacity of the creature. He held it in place for a few minutes as it became a part of him.

If one had seen Navarro at this point, aside from him being a skeleton covered in a mass of fungus, he would have looked a new kind of funny. The coyotes swung over his shoulders and hanging down in front of his chest looked like giant furry suspenders. If the possum had been six inches higher, it might have been mistaken for a horribly matched bow tie.

Navarro picked his arm up off the ground where the second coyote had dropped it. He brushed if off and held it in place, watching as his body reattached it. Five minutes later he stood in the moonlight with his hand in front of his face, watching as he flexed each finger and made a fist. He was amazed how much his hearing had improved in the last ten minutes. He could have sworn he heard a rabbit half a mile away.

He smiled at his good fortune and decided to see if he could find said rabbit.

32

Tim Hears a Coyote

Tim had been sleeping when he heard the sound of coyotes howling and fighting in the wash behind the hill. He hadn't found Rage tonight and even though his truck was here, Tim assumed one of Rage's stoner friends had picked him up and taken him on a rampage. He knew if Rage had been home, Rage would have gone out to check on Fatty. Tim cursed both the animal and his dog under his breath and got up and got dressed.

Stepping out on the patio, he found Fatty pushing his empty dish around, trying to find a bite of food in some hidden corner that just wasn't there.

He said, "Okay, Fatty. I'll get you your food."

Tim took the bowl and went into the kitchen to open a can of the generic dog food Rage bought by the case at Costco. Rage made weekly trips and bought industrial size containers of Mountain Dew, frozen burritos, frozen pizzas, gummy worms and just about anything else a hungry nine-year-old might crave.

When Tim brought the food back out, Fatty was gone. Tim searched around the sides of the house, calling out to the dog. Fatty wasn't there.

He went back to Rage's happy place and peered down into the wash. The night was dark, so dark that Tim didn't notice Rage sleeping in his shallow grave. What he did see was Fatty running down the trail that went to the old, ruined houses. Tim called him, but the dog kept going. He knew from living on the hill for a few months that the area was a haven for coyotes. The coyotes loved the area as there was enough wild area to support them even though it was right smack in the middle of Los Angeles. There was a good supply of food. Aside from the possums, raccoons, rodents and skunks, dogs and cats were plentiful. Everyone always feared for their children as well, even though, to Tim's knowledge, no kid had ever been so much as looked at cross-eyed by one. The coyotes were considered a protected species and therefore there were strong fines for attempting to deal with them in a non-throwing up your hands and saying "oh well" manner. He thought given the amount of time Rage had spent bitching about the coyotes, he could have built a fence to protect his dog. That, of course, would have had to have been some other Rage than the one he was thinking of.

Tim needed to go and get Fatty, and even though he knew the coyotes didn't attack humans, it seemed stupid to go empty handed. Besides, there were other big dogs in the neighborhood, and even though coyotes wouldn't attack him, the dogs might. The closest thing to a weapon he could find on a quick search of the back yard was a shovel. He held it in both hands and gave it a test swing. It would do.

Tim started down the path and called out "Fatty."

As he walked down the hill, he called out again, "Fatty, you little bastard, come and get your damn food."

***

Fatty had heard something down the hill. And it wasn't the coyotes from before. He knew not to play with those things. They didn't play fair. They sometimes ganged up on other dogs and actually killed them. There was something just not right about a dog that would do that.

But the coyote smell had changed to fear and then dissipated. In its place was a new smell. No, not new exactly. It was a smell he remembered as having been on his bones. The ones he had left in his cave. He had forgotten all about them. One of the joys of being a dog was that you were constantly finding new and exciting things. The downside, of course, and it was lost on the dogs themselves, was that the reason they constantly found new and exciting things was because they had some of the worst memories in the animal world. Oh sure, they could remember things like coyotes are bad and

147

eating is good. But the day-to-day items like where to pee, what tastes bad or where they put something... well, those were in one minute and out the next.

So, when Fatty smelled the fungus that his bones had been covered with, he remembered that he hadn't really been all that fond of the fungus, but the bones had been delicious. He decided since nobody had fed him today, and there was a perfectly good stash of bones just down the hill, this was a perfect act of providence. He smiled a giant dog smile as he ran down the hill, noting all of life was just one giant act of providence for a dog.

33

Dog Fight!

Navarro looked up with a start. It was that goddamn dog. The one that had tried to eat him. Navarro had heard him coming down the path, but now he could see him. Navarro stepped into the path, holding his leg bone mace, making sure the animal could see him. He wanted to do more than just kill and eat the dog. He wanted to make sure it feared him. He wanted to destroy the dog before devouring him.

Fatty, running down the hill, skidded to a stop at the sight of Navarro. He didn't know what to make of the thing that stood ten feet in front of him. It was a man. No, it was like a man. But it smelled like the bones he had come to eat. It also smelled like possum and coyote. It had fur in places and was holding a large bone.

They stood looking at each other. Navarro tried to taunt the dog, tempting it with the bone in his hand. He leaned over and tried to say, "Here boy," but of course couldn't speak. If the dog would just come within three feet, he would strike it with the bone. He didn't want to kill it outright. He didn't even want to kill and eat it today. He wanted to wound it, to cripple it and then keep it for a while. He wanted it to know it was at his mercy, the way he had known he was at the dog's.

Fatty stepped forward to get a better look at the bone. It didn't look like one of his, and he didn't yet recognize Navarro as his actual bone collection. Navarro quickly turned the bone from bait to a weapon, but because he didn't want to strike a mortal blow, he didn't strike with enough force to hit Fatty in time. Fatty jumped forward to his left while Navarro stepped forward to get a better second shot at the dog. Fatty didn't make it a habit of attacking other animals. He was more of a pacifist. It was almost as if he understood the origins of his name. He preferred to hang out and get fed. But he wasn't so centered as to be able to turn the other cheek, particularly when something was trying to hurt him. He believed in a sort of tit for tat kind of justice. The fungus man had tried to hit him, so he would give the fungus man a nip in kind.

Fatty lunged for Navarro's right ankle. It was a fairly harmless attack, one that dogs did mainly to make a point. It said, "Hey, we're down here, don't tread on us." Fatty jumped in, gave a quick playful chomp on Navarro's ankle and ran past him, getting out of harm's way.

Fatty turned around quickly, making sure to not keep his back to Navarro. Lacking any feeling in his legs, Navarro didn't react from pain, but from outrage. The dog had taunted him. This was going to take a little longer than he thought. *But wouldn't that just prolong the pleasure of it all?*

Both Navarro and Fatty heard Tim coming down the path, calling out "Fatty you little son of a bitch, I've got a treat."

Fatty thought, *So do I.* He had recognized the flavor when he bit Navarro's ankle. Somehow, and he didn't claim to be the sort of dog to figure out such complexities, but somehow, this man was actually Fatty's bone pile. He decided he would take one for all his trouble.

Navarro took two steps back from the dog, not out of fear of it, but in order to be shielded by a small patch of trees from the human coming down the path. He peered around a tree and noted that the man had a spade and was holding it like a club. He thought, *Two against one, and he's got a bigger stick.*

Before he thought anything else, Fatty struck and got hold of his right ankle again. Inexplicably, Navarro lost control of his left leg. It turned and he felt the knee bend, like it was trying to sit down on its own. As the dog tugged on his right leg, Navarro, having been caught off guard, and lacking any support from his other leg, went down on his back. As he fell, he could have sworn he heard "Fuck you, old man" in his head. Fatty got hold of

Navarro's leg, just below the knee and gave it a solid dog style shake. The leg came off at the knee and Fatty took off, Navarro's calf in his mouth, and ran up the trail, passing Tim in the first twenty yards.

Tim stood, shaking his head as Rage's stupid dog ran by him, without so much as an acknowledgment that Tim was there. He turned and headed back up the hill. He wasn't quite sure what the thing he'd seen in Fatty's mouth was exactly. I looked like some kind of rotten moss-covered log.

Navarro sat under a cedar tree, watching as Tim walked up the path, following that god damn dog, "Fatty." Fatty had now taken part of his second original equipment leg bone. As he began crawling back to his cave he thought, *Oh, God, how good it will be when I eat that dog.*

Several times on the crawl back to his cave he thought he heard a wet slurping sound. Each time he stopped and examined his knee, wondering if he was somehow leaking. What he could be leaking, he didn't know. Everything checked out. It wasn't until he was back in his cave that he placed the sound. It was the coyote with the broken neck. It was chewing the flesh away from Navarro's shoulder, trying to eat him. The animal wasn't able to move, or for that matter swallow, but it had managed to eat away a section of Navarro about the size of a softball.

Navarro shook his head while willing a half dozen tendrils to bind the coyote head's mouth shut. Turning his head as far to his left he was able, he could just make eye contact with the coyote head. Eventually he was able to stare down the coyote.

He went to his spare bone pile and found its remaining leg and foot bones. He carefully used the bones to repair his leg and spent the rest of the night healing, resting, contemplating his new skills, and listening to the new voices that ran through him.

III

Monday

34

Rage is Uncovered

On Monday morning, Tim slept in, partly because he had a lifetime proclivity to do so and partly because he had had a long, action-packed weekend that had ended with him trying to make up for it by studying into the wee hours. On top of that, a super late-night trip down the hill to "rescue" Fatty had broken up the few hours he had actually had to sleep. He didn't need to be in class until noon, so waking up at ten wasn't going to put too much of a dent in his day. He put on the coffee and then jumped in the shower.

By 10:30 he was dressed and ready to go. As he headed through the house, he glanced into the backyard and saw that Fatty was running in circles out by the edge of the hill acting quite agitated. The dog was running, jumping, and barking frantically. Tim was afraid the dog had cornered some cat, or worse yet, a skunk and so headed into the backyard to break things up.

As he approached the object of Fatty's attention, he realized it wasn't an animal, but a large outcropping of the mushrooms Rage had been eating earlier in the weekend, and in fact had been trying to eat him back yesterday. Some of these, though, were significantly larger. As he bent down to touch one of the larger ones, which had to be at least a foot across he saw it was at the head of the outcropping and that the whole thing was in the unmistakable shape of a grave. He brushed back a few of the larger mushrooms and saw they had been growing in the dirt around Rage's face. Somehow, Rage had gotten buried, and the mushrooms were covering the spot. He wildly brushed the dirt and fungus away from Rage's head and Rage opened his eyes. Rage said, "Dude, what are you doing?"

Tim said, "I'm getting this stuff off you. I thought you might be dead."

Rage seemed to Tim to be delirious. "No dude, I'm not dead. But don't fuck with the mushrooms. They aren't hurting anything."

Tim kept brushing the area around Rage's head clear. He started to dig Rage out of the mound. Rage reached up with his right hand and grabbed Tim's arm, stopping him from digging. "Hey man...listen to me. It's cool. Let me be. I'm fine."

Tim tried to wrestle his arm free, and Rage clamped down harder. His tone changed, and he slowly, forcefully added, "I said I'm fine. Now just leave us the fuck alone."

Tim stood back and really examined Rage. "Us?" His face looked thinner and although he hadn't to his knowledge ever really paid all that much attention to Rage's body, his arms seemed much less muscular than Tim recalled.

Fatty was running around the grave, biting mushrooms off of Rage and spitting them out. Rage was impotently trying to wave the dog away.

Tim didn't give any thought to honoring Rage's request to leave him in this predicament, but decided it was time to bring in the professionals. He left Rage in the capable paws of Fatty and called 911. It was an odd call, and he wasn't sure what to say or how to describe the situation. He thought calling to say your roommate was being eaten by mushrooms might get the wrong sort of professional attention. In an effort to get someone to come out and not think he was some crank caller, he described it as a potential overdose.

Don Hardman came rushing around the back fence carrying a shovel in both hands, and called out to Tim, "I heard the racket all the way over in my shed. Need a hand there, son?"

Tim shrugged, "I honestly don't know, sir."

Don reached the spot where Tim stood over Rage's grave.

Tim continued, "I've tried to get him out of this hole, but he is fighting it. The paramedics are on their way."

Don nodded, "That's good. Let the professionals handle this." He leaned over Rage and spoke loudly and slowly. "Son. What have you been into?"

As Rage wound up to start a really good rant about fascists and the like, Don quickly assessed the situation and whispered in awe, "It's the god damn mushrooms."

Rage said, "Get off my property, old man."

Dora called over the fence, "Don, honey? Is everything alright?"

Rage closed his eyes and tried to recapture the calm that until a few minutes ago had engulfed him.

Don called back, "No ma'am, things are not all right. Reggie here is being eaten alive by those mushrooms we found yesterday."

Tim thought that was a good assessment. Rage looked twenty pounds thinner.

Rage hummed quietly to himself, thinking that was how all those yoga dudes were able to zone out. As it wasn't working, he hummed louder.

Dora said, "Eaten alive? What do you mean eaten alive?"

Don looked back at his wife over the fence, trying to hold in the look of impatience that was rare in their relationship but common between most married couples. "Well, I guess I mean it in the usual sense. The boy is alive, but he is being... consumed... by a pile of red, blue, and blackish mushrooms." He paused, and as if to add proper punctuation, added, "Eaten... by... mushrooms."

Dora recognized the look, but just not from her current husband. "Oh, well then, I guess that makes sense." She assumed, had she been standing where Don was, it would make sense and she might also lose patience with someone asking what must appear to be a stupid question.

Don surveyed the scene with a wider lens. "You know, I was planning on spraying my part of the wash this morning, but this stuff is worse than I thought." He turned to Tim, "I'll spray out here too."

Rage opened his eyes and screamed, "Leave us alone. You stay off my property, old man."

Don was used to abuse from the boy and knew ignoring it was the act of the bigger man.

Don and Dora stayed on the scene until the paramedics arrived. Don, of course, stuck around long enough to ensure the paramedics got the full story.

Full description or not, once the paramedics arrived, they weren't sure what to make of the situation. One of them had been tempted to call the whole thing in as a prank call, but after talking to Rage for a while, he became sufficiently pissed off at the little slacker and decided to drag the little fucker out of his cocoon and take him in for as many painful tests as his limited knowledge of actual medicine could imagine. He had hoped that the kid would close his eyes long enough that he could get away with using the paddles on him.

Rage was extremely agitated as they pulled him from his hole. "You fucking assholes. This is my property, and this little pussy has no legal right to invite you here. Let go of me."

The paramedic looked him in the eye, smiling, and said, "You know Frank, I think this one may need restraints."

Rage tried to punch the guy but didn't really have the energy. He'd used up about all he had just fending off Tim. He alternated between whining, pleading and screaming all the way to the ambulance and on to the emergency room.

Tim followed the ambulance in his car, in awe at just how quickly Rage could suck the normalcy out of any given day.

35

Lisa Tastes the Dark Side

Lisa watched Navarro picking through her bones. She wished that had been the worst of it, but each time he moved, she felt jerked along with him. She took solace in the fact she was in this place, on this plane, so rarely. Since Navarro had taken her first leg, she had spent most of her time floating in a place she liked to think of as Heaven. That was she spent most of her perceived time in her Heaven. When there, time was different. Here, she might slip away between steps, and during that space she could lose track of time. But now, she was spending more time on this plane because of Navarro.

Heaven was where she was able to just be. She felt connected to all things, loved all things, and all things loved her. The only time she left was to relive pieces of her life, work on them, study them and then return to her Heaven. In Heaven, upon each return, she found that the peace and awareness there was greater than before. It was almost as if each reliving, allowed her to cast off more of what it was that was holding her back. Each time she was there, she thought, *Ahh, now this is...perfect.* But each time she came back, she came back with the realization there was more there, more to love and less to distract her. Love wasn't the right word either. She was past the concept of words. Language was for the living.

When she had lain in her body, she had made it a point to say her name over and over again. "Lisa Whitely. My name is Lisa Whitely." She had to.

When she was in Heaven, she couldn't remember her name. She didn't need one. She could barely remember anything. She guessed she didn't need to. She just was. Her memories, the things that made her her, seemed more tied to her mortal shell than to the her that went to Heaven.

Her Heaven was wonderful, and to a lesser degree, so were her travels back in time. But now, as Navarro tugged at her bones, it tugged her back to this place. And what had made it even worse was that during the time since he had used her leg as a replacement part, she had been dragged back and forth between her body, bone pile that it was, and his new fungus body.

She had seen him killing several animals and attacking the dog. She had even been able to trip him when the dog came after him, managing to undermine his left leg—her left leg—while the dog took his right. Even now, not two hours later, she had been called back to relive the scene more times than she could remember. Each time, she pulled back her leg just as the dog attacked his right. Each time she felt that somehow her interference was more definite, and the dog somehow hit Navarro's right leg a little harder. Each time, Navarro fell, and the dog made off with his calf and foot.

Watching the animals killed and sensing Navarro was up to no good wasn't the part that was the most unbearable for her. What was worse was that she could feel herself becoming a part of him. It wasn't that her bones were being used that was the worst of it. It was that when she wasn't in Heaven, or in her bone pile, or reliving some element of her past life, she was Navarro. She could feel them as becoming the same person. She could feel his voice in her mind. If she had still had her body, she would have said he was making her flesh crawl. She had no flesh now, of course, and the absence of it was almost a blessing.

She thought Navarro had changed. Of course, she had to remind herself she hadn't really known the old Navarro. Her actual experience with him, at least in real time, had amounted to less than an hour. She knew one shouldn't judge a life by a single hour of it, particularly one that represents such an extreme. One's best or worst minutes shouldn't be how they are remembered. Although in Lisa's case, she had had fifty years to relive that one hour, to study and analyze it. It was a fucking a bad one.

Suddenly, just thinking about that hour pulled her back to it. She saw Navarro's entry way, but the image was different. The front door was closed, and she was looking at it from the inside. Usually, she started the scene standing on the porch waiting for the door to open. Sometimes when she relived it, for just a moment, the her in the scene didn't see what was coming. This time turned out to be one of those times, but mainly because what she was seeing wasn't part of her memory.

She leaned forward and put her eye to the peephole. This wasn't all that familiar a practice, particularly since she didn't remember ever having done it in her life. Of course, if she had lived through that horrible day, it probably would have become a daily ritual. Looking through the tiny lens, she found herself getting a catch in her breath. What she saw was herself, Lisa. The Lisa on the other side was staring at the peephole and smiling. It was a technique they taught all the canvassers. People were more likely to open the door if you appeared forthright and were smiling. God how she wished she hadn't followed their advice.

She reached down and fumbled to open the door. She only got a brief look at her arm as she did so but could see her skin was dotted with age spots and that her arm sported a good deal of hair. It wasn't the fine baby soft hair that had dotted her own arms. This was dark, and thick. This was man's hair. She, the part of her that was reliving or watching this, felt panic rise in the part of her that watched. She was Navarro here. But the part of her that was Navarro was agitated too. But differently.

When she opened the door, she found herself looking at the nineteen-year-old Lisa. She was beautiful...far more beautiful than she could have remembered. She was so young. She was having a hard time not looking at her breasts. She was wearing a thin yellow tee-shirt and short cut-offs.

The other Lisa was talking about some charity or political movement. She couldn't quite follow the conversation, because she was using everything she had to keep her eyes on the girl's face. Her eyes kept grazing down to catch a quick peek at her breasts. The nipples were stretching through the thin material. She kept flicking his concentration back and forth between her beautifully sweet innocent smile and her tits.

She felt herself getting an erection. That didn't help. Not only did it make her even less able to focus on anything the girl was saying, but it also made it harder not to stare at her body. She spoke up, "Yes, yes, excuse me for a moment while I get my checkbook." With that she turned around and left the room.

She went into a room just down the hall. There was a desk in the room, and she found herself right there, looking at the checkbook. But she didn't touch it. Instead, she reached down, unzipped her pants and pulled out her penis. She stroked it slowly amazed by the sensation. She was just teasing herself, clearly not going for the gold, just momentarily enjoying, but intentionally prolonging her erection. She couldn't get over how big she was. She felt an odd sort of pride as she forced her dick back in her pants and zipped up. She hoped Lisa might notice it. It was an odd thought and she wondered why she wasn't thinking clearly.

She took the checkbook from the desk and went back out into the hallway where she had left Lisa. The other Lisa had turned around and looking at her rear end, she found her whole body do an involuntary shudder. She approached the girl and reached out and touched her shoulder.

The other Lisa turned around and when she saw her eyes, she gasped. The girl that she knew was the nineteen-year-old Lisa for just a second didn't look right. She heard herself whisper "Innocencia." She leaned forward and kissed the girl. She felt the girl's tongue retreating in her mouth as she thrust hers deep. She had felt that she was tasting the thick cherry flavor that she remembered from somewhere in the past but was suddenly overcome with the fact that the girl's mouth tasted of cigarettes.

She looked down and Lisa was gone. She tasted wild cherry life savers. As she pulled her head back, she saw a young girl. A very young girl. Maybe twelve or thirteen? If that. The girl was wearing a pink dress and had a matching ribbon in her hair. She had big brown eyes and dishwater blonde hair. She said, "I liked that, Emile."

Lisa forced herself to turn away just long enough to see that they were sitting on the grass on a hill. There was an outcropping of trees behind them and an amazing view of what she somehow knew was the San Gabriel mountains in the distance. She turned back to the little girl and leaned forward to kiss her again. The girl had been eating cherry lifesavers and her kisses were thick and sweet from the sugar.

They kissed for a while, and whenever Lisa found herself reaching out a hand to touch the girl, Innocencia, her hand was pushed away. Lisa was getting an erection and it was making her bolder. She pulled up the girl's dress, exposing her panties. "Emile, stop," she said in a voice that broke with an adolescent boy's unmistakable quality. "I just want to look."

"You said that last time, but then you tried to do more."

She could remember the sight of the girl's panties from before. But better, she could remember how she had smelled when he had put his face closer to see her panties better. She said, "I know. But...you let me look before, so looking again won't hurt."

Innocencia tried to push her dress back down while Lisa pushed it back up and in doing so touched the leg halfway up her thigh. The girl pushed back and started to get up from where they sat. Lisa pushed her back down - a little too hard. Innocencia fell onto her back. "Emile, stop that. That hurt."

Lisa leaned over the girl as she tried to get up and pushed her back down. She reached down and pulled down the girl's panties. Innocencia screamed, "Stop. Emile, stop!" She slapped Lisa in the face and tried to wriggle free.

Lisa watched herself hit the girl once. She screamed. She hit her again, harder, and the girl froze and looked into Lisa's eyes. Lisa said through gritted teeth, "Stop trying to get away. I just want to look. Now hold still."

She did.

But Emile did more than look. He examined her closely, wondering how it was supposed to work. The girl's part didn't appear to be a proper fit for the boy's. He had always expected something different. He touched her vagina, not even sure that was what it was. He basked in its scent. The little girl whimpered, and he spread her legs, realizing that that was necessary to get a better view. He found that surprising. He laughed, thinking that it just didn't make sense. Why would it be down there, instead of on the front where his was.

Lisa noted that although Innocencia was crying softly, she didn't seem to be objecting anymore. This didn't really make sense to the Lisa that was watching, but the whole time that she was examining the girl, she knew this was more than an examination. Her dick was killing her, and she had to know how it worked. She had to understand how everything was supposed to fit.

Lisa pulled down her pants and saw that although her pubic region, like the girl Innocencia's, was prepubescent and lacking in hair, there was no reason to suspect that it wouldn't function. She was hard and felt like she would burst.

Innocencia cried out at the sight of Emile up on his knees with his pants down. "No, please."

He said, "Stop being such a baby." He leaned down, face first, wanting to get a face full of her aroma before he found out what it would feel like on his dick. He pushed his face into her and tasted her. He rubbed his face around her and shoved his nose inside her, before sliding forward to look into her beautiful eyes. He wanted to see her beauty and smell her when it happened.

Innocencia was crying hysterically and he didn't want that. He wanted her to enjoy this too. He slapped her to calm her down and felt a spasm that Lisa didn't quite recognize. She heard herself gasp and felt her whole body shudder. She looked down to see that she had ejaculated all over the girl's belly.

She rolled off the girl and lay thinking how wonderful everything was. Innocencia got up and without so much as a word to Lisa, ran away through the trees.

She closed her eyes, still feeling the aftermath of her ecstasy, and heard herself whisper, "Innocencia."

She opened her eyes, saw that she was kissing a wide eyed and frightened nineteen-year-old Lisa and thought, *Oh shit, here we go again.*

36

Back in the ER

Dr Patel studied Rage while the two paramedics tried to explain the situation in which they had found the boy. Rage lay covered by a sheet on an examining table. He was covered with mushrooms. They appeared to be growing out of his skin.

"So, Mr. Sutherland here continued to fight the whole way. Says he's fine."

Rage added, "That's right. Because I am fine."

Dr. Patel asked, "But, you would appear to have mushrooms sprouting from your body. Doesn't that strike you as perhaps abnormal and worth a bit of investigation?"

Rage shook his head, "Hey man, there's a lot of shit in this world that isn't normal. Do you geek types ever think to... I don't know... just let things happen? Better yet, tell me this... is this a disease or some condition you've ever read about?"

Dr. Patel shook his head, thinking Mr. Sutherland was right, this was new. He answered, "No, I don't believe it is. But..."

"There you go. If this isn't something all your big doctor books tell you needs to be treated, what's the fucking deal here? I mean really, is this Nazi Russia and don't I get any freedoms?"

Dr. Patel added, "As I was saying, yes, this is something we haven't encountered before - to my knowledge. That, of course, is all the more reason that we get you checked out."

Rage tried to get up, "I know my rights, you can't keep me here without my consent." He was weak enough that the smaller of the two paramedics could hold him down with one hand resting on his chest. Rage struggled, "Let... me... up."

Dr. Patel countered, "Mr. Sutherland, please. You will be out of here quickly enough. But first, we really have to find out what's going on here. For all we know, you could be putting more than yourself at risk. You could be spreading whatever it is you are suffering from."

The paramedics eyed each other at the mention of Rage's being potentially contagious. The doctor continued, "You may have already put your roommate at risk."

Rage spat, "Fuck him. I'm throwing him out of my house as soon as I get out of here. He had no right to call you. And he's not my roommate, he's my fucking tenant." He paused, "He was my tenant. Now, he's dead to me."

Dr Patel excused himself and stepped out of the examining room. Rage continued to try to force his way out of the bed. He wrapped his hand around the paramedic's arm, trying to push him away. The paramedic wasn't too thrilled about the potential carrier of some new disease getting so damn touchy and pushed down hard. "Sir. You need to relax. No one is trying to hurt you. Please calm down."

"Calm down? You calm down. I was just minding my own business." Rage was exhausted but continued to feebly struggle to get free. He tried to rock back and forth, failing to get any momentum and punctuated each beat of his rocking with a strained, "Fuck... you..."

Dr. Patel returned, holding up a large silver syringe and smiling. He said, "All right, Mr. Sutherland. We will give you a little something to help you relax. That will make you more comfortable and will make the examination go much smoother."

Rage tried to object but had pretty much exhausted both his energy and vocabulary. He also had to admit that turning down something designed to make him relax really wasn't in his arsenal. He stared pitifully at the doctor, wondering what good one more "fuck you" might do. Pouting, he added

"Fuck you, Patel."

Dr. Patel stuck the syringe into Rage's arm, perhaps a little more forcefully than was absolutely necessary, smiled and thought to himself, *No, no, asshole... fuck you.* He said, "There, there, Mr. Sutherland. This should begin to take effect almost immediately."

He turned to the paramedics, "I've got this from here, you two are free to go."

The larger paramedic asked, "You think we need to get checked out or anything? I mean, is this guy really contagious?"

The doctor shook his head, "It's certainly possible, but not likely. Something this off the books, if it was contagious, would be a lot more well documented. This is probably just some contamination he's gotten into. You just take the normal precautions and come back if you notice anything unusual."

Dr. Patel turned from the paramedics back to Rage. The paramedics knew the score. Once the doctor decides he's done with you, you disappear back into the background. The younger, smaller one thought it must be exhausting being God all the time.

Rage was muttering, "Yeah... you can all go now. There's nothing to see here."

Dr. Patel asked, "Now, Mr. Sutherland, are you feeling better?"

Rage looked the doctor in the eye, assessing the question. "You know, Doctor—if that is your real name—I've never, ever felt better."

Dr. Patel said, "That's good. Can you tell me about the fungus that is covering your body? Do you know where you might have picked it up and when did you first notice it?"

Rage wasn't really the sort to cooperate in such circumstances. However, he wasn't really himself. Aside from the fact he had become a hothouse for the fungus he'd found in the yard, he was floating on a cloud of sedation. He gazed up at the doctor, intending to cooperate and said, "Fungus?"

Dr. Patel asked, "Yes, the fungus on your body."

Rage nodded, "That's right, it is." He paused and faded back to the time when that doctor guy asked him about the fungus. He shrugged, "I guess I first noticed them a couple of days ago. It was just before I broke my leg."

The doctor interrupted, "Broke your leg? How long ago was that?"

"That was Saturday morning."

"And you haven't had it treated yet?"

Rage looked at the doctor, stoned and puzzled. He wondered for a moment if this was the same doctor he had seen before. He looked like him. And he thought he remembered that other guy saying his name was Patel. He decided to go with his gut, hoping he didn't come off too much like a skinhead. "Uh... you treated it." He paused, waiting for a look that he was far too out of it to really parse, "Day before yesterday. Don't you remember me?"

Dr. Patel shook his head, "I see a lot of patients in here. I certainly can't commit everyone to memory." He turned and stuck his head out of the room and called out, "Leticia, can you come in here and bring Mr. Sutherland's chart?" He turned back to Rage and asked, "So which leg was it?"

Rage smiled and slapped his left leg, snapping off a few mushrooms, "Doesn't matter now, cause it isn't broken anymore. Good as new."

Patel leaned over and felt Rage's leg. It was covered with dirt, fungus, and more types of filth than he cared to think about. When the attendant brought in the chart, she said, "This is the one who sneaked out of here on Saturday without getting his x-rays."

Patel looked at the chart and nodded, "Alright. That makes sense then. This leg isn't broken and it sure as hell didn't heal in two days." He thought it didn't make enough sense, though. Although he couldn't remember the patient, he didn't like to think he may have misdiagnosed something as simple as a broken leg. He didn't make those kinds of mistakes and wasn't going to accept that others might think he had. He spoke to Leticia, "Let's get that x-ray now. In addition, we are going to want to run a full blood panel."

Leticia asked, "Should he be admitted?"

Patel feigned confusion, "Let's see, I don't remember. Did I say that he should be admitted?"

Leticia turned and exited the room. She thought it was no wonder she drank in the ladies' room on her break. Stupid dicks like Patel made working in the ER harder every day. When she was studying to be a nurse, she used to work as a cocktail waitress. Back then, she and her coworkers used to joke that the restaurant business would be perfect if they could just eliminate the customers. It was a perfect environment... food, drinks, nice decor and with, depending on the venue, great music. Unfortunately, it was populated by demanding assholes. Turns out, it was the same in the medical profession. Here though, although the patients could be rude and demanding, they were Mother fucking Teresa compared to some doctors.

Patel explained to Rage, "We'll get your blood work started in a few minutes, but while that's happening, we'll also get that leg x-rayed. Since you didn't get it x-rayed on Saturday, we need to do it now to find out what the real situation is with that leg."

Rage smiled and said, "Situation's simple, bro." He paused to see if Dr. Patel appreciated his being down with the homies. "It was broken. Now it isn't broken. Situation explained and situation under control."

Patel gave Rage a polite, yet clearly condescending half-smile, "Yes, well, let's let the x-ray confirm the miracle, shall we? Leticia will be in here to get some blood and then she'll take you to have that leg examined." He stepped out of the room without another word.

Once the doctor was out of the room, Rage took a few minutes to do his own self-examination. Ever since he'd been so rudely dug up, he'd been pushed, poked, and prodded by Tim, those paramedic dudes and the doctor. They'd wrapped him in a blanket back at the house and although the doctor had taken a couple of peeks under the blanket, for the most part all he'd seen was freaked out emergency workers.

They hadn't really had much of an effect on him, given that he was feeling so good. Although, whatever the doctor had given him has certainly enhanced his sense of euphoria, and he had already been half-way to Heaven. He remembered he had never felt so safe as when he dug his way into the dirt last night. His sleep had been amazing. It was as if his whole body was getting a slow, terribly intricate and detailed massage. Thousands of fingers wrapped around him and periodically roused him from his slumber just long enough for him to remember that everything was fantastic and that everyone loved him. He felt the cool breeze on his face and had an awareness of every inch of his body. He had felt places he knew he had but couldn't remember actually feeling before. As he lay in his hole all night, he would awake for a few minutes and feel each of the hairs on the third toe on his left foot. Or he would feel all the skin on his thigh as a worm nudged him.

Now, wondering why they had brought him in without letting him get dressed, he pulled up the top of his blanket and looked to see what all the fuss was about. Given his mental state and the heavy sedatives that the doctor had provided him, he was in no danger of freaking out, whatever it was. As he scanned down his body, he smiled and only managed to say, "Cooool."

He was still sprouting mushrooms. He still had little bunches of them clustered in his armpits, crotch, and anyplace that could be considered to be a nurturing, potentially humid, dank environment. But now he also seemed to be sprouting tiny shoots. He had tendrils dangling from the edge of the table. He thought he looked like something out of Gulliver's Travels. He seemed to be lashed to the gurney by the various strands that circled his body.

The other thing that struck him was that he seemed to be losing his love handles. It wasn't that he was fat. After all, he was pretty active, at least in his own way. But age and beer take their toll and one couldn't deny he had put on ten or fifteen pounds over the years. But looking down at himself, he couldn't help thinking he was looking trimmer than he had in quite some time. It added to his smile. Life just kept getting better.

37

Navarro Has a WTF Moment

Navarro was picking through his bone pile and found himself thinking about Innocencia. He wasn't sure why, but it made him think for a just a second about the girl who had died on his patio long ago. *Not died, you killed her.*

Navarro froze at the thought. He dropped the leg bone he had been evaluating and slowly turned to look at the skull. He stared at it for a few seconds and then began to smile. *Is that you?*

There was no response. He flicked the skull with his finger and thought again, *Is it you girl?*

"Fuck you, Navarro."

He started to laugh but caught himself. He thought about the girl...what she had looked like alive. He remembered how she had looked on that day. How she had looked when he dropped her naked body into the grave. He realized that although he could play back what happened in his head and rewrite the memory however he pleased, he couldn't change what the girl saw. He felt naked.

He picked up the skull, both wanting to destroy it and wanting to hide from it. He thought, *IS...THAT...YOU?*

He felt a chill run through him. He felt afraid. He felt exposed.

He was concerned that the bones were essential. He would need parts from time to time. But he couldn't stand the thought that they were perhaps judging him. And worse, that if they were judging him, they actually had something legitimate to judge him for. Of course, it wasn't as though the situation was as cut and dried as it may have appeared. He knew the incident was more of an accident than a crime. Of course, from the girl's perspective, she wouldn't understand that. She would think he had somehow set out to harm her. Girls sometimes didn't understand things like that.

Navarro took one rib that lay in the pile and used it to dig a hole in the back of the cave. He took the skull and placed it in the hole, burying it under a foot of dirt, rocks, and fungus. He then looked around the cave, from bone to fungus to bone. He didn't feel any better. Everything knew about him.

Navarro crawled to the mouth of his cave and wondered how far he could make it in the bright morning sun. It wouldn't work. He turned back and decided he had to get rid of the bones. He would just have to take his chances that they wouldn't be needed later. He gathered the bones and piled them at the back of the cave.

Once again, he used a rib bone to dig up the skull. This time, he dug up a much bigger hole. He needed to bury all the bones. He needed to get rid of the evidence and make sure he was rid of her.

As Navarro was placing the bones into the grave, his mind flashed on the memory of the last time he had buried the girl. He remembered the smell of her and how her skin had felt. He remembered the way her bare skin had looked as the dirt was thrown over her. He remembered she had worn pink panties. No, that wasn't right. She hadn't worn panties at all.

He remembered the way she tasted when he rubbed his face into her. Wild cherry. He thought, "Oh, my Innocencia."

The voice cried out in his head, *You raped that little girl, you fucker.*

Navarro shook his head. He had loved the little girl. She hadn't understood his love. He barely understood it. He had tried to love her, but she wouldn't respond. And then she hated him. She had ruined him for other women.

She was a child.

Navarro shook his head slowly. *No. That was just what she wanted to believe. She was so much more of a woman than she could admit. I tried to make her see. She was my Innocencia.*

Navarro covered the bones with handfuls of dirt. As he watched the last white patches of bone disappear under the soil, he remembered the way the dirt had obscured the white and pink of her breasts fifty years ago. He wasn't sure why it made him so mad at her thinking about it, but he remembered how much the episode had upset him for so long. He wasn't sure if he had ever forgiven her.

Once the bones were gone, Navarro sat in his cave alone, feeling somehow vindicated. But... feeling that someone was watching him.

38

Rage Crashes

Two things were certain. Tim was missing class and there was no way he could leave Rage at the hospital in this condition. Rage had been covered with fungus, assorted mushrooms and long strands of stuff that God only knew what was. He looked completely messed up and although Tim was no doctor, if he had to bet, he'd have wagered that the mushrooms were really eating Rage - from the inside.

One other thing was certain. Rage was too much of a drama delivery system for Tim. Tim needed an environment more conducive to maintaining the work ethic he had always embraced. Tim had to move. He didn't want to be a jerk about it, clearly getting Rage to the hospital was more important than some Monday morning chem lab, but Tim needed to find a way to get back in control of his own life.

It may not have been normal for Rage to be eaten by mushrooms, but it was normal for him to act like an irresponsible adolescent, and it was becoming just as normal for Tim to get swept up into the madness. And not as a participant, but as the adult who had to somehow step up and clean up the mess.

Twice in the last month alone, Rage had brought some drunk lowlife girl back to the house and somehow ditched her there. Yeah, that was Rage. He didn't go to her place and sneak out; he brought her home and then skipped out before she woke up. Tim would end up making them breakfast and securing them a ride home. He should have just let them deal with the consequences of their actions. That might have taught them a lesson that would have served them well. But each time he found himself drawn into the situation, letting whatever happened to them seem like something that they weren't at all complicit in. And, of course, the inconvenience of dealing with the aftermath invariably fell to Tim. On one occasion, Rage's victim was still drunk enough in the morning to mistake Tim for Rage and try to take him back to bed. He politely declined.

Usually, Tim found himself pretty much going with the flow. He really hadn't picked his high school girl friend. She had picked him. As seniors, when they broke up, it wasn't because he found her smothering, annoying and immature, all of which he did. It was because she decided they should see other people. He agreed but didn't see anyone else until someone else let him know she was interested.

He was an engineering student, not because it interested him, but because his parents wanted him to be an engineer, and he really couldn't think of anything he wanted to do instead. He was a good student, but not because he was all that interested or motivated, merely because he had made meeting challenges a habit. He rarely chose the challenges, but once they were chosen for him, he found that for him, meeting them made up the path of least resistance.

Given his predilection for going with the flow, he believed it would be in his best interest to position himself in a place where there would be considerably less flow. Once Rage was admitted, which seemed inevitable, he would go to campus and check the housing boards. It was time to take the unusual step, for Tim, of taking a step.

***

Dr. Patel came into the waiting room. It was rare for him to exit his domain, but he often noted information was somehow more meaningful to friends and family when he delivered it himself. He thought it was often the least he could do. He approached the young man that Leticia pointed out to him and asked, "Excuse me, but are you the tenant of Reginald Sutherland?"

Tim looked up. Tenant? He answered, "I'm Rage's roommate?"

175

Dr. Patel asked, "Rage?"

Tim nodded, "Yes, Reginald."

Dr. Patel eyed the youth suspiciously, wondering if this one was on the same path as the one in his examining room. He said, "I'm afraid we are going to want to keep Mr. Sutherland here overnight for tests and observation."

Tim nodded. It seemed the least they could do considering Rage's condition. He was about to ask if he was free to go when Leticia came running into the waiting room. She addressed Dr. Patel, "Doctor, your patient is coding."

Patel turned and hurried back into the examining area. Tim cursed his luck at not having left already. Then he decided leaving would be what Rage would call a dick move.

***

Rage drifted in and out of consciousness. He could feel a presence within himself. Awake he felt a warmth and a glow in his innermost being. He felt part of a whole, something he couldn't have told you had been lacking two days earlier. When he dozed, he felt that his parents were with him. Every time he woke, he would be momentarily confused, then remember they were dead and then he would giggle, empowered by some sense of well being he couldn't explain.

Every now and then, he would feel the presence of Dr. Patel and members of his growing entourage. Once he thought there had to be at least fifteen hospital people in the room, but once he looked closer, he realized some people were just his parents, grandparents, and some old man who he used to watch on TV when he was a kid.

The snippets of conversation he heard didn't seem to go together or really make sense to him. He didn't really care because he knew it was all stuff that was over his head and didn't really concern him, anyway.

He saw the doctors arguing and getting quite agitated, talking about broad spectrum antibiotics, anti-fungal treatments, and something about insurance, unheeded advice and liability. He smiled to himself, shaking his head and thinking he had a lot of experience with unheeded advice. It was kind of his specialty.

His father said, "You got that right, Reg."

Mom shook her head and smiled at Rage, while addressing his father, "No, Bob. This boy was always a blessing."

"Nancy, you know I didn't say anything to the contrary. Just saying he was always a handful and an unruly one at that."

Rage's mother put her cheek to his forehead. He drifted off while an old faggy looking man in white sneakers and a sweater sang about the joys of being a neighbor.

Later, Rage woke to the sharp pain of a needle being placed in his arm. His parents were gone, and he was alone with the doctor and a nurse. The nurse was adjusting an IV, and the doctor was watching him intently. Rage peered up at the doctor as he felt a cold stabbing pain shoot down his arm. He looked down to see his arm start convulsing and he reached out with his left arm to try to yank out the needle.

Dr. Patel grabbed his hand and called out, "Mr. Sutherland, you need to leave the IV alone."

Rage pulled the needle out of his arm and tried to get up, but he was too weak. Dr. Patel sent the nurse to get help and within a minute, two orderlies were in the room and helped the nurse strap Rage to his bed. Dr. Patel watched the three work, waiting until the situation was under control.

Rage screamed "Stop, you're killing us." He fought the orderlies with all his remaining strength.

Once the orderlies and the nurse had Rage safely tied up, Dr. Patel injected Rage with another dose of sedatives. Rage was crying as the sedative took him away, "You don't know what you're doing, please, don't kill us."

***

Once he was asleep, the nurse reattached the IV and restarted the drip. Patel said, "Now we wait."

The nurse asked, "Have you seen this sort of thing before, Dr Patel?"

In spite of his predilection for not explaining himself to staff, this was an extremely unusual kind of day, and he was feeling extremely unusual himself. "No, I haven't. I doubt anyone has seen this - exactly. The man is completely being consumed by fungus."

"And this will help him?"

Patel gave a noncommittal shrug. "Yes and no. We've given him a pretty strong anti-fungal treatment and we'll keep that up. However, the infestation is certainly off the charts and even though I'm sure we can kill the fungus, I'm not sure if we can reverse any internal damage that may have been done. We can see he has fungus wrapping around his internal organs, consuming him from the inside. We will have to see the extent of that damage."

He glanced down at the small mushrooms that were peeking out from under Rage's hairline, plucked them out and added, "Time will tell."

***

Tim sat in the waiting room. He thought it aptly named. After the doctor and nurse had rushed off, he had questioned his decision not to leave. He certainly couldn't help and wasn't being fed any information from the hospital personnel. Just about the time he had convinced himself leaving might be the right thing to do, Dora Hardman came into the waiting room. She saw Tim and changed her trajectory, coming his way with a concerned smile on her face.

She asked, "How's Reggie?"

Tim said, "I don't know, they aren't saying anything."

"I'm sure he'll come walking out of that door real soon."

Tim shook his head, "Oh no, I didn't mean they hadn't said anything. I meant ever since the doctor told me they were keeping him overnight for tests and observation and then ran out of the room because Rage had 'coded' I haven't heard anything."

Dora asked, "Coding? Oh my Lord. They said he was coding?"

Tim shrugged, "Yes, that's what they said. Why? What does that mean?"

Dora stared at Tim like he was a mental patient, "Son, don't you ever watch TV?"

"No."

Dora was tearing up when she explained, "It means he died."

Tim asked, "Really?"

She nodded, "I think so."

Tim looked at Dora and blinked a few times. "Maybe we should check. You know, just to make sure."

39

Navarro Comes by His Senses

Navarro sat in his cave, thinking on all he had done. And it was good. He glanced down at the soft furry animal that was attached to his chest.

As he examined the possum, he got a sense of himself. All day he had caught glimpses of himself and the cave, as though what he was seeing was periodically being interrupted by some other channel. Just flickers and flashes and sometimes superimposed images. Last night he had had the same thing happen when he was fighting the coyotes. He had looked left but could somehow see to the right as well. Now he understood it was the possum.

Concentrating hard, he could see himself with the possum's eyes. He smiled. His smile wasn't what you would call disarming. He noted that he didn't really look like himself. It wasn't just that he only had the one eye and the fact his face looked like it was made of slightly melted wax. His mouth sagged and his eye drooped. He had no hair, but he didn't look bald, more like the underside of a portobello, rough with black ridges. No, it wasn't any individual item that made Navarro dislike his appearance, although each in its own way was disgusting. What he found so discomforting was that by no stretch of the imagination did he look like a living person. He looked like a rotting corpse, one that had been taken over by decay.

He willed the possum to look away. He may have looked like bloody death, but he was feeling more alive by the hour. His senses were returning. He had been struck last night almost immediately by the fact he could hear. It was jolting. Suddenly the silence had been broken, and just in time to save him from being torn apart by his new coyote buddies. Slowly he had begun to feel the effects of the six new eyes he had gained during his little hunting session. It had taken until just the last hour or so for him to have finally understood it was the eyes of the animals from which he was getting the additional imagery. In fact, if he thought about it, the pictures were more like bits and pieces from their thoughts and less like transmissions from their eyes.

Best of all, he was just beginning to understand he had been smelling things for the last few hours. It was less sudden and dramatic than had been the realization he could hear. After all his time in solitude, he had become more than aware of the fact the mind can play tricks and fill in the blanks for you. He had spent days now in this cave, surrounded by moist, rich earth and virtually bathed in fungus. In his mind's eye—or was it nose?—he had an idea of what it smelled like and somehow had been almost smelling it. Like he remembered similar smells and somehow assumed he smelled them.

Now, however, as the smell was becoming more solid, more real, he caught the occasional whiff of something unexpected. He had been digging through his torso earlier, searching for a good spot for another two ribs when in spite of the fact that his mind was busily producing the illusion of the smell of diced mushrooms, he caught a whiff of grass and flowers. He thought he felt one of his ears stand up, but remembered he had none, when the smell of animal fur hit him. He could smell the possum. This had made him curious. He hadn't known what a possum smelled like in life, and if you had asked him yesterday, he would have said it had no discernible odor. Yet now, he could smell not just possum, but wounded possum. And fear. Not just possum fear, but...his own fear? Yes, he smelled what he was certain was his own fear. He had shaken his head at the time - he wasn't afraid.

Now, looking back on that moment, he realized he was capturing the coyote's sense of what it was smelling. It smelled not just the possum and that it was hurt and afraid, but it had been smelling its own wounded state. He concluded that there must be some threshold in the coyote that made it capable of merely being afraid, rather than having lost its mind by now. A broken neck, then lashed onto, and being held motionless by some unknown creature. Top that off with the fact said creature was slowly absorbing your flesh...well, it was a wonder the poor thing didn't have a heart attack.

The coyote whimpered at the shared thought.

Navarro thought, *Exactly.*

Navarro stepped to the mouth of the cave and willed himself to smell. He heard the coyotes sniffing. He smelled grass and flowers and dirt and raccoons and skunks and cats and that god damned dog—and wind. He could smell the wind. It all was wonderful.

Of all the wonders he had missed during the last twenty years, lying at the bottom of his grave, it had been the smells he had missed most. He flashed on the memory of Innocencia. He had been missing the smell of her for over seventy years. Of course, he knew Innocencia was long gone and that the smell he had missed was longer gone still. But suddenly, he had a reason to live. He needed to smell the smell of Innocencia again. He had to find a way to languish in it and appreciate its rarity like he had failed to do in life.

He had thought all this time he had been waiting for some kind of chance to relive his past...to make better choices and not miss out on so much this time. He didn't know how that would work, but had somehow thought it involved reliving his life, somehow starting over. Now he realized, far too late for the first pass through life that it didn't work that way. Now he had to make things happen, but in a forward direction. Now. Not tomorrow and sure as hell not yesterday.

If you had asked him at any time during the last fifty or sixty years about the biggest regret of his life, it would have been that he hadn't gotten enough of Innocencia. Now he believed he had gotten it all wrong. He probably had about all of Innocencia that there was. She had been a young girl and he doubted that the freshness of the girl would have lasted much longer. In fact, there was a good chance it had already passed and that the aromas and tastes that had marked the highest moments of his life had already been a pale shadow of the real thing.

He decided it was time to stop pining for the smells of a virgin, dead and gone. It was time to forget living a seventy-year-old moment. It was time to look for love in the here and now.

He smelled the wind and wondered just how far these new olfactory powers could reach. It was not yet noon, but already he knew this would be a great night for hunting. His tools were sharp, his need was great and now, finally, his goal seemed to be shaping up. Tonight would be the night he started his hunt for his next virgin.

40

Don Fights the Good Fight

Before seeing the effects the mushrooms had on the Sutherland boy, Don had planned on picking up a new starter for his sprayer and washing down the back of his property. Knowing this was no longer just a nuisance situation, but potentially life threatening, he had decided a newer, bigger sprayer was in order. He rarely had such a good excuse to indulge in his passion for tools and gadgets.

Unloading his truck, Don pulled out not just the new weed sprayer, with the larger reservoir, but a five-gallon drum of Weed-Away. He worked to maintain an air of solemn purpose as he lugged his new toys around back to his shed.

Don filled both tanks and started his long slow sweep down the hillside behind his property. As he pivoted slowly from right to left, letting a stream of spray fire out fifteen or twenty feet in front of him, he was reminded of his time in the jungles of Southeast Asia. He had spent six years routing out what he had considered to be a hard to rout, heavily entrenched, invasive force. He had won quite a few battles before ultimately losing the war.

He shook the weed sprayer and gave it a hitch. This day, there would be no compromise. This was a day when the Marines would get things done with no outside interference. He turned up the spray, increasing his reach and continued his march to the bottom of the hill.

It amazed Don how much the mushrooms had grown overnight. He had to admit that the morning sun made things a lot clearer than had the twilight under which he had examined the wash last night. That said, there was no denying what had been a mushroom patina over a bed of green was now an explosion of fungus.

As he moved down the hill, he could see many of the plants that had provided a bed for the mushrooms where now gone. In their place were more mushrooms. And bigger ones too.

Don looked back over his shoulder. This wasn't napalm he was spreading, so he had no illusions that behind him he would see a bare patch. The green should still be green and the blue and red should still look the same. Deforestation could take anywhere from one to seven days. Still, he was a little unnerved to see the effect of his spray on the killing fields.

He powered off the sprayer and took a longer look at his handiwork.

Mushrooms and long thin strands of fungus seemed to be writhing on the ground. He hadn't seen the strands before as he headed down the hill, but looking back he could see dozens of them poking out of the ground and seemingly tending to the mushrooms before beginning to writhe and wither themselves. There were also hundreds that lay motionless. He thought it was one of the damnedest things he'd ever seen.

Don stood watching the field of dead and dying fungus above him and felt the touch of something on his right leg. He looked down to see long fungus tendrils winding around his ankle. For just a second, he found it unnerving enough to grunt and jump back. The tendrils pulled loose and lay writhing at his feet. He looked at them in wonder, thinking they resembled animals more than plants.

He turned the sprayer back on and dowsed the ground at his feet, before turning back toward the base of the wash and moving on toward the old houses. He harbored no illusion that his weed spray packed the destructive power of a flamethrower, but still looked forward to giving Emile Navarro's house a good drenching. If that queer old bugger could still upset his wife after all these years, then absent the opportunity to give him a good thrashing, at least he could take an honorary piss on the man's old house. After all, it was probably his grave as well.

When he finally reached the Navarro home, Don saw that it would be quite the challenge. He noted that in the daylight it was clear the house wasn't just covered with the fungus and mushrooms, but the inside was teaming with them. He emptied the canister of his sprayer on the outside of the house and headed back up the hill to refill it. But not before he took that first piss on old Navarro's final resting place.

Heading up the hill he was careful to avoid getting tangled by the dead and dying fungus.

***

Navarro could barely stand the noise. He had heard the spraying soon after it started, but before that sound had reached his many canine and marsupial ears, the screaming in his head alerted him to the activity outside on the hillside. He had rushed to the edge of the cave, trying to see what the commotion was all about. At one point, he stepped out and risked being seen just to get a better idea of what was happening.

Once he got a bead on Hardman and saw what he was up to, Navarro huddled back into the shadows at the mouth of the cave and watched in horror as the old marine systematically destroyed what must have been a quarter of the fungus in the wash. He could feel himself diminishing in warmth, at the same time hearing the growing screaming in his head.

Even in his cave, where they were far away and safe from the poison that Don was spraying, the fungus all around him was clearly agitated. He heard the sounds of fear and pain, but also the mourning that came from such a massive loss. Thousands of lives that were all part of Navarro's benefactor were being lost every minute that damned sprayer was engaged.

While Hardman was out of sight, Navarro wondered what he should do. He hoped Hardman wouldn't return, but if he did, there was nothing to be done. Even if in the heat of the day, Navarro could somehow hold his own against Don Hardman, who not only possessed a body comprised of living muscle—and it appeared that there was still quite a bit of it—Hardman was for all intents and purposes, spraying kryptonite. If Hardman hit him with the spray, he would once again be a pile of inanimate bones. No, for the time being, Navarro would have to stay in his cave and wait for nightfall.

But when Hardman returned to the house below and started spraying again, Navarro had a sinking feeling that the old man would not stop there. He looked at the mouth of the cave and at its heavy lining of fungus. As Hardman entered the house, Navarro started trying to come up with a plan.

***

Don stepped into the old Navarro living room and was struck with the familiarity of the place. After all, he and Betty had been in this very room many times. Of course, that was before the roof was partially caved in and the walls were covered with mushrooms and wildly waving strands of fungus. A sheet of thick fungus peeled off the ceiling and dropped onto Don's head and shoulders. The sheer weight of it brought Don to his knees. Strands of fungus reached up from the floor and wound around his arms and legs and pulled him down onto the ground. Don laughed in frustration at the idea he was somehow being overtaken by a bunch of mushrooms. Dainty little red and blue ones at that. He laid on the ground, unable to get up. He thought back to this morning's discovery of Reggie being partially eaten by these bastards.

He couldn't move. Well, that is to say he couldn't move his arms or his legs. However, he could still move his finger. The finger on the trigger of his Weed Master 3000. He pulled the trigger and a blast from the sprayer shot through the sheet of fungus that lay over his torso, obscuring the stream and dissipating it into a veritable shower of weed killing liquid. He could taste it and hoped having been saved from the clutches—really? Clutches?—of mushrooms, he wasn't slated to die from an overdose of Weed-Away.

Slowly Don regained his feet, never letting off the trigger, dowsing every inch of the room. Once the whole room was a writhing mass of dying fungus, Don stood and spit up whatever foul-tasting poison had made it into his mouth. He wiped his nose and thanked the Lord he hadn't gotten any of the foul stuff in his eyes. Thankfully the fungus that covered his face had for the most part shielded it from the spray.

Don spent another twenty minutes spraying down every room in the house. Once he finished, he went out on the front stoop and surveyed the hill leading up to the Sutherland place. He planned his route and started to move up the hill, serpentine, heading toward what looked to him like a fungus covered hole about a third of the way up the hill from the house. He paused to survey the way the hill had changed since the last time he had given it a good look. The hill had split just about at the little cave and the fungus was thickest between there and the house. It looked like the fungus had somehow forced open the earth and caused the slide that exposed the houses.

***

Navarro was watching as Hardman started heading up his hill. He was pretty sure the shadows were protecting him, but found it unnerving that Hardman seemed to be looking right into the mouth of his cave. He turned and peered around. There was no place to hide and if Hardman had taken all that time cleaning out the house, there was no way he would not want to spray down the cave.

Navarro looked at the soft dirt in the back of the cave. At the place where he had buried the girl's bones. He cursed his luck, a practice that a lifetime and then some had perfected, and then crawled to the new grave and used the end of his mace to dig it out. He piled the dirt on the side of the grave that was closest to the mouth of the cave. That way, after he crawled in and pulled the dirt down over himself, any he missed might possibly obscure his handiwork.

He didn't have time to be all that concerned about moving the existing bones out of the way. He was digging for his life. He had no doubts that if Hardman found him, he would be reduced to bone. And, with no fungus left to save him, bones would be how he stayed.

Navarro could hear the sprayer getting closer as he pulled the last of the dirt over his face. He laid as still as he could as he waited for Don to pass. As he laid in wait, he began to feel the animals attached to his body, attempting to wriggle free. He realized they were slowly suffocating in the dirt with him. He of course, had no need to be out in the air, but they were still living creatures, no matter how much of them were intertwined with the dead and rotting Emile Navarro.

***

Five minutes after the sound of the sprayer had reached its crescendo, the sound began to die down. The sound changed first in volume, but then in quality. He realized the possum had died, and the coyotes were dying. The sound had completely died, but before he was entirely sure that Hardman had finished his work Navarro knew the coyotes were dead. That could have been as responsible for the quiet as could have Hardman's being gone. Knowing his pets were dead and that he couldn't trust their ears anymore, Navarro decided to wait. It was something he was good at. Laying in the dirt had been his primary occupation for the past two decades. He waited what he estimated to be at least two hours before pushing up out of the grave.

Scanning the cave, it was clear there was no sign of life in the cave. He glanced down to confirm his animals hung lifeless in their fungus harnesses. He absentmindedly rubbed the possum's head while he wondered what he would do next.

41

Tim Tries to Get Away - Again!

Dora was the one who finally had the sense to throw her weight around at the front desk and discover that Rage wasn't on his way to the morgue, but was in fact resting after a rousing bout of having his life saved. Of course, they didn't really give her all the gruesome details. All she and Tim were apprised of was that Rage wasn't dead, appeared to be out of danger, and that even if he wasn't, they as non-relatives wouldn't be able to see him until tomorrow.

Dora and Tim discussed their options, and both came up with the same conclusion. Dora would drive Tim back home, and he could check on Rage's progress this afternoon by phone.

Once back at home, they both headed out to Rage's happy place to see the results of Don's spraying. He was standing on the outlook, just next to where Rage had been buried this morning. He looked like a man who felt he had accomplished something truly monumental.

Dora asked, "So, Don, what's the status of operation mushroom eradication?" She knew Don liked it when she discussed his endeavors like they were official.

Don nodded, "You know, dear. I can't really emphasize just how damned dangerous these little - you should pardon my French - fuckers are. They not only tried to eat young Reggie this morning, but the god dammed things also attacked me when I was in the old house."

Tim, amused, asked, "Attacked you? The mushrooms?"

Don said, "Damnedest thing. Some heavy bundle of the things hit me high and all of these, these thin little strands wrapped around my legs and arms, pulling me down to the floor and holding me there."

Tim stared at Don, wondering how it was that Rage hadn't discovered snorting weed killer yet. "Held you there. The mushrooms. They... held you there."

Don glared at the boy. During the boy's brief stay on the hill, he'd always appreciated the kid's respectful attitude toward authority and his elders. Now, he wasn't so sure he liked his tone. "Yes. They held me down." The frustrating thing for Don was, he knew how crazy it sounded. He wouldn't have believed it either. In fact, looking back on it, he wasn't sure how much had really happened and how much may have been induced by his being a little spooked when he got knocked down by - by whatever it was that fell on him.

What the hell, he thought, *in for a penny...* "Damned right they held me down."

Tim nodded, "So, how did you get away."

Don clenched the Weed Master tightly as he replied, "I shot the bastards."

Tim nodded, "Right. Makes perfect sense to me."

But it didn't make sense to Dora. She had pretty much tuned out the saga of the battle of the fungus. All she had heard was that Don had gone into the house. She looked down the hill and asked, "You really went into the house?"

Don nodded, "That I did."

She asked, "Did you find... anything?"

Don squinted at his wife, "You mean, did I find anything aside from the man-eating fungus? The fungus that I single handedly eliminated?"

She stared at Don, "You know what I mean."

Don flinched. Of course he did. Stupid. He softened his tone, "No. Nothing."

Tim stepped into the hole where Rage had been buried and kicked at the dead mushrooms. He had to admit they were enormous. They had definitely been eating Rage this morning, but of course, the idea of flesh-eating fungus was within the realm of the possible. More to the point, it was well within the realm of extreme ideas that could fit his world view, as outlandish as it seemed. But mushrooms that attacked old men? That was something that either needed a good deal of study to embrace, or to just be ignored. He glanced up at Don, "Well, I guess I better head off to campus and get a little work done."

Don and Dora both stared at him as though he was somehow missing the significance of the situation. Of course, both were thinking of different situations. Tim spoke again, "Thank you both for everything. I mean, this morning - and really, well, everything."

Then, Tim left the area known as Rage's Happy Place with the intent never to return. He moved purposefully through the house, only momentarily slowing down to feed a very demanding Fatty. The dog was dancing around his dish, waiting for someone to appear, and as often happened, one of his people appeared at his bowl and poured in a pile of the good stuff.

Tim drove to campus, and once again checked the boards. Then, he hit the coffee shops around campus, looking at every bulletin board he could find. He also picked up a few of the neighborhood newspapers and fliers, the sort that had want ads.

He had just two classes on Monday afternoons and sat through them, copiously taking what were, for all intents and purposes, automatic notes. A lifetime of study habits had given him the ability to write down fairly usable notes from lectures where he was barely paying attention. While he carelessly documented apparently not so fascinating facts about engineering and anthropology, he was wondering about the mushrooms that had almost eaten Rage this morning. And finally, he was planning his escape from the madness that was Rage's world.

Tim spent the afternoon calling potential roommates, only to find it was too late in the semester. Every room had been taken or folks had determined that they could make the rent without adding to the burden that an additional body would present at this point in the semester.

He called the hospital to check on Rage and was told he was responding well to treatment, but that it would be at least a couple of days before they would consider letting him come home. They pointed out there were to be no visitors until tomorrow. He thought, *hey, nobody asked.*

Tim didn't want to be too callous about Rage's situation but given his discovery that he was stuck living with Rage for at least a couple more months, he looked forward to a few days of solitude. He read until ten o'clock and then went to bed early, meaning to get an early start on Tuesday.

He drifted off about the time that down the hill, Mr. Navarro was leaving his cave.

42

Navarro Uses Lisa - Again!

Navarro sat in his cave and took it all in. He sat alone in a sea of lifelessness. As he sat on top of the grave he had been hiding in earlier in the day, he contemplated the bones that lay all around him. When he had come back from last night's hunt, he had felt like what had been called, in his day, a million bucks. Voices ran through him, talking to each other and to him. He had spent years up on this hill, entombed and alone. Before that, he and Dora had lived up on this hill, outside of the flow, outside of the mainstream. They were old people, and the world had no interest in them. Even before he had been buried alive, he had been left to rot. But now, he felt like he was at the hub of a million lives.

Or he had been. Now, the buzz in his head was greatly diminished. His animal friends were dead. The fungus that had brought him back from the dead was itself dead. All that remained was its creation. He sat and mourned his loss.

As he contemplated the bones, he stared at the skull, wondering again if there was someone inside. He still heard whispers in his head and wondered if they had been human or were just the voices of animals he had killed, along with those of others that the fungus had consumed. He wondered what the skull would have to say. He wondered if it was still occupied.

Navarro scooted across the floor, dragging long tendrils that attempted to find purchase in the soil, but that recoiled from its deadly surface. Until now, whenever he sat in the cave, it was like he was plugged into the earth. He knew the fungus was much bigger under the earth. He felt the larger presence when he was outside, prowling, but it wasn't as strong. In the cave, he was next to the power source. He feared that from here on in, he may be the power source. He would need to feed and keep himself healthy.

He picked up the skull and examined it. He noted the front of the skull had cracks and a piece missing from the back. He wondered if that was what had killed this person. His eye opened wider as he considered the placement of the wound. He had been right before. It was the girl. He dropped the skull and let it roll away from him.

***

Lisa watched as Navarro examined her. She had expected him to sniff at her at any second. God, how she hated him. Even now, fifty years after killing her, he still was pulling her back to the scene of his crime.

***

Navarro thought about his crime. Not a crime. It had been an accident. There was no doubt about it. But still he had regretted it. It had been one of the many things that had haunted him during these last fifty years.

He wondered if he could make it right somehow. He wanted to try. He examined the girl's bones, wondering if he could give her new life. With the fungus gone, it was up to him if it was to happen now. He remembered he had already used part of both of her legs. He was using her feet. He smiled. He was a sort of tribute to her already. It made him feel like he had maybe completed the first step in earning her forgiveness.

He took her left arm and considered it as a whole. It was shorter than his arm but might still be utilized. He dug a hole in his left side, about six inches below his left arm. He found a spot where there was an accumulation of new animal bones. He took the arm and placed the end of it in the hole, carefully holding it at an angle where it shadowed his left arm. He could feel the bones being rearranged to form a semblance of a socket as new tendrils began to weave flesh around his new appendage.

It took about an hour for him to finish his left arm and learn to use it. He sat flexing his new second left hand, nodding his approval as he used his

195

original left hand to begin digging the foundation under his right arm to mount the other. He took his time, taking care to get the right balance.

***

Lisa watched in horror as Navarro took her limbs, one by one. He had already used her legs, even using part of one for his weapon, and now he was adding her arms to his collection of animals and bones. She, of course, had no use for them, but as long as she was somehow connected to them, it meant she was more connected to the monster who had killed her.

Even while her second arm was being attached to Navarro, Lisa's left arm was seething at its complicity in the endeavor. It tried to control itself, only managing to periodically be less compliant. Lisa tried to twist her arm out of Navarro's control, but she was too dissipated, too diluted in that she wasn't a body, but a series of disconnected pieces. And, of course, she was dead. It wasn't like any of her bones had moved of their own accord in fifty years. Last night, she had managed to kick out her left leg a bit, helping Navarro to fall when the dog attacked him. But she couldn't be positive that that had for sure even been her doing. What happened was what she willed to happen, but for all she knew, it may have just been a coincidence.

Now, she felt herself being integrated into the new Navarro. She wished she could scream but had given up trying years ago.

***

As Navarro sat in his cave admiring his handy work, he wondered at all that he had done. He stood up and stretched to his full height. He now had four arms and had spent the better part of the afternoon and evening using them to insert the girl's additional ribs into himself, allowing him to better balance himself. He used her backbones to reinforce his own. He had used the additional bones strewn about the cave - and that were inside him - to better fortify his new body. Fungus was soft, but bones were strong. All that was left of the girl was her skull, and he wasn't sure how to make use of it.

He still had the coyotes and possum bound to him. When he looked down at the possum, he could tell that it was slowly being consumed. The usefulness that the possum and coyotes had provided in their senses of smell and sight would be missed for a time. He would have to replace them tonight. In the meantime, they were his only food to last until sundown. Yesterday, they had been living, breathing animals that could serve a higher cause. Today, they were just food for the fungus. He nodded, thinking that was the way with all things, really.

43

Navarro Goes Back to the Well

Stepping out into the night air, Navarro was once again feeling defenseless. Once again, he was deaf. Once again, he had no sense of smell. This morning, for a time, he knew what animals were where. His sense of smell had been not just acute in its strength and subtlety, but also in its unique triangulation capabilities due to coordinating the senses of three separate olfactory systems. He needed new noses, but he also knew that without the old ones, finding the new ones would be particularly challenging.

Surveying his surroundings, he found that it bore little resemblance to the landscape from his previous foray into the world. The mushrooms were gone. The greenery was gone. As he stood in a section of dead grass, tendrils from his feet attempted to scoop up dead material to replenish him but came back with poison debris. At first the tendrils held onto what they found and clutched them tightly, only then beginning to die, themselves, from contact with the weed killer residue.

Navarro thought, *No. Stop... Not here.* He would travel up the hill, looking for better hunting grounds. He needed both meat and plants to ensure he kept up his strength. As the evening had worn on, he had begun to understand that he was carrying the seed. He could re-cultivate the fungus that had cultivated him. But, to do that, it was imperative he feed as there was no longer any possibility of being resurrected again if he didn't.

Navarro, sporting his new limbs, began to climb the hill, taking care to touch as few of dead spots as possible. As the hill was steep, he leaned forward to brace himself with his hands. That was how he discovered he could climb more comfortably on his hands and knees. From then on, he progressed on all sixes.

Once he reached the top of the hill, standing in a place he didn't know as Rage's happy place, he found clean grass, leaves, and muck. He allowed himself to sit and rest. The two extra arms allowed him to increase his feeding speed. While the tendrils worked at his mental command, having four hands able to scoop up mulch and hold it in place, made the tendrils able to fortify him all the quicker.

Although he had four hands contributing to the effort, one was far less efficient, due to the care that was required for its operation. Earlier in the day, knowing how vulnerable he would be without any sense by sight, he had taken the precaution of lashing his mace to the end of his original right arm. It extended from his forearm, with his hand free and dangling slightly. It meant he could swing the mace without worrying about losing his grip and meant his hand could be used to grasp his target after a successful swing. As a gathering mechanism, however, he had to take care to move slowly so as not to hit himself in the face with the mace whenever he reached up to his chest to push leaves or compost into himself.

Sitting in the weeds, feeding himself, he turned his head constantly, remembering he was vulnerable to attack from behind. He had planned on only sitting until he was satiated, but after nearly an hour of feeding, he realized he would never completely be satisfied. He was to feed forever, and when he had eaten enough to fortify what he was, he would eat to become what he was to be.

Once he reached the tipping point and had become aware he was now starting to carry the extra baggage, he began to move along the ridge along some of his old neighbor's property lines. He kept a little below the crest. That way, he could see all the hillside and still check for domesticated animals in people's yards. Because the hill was at times difficult to navigate, he took to all sixes again, this time finding it even easier given his recent feeding.

Navarro paused every few feet, taking a few moments to survey the terrain above and below the crest line, looking for movement. It didn't take long before he found two young raccoons rummaging through a trash pile behind a house Navarro couldn't place but knew he had seen before—in another life. He approached the raccoons slowly on all sixes. The raccoons watched him suspiciously. However, they didn't bolt. They had a sense that the creature that approached them, something that bore only a slight resemblance to the creature that killed their mother, somehow didn't seem to be a threat. They felt only a slight fear, mitigated heavily by a strong feeling of affinity.

Navarro felt it too. A voice in his head, one that spoke with emotion, not words, longed to hold them. He felt a paternal instinct to protect them. He approached them slowly in an open and nonthreatening way. He was aware of the location of his mace but was loath to swing it. He was sure he could take down this fresh meat with a single swing as the two raccoons were within two feet of one another.

The raccoons both stood to examine the creature that approached. One of them growled a halfhearted threat but hoped the thing would take care of them. Foraging had not been so easy without their mother.

Navarro readied his mace as a Plan B but didn't need to. Maintaining his posture on just his new arms and legs, he reached out with his original hands and scooped up both of his babies, one in each hand.

He took a few minutes to affix each little raccoon to a shoulder. He let the tendrils hold them down and began mingling with their bodies. He could feel a reunion among the voices in his head and felt pride in what he had done. He then moved slowly back along the ridge, the way he had come, heading slowly for the home of Don Hardman and Dora. He had a bone to pick with Don Hardman. That murderous old meddler.

Every few seconds he greedily checked for some new sign his hearing would return. By the time he reached the Hardman yard, he heard the faint chirp of crickets. He found himself remembering how delicious they were and decided the raccoons must be working. He looked at each and although if you had asked him an hour ago if raccoons had expressions he would have laughed—silently—in your face. But now he could see the young raccoons wore expressions of delight.

Navarro entered the Hardman yard and rooted around in the garden. Hearing the muffled excitement that the sight of the garden created in the young raccoons, Navarro noted they still didn't fear him. In fact, he could feel their love - of a sort. They wouldn't try to escape, at least not right away. He willed the tendrils to loosen their front legs and handed each a tomato. The raccoons each greedily took their tomatoes and dug in. Their hunger was palpable, having gone two days on their own without a guide to keep them properly fed.

Navarro could feel their happiness. It ran through him. He also could taste the tomatoes. He didn't know how many times removed this food was from fortifying him, but this was the first time he had experienced taste in twenty years. He sat in the garden feeding the raccoons tomatoes until neither of them could be persuaded to take another.

Once the raccoons had been fed, Navarro began to explore the yard, wanting to learn as much about his adversary as possible. A swimming pool dominated the center of the yard. Quite a waste of space, in Navarro's opinion. Navarro's shed was butted up against the house, away from the hill.

Navarro approached the shed. As he neared the house, he could feel the raccoons start to tense up. He used a couple of free hands to pet them, trying to sooth them with his thoughts. They settled down as Navarro rose to his full height and opened the door of the shed.

Inside the shed, Navarro found an assortment of tools, as well as quite an array of garden equipment. And chemicals.

Navarro stared at the drum of Weed-Away and seethed. Hardman, the butcher, had used this foul stuff to kill his mother, and millions more besides. Navarro had no idea what the future would bring, but he wanted no more of this poison in his life. He took the container which felt to be at least half full and dragged it out to the yard. He carefully removed the cap from the deadly stuff and tipped over the drum, draining it into Hardman's pool. He thought "fire with fire." Once the drum was completely drained, he kicked it into the pool.

Back inside the shed, Navarro raised his mace and with a single blow was able to render the Weed Master 3000 a retired unit. Of course, decommissioning the agent of destruction couldn't satisfy Navarro's rage at what had happened to his kind, so another minute of frantic mace work rendered the device not just unusable but virtually unrecognizable. Navarro then stood still, listening carefully to make sure he hadn't roused Hardman with all the racket. He fondled his mace in the meantime, wondering if he really feared Hardman's intrusion or longed for it.

He was stronger now than he had been when he beat the coyotes. They had almost bested him, but he had learned from his mistake. Now, the mace couldn't be knocked away. Now, he had additional hands to grasp his prey and fend off attacks. Plus, and this was something that shouldn't be underestimated, now he felt responsible for the survival of his species. He would kill and eat anything that tried to stop him.

It was during such thoughts that Navarro, eyeing the tools on Hardman's wall, spotted the scythe. He eyed the tool. It had a three-foot handle that sported a two-foot curved blade. Navarro removed the tool and examined it, feeling its weight. He smiled at its utility. It would make light work of the harvest of vegetation, and in the right hands, say, in his lower left one, it could be used to slice the head off a particularly troublesome neighbor.

Navarro used an axe on the wall to break the handle off the scythe. He then carefully lashed the blade to his lower left arm, adding to his arsenal and on a more aesthetic level, adding a sense of visual balance. The arm with the blade was now roughly the same length as the arm with the mace. He now looked balanced. And not just in shape and size. What the mace provided him in power, the blade could offer him in finesse.

Navarro felt himself on the verge of true change. Whereas once he had allowed things to just happen to him, now, he was that agent of change. Dora used to try to get him to appreciate the arts. Now, he was becoming a true artist. Where she had accused him of being cold and unfeeling, here he was taking care of all these animals, not to mention saving a whole species.

Navarro thought that if Dora could see him now, she wouldn't recognize him. He was just that changed. Just that evolved.

44

Rage Suffers a Bout of Introspection

Rage laid in his bed, watching the moon through the window. He had slept most of the day, groggy from the range of drugs the hospital dudes had been pumping through him. They had none of the features he looked for in a nice chemical cocktail. Rather than taking the edge off reality, they merely ran through his veins, killing any organism that didn't meet the good Dr. Patel's idea of normal. He wasn't entirely positive that his exhaustion wasn't somehow connected to his previous night's encounter with his mushrooms.

Rage tried to watch a little television, but everything on was shit. The hospital had about twenty channels and nothing on was remotely in Rage's range of interests. He didn't much care, as he probably wouldn't have been able to really get into it. Once again, good drugs should make everything interesting, but whatever had been done to him was casting a pall over everything, taking the fun out of things and sucking the life out of them.

To make matters worse, while he was thrashing about, his leg had broken again. Once he was sedated, they had put a cast on it. Now he sat staring at the new cast, wondering if it was really necessary.

He thought about his parents. Thinking back over the past twenty-four hours, he was pretty sure he had seen his mom. But then, he had been pretty fucked up at the time. He guessed one had to be in order to see a dead person. He wasn't just fucked up with the stuff the hospital had given him. Rage had been eating hallucinogenic mushrooms pretty much nonstop for about three days. He shrugged after giving up deciding where the mushrooms ended, and the sedatives started. He wondered where the other side ended, and reality started. Was his seeing his mom mushroom related, or just a dream brought on by the sedatives?

Or was she real?

Rage had been taking drugs since long before his parents died. He had been high, one way or another, from shortly after his eleventh birthday. He and his friends had smoked weed back in what was to become his happy place. He would say it was as far back as he could remember, but that was in part because years of weed meant that his memory was suspect. He took his first hit of acid in Jr. High and had taken more assorted hallucinogens over the years than his limited math skills would allow him to estimate. The thing was, Rage took drugs because they were fun. He wasn't some new age, truth seeker. He didn't believe in any crap about them being some kind of window to another reality or any horse shit like that. That being said, he also didn't remember ever seeing anything that wasn't really there. Oh yeah, he saw things that didn't seem right. Colors were tweaked and shapes got messed up. But he didn't see imaginary people, and neither did his friends. That was just bullshit that old people made up to scare kids.

So, he wondered again, did he really see his mom? He knew there were colors that weren't visible to the naked eye that people may see while tripping. He didn't believe any hallucination he'd ever had was made up of whole cloth; it was just a clearer way of seeing things. Not in an airy fairy religious or spiritual way. He just could really see things without all that shit you bring to the table from all the crap you got taught your whole life. You saw what was, without all the filters.

Maybe the dead were here, just not visible because if you saw them every day, it would blow your mind. Rage was no scientist, but he had to say that no, that was bullshit. You wouldn't be able to take a step without running into them. There must have been billions of dead people over the last how ever many million years there had been. The air would be thick with them. Nonetheless, Rage tried turning his head really quickly a few times, seeing if he could catch some dead dudes off guard. It didn't work.

This whole line of thinking was just a distraction from the real thing that was bothering him. He was lonely. Not in the way that had plagued him his whole life. He had always craved the company of playmates. He either wanted to hang out with party pals or jump some girl's bones. Either way, he hated to be alone. But this was a whole new level. After the tripping he just did, he was aware of a kind of company he had missed his whole life. He had never really felt loved and connected to anyone. He guessed he was supposed to have felt that from or with his parents, and now was trying to rearrange his memories to accommodate the idea that he had, but this had been so real for the last few days that its absence was palpable.

He tried to sleep, but his dreams were no better. He dreamed his parents were alive and they had moved away and left him. He dreamed the fungus that had embraced him had left him too. He cried as he saw his parents watching him from a distance, disappointed at the man he had become.

A little after midnight, he gave up on sleep and tried to get up to take a piss. He found moving was difficult. He knew it was probably as a result of the killer cocktails they were giving him, but looking down as he hobbled toward the restroom, he saw he had lost considerable weight. Rage usually weighed in at about 160. Staring at his arms and legs, he thought he must be down maybe thirty pounds or more. He thought his arms looked like those starving kids on those commercials where they beg you for thirty cents a day to feed, clothe, and educate them. Standing at the urinal, Rage moved his gown aside and let out a sigh of relief. His weight loss hadn't affected his dick. He crossed himself, or at least thought he did, and thanked God for not messing with his junk.

Before climbing back into bed, Rage spent twenty minutes standing at the window looking out at the lights of Eagle Rock. He wondered about the mushrooms. Eating them had made him aware of a warmth he had never felt. He had been right with everything. He'd heard of people being that way. Happy people who were cool with everyone and everything. He had thought he was one of those dudes. Now he wondered if anyone could feel that way without getting high.

Rage laid back down, exhausted and dreamed again. This time, he dreamed about blue and red lights circulating in and around his parents' graves. There was no body in his mother's grave, only a pool of red and blue light. He crawled into his mother's grave and rolled around in the lights, letting them warm him. He tried to feel the incredible warmth he knew they were capable of, but instead he wondered why there wasn't more light. He panicked that there wasn't enough light left and feared as the remaining light diminished, he would never again feel her love. Rage started scooping up the remaining light and swallowed it by the handfuls. He could feel the warmth coursing through his body and craved more.

Rage climbed out of his mother's grave and into his fathers'. This time he wasted no time and ate all the light that was dripping out of his father's rotting corpse. Once he had consumed all the liquid and his body was satisfied in its need for the warmth of the light, he wrapped himself around his father's body, watching as the grave was filled in over him.

Even in his dream, Rage was exhausted and relished the fact that as the grave filled in, he knew he could finally rest.

45

Navarro Pads his Nest

Standing in Hardman's shed, Navarro took one last look around before heading out to try his new configuration and appendage. He saw something on the floor that gave him a curious thought. There was a half-gallon container of Miracle Grow fertilizer sitting next to the door. It had a spray top and Navarro picked it up and held it where one raccoon could get a good whiff.

The raccoon recoiled from the smell, but Navarro decided that was probably the proper reaction for a small mammal to have to a chemical fertilizer. On the other hand, Navarro only contained a small percentage of small animals - at least for the time being. He gave it a try and gave one of his forearms a small test spray.

Navarro watched as tiny tendrils moved quickly to see if the spray was a threat. He could feel some sense of a community memory of the last time the fungus experienced a chemical spray. It didn't take more than a minute to see the fungus was not negatively affected by the fertilizer. Navarro decided what didn't kill him, might just make him grow faster. He grabbed a shovel from the wall of tools and carried it and the Miracle Grow with him as he headed down to his cave.

Once there, he used the shovel to clean out the top couple inches of soil from the floor of the cave. He put the fouled earth outside and then scraped another inch or two from the walls. Navarro leaned on the shovel and examined his work. He decided to turn the soil, as he wanted his new patch to get off to a good start. He was going to try to bring his mother back from the ashes and hoped here in this womb-like cave, they could create the seeds for a new civilization.

Navarro used the shovel to dig a trench. He reached into his belly and up under his ribs, grabbing handfuls of rich tendrils and lovingly placing them in the trench. Over that, he spread a layer of leaves and muck that had been collecting on his body all night. He sprayed down the whole row with Miracle Grow and then sprayed it into the gaping wound that he had created in his torso.

Once he felt that he had created a proper start for his mother/child, he decided he needed to get back out and do some serious hunting. He was eating for millions now.

Having been up the hill already, he headed back up to check the yards of his old neighborhood. He'd already checked the Hardmans' and the one he had finally placed as belonging to Bob and Nancy Sutherland. He never much liked Bob but remembered that little wife of his was quite a looker. But that had been twenty years ago, and even then, she was pushing thirty. He was sure she was no peach, but wasn't looking to rekindle any old passions, or get into her pants, just see if she had a cat that he might snatch and eat.

Despite his interest in looking at what time may have done to the little lady that had once been his nearest neighbor, Navarro found himself having a bit of an anxiety attack the closer he got to the Sutherland yard. He got as far as the Rage's happy place but was overcome with a fear he couldn't understand. He headed along the property line, not yet realizing his motivation was that his raccoon passengers were terrified of the dog whose name they didn't know to be Fatty. If Navarro had yet been able to read the thoughts of his latest nose bearers, he would have happily stepped into the home turf of his enemy. As it was, he found himself calming down as he crossed into the vacant space on the hill where his home had once been perched.

The street where Navarro had lived had been a through street. The road had sloped down and curved around his property. Across the street had been where the Fondas, Edwards, and Lees had lived. Now, it was clear both his and the Fondas' homes had gone down the hill, along with the road that had separated them. In their place, the city had turned the neighborhood into a cul-de-sac with a wooded bit of green space where the houses and road had once sat.

A small brown Chihuahua approached Navarro and barked at him defiantly. Navarro didn't like the smell of the animal. He wondered at the fact that the raccoons weren't the most reliable source of information. He thought it must be that the coyote senses had been somehow more in tune with what he himself could understand. That said, he had to laugh at the fact the raccoons provided their own kind of benefit as well. The little dog was drawing too close to Navarro because he was taken in by the scent of the raccoons and the fact they were adolescent. Navarro couldn't say much for the reasoning power of the dog, given that it took no apparent note of the fact that the little raccoons were perched atop a four armed, weapon wielding monster.

Navarro shrugged. He wanted it for its senses, not its brains. He brought his two lower weapon bearing arms down around the little dog, giving him a half second where the dog was confused by the barrier that the arms, mace and scythe made. He could have jumped the wall of Navarro, but during the moment it took him to make that call, Navarro scooped him up with one of his other hands and held him up to his face.

For the first time since encountering Navarro, the dog took its eyes off the raccoons and looked up into the face of her captor. She began to whimper at the sight of the creature that looked down at her. She tried to wriggle free, but the thing held her to its body and she found herself sinking in. Something was holding her legs and she started to bark. Her intent was to scold the thing. She had to. It was all that a dog her size could do. Unfortunately, before she could get out her second "yip", she felt tiny fingers around her snout, and she found she couldn't get out another sound.

Navarro held the little dog against his chest while binding the dog to himself. He turned and started toward the mouth of the cul-de-sac. This high on the hill, the city scrimped on the streetlights and he figured he could get across the street without being seen. It would give him access to what he remembered was a closed in canyon that went deep behind the houses across his old street. Time passed of course, but back when Navarro had been alive, the canyon had been steep enough that nobody ever entered it and big enough that it was a haven for coyotes.

To get to the canyon, Navarro had to pass through and between a couple yards. He looked until he found a house that was not just dark but had no car in the driveway. He tried the gate and slipped through once it proved to be unlocked.

As he moved through the yard, he could hear the distant eerie squealing yips of a band of coyotes. He could feel a tightening in his chest and knew the little chihuahua was having a panic attack at heading toward a group of dog killers. Navarro smiled to himself. *Out of the frying pan and into the fire.*

On this side of the street, folks put up solid fences behind their homes. On Navarro's old side of the street, the distinction between yard and hill was more defined by slope and less need for definition. Here, without a fence, nobody could keep a small animal, without the constant threat of attack.

Navarro slipped through the back gate and out into the wild. He looked at his weapons and thought it was time to put them to the test. He went down on all sixes, and started down the hill. It wasn't long before he heard the sound he was waiting for and slowed down. He could hear movement in the tall grass to his right and a little ahead on the left. He stopped and stood up, wondering which animal would strike first. He used his animals to sniff the air. He heard a muffled whimper from the dog as it breathed in the smell of circling death. *Just wait, my little friend. I think you're going to like this.*

He willed himself to look to his right, focusing his attention on the one that the scent suggested was closest. However, he knew he still had at least two raccoon eyes looking forward to where the other animal might be coming from. He waited. Before either animal showed its position, Navarro heard the sound of something rushing at him, coming from directly behind. He turned slightly to his left, leaving a raccoon scanning to the right. He turned quickly and sliced the air behind him with the scythe. He heard a thick wet splat as the weight of a coyote head bounced off his back. *I guess that one's just meat now. Need to be more careful.*

He caught sight of his chihuahua out of the corner of his eye and deciding this wasn't the time to worry about noise, decided to have a little fun. He had the tendrils that bound the dog's snout relax. Navarro, still keeping eyes on the locations of the other two coyotes, reached down behind him and picked up the coyote head he had loosed with his scythe. He held it up and showed it to the little dog. The chihuahua began to bark furiously, feeling the adrenaline and shared sense of victory.

Navarro could feel the warmth of the blood that was pumping onto the ground from the body of the decapitated coyote. He wanted the meat but felt a need for the blood too. He didn't want to waste it. He reached down with a free hand and hoisted up the bloody carcass and put the neck wound to his face. He sucked at the oozing neck wound and could almost immediately feel the effects. Over the last few days, he had shown the fungus that although civilizations could be built from the bounty of decaying matter, there was even more to be gleaned from the living. The blood-soaked meat had so much more to offer than when left to dry out and rot.

Both of the other two coyotes broke for Navarro at the same time. He smashed the one on the right with a mace shot to the chest. He took more care with the one that approached from the front. The chihuahua was barking a high repetitive war chant, insisting Navarro show no mercy to the beast that was closing fast. Navarro swung intentionally too low. The effect was that he took three of the coyote's legs off just below the knees.

The coyote lay face down, squealing for help. Navarro looked at what lay before him and considered his bounty. He saw meat, he saw noses, eyes and ears. Better yet, he could hear that help was coming for the coyote squealing at his feet. At the suggestion of the chihuahua, he kicked the coyote, encouraging it to raise up a larger cry for help.

He stood in the center of his trap and waited for the next wave.

IV

Tuesday

46

Rage Gets the Cure

Tuesday morning, the sun was shining through the hospital window when Rage woke up. Dr. Patel stood looking at Rage's chart, shaking his head and saying, "All I can say, Mr. Sutherland, is that we dodged a bullet here. This was one invasive fungus, but I think it's safe to say we beat it."

Rage lay in bed gazing out the window. He asked, "But was I in danger? I mean, I don't think so."

Dr. Patel shook his head incredulously, looking conspiratorially at his nurse, "Were you in danger? My God, son, you were being eaten alive. I know you were delirious when you came in yesterday, but do you have any recollection of all that transpired in the last twenty hours? Your heart stopped yesterday. That little mushroom patch you found killed you." He paused for dramatic effect. It was a trick of the trade, "I brought you back to life." He paused again. This was his favorite part, although most people forgot to thank him. "I got your heart started again and even though the fungicide that ultimately killed the fungus hadn't yet done its work, it kept the fungus from continuing to spread, which meant that my work wasn't for nothing." He paused again. Nothing from the patient. The man clearly was a self-obsessed example of his generation. Even in the face of such a monumental feat, nothing but video games or beer could impress him. Typical.

Rage, still looking out the window, asked, "So, I guess I can go home now."

Dr. Patel shook his head. "We'll want to keep you around for a day or two, just to play it safe. Although we see no signs of the fungus remaining in your body, we'd like to monitor you. Don't forget, your heart stopped yesterday. For safety's sake, it isn't wise to run out like a maniac after an episode of that nature. Let's wait and see how we feel tomorrow."

Rage said, "We? We don't feel anything. I feel like I got eaten by some giant and shit out onto this bed. But there is no we. I guess I just thought there was."

Dr. Patel looked at the strange young man. It occurred to him it may be that his assessment of him as a young man was giving him too much credit. According to his chart, he was thirty. Dr. Patel was thirty-two. And this man that lay in bed had no career, or even it seemed the ambition to pursue one. He was old enough to be a man, but he was a boy. "Well, there, you see. Rest is the answer to the way you feel. You've been through a lot. On top of that, you've been running around on an unset broken leg. Most people never experience something as harrowing as what you just went through. Some who do, don't survive. You will feel better in time."

Rage felt drained. He didn't think he would ever feel better again, but sometimes he, for brief moments, recognized that listening to smart people could make sense. He nodded and closed his eyes.

Dr. Patel looked again at the chart. He didn't really need to, but somehow felt that looking down at the chart made it look less like the patient was ignoring him, and more like he was too busy and intrigued by what he saw to note that the patient was dropping off. After thirty seconds or so of nodding while reading the chart, making sure the nurse wouldn't think he had been dismissed by Mr. Sutherland, he replaced the chart, turned around and walked out of the room.

Nurse Leticia stepped forward to once again check Rage's vital signs, confirm that his IV was functioning, and just generally to give the doctor time to find someone else to impress because that bullshit doesn't work on her. Rage opened his eyes and put out his hand to touch the nurse's arm.

She asked, "Is there something I can get you to make you more comfortable, Mr. Sutherland?"

Normally he would have made some inappropriate suggestions about what someone in a nurse's uniform could do to give him comfort. But it usually only had a marginal chance of not having a negative effect. Right now, he felt a lot more lonely than he did horny. He kept his hand around her wrist and asked, "No, but could you stay with me for a few minutes?"

She nodded, taking his hand off her and patting his arm congenially, "I can stay for a few minutes."

He thought she was better than nothing. He felt alone. He realized this morning when he had woken up that he was alone. Not in the sense that he had been alone for the last decade or so, but in the sense that whatever warm sense of belonging that he'd felt for the last few days was gone. He had been feeling loved. He hadn't known if there was an entity that was doing the loving, just that he could feel its effect.

He looked up at the nurse. He looked at her eyes and saw that she was splitting her attention between him, his monitor, and the clock on the wall. She wasn't here because of him as a person, but because of him as a customer. She didn't want to be here. She was just doing her job. He thought about all the girls he'd been with. Truth be told, many of them were pros just doing their jobs. Others just wanted to hang out with him because they were fucked up and he had drugs and a place to party. He had known that they didn't fuck him because they loved him. It hadn't mattered. It wasn't out of love that he had wanted to do them. Now, looking at the nurse, who was comforting him with the same level of professional enthusiasm as a working girl had ever shown while servicing him, it made him want to cry. He pulled his arm away and said, "That's okay. You can go."

She adjusted his bedding, patted him on the arm again, and smiled pleasantly. "Feel free to press the call button if you need anything."

As she left the room he thought, *I need to go back home.* What he meant by home, he couldn't say. He missed the way he had felt for the last couple of days. He also believed he missed the way it had been when he was a kid, the way his parents had tried to raise him. He wished he could go back and start over.

47

Eagle Rock

Tim dropped by the hospital on his way to class. He figured it would be easier to get a quick status from a human that couldn't put him on hold or transfer him to an endlessly ringing phone. He wasn't sure what his responsibility to Rage was. Tim also wasn't sure what the whole episode meant to him.

Tim was a good student. He had always been a hard studying, church going, rule following example of what he believed his parents wanted him to be. He kept is eyes on the prize and never doubted his direction in life, even if he hadn't played that big a part in charting it.

Life with Rage seemed to provide challenges he wasn't necessarily prepared for. Most of the areas where Rage seemed to test him the most, were areas where his life plan had no real play. Of course, he had a script for avoiding drugs, only drinking at a gentlemanly level and using his time productively. But Rage constantly put Tim's boundaries to the test.

Tim smiled at the fact that Rage couldn't really tempt him to go over to the Rage side. But the thing that was bothering him now wasn't how he was reacting to Rage's lifestyle. That was something he was particularly proud of. What was bothering him was how he was reacting to Rage's illness, and potentially to his problems.

Tim liked to think he was a better person. He kept listening to his inner voice telling him to shake off Rage and get back on track. Even as he was wondering how Rage was doing, it wasn't because Rage was a friend. Tim was pretty sure he wasn't. It wasn't because Rage was a human being and Tim genuinely cared about his wellbeing. That made Tim a little squeamish to think about. No, it was because the timing was inconvenient for Tim. Rage might die, and Tim's main thought was, *How does this affect me.* Tim thought the voice in his head sounded a little like his father's.

Mt. Washington isn't much of a mountain by real world standards. It is just a big hill that sits in the northeast corner of Los Angeles. Nestled between Glendale and Pasadena, actual cities, it is flanked by the Los Angeles neighborhoods of Eagle Rock, Highland Park, and Glassell Park. Mt. Washington is residential and as such, residents, depending on which side of the hill they lived on—and their ethnic makeup—did their shopping and other local business in one of the surrounding neighborhoods.

Given the location of Rage's house, which overlooked Eagle Rock, Rage and Tim spent most of their time on the Eagle Rock side of things. Eagle Rock was also home to Occidental College, where Tim was a student. Rage, when out prowling for tail, found it often more productive to cruise York Blvd in Highland Park, a more productive hunting ground for one who couldn't properly chat up actual college students. Highland Park had a more forgiving party crowd.

Eagle Rock was essentially defined by two streets, Eagle Rock Blvd, which ran North and South, and Colorado Blvd, which ran east and west. The intersection of the two was essentially ground zero for Eagle Rock and was an easy ten-minute walk to campus. That was also just a few blocks from where the hospital lay.

Nestled into the north side of the crotch of Mt. Washington and Eagle Rock, is a series of natural springs that come up from hundreds of yards below the "mountain." Therefore, it isn't unusual to see trucks from a number of different bottled water companies clogging the side streets of Eagle Rock. It is a bottled water paradise and the font of a number of water fortunes. Looking down from Rage's happy place, if you stand on your tip toes, you can see two separate water plants.

The water plants are one of the two distinct features of Eagle Rock. The other, isn't actually in Eagle Rock, that is to say, it is there, but officially it is in Glendale. Forest Lawn is a uniquely Los Angeles cemetery franchise. The one in Glendale is vast, and creeps over a large hill on the south side of Eagle Rock. One is hard pressed to not see it from anywhere on Eagle Rock Blvd, and from Mt Washington, it is the southwest view. From Rage's front yard, you can see a patch of Forest Lawn and one of its many chapels. The uppermost cross that rises above yet another of the Forest Lawn chapels can be seen for miles.

As Tim turned onto Eagle Rock Blvd, preparing to head north to the hospital and ultimately to campus, he wondered at the purplish hue Forest Lawn seemed to have taken on. At the corner of Verdugo Blvd and Eagle Rock Blvd, he could see the Eagle Rock corner of Forest Lawn was covered with tiny mushrooms with little blue and red flecks.

Mr. Hardman had wiped them off the back of their hill, but it looked like there were more over here, one hill over. He wondered if there was cause for concern. There weren't that many people as crazy as Rage. He doubted anyone else was wired in such a way as to bury themselves and spend the night, allowing the mushrooms to actually start to eat them. He also assumed the days when everyone and their brother would eat a hallucinogenic mushroom, just because they found it growing on the lawn, were about forty years gone. In that respect, Rage was a bit of a throwback.

And besides, even if statistics did show that most people that did use hallucinogens came to a bad end, was that any reason to assume the mere existence of those substances should be any cause for alarm? He decided it was. Just not an immediate one. He would mention it to Mr. Hardman tonight. Mr. Hardman knew everyone in positions of authority and would know who to talk to about how to give the cemetery a similar wipe down.

Tim stopped by the hospital and asked at the front desk about Rage's status. He was in a hurry and wanted to avoid having to see Rage, just in case that was fate's way of once again pulling him off course. The nurse manning the desk was, however, able to give him a bit of information. Although she couldn't go into any real details, him not being family and all, she could say that Rage was alive and showed no signs of getting worse. He thought to himself if he had been Rage, he could have charmed more information out of the woman. It bothered him a bit to know someone who refused to play by the rules was often received better by members of the opposite sex than a forthright future contributor to society.

He stood at the front desk, staring at the merely moderately cooperative nurse and considered what kind of man he was that he would not stop in and see his roommate. He thought it made sense to note they weren't friends. They had a business relationship. On the other hand, it did seem kind of a shame that Rage had no family to visit him. Tim realized he was the closest thing to family Rage had right now. Tim decided that a couple of minutes wouldn't throw him too far off schedule.

Tim stepped into the room and saw Rage lying in bed on his side, facing the window. He stepped slowly so as not to wake Rage. He would just take a look to see if he looked any better. Yesterday morning, aside from being filthy and covered with God only knew what, Rage had looked like a refugee from a concentration camp.

As he stepped to the foot of the bed, he saw that Rage was awake. He looked like he had been crying. Tim stopped, wondering if he had made a mistake by coming in.

Rage said, "Yeah, come on in - I can see you."

Tim asked, "Yeah, hey, how you feeling?"

Rage said, "Like a faggy, little cry baby orphan."

Tim wasn't sure how to reply. This didn't sound like Rage. He suspected a trap. He held his tongue.

Rage stared out the window for another minute. Tim could see a fresh tear running down his cheek. He stood blinking, wondering if Rage was going to drift off. He was hoping Rage would.

Rage turned to look at Tim. "Don't you have class?"

Tim shrugged. "Yeah. But it can wait a bit."

"Late for class. Why?"

"I wanted to make sure you're okay first."

Rage slowly started to smile. He started to call Tim a fag but caught himself. "Really? Why?"

Tim said, "Well, I don't know really. I mean…"

Rage nodded and looked back toward the window.

"Yeah, but enough about me. How do you feel?"

Rage shook his head, "I don't know. I guess I don't feel anything anymore."

Tim looked puzzled. "So, that's good?"

"They said I was loaded up with fungus and that they were somehow killing me. They killed the fungus and now they want to keep me here for observation for another day...maybe two."

"Well then, that does sound good."

Rage shook his head. "I guess so, but I sure felt better before they killed them."

"You have a cast on your leg again?"

Rage nodded, "They said it's still broken. Hurts like hell."

Tim checked his watch and decided he could still make class if he left in the next few minutes. "So, I'm going to head out to class. You need me to bring you anything tonight?" After a beat, trying to lighten the mood he added, "Anything but mushrooms. Mr. Hardman killed the whole lot of them."

Rage didn't laugh. He looked at Tim. His eyes looked as though he might lose it and start sobbing any moment. Instead, he closed his eyes and said, "No thanks. I don't need anything."

Tim left the room and could hear Rage sobbing as he rounded the corner. He headed off for school, thinking he maybe should rethink his plans about moving. Tim could still hear his father's voice running through his head, reminding him his number one priority had to be his studies. He shook his head at the thought. Rage was in trouble and all alone. He figured he could find a way to study and still be a decent person. He decided today was the day he would commit to finding a way to be Rages roommate, instead of his tenant.

48

Navarro Reminisces

Navarro sat in his cave, wishing the sun would go down. Of course, it wasn't even noon yet, but his night had been such a success that he had hated to see it end. He could have gone on hunting all night.

After taking on and defeating seven coyotes, he had had more meat than he needed and a fantastic new collection of pets. All but one coyote had survived his attacks, so he had managed to put them to good use. He had taken two that had broken necks and, just as he had two nights earlier, hung them over his shoulders so their bodies draped over his back and their heads faced forward. They were placed facing slightly outward, so they increased his field of vision. But also, and here is a place where lessons were getting learned, so they couldn't eat his neck or head. This was a sign of personal growth for Navarro. After ninety years of repeating the same mistakes, each time cursing the fates, he was finally starting to learn from his mistakes.

Navarro had tried to find a way to use the coyote whose legs had been cut off. That one had proved to be a handful. He had thought he could control the blood, but the thing just kept alternating between whimpering, howling, and this sound Navarro couldn't really place, but if he had to describe it, sounded like shrieking in terror. He worked quickly to avoid killing it. First, he bound its wounds with fungus. Then he held it to his left side and wrapped it around his torso. From behind, it looked like the coyote was peeking around Navarro to spy on what was behind him. That was fitting, as that was what Navarro intended to do with the beast, create a virtual rear-view mirror. Tendrils bound the animal to his side and to his left leg. He found that just as the animals he had placed on his shoulders added a good deal of padding to his back, this one, wrapped around his leg much like the animal would have done had it tried to hump him, provided good padding for his leg.

Navarro picked through the additional dying coyotes to find a fitting one for his right side. He had a hankering for additional meat and fur to cover as much of himself as possible. It not only would provide him an opportunity to improve senses, it would give him armor to match his weapons. He would also slowly consume them, giving him a constant source of additional food. Navarro picked one up and tried to make it fit on his right leg, similar to the first. He had to trim it a bit to get a better fit. Once he had started pruning its legs, it had started to kick up quite a fuss, but he persisted and got it in place, and was able to muzzle it properly.

He found that once he started commingling with the animals, he was able to calm them down a bit. He could patch their wounds, but it didn't quell the wash of self-hate that hit him each time he felt his tendrils absorb bits of the animal. It was the price he paid. It didn't last long, and once finished, he could feel another companion, one that would quickly grow in awe of him.

His little raccoons had at first been frightened of the coyotes - and of Navarro himself - but that abated over the course of the night and now, sitting in his cave, he realized he was just one big happy family.

As he sat facing the mouth of the cave, he found that he could see all around him. Twelve extra eyes gave him a full 360-degree view. They had come in handy later in the night as he had made additional forays into the woods.

After his remodel in the field, he had had three left over coyotes and had dragged them back up the hill and then across the street and back down to his cave. Two were dead and one was dying. He used his scythe to split each one up the middle. He carved each as though he were filleting fish. He gutted each one and cut off the heads and legs. When he was finished, aside from a pile of heads, legs, and offal, not to mention six large slabs of meat, bone and fur. He used the slabs to cover his body, fur side out. It added girth, not to mention a layer of meat and bone. This, he felt, would add to both his food supply and his armor.

Standing back, he wished he could see himself. He was sure he cut quite a figure – seven heads, four arms, two heavily armed, covered with a thick coating of fur. He figured he probably weighed around 300 pounds. He smiled at the thought of his next meeting with that god damned dog that had tried to eat him.

Between then and now, Navarro had killed two more coyotes, a raccoon, a half a dozen rats (something he wasn't sure he believed had been up on this hill before) and three feral cats. Easier than that haul had been three dogs. Each had been like taking candy from a baby, because it turned out the little Chihuahua that had been his first catch of the night was in heat. Each of the three dogs had almost run into Navarro's arms. If he hadn't had a full set of heads, he may have tried to save them. Instead, he just sliced them as they approached and added them to his meat haul.

His final prey of the evening was a little dog he found in the backyard that had bordered the Hardman house. He had slipped through the back gate after catching a scent on the wind that caught him off guard. He wasn't sure at first but caught a scent he hadn't smelled in over seventy years. It was a little off, but he attributed it to the coyotes and their habit of judging their smells through the lens of possible food. They didn't appreciate the scent of a sweet little girl. But Navarro did.

He walked around the yard, staying in the dark edges, trying to find proof that his olfactory sensations weren't just some phantom dream but that he really had found a new Innocencia.

It didn't take much to prove out his theory. The yard was split evenly between a pool area and a grassy yard, complete with a swing set and jungle gym. There was a pink inflatable donut in the pool, and it had pictures of a little girl on it. The girl had red hair pulled up into ridiculous pig tails.

Navarro scouted the house, daring to venture near the windows. It was almost dawn, and all the lights were out. There was nothing he could see. But, standing near the window nearest the Hardman house, he could smell the child in her room. The smell wasn't quite right. He couldn't place what it was that was different about it, but there was no question it was what he craved.

Unfortunately for Navarro, the sun would come up shortly. Although he didn't need to worry about the heat for hours and wondered with his new fur coat if he had to worry about it at all, he did need to be concerned that people waking up might see him. He felt he could hold his own one on one in the dark - a theory he had yet to test on a two-legged animal. However, he knew in the light of day, a crowd could form much more easily. He had waited decades for this moment, waiting another night wouldn't kill him. He chuckled silently at the thought.

As he started to leave the yard, a small white dog approached him with an air of outrage and superiority that only a small white dog can muster. The dog began to bark at Navarro. The bark very clearly was saying "get out of my yard." That had, in fact, been Navarro's plan. But the little dog was making too much noise.

Navarro intended to kill the dog quickly, but as he swung his blade, he felt a sudden wave of love and fear for the little dog and instead grabbed it with a free hand. He held his hand over the dog's mouth as he ran out of the yard and descended to his cave.

The whole way down he found himself divided in his attention. He found himself delighted by his new companion for reasons his conscious mind couldn't fathom. At the same time, he tried to hold on to the smell of the child. He wondered just what it was he was going to do to her.

Sitting in his cave, and feeling impatient to explore, it struck Navarro that there was much he could do without leaving the cave. First off, he could tend his garden. He studied the rows of fungus he had planted earlier. He covered them with the carcasses he had brought back this morning. He was able to pepper his garden with the bodies and ended up with enough to cover the floor of his cave with fungus, offal, and liberal doses of Miracle Grow.

Once he had done all he could do to feed his garden, he decided it was time to turn his attention to remodeling his new home. He figured if he was going to be confined to his cave for two thirds of the time, and if he wasn't going to sleep, he should at least find a way to make it more spacious. After all, he was expecting to bring guests to his home, and he thought he may need a little more space, not to mention a little more privacy.

Navarro took Hardman's shovel and began digging at the back of the cave. At first he tossed the dirt over his shoulder, letting it cover the garden. He knew the fungus would grow just as well under the earth as on top of it. If his mother was to return in his children, he would need for them to extend deep into the earth.

After two hours of digging, Navarro had covered his garden with over a foot of dirt and had to begin hauling dirt out of the cave and throwing it out onto the rocks. The hole he had dug in the back of the cave went back over twenty feet and down about eight. It was big enough for Navarro to move through, if he hunched over. Over time, as he worked in the increasingly cramped space, he discovered that although using the shovel became more of a challenge, by using both his mace to break up hard patches and plunging his scythe tip first into the softer earth, he could use all four hands to squirrel away the dirt much faster. As he went deeper, rather than carry the dirt all the way out of the cave, he piled it up in front of the hole. He knew taking the dirt out and spreading it in such a way as to not draw attention to his cave would take a long time, but he smiled at the realization he had nothing but time. It would take as long as it took.

He smiled at the remembrance of the old saw "many hands make light work." He had to agree. It wasn't just that four hands made his physical labor go faster. It was also that having the inner warmth of the fungus and his pets that gave him the kind of companionship in life he had never really known, or even sought out. He guessed he had always been a bit of a loner. But, he decided, that was changing. Now, he craved company. He craved union. He got positively tingly just thinking what it was going to be like merging with the little girl. At times during the morning, amidst the overwhelming smells of fresh earth and decay, he could almost swear he smelled the child on the breeze.

49

Where's Bruno?

Pippi sat at the breakfast table staring at her oatmeal. She had wanted pop-tarts. Alan wouldn't let her have them. She couldn't have most of the stuff that they advertised on television. It made no sense.

She took a bite, and then another. Not that she didn't like oatmeal. It was just that it was not something important enough for advertisers to take it seriously. Once she had seen Pippi Longstocking eat a whole onion, just like eating an apple. Pippi thought to herself, *That's where I draw the line.*

She wasn't even sure she knew what a pop-tart would taste like. But she knew it would have to be better than an onion, and far more fun and exciting than oatmeal.

Alan asked, "Did you want some yogurt, too?"

Pippi rolled her eyes, "No, Dad. Just this delicious oatmeal."

Alan opened the door and stepped outside. After a minute, during which Pippi finished her oatmeal, Alan came back in and asked, "Have you seen Bruno this morning?"

Pippi got up and headed out to the backyard, "No, but let me check. He's always finding some new hiding place."

"I know. But I put his dish out a half hour ago, and he hasn't touched it."

Pippi shook her head, "That's weird. He must be asleep somewhere."

Alan and Pippi both found the open gate at the same time. Alan immediately thought about the coyotes that were always roaming the hillside looking for strays. "Did you open this last night?"

Pippi looked worried, and offended, "No, of course not." She ran through the gate, "Dad, what are we going to do?"

Alan thought a second, not wanting for Pippi to find her dog partially eaten, or some sign of some other tragedy that may have befallen him. He thought this might not be as bad as it looked, but in case he was going to have to come up with a 'doggie went to live on a farm' story, he needed no witnesses. "Well, we aren't going to do anything. You are going to school. I will look for Bruno. He probably got into a neighbor's yard."

Pippi said, "Dad... I can't go to school now. We have to find Bruno."

He thought perhaps this was the sort of thing that warranted staying home from school - it was always hard to tell. But he needed to give her a job that didn't involve combing the hillside. "Tell you what. You go over to the Hardman's and see if he is over there. I'll check around back here."

Pippi started to object but Alan said, "Go."

Alan walked down the hill behind his house. He could tell something had been this way and frankly thought he saw some blood on the ground. He followed the trail until he lost it while trying to navigate through a large patch of trees and brush. He spent another ten minutes rummaging around before he decided it was a lost cause. Bruno was a little dog, just over four pounds. If the blood he was following was the dog's, then... well... that was a no-win situation here. If it wasn't, then there was no point finding the trail.

He didn't like to think how this would affect Pippi. She had just been a baby when her mother died. Although she understood it was something missing from her life, it wasn't something she remembered as a loss. She never lost anyone who she loved; she only knows she missed out on having a mother. He assumed this was part of what having a pet was all about, getting to know about love and loss. Even so, he wasn't ready for her to experience the loss part just yet. He heard her coming and headed up the hill to head her off. When he saw her, he asked, "Well, did Don and Dora see him?"

She shook her head, already portraying the look he feared she would sport for days.

"Well, they aren't the only neighbors we have, you know. Let's get up the hill and check them all. There are a lot of dogs in the neighborhood and Bruno is probably friends with them all."

Pippi nodded solemnly but said nothing as they headed back up to their yard. Alan didn't like the sound of his voice. He thought he sounded like a politician.

***

Dora asked, "Do you think Bruno could have gotten into that poison you sprayed all over the hill yesterday?"

Don said, "Not poison. Weed killer."

"I'd wager if I looked at the bottle, it would have a little warning in very fine print that used the word poison almost as freely as you were spraying it yesterday."

Don said, "Oh, for Christ's sake, a dog knows better than to lick up a puddle of poison." He thought to himself, *Even a little half a dog should know better.*

"Oh, so it is poison after all. I see."

"Oh, all right. I'll go have a look for that little fucker."

Dora said, "Don!"

Don shrugged, a little embarrassed. Dora didn't like that kind of language, and he only forgot it when she got under his skin about something. She was no prude, and Don could attest to that, but there were quite a number of activities she would rather partake in than discuss. "Well, uh, if you ever saw him with that Simpson Chihuahua, you'd know what I meant."

Dora said, louder this time, "Don!"

Don thought, *Leave before you step in it again.* And he did.

Don headed out to the shed, to see if there was some kind of warning on the Weed-Away. He assumed it was poison for animals but thought if he was wrong it would go a long way toward calming the ladies on the hill.

As he approached the shed, it struck him as odd that the door was open. Don believed in order, and he didn't leave his shed open. Dora didn't either, although it had taken a couple of years for her to take the hint.

He pulled the door wide and let the light in, half expecting to see little Bruno, dead in a pool of Weed-Away, his little pink tongue puffed up from the stuff. Instead, he saw his Weed Master 3000, dead in a pool of... he guessed it was Weed-Away? But that wasn't what killed it. Someone had smashed the holy bejesus out of it.

Don surveyed that damage and scanned around the shed. He kept an orderly ship and didn't take a minute to see that some asshole had taken a shovel and his scythe. If the thief hadn't taken tools, which carried with it an implication of an intention to work, he would have suspected Rage. He did anyway for a second, but then abandoned the thought, knowing the boy was in the hospital.

Don considered grabbing an axe and seeing if he could track the culprit but knew he was dealing with some stupid young punks that could probably use a bit of tough love, rather than a head splitting. He headed out through the gate, just as Dora came out to the yard to start her search for Bruno.

Don and Dora headed down the hill together. Don couldn't help taking a little pride in seeing his handiwork. There was no sign of life from the fungus that he had sprayed yesterday. He decided not to point out to Dora that most of the other flora in the wash looked like it was dying too. There was always more where that came from, and he would make a point of seeding the hill in plenty of time for the rainy season.

Dora could hear Pippi up the hill calling out, "Bruno. Here boy." She feared the dog had been caught and eaten by a coyote. These damn canyons were lousy them, and people were prohibited by law from doing anything about them. They were a protected species, and the hill was full of horror stories about little dogs and cats being caught and ripped apart in front of their owners. She'd even heard of one jumping out of the bushes on one of the main streets and taking a cocker spaniel right off its leash while being taken on a walk.

Dora muttered, "I hate those G D coyotes."

Don had been thinking essentially the same thing. He nodded, "Yes, dear. I would have to agree."

Pippi came running down the hill to join them. She was smiling and looking expectant, "Did you find him yet?"

"Not yet, sweetheart."

Pippi said, "You know, Bruno's pretty tough. You don't think a coyote got him, do you?"

Don did, in fact, think just that very thing.

Dora said, "Oh, Pippi, it's too early to think that way."

Don backed her up, "She's right. Dogs run away all the time. That doesn't mean that they've necessarily been eaten."

Pippi looked at Don, wide-eyed, "I don't want Bruno to run away *or* be eaten."

Dora looked at Don, wondering how he had raised two children. "He didn't mean they run away and never come back. It's just that they smell a little something and go for adventures sometimes."

Pippi nodded, understanding the need for adventure, but still looked concerned. She scanned the area in front of them and pointed to a cave she'd never seen before. "Hey, look over there, maybe Bruno went looking for adventure in that cave."

Pippi ran for the cave and Don and Dora followed, allowing the child to run on ahead. The girl called out, "Bruno, hold on, I'm coming."

50

Navarro Almost Gets Pippi

Navarro was thirty feet down in his new hole when he heard a child's voice crying out. She called out the name Bruno, and the little white dog that been picked up in the girl's yard began to wiggle furiously. He had placed the dog on his chest, near the Chihuahua that had apparently pleaded for his life.

The two dogs had been making the canine version of goo-goo eyes at each other ever since. It wasn't really the truest canine version, as each dog had their rear end embedded in a mesh of Navarro and fungus. They couldn't actually lick each other's butts, but they could nuzzle each other and lick each other's faces, and that was almost as good.

But now, Bruno was tugging furiously, trying to untangle himself. Navarro held him tighter and placed a hand on the dog's head, petting him and trying to calm him, both inside and out. His tendrils took care of the inside part, tightening their grip and reaching deeper within the dog, increasing their union.

As Navarro slowly made his way up the tunnel, he could hear the girl entering the cave and was overwhelmed by the scent of the child. Scent was too subtle a word. Reeked was perhaps too crude, he thought. The air was thick with the odor of youth. He could smell her completely and with every fiber of his being he wanted to expand to make more room for her deliciousness.

As they climbed to the mouth of the tunnel, all of them, Navarro, the dogs, the raccoons, and Lisa were both excited and afraid of what was about to happen. Both Navarro and Lisa could remember similar moments.

***

Lisa had been dragged around all morning with Navarro. She was finding it somehow harder to think of him as him. She found herself, whenever dragged back to this plane, as thinking of him as us. She found this to be an uncomfortable level of familiarity – even considering she had been experiencing moments of his past as though they were hers. She realized the more of him she knew there was, both less to like and less to hate. He was less a monster and more a fool.

As if to prove the point about their unfortunate union, the overwhelming nature of the little girl smell that seemed to saturate each molecule of the cave and its inhabitants, reminded Lisa of Innocencia. It *was* Innocencia. In her mind's eye, she found herself face to face with the little girl she now knew to be Innocencia.

Innocencia was standing in front of her house, wearing the same dress she had had on when they had pulled off her panties and tried to make love to her. Lisa felt herself blush at the fact she had failed to hold on and had prematurely ejaculated that first time. She intended to make it right the next time. This time, she hoped.

The girl said, "You stay away from me, Emile." She looked a little frightened, but a lot more mad, and turned to walk back into the house.

Lisa grabbed her around the wrist. "Wait, Innocencia, I love you."

Innocencia turned around and looked like she might explode with anger. "No... you... don't! If you did, you wouldn't have done what you did."

Lisa was confused. What they had done was beautiful. Innocencia's little perfectly clean body was the only thing that made any sense to her anymore. She was hard just thinking about it. "You know you love me."

Innocencia shook her head, "No, I don't. I hate you, Emile Navarro. I will always hate you." She shook her arm free from Lisa's grip and ran into the house.

***

Navarro climbed to the lip of the tunnel and peered out to see if he could

234

catch the child right now. He had never stopped loving her and had always known she would forget whatever had made her hate him.

Navarro was perhaps twenty feet back from the mouth of the cave, in the dark and peering over the dirt pile when he caught sight of the girl who he somehow knew was named Pippi. She was magnificent. She had a strong profile, wild little girl hair and that smell. She wore short pants, and he could see how smooth and hairless her legs were and knew she would be wonderful to play with.

He waited for her to come deeper into the cave, so that when he pounced, she wouldn't be able to escape. Before that happened, though, the little girl was joined by Don and Dora. He dropped back down into his tunnel, cursing his luck.

Pippi called out, "Bruno. Here boy."

Bruno wiggled again but wasn't able to free himself. The tendrils were holding his mouth closed tightly, and even though he whimpered for Pippi, Navarro had a hand over his mouth.

Don said, "I found this cave yesterday. It was positively bursting with those damn mushrooms."

Dora replied, "You must have done a bang-up job in here. You can't even tell there was anything here.

Don nodded, thinking that was odd. He stepped into the cave, noting the ground was soft. It seemed odd.

Pippi reminded them, "Who cares about the mushrooms. We're here looking for Bruno."

Don kicked the dirt off his shoes and nodded as if coming out of a dream. "Right you are, girlie, let's get back to the hunt."

Don assumed that at a certain point the child would give up, and in the meantime, he had nothing on his agenda for the day. Aside from replacing his missing tools, and there was no hurry on that operation. That was one of the joys of retirement.

Don, Dora, and Pippi continued down the hill.

***

Once they had left, Navarro climbed out of the tunnel into the cave and basked in the thickness of the child's scent. He shook his head when he discovered it had been spoiled by the smell of decay. Don and Dora practically reeked of death.

He thought about the girl. Pippi. That was an odd name. It had never ceased to amaze him how each succeeding generation seemed to be odder than the last. It was a wonder to him that civilization kept advancing rather than crumbling. The qualities of leadership seemed to just get worse and worse. He guessed it shouldn't matter to him anymore. He was now his own civilization. There was no politics, no taxes, or societal niceties. His job was simply to feed. He glanced back at his tunnel. He thought that yes, his only job was to feed - and grow.

He crawled back down to the bottom of his tunnel, feeling a sudden pull. He wondered back at his reasoning for building the tunnel. It had just become something he needed to do. He had considered it an effort to increase the size of his cave, but really had proven to be a tunneling project. He had just felt the need to go deeper. He had taken two turns, each time with no real intent, just the need to adjust.

Now, staring at the base of the tunnel, he felt compelled to go deeper. In his head, he felt that he heard, as he usually did, a cacophony of voices. Some cried out for freedom, some for union, some for food. Now, however, there was a growing consensus of "down."

An hour later, Navarro broke through. As he leaned forward to scoop up four more handfuls of dirt to haul up the fifty-foot tunnel, he fell through the thin wall of dirt into a huge dark cavern.

For just a second, he wasn't sure how far he would fall, fearing he had found some deep fault line from which he couldn't escape. However, he had only fallen five or six feet before he hit a slope and rolled probably another twenty or so.

He found himself lying on the floor of a huge cavern, maybe seventy-five feet high and fifty feet wide. Although there was virtually no light in the space, the fact he was blessed with a dozen canine eyes made him able to see the chamber. Knowing he was inside the hill and essentially deep under where his house once sat was a strange sensation. But not as strange as what sat almost hovering in the center of the room and occupying at least a third of its space.

It was his mother.

51

Don Goes Spelunking

After Don and Dora dropped Pippi back at home, both Pippi and Alan were already late for school and work, respectively. Pippi was crying when Alan took her to school. "But we have to find Bruno."

Alan shook his head, "Patty, Bruno is going to find his own way home at some point. We've looked everywhere we can think of."

Hopefully, Pippi countered, "We could look again."

Alan didn't want to close the door yet but didn't want to lie much longer. "Listen to me, baby. Bruno may look like a puppy, but he is a full-grown dog. In fact, as far as dogs go, he is a lot older than I am. He can take care of himself for one day." He paused, thinking that was about as far as he could go with this line of conversation without going on about what a good life the little dog had had, blah, blah, blah. "Now, we need to get you to school before you miss any more classes, and I need to get to work while I still have a job." He took a deep breath, to prepare for what he hoped would be the last lie of the day, "I'm sure Bruno is fine and will be waiting for you when you get home."

***

Once Alan and Pippi had left, Don decided to go down and check out the cave. He found it particularly odd that there were no dead mushrooms there, and it had got him to thinking. If, as he suspected, the mushrooms had been planted by some punks trying to grow them to get stoned or sell to some other punks, then whoever planted them, must be upset about the death of their little stoner crop. Whoever trashed his shed had had a real bone to pick over the weed killer, but had also stolen some of his tools, a scythe and a shovel. Both ideal for someone planning to do a little gardening out in the wild.

He didn't know why he hadn't considered it already. It was a cave. A cave was where you would try to cultivate a mushroom crop. He smacked himself on the forehead. There had been a time when he could have worked this out without having to let it come to him on its own in its own sweet time.

He considered letting Dora know where he was going, but then realized he'd be back before she knew he was gone. He grabbed a fireman's axe out of the shed and headed out of the yard and down to where those little college pukes must be laughing at him even now.

52

Navarro Learns

Navarro stepped up to stand in front of the giant ball of fungus and tried to take it all in. It was at least twenty feet across. It looked solid until you got close and had a better view. Billions of tiny tendrils twisted together into larger strands. Those strands wound around each other and formed other larger appendages. Bands of tendrils, some over two feet across stretched out in all directions, disappearing into the earth around the cavern. They held the core of the fungus suspended in the center of the cavern. Smaller tendrils swept the area around and below the fungus in a constant quest for food.

Navarro stepped into the fungus and felt it wrap around him. Although he was a creature with no tear ducts of his own, he found himself enrobed in love and broke down at the overwhelming warmth and acceptance of a billion lovers, children, and mothers. Each of his companions felt the same wash of love and were all overwhelmed with what they were all now feeling.

Navarro had grown used to the voices in his head, but the volume was so much larger now that he couldn't believe they could all fit into his mind. What was different now, though, was that despite the exponentially larger number of voices, they were virtually all in unison. He heard a choir with a billion voices all accepting him and welcoming him home.

"Navarro, our child, you have served us well. Let us feed."

He thought, *Yes, let us feed.*

The fungus wrapped itself around each of Navarro's many appendages and pierced him with thousands of tiny tendrils. He felt his mind expanding with thousands of tiny new facts and memories. He understood how they had suffered. Once covering thousands of square miles, they were now isolated under this mountain with only a limited supply of clean water. They had sent out feelers, looking for food. They had found, and freed, him.

He stared deep into the core, noting that in the center the fungus was darker, almost black. It was covered with red and blue spots. Staring at the blackest part of the core, he knew in the desperation to find new sources of food, millions of years of traditions had had to be abandoned. Navarro had been resurrected because of the hunger the fungus had sensed in him. He was a kindred spirit. The fungus only lived on decay but knew the limited hunting grounds could only supply so much.

Looking into the red spots, he knew his job was to walk the earth, bringing back food. Food in the form of rotting material—or material that could be made to rot. It made sense. He could travel on the surface of the world and bring things back. This fungus could only exist underground and was surrounded on all sides by toxicity, so couldn't spread out further. It needed to grow down but couldn't provide the needed food for itself.

Navarro nodded and tried to step away from the fungus. He couldn't move and heard the fungus say, "It's too late. We have failed. We will die here, together. We can be together."

Navarro understood and countered, *But we can grow. I will bring you food. I have brought you food.*

The choir sang, "Yes, you brought us food. We could feel our sprawl returning, but it has become tainted. The earth around us has grown worse. Hope is lost."

Navarro thought, *No! That fucker Hardman poisoned you. He sprayed the hill. But I can fix it. Somehow. I have so much to do.* He quickly added, *for you. Let me bring you an offering. Tonight, I will bring you a pile of fresh meat.*

He heard a break in the unison, with some voices disagreeing. The choir now responded, but with many fewer voices, "Fresh meat is no good. We seek decay." He saw the red spots seem to throb and knew they understood that fresh meat could work. It was slower than the wonderful decayed material, but large quantities could do. He didn't need the fungus to tell him that. He had been learning it on his own for several days now.

He heard a human voice behind him. It was coming from up the tunnel. "Hey, who's down there?"

Navarro smiled, *Hardman!*

A choir of a billion cried in his head, "Hardman. The destroyer?"

Nine heads nodded in unison. The mother fungus slowly released its grip on Navarro. It cried, "Bring us this butcher, Hardman."

Navarro felt a jolt of emptiness hit him as the mother let him go. He felt thousands of voices in his head, some weaker, some stronger, all trying to express the same thing. They all cried variations on the theme of "Go back, jump into the core."

Navarro couldn't do that. He had to keep the core alive. He had to keep himself alive as well. He wasn't ready for the core, and without him it would die. And he wasn't ready for that either. He needed to live. And of course, there was something about a little girl named Pippi.

He wasn't exactly sure what he would do with her, but he knew when he was finished, if she didn't love him as much as mother, then she would go in the new meat pile he intended to keep stocked.

He crawled on all sixes up the slope to where his tunnel ended at the mouth of the cavern. Peering up the tunnel, he could see Don Hardman staring down. Hardman cried out, "You can hang out there as long as you like, but I'll be waiting up here whenever you little punks get hungry."

Navarro smiled. *We're hungry now.* On all sixes he started up the tunnel, keeping his scythe and mace arms at the ready.

***

Don Hardman stared down the dark tunnel and wondered if there was any point to it. The boys, or men, who he was looking for were probably not stupid enough to be down in the tunnel. He had found their handiwork, all right. The sons of bitches had not just planted a new cave full of their poisons. They had tried to jump start it with the bodies of a bunch of animals they had butchered for the project. No doubt if he dug up enough of it, and

242

he had no intention of doing so, he would find poor little Bruno's body here as well.

He found the tunnel pretty quickly and figured they must have dug it out in order to increase the size of their growing area. He guessed that to the sort of fucked up punks who would kill dogs and cats to feed their little drug business, digging a hole, potentially undermining a hill where homes were placed at risk, didn't seem like a fucked up thing to do.

He figured they may be sociopaths, but he doubted they had night vision. There was no light coming up from the tunnel, so figured if they weren't there, they would probably be back tonight under cover of darkness to tend to their little business venture. He turned and took a moment to take in the bloody mess that lay all around him. He thought he had lived too long to have lived to see this kind of mess.

As he was about to leave, he turned to take one more peek down the tunnel. He took an involuntary step at what he thought he saw. The man crawling up the tunnel was so covered in muck he didn't look human. Then Don saw he was sporting four arms. The thing was grinning at him and as he came higher toward the light, Don could see the glint of eyes in places where there couldn't be eyes.

Don was an ex-marine and didn't run from fights. There was no man who had inspired an ounce of fear in him in almost fifty years. That said, he took a step back from the mouth of the tunnel and put a little distance between him and the thing that was about to emerge.

The creature stepped out of the tunnel and stood its full height. It was six feet tall and must have weighed over 300 pounds. Four arms. More heads than he could count. Some of them were animal heads with bared teeth. Some of them were growling or barking at him. The one in the center, the only one he believed should have belonged to the beast, was the worst one of all. It had one eye that sagged a bit lower than seemed right. The mouth was agape and revealed a gaping maw that would have put that screaming guy in that famous ugly painting to shame. The thing's torso seemed to be covered with fur, but most of it, and its head in particular, looked like it was just a mass of rotting fungus.

He cinched up on his axe and decided the top head was probably the most effective first target. No doubt, something this unprecedented had no set of rules he could draw upon, but in the absence of existing intel, go with what you know. He didn't know what this thing was, but he was reminded of the old line from some picture he got dragged to back in the seventies, "Kill the brain, kill the zombie." He didn't believe in zombies, of course, but he'd be damned if he knew of a creature that wouldn't respond similarly.

The thing tensed and raised its arms as Don began to circle the room, waiting for his opening. They circled each other slowly for a minute or so. Don would normally have said something to unnerve his opponent, but for the life of him couldn't think of what to say to this monster. He thought, *Jesus Jumping Christ, did I just call this thing a monster? Okay, no more thinking about it.*

That was when he noticed one of the heads that protruded from the front of the beast was Bruno's. Don shook his head, hoping that was all that was shaking and thought he'd better take care of this quickly or he'd end up pissing himself - or worse.

***

Navarro saw that Don was looking momentarily at the little dog and used the brief lack of attention to take a shot. He lunged forward and swung out with his mace.

Don regained his focus and jumped back in the nick of time. While Navarro was still leaning forward and recovering from his wild swing with the mace, Don slipped to the left and gave Navarro a swat on the back with what sadly turned out to be the flat end of the axe head. It turned Navarro around so that his back was turned toward Don for a second. It didn't matter, because Don was momentarily frozen by the realization there were more heads with more eyes on the monster's back. That pause was enough time for Navarro to turn around and right his balance.

Navarro made a mental note that as Hardman was going to be more of a challenge than had been the coyotes, he should lead more with the scythe, because its weight was less likely to throw off his balance. He thought, *What the hell, there's no time like the present.* He lunged forward, slicing up with the scythe, barely missing the old meddlers left arm.

***

Don was assessing the situation, noting the monster didn't have too much strength behind its swings. He didn't know if this thing was the sort of creature that got tired, but decided being seventy years old, he was, and had better end this thing soon. He hadn't traded blows with another man in almost half a century and had quit working out at least ten years back. He was starting to feel the heaviness in his shoulders. He stood still and decided he would dodge the next whatever came at him and take an all-out offensive swing while the creature tried to right itself.

***

Navarro considered his next move. He decided that however he finished off Hardman, he'd never get him down the tunnel in one piece, so he might cut him up up here and then throw him down in pieces. He readied himself for his next attack and found that as he stepped forward, his right and then his left leg both refused to cooperate. *Fuck you, Navarro*, and glanced down for just a fraction of a second at his uncooperative feet when the axe came down.

***

Don didn't split the monster's head like he had planned, but he did remove it. The axe came down on the right side of its neck, between—*holy shit was that a raccoon?*—and his head, slicing through his neck and down into his torso. The single eye bulged as the head rolled back off the beast and into the corner. The beast stood still for what seemed like an eternity before dropping to its knees.

Don took a moment to catch his breath and was about to step out of the cave to catch a better class of air, when the beast, still sporting an assortment of heads, swung its mace straight up, catching Don in the family jewels, knocking him back into the tunnel.

Don's body was just hitting the floor of the cavern below as Navarro was placing his head back on and beginning to mend himself.

53

Alicia

Rage didn't like the way the doctors and nurses looked at him when they came into the room. He could sense a level of pity or concern that pissed him off a little. He just wanted to look out the window for signs of life but guessed it made him look like some kind of loser. The realization over the last twenty-four hours or so that he probably was a loser was no reason to let others think it about him.

Rage had the television on low, having scanned for the channel with the best chance of flashing a little cleavage, then turned to look out the window. He figured if anyone came in, they would just assume he was watching the tube, and that would seem normal.

He was feeling much better physically. Inside, he knew something was wrong. Not from the mushrooms, but from all the thinking he'd been doing. It was something he had actively avoided for, well... his whole life. As a kid, he figured all the thinking was his parents' responsibility. Later, it was just a bummer thinking about stuff. He'd been high to the best of his knowledge for at least the decade or so since his parents' death. He was mostly high for the five or six years before that, too.

Gazing at the trees blowing in the breeze outside, he wondered if he knew how to be happy without getting high. He thought about the things that gave him pleasure. It really came down to four things: weed, beer, pizza, and girls. He was finding that the beer and pizza weren't really doing his body any good, and that was making it harder to find girls that would fuck him without getting paid. And the weed made the whole pizza thing more of a problem.

He realized there was a fifth thing. He'd forgotten about adrenaline. That was cool, too. Rage guessed he could simulate it with cocaine, and had on too many occasions, but getting it the natural way was less of a total body beat down. It made him tired just thinking about it.

He was thinking about his parents again, wondering if he'd really seen them yesterday, looking out the window, when he heard someone say, "Hey, Rage."

Rage turned to see what he could only categorize as a smoking hot babe, standing in the doorway. She gave him a nervous smile and a little half wave and stepped into the room. She was wearing jeans and high heels—he loved that!—and a top her mom probably thought was wholly inappropriate. Truth be told, her mom didn't, which was in part why she dressed this way.

Rage looked up from her cleavage to her face as she stepped next to the bed. He thought he must be regaining his strength, because maintaining eye contact was no mean feat. He remembered to smile.

She said again, "Hey, Rage. Remember me? Alicia?"

Rage nodded, smiling, but guessed that his puzzled look gave him away. She looked a little familiar, but a lifetime spent living in a fog didn't result in the most finely tuned memory.

She said, "Alicia Finley?"

Rage wasn't getting it fast enough. She said, "I blew you in eighth grade." Rage smiled, remembering her. She added, "And I guess we boned a couple of times in high school."

Rage kept nodding, not really remembering that last part, but wanting to. "Hey, yeah. How you been?"

She could see he didn't remember their history, but then again, sometimes guys were pigs. But there were some things a girl just remembered. Alicia had had a crush on Rage through most of middle school and right up until her family had moved to San Diego. "I've been good. Kind of working on getting my shit together now."

247

Rage nodded, "That's cool. That's something people do, I guess." He glanced down at himself, laying in a hospital bed, attached to tubes and shit, and thought getting his shit together was something he was kind of due to do as well.

Rage peered up at Alicia again, letting his gaze take in the whole package once more. Damned if he couldn't place the body. He remembered some cute blonde giving him a BJ down in the wash, but really wasn't sure he could pick this one out of a line-up. But, of course, that would have been almost twenty years ago. This chick was no twelve-year-old. She looked like she'd been ridden hard and put away wet. Even so, she'd cleaned up nicely.

Rage racked his brain for a little small talk material. This wasn't usually so hard. Talking up girls was kind of his specialty, but he wasn't usually so sober. "So, what... ah... brings you here?" he asked.

"Well, I had to get out of San Diego. Too many bad influences. I decided to go straight. I moved back here and moved in with my Grandma just until I could get back on my feet." She paused, considering going on, but remembered that Rage had always bored easily.

Raged nodded, "Yeah, that's cool. But I meant here. My room. Why did you come here?"

"You know, that's kind of funny. I mean, I've been thinking about looking you up. It's been a long time since I've been up to your happy spot; you remember that?"

Rage nodded, "Happy place."

"Right. Happy place. So, anyway, I've been thinking about looking you up. But I wanted to wait until I was together. You know..." she paused, realizing that he didn't know, and that she was babbling. "Anyway, I was getting high this morning up at Forest Lawn. You remember how we used to like to get high up there?"

Again, going to have to be more specific. He thought. He said nothing... she seemed to be self-propelled in the talking department.

"So, suddenly it hit me, I have to see Rage. Now." She smiled, "So, here I am."

Rage furrowed his brow, wondering how he'd never noticed how funny

248

women explain things. It didn't occur to him that it was because he rarely paid any attention to what they said. "Yes. Here. But how did you know I was here? In this hospital. In this room."

"Well, first off, I'd been feeling all warm and fuzzy. Really, I was feeling as good as I've felt in years. Maybe ever. And sometimes when I'm laying down, and you know, feeling good, I think about you." She looked at him, making sure he wasn't looking at her like she was weird or something. "So, I thought, I wonder what Rage is up to and suddenly there's like a hundred voices in my head all screaming 'He's at the hospital.'"

"Voices told you I was here?" he said.

She shook her head, "No, just that you were at the hospital. But this is the only one I knew about so its where I came. Once I got here, I asked for you and, well, that's all there is to that."

"So, voices in your head told you I was here."

She looked at him like maybe he was not right. "Right. Like I said."

"So, are you high now?"

She shrugged. "Maybe a little."

"Weed?"

She shook her head, "Mushrooms. Little black ones with red and blue spots."

Rage nodded. "Yeah, those are some mother fuckers."

She smiled, "I swear, I never felt so good. I feel like, like..." she trailed off, not finding exactly the right words for how she felt.

Rage finished for her, "Loved. You feel like someone loves you."

She laughed, "I feel like everyone loves me." She looked down at Rage and tried to look right through him, "And, like I could really love everyone."

Rage stared out the window. "Yeah, I felt that way too."

Alicia pulled a chair up to the side of Rage's bed and sat down next to him. She put her hand on his and said, "Why'd you stop?"

She was blocking his view of the world outside. He looked her in the eyes, not really recognizing her. She really looked like any number of girls who had been in and out of his world over the years. He shook his head. "I don't know. I guess it wasn't real. I mean, I was just fucked up on mushrooms."

She opened her purse and showed him a baggie with a dozen or so mushrooms. She said, "I say, if it feels like love, what the fuck? How often do you get to really feel that way? And, if you feel that way and the real thing is a feeling too, well... I don't know... fuck it."

She held out her hand and in it were a couple of fat little mushrooms, the kind with red and blue flecks. They were a little out of focus, because behind them he couldn't take his eyes off Alicia's cleavage. He leaned forward and ate them out of her hand, never breaking his gaze.

Thirty minutes later, Rage was feeling the glow of the mushrooms and was holding hands with Alicia. "You know, I keep looking at you. I swear to God, I can't believe I can't remember doing a girl as hot as you."

She laughed, "Well, I don't know if I was hot. I mean, Christ Rage, I was a little girl back then. I mean, I think I was twelve."

Rage cringed, "Jesus, you mean I did it with a little kid?"

"You were twelve, I don't think it counts as doing it with a kid."

Rage nodded, "I guess that makes sense." He didn't, really. He had spent a lot of time in the fog over the years and guessed it was best not to try to pierce this one. The last thing he wanted to do was end up thinking about kids when he was getting laid.

He was feeling incredible. Not just the great mushroom high, but also, Alicia was holding his hand. Her touch was electric. He could feel her energy moving through him. Truth be told, it was making him a little horny. He thought that was a good sign, considering he was dead yesterday.

She was telling him about the cemetery. "So, when I was laying in the grass, you know, getting comfortable, I had this urge to just lay down in the dirt and let it cover me."

"Yeah, you're gonna want to avoid that."

"How come?"

"It's how I ended up in here. Some mushrooms started to, I guess the right way to say it is that they tried to eat me."

"Shit. Eat you?"

"Yeah. So, I guess my advice would be, eat the mushrooms, dig the glow, but don't lie down in the dirt and let them eat you back."

She nodded.

He lifted the side of the blanket. "So, speaking of laying down... care to join me?"

She gave him a suspicious smile, "I'm not having sex with you, Rage."

"I didn't say anything about sex. I just thought you might like to lie down a while."

She did want to lie down next to Rage. "Well, okay, but just for a little while." Alicia slipped into his bed, avoiding his IV. She put her head on his chest, and he put his hand on the small of her back. In less than five minutes she was asleep on his chest. In less than ten minutes more, Rage finally got it through his head that sex really wasn't forthcoming. Once that realization hit, he passed out too.

54

Navarro (and Bruno) Say Hi to Hardman

When Don woke up, he was being dragged across a dirt floor. Everything hurt and when he opened his eyes, he thought for a moment he'd gone blind. Everything was black.

Something wet was wrapped around his right ankle and was pulling him by his leg. He tried to sit up but found that something wasn't right. He couldn't move anything. He tried to remember how he got here, and suddenly the whole fight with what he could only describe as a zombie came back to him. It was ridiculous, but what was he going to do? Die at the hands of a fictional creature? Not likely. He remembered the fall and feared he had broken his neck.

He tried to move his arms again, this time with a determination to prove, if nothing else, he wasn't paralyzed. He didn't need to stop the forward motion, just wiggle a finger. The pain was incredible. He took that as a good sign. Feeling was good, even if he felt like he'd been hit by a truck. He dug his hands into the dirt and tried to stop his forward progress. It didn't work, and he didn't even slow down. In fact, he felt something cold and clammy wrap around his other leg and found himself moving even faster as he dug his hands into the earth trying to stop. He wasn't sure where he was going but preferred to pick his own path.

As his eyes adjusted to the darkness, he saw he was being pulled forward by what looked like vines. He just got his butt kicked by a zombie, so he wasn't going to question the fact that some slimy plant was overpowering him. He was grateful he wasn't paralyzed and recalled a few tight spots back in Vietnam that seemed just as dire, but a hell of a lot less weird. He was being pulled across the floor but could finally pull himself up so he was sitting up.

Hardman was face to face—or whatever passed for a face—with a giant throbbing mass of fungus before he could take it all in. He felt himself being pulled up to his feet and turned around. He could see a light patch from where he had come and realized he must have fallen down a well. He felt a tightening around his arms and legs. Looking down, he could see that long tendrils were holding him in place while other, thinner, more wily ones were attempting to breach his defenses. Tendrils held his head in place while skinny little shoots were attempting to enter his ears, eyes, nose, and throat. He could feel some little warm wet something crawling up his ass and was sure that something was trying to corkscrew its way into his penis.

While struggling to get free, Hardman looked up and saw the beast that bested him earlier. It slid into the light patch, stood, and seemed to be laughing at him. It came over and watched him up close. Hardman stared at the thing and felt as though there was something that didn't make sense. None of it made sense. But that wasn't what he meant. There was something... oh yes, that was it. He had killed this thing. He had cut its head off.

The beast came up and used two hands to push Hardman deeper into the mass of fungus. Hardman stared at the monster and slowly became aware of the din of a thousand voices in his head. He was watching the monster watch him when he heard the word "Navarro" resonate in the recesses of his mind. He was staring the thing in the eye when he heard it. His eyes grew wide at the realization that this thing was, somehow, Emile Navarro. He could see it if he really tried. He closed his eyes, not really wanting to try.

He quickly found that he wasn't able to wake up from this nightmare or wish it away, as Navarro punched Hardman in the face. He opened his eyes, thinking if he had nothing else to be thankful for right now, at least Emile hadn't become any stronger in death. It wasn't the sort of shot that Hardman had taken in his youth when boxing had still seemed like a sensible career choice. He opened his eyes and glared at Navarro.

"Jesus H. Christ, you are one ugly son of a bitch." He was too. Looking at Navarro now, he found it wasn't just that Navarro's corpse was, well, a walking corpse; he was covered in rotting animal skins and there were animal bodies strewn here and there. Some were alive and growling at him. Others were clearly decomposing and gave off enough of a stench that Don found not puking to be quite a challenge.

Leaning forward to get a good look at Hardman, Navarro sneered at him. As Navarro's corpse leaned in closer, Don thought he recognized Pippi's dog, Bruno, sticking out of the creature's chest. Navarro's lips moved as though he was speaking, but no sound came out. He looked determined and bore down, trying to speak again. For several minutes, Navarro would try to talk, then take a turn around the cavern, shaking his fists and talking silently to himself.

Navarro approached Don again and stood gazing with naked hatred at the old marine. He spoke again. This time there was sound. Bruno, Pippi's dog, opened his mouth and, clearly straining and struggling with each syllable, said, "H H H Hard M Man. D D Des T T Troy er."

Hardman watched, wide eyed, as the dog repeated, this time more easily and being perfectly lip synced by Navarro. "Hard man, dest royer. K Killer."

Hardman laughed. It wasn't a hey-you've-got-a-talking-dog laugh, it was a there's-nothing-left-to-say-you-crazy-lunatic kind of laugh. "Well, Emile, I always thought you were a bit of a lunatic, but this may just take the cake."

Bruno coughed out a new word, "Ad adulterer."

Hardman shook his head. He took that kind of accusation seriously. "No. Not an adulterer. For better or worse, I never cheated on either of my wives. Dora was a widow when we got together."

Navarro, through the mouth of Bruno, barked out, "Liar."

Hardman laughed again. It was hard not to. He looked at Navarro and said, "You do know you're dead, right? Long dead."

Bruno twisted his head, thrusting his neck forward, trying to find a comfortable way to speak new and different words. The different syllables made his tongue and teeth feel like they didn't belong in his mouth anymore. "No. N Nothinggg dies. Ev Ev Everything ng lives. Through me."

Hardman nodded slowly. "Nice. Not just raised from the dead, now you think you're God."

Navarro smacked Hardman in the side of the head with his mace. He said, "N Not G God. Bigger."

Hardman, reeling from the blow, starting to lose conscious, thought he wished he'd paid more attention back in Sunday School.

55

Dora and Pippi on the Hunt

Once school let out, Pippi ran home. She fluctuated between watching the street closely, searching for a little white body, and looking up and down side streets for signs that Bruno was on the prowl. Neither extreme panned out. Pippi ended up at home only twenty minutes after school let out. She hit the door expecting Bruno to be sitting on his little throne waiting for a treat, but he wasn't. He wasn't anywhere to be found. And she really looked everywhere.

After giving the whole house a good going over, she ran next door to Don and Dora's. Dora answered the bell and Pippi asked, "Have you seen Bruno?"

Dora gave her a worried look, "No sweetie. I was hoping he would have come home by now."

Pippi asked, "Maybe Don's seen him?"

Dora let Pippi in and led her to the kitchen. That was where the two of them spent a lot of time over the years. It was where they baked cookies and where they often shared a lemonade. It was where Pippi got to have her only off-the-clock time with a grown-up woman. Dora opened the refrigerator. "Honey, I don't know if Don's seen Bruno. He's been off running errands or some such thing all day." She hesitated, knowing there were all kinds of things that could have happened to the dog, most of them bad. Even so, she decided the girl needed to do something, and Dora preferred it not be unsupervised. "Why don't you and I take another look around the neighborhood?"

Pippi looked relieved to have an adult offer to help. She was feeling overwhelmed by the responsibility of finding Bruno. "Yes, please. Can we start in the wash?"

Dora sighed. "I guess that makes sense. That was - is - one of Bruno's favorite spots, I guess." She really didn't like going down the hill anymore. The idea of that house suddenly reappearing, not to mention the eerie sensation she'd had the other night when she imagined she'd seen Emile... she was a little on edge. "Why don't you go out back and make sure Bruno isn't curled up on my back porch. I need to change shoes if I'm going to climb down into that wash."

Pippi, her spirits boosted at the prospect of taking action, said, "You bet. I'll check the garden too."

Once Pippi was outside, Dora topped off her lemonade with as much vodka as would go, then stirred it with her finger and drank half the glass. She set it down, then took another sip before heading out and gathering up Pippi.

Pippi looked up. "I thought you were going to change your shoes."

Dora marched determinedly toward the place in the yard where things just dropped off. She didn't look down. "These old shoes could use the workout. Let's find that dog."

Halfway down the hill, they came to the cave they'd found earlier. The ground was all broken up, and the place stunk something awful. Dora stepped inside and saw there were what looked like dead animals partially buried in the cave. Pippi stepped in behind her, but Dora turned to head her off. "You don't need to come in here."

Pippi started to object, but Dora took a tone Pippi had never heard before, "Stop right there. You turn around and march back a few feet."

Pippi did as she was told, but asked, "Why? What is it?"

"I'll tell you what it isn't." She scanned the cave quickly, hoping to convince herself she wasn't about to lie to the girl. "It isn't Bruno. That I can tell you." She was pretty sure that had been a factual statement. Gazing around the chamber, she saw bloody, partially eaten, or dismembered animals. She couldn't imagine why. Coyotes would have eaten their kills. She wondered if the drug dealers that Don had suggested had been growing the mushrooms were members of some cult or some such thing. She looked down at her hands and saw she was shaking a bit. She just about jumped out of her skin at the sound of Pippi calling out, "Bruno! Here boy!"

Dora looked around the cave again, not able to see all the way back because of the contrast of the darkened cave and the sunny afternoon. She turned to Pippi. "I'm going to go in again. Stay out here." She paused. "And for goodness' sake, don't yell again until I come back. You scared the dickens out of me."

"Why can't I come in?"

Dora said, "Pippi, honey, sometimes you just have to trust your elders. I'm telling you for your own good. Nothing in here is for a child's eyes, and nothing in here will get us any closer to finding Bruno. I just need to take one more look."

She thought of the things in this life that she had seen and wished to Christ she hadn't. She'd heard years ago from a priest friend that there were things that couldn't be undone. She believed him. More to the point, she knew from a few unfortunate times in her life that there were things that once seen, couldn't be unseen. A mutilated accident victim. One's parent in a coffin. These were sights that only took a moment to create a permanent scar on one's memory.

Dora stepped into the cave and saw that it mercifully didn't go back that far. Maybe twelve or fifteen feet deep and the killing field didn't even extend back that far. She turned to leave and stepped to the mouth of the cave. She was overwhelmed with a sense of déjà vu. She couldn't put her finger on the moment but felt that she was being watched from inside the cave. She used all the resolve she could muster, aided by the resolve that a couple ounces of vodka had supplied and turned around to look back into the cave.

It hadn't changed. Just a cave piled up with meat, dirt, and fungus. Pippi said, "Let's keep looking, he may be down in that house we found the other day."

Dora followed Pippi down the slope toward her and Emile's old house.

Once down at the bottom of the wash, the challenge for Dora became how to handle Pippi's desire to enter the old house. Dora wasn't about to allow the little girl to go into the old house. It wasn't safe, and she had no way of knowing if the hill would give way at any moment.

Pippi was determined. "He's just a little dog. He could be trapped in there."

Dora shook her head, "Just how do you figure that?"

"Well, he could have gone in there and something fell on him?"

"So, you want to check in a place that you believe to be the sort of place where things just fall on folks?"

Pippi went to the window. "I just want to check."

Dora said, "Patricia McNealy, you step away from that house."

Pippi looked at Dora like she had betrayed a trust. Dora never called her by her full name. That was something her dad would do when she was in trouble.

Pippi did as she was told. But she talked back. "Someone has to check inside. We have to."

Dora stepped between Pippi and the old house. She climbed up to the front steps and peered into the dark entryway. She knew there was nothing to be afraid of. The house had been buried for twenty years. She had a sense it was empty. That sense didn't necessarily motivate her to step inside. She hesitated and worked to summon the courage to step into the old house. It wasn't just the memories that gave her pause. It really did seem needlessly dangerous. She could just imagine that after all these years at the bottom of the hill, she could end up joining Emile in his burial site.

She heard a familiar voice call out, "Good God, Dora, don't go in there."

Pippi called out, "Dad!"

Dora turned to see Alan walking through the clearing to the house. Pippi ran and hugged him.

Alan was watching Dora. He looked at the house. "Dora, is that..."

She replied, "Yes, it is."

Pippi asked, "Is that what?"

Alan ignored Pippi. "Why would you even think about going inside? It looks like it could cave in anytime."

Pippi said, "Because Bruno's in there."

Dora said, "Pippi!"

"I mean, he might be in there. We have to be sure, Dad."

Alan asked, "Still no sign of him, huh?"

Pippi shook her head. "And this is the last place I can think to look for him."

Alan considered all the stupid things he'd done over the past decade, all in the interest of either making his daughter happy or helping to avert tragedy. He stared at the house and decided if he really looked at it realistically, there was only the remotest chance this would be the moment the building would choose to collapse. He also knew that chance was infinitely slimmer than the chance his daughter would let go of the idea that her dog was trapped inside.

"Dora, please keep an eye on Patty while I check inside." Then, Alan went into the old Navarro house.

As he stepped into the center of the living room, Dora called out to him, "Be careful, Alan."

He went from the living room, through the dining room into the kitchen. It occurred to him this was basically the same floor plan as his own home. He walked through the hall into the master bedroom, noting that the place was filthy and that the floor was missing in the back. The whole room was covered with dead and decaying plants and fungus.

The room that would correspond in his own home to Patty's was crushed by what looked to be part of another house. Throughout the house, he looked along the floorboards for any sign of Bruno. He hadn't expected to see any signs of the dog and his assessment proved to be correct. There was no Bruno, or any sign he had been here.

Alan emerged from the house, and when he saw Pippi's expectant look, he shook his head. Pippi started to cry. "Oh, Dad. Where's my dog?"

56

Three's a Crowded Hospital Room

Tim walked into Rage's room and was only half surprised to find Rage wasn't in bed alone. He was probably a little more than half surprised, however, that both Rage and the woman in his bed were sleeping, and apparently wearing clothes. He looked under the bed, just to make sure there were no extraneous clothing items that hadn't made it into the bed. As he turned to leave, he heard Rage, "Hey, Dude. You came to visit?"

Tim looked over at Rage and saw that he looked in much better spirits than when he had left him. He looked less adrift. Yesterday, Rage had looked drawn and as close to depressed as Tim thought Rage capable. Now he had color and was smiling. Not to mention, even though she looked to be asleep, it looked like the woman in bed with Rage was doing something unladylike to Rage under the covers. The area around Rage's crotch was moving rhythmically as Tim asked, "Are you sure you're medically okay for that sort of thing."

Rage looked down and laughed. "Oh, don't worry about that. I think she's just having a good dream. She's not going for the gold or anything, just keeping her hands warm."

Tim shook his head and tried not to let his mind take him on a vicarious trip under the blanket. "So, do you want me to bring you anything when I come by in the morning?"

Rage shook his head, "Nah. I'm probably gonna see about booking this evening. I'm feeling pretty good, and this place is a real drag."

Tim nodded, trying not to look at the little tug of war under Rage's blanket. "Yeah, I can see you must be miserable."

Rage said, "No, not really. I was. But Alicia came by to catch up and..." He considered mentioning that she had brought him some mushrooms and that they had really taken the edge off. He didn't though, because Tim was such a little bitch when it came to drugs and such. "And, anyway, whatever was wrong seems fixed."

Alicia woke up and took a few seconds to place herself and assess the situation. For just a few seconds, Rage thought things might get weird because awake, Alicia was apparently much more skillful with her hands than asleep, but she quickly caught herself and slipped her hand off his junk. She glanced up and saw Tim, "Oh, hello." She sat up in bed and offered her hand, "Hi, I'm Alicia, an old friend of Rage's."

Tim stared at her hand and lifted his up instead, offering a quick little wave. "Hi. Tim. Rage's roommate."

Rage said, "Yeah, Tim's been living at my place for a few months now. Alicia here and I went to school together. She just moved back to her grandma's house from San Diego."

Tim nodded, having no real use for the information. His experience had been that a friend of Rage's was no friend of his. In addition, there had never been a reason to learn a woman friend's name, as he only rarely saw one a second time. Few if any women found a second round with Rage worthwhile. Tim said, "Well, listen, I'm going to go home and get a little studying done. Don't worry about Fatty. I'll make sure he gets fed." He turned to Alicia and said, "Nice meeting you, Alicia. I'm sure I'll see you again real soon."

She nodded, "You too."

"You don't need to come back in the morning. I expect to be gone, but if not..." Rage looked at Alicia, "Well, Alicia and I have a lot of catching up to do."

Tim shrugged, "Sounds good." Then he exited the room.

Rage turned is attention to Alicia. "Uh, so, where were we?"

Alicia looked a little confused, an expression she wore a lot. "Well, I think we were sleeping."

Rage nodded down at the spot from which Alicia had so recently rescued her hand. She laughed, "I don't think that's such a good idea."

Rage said, "Agree to disagree?"

"I don't know what that means. But I know my grandma said I always rush into stuff like that. I mean, for fuck's sake, I was blowing you at twelve. I think we should take things a little slower this time."

"What do you mean by this time?"

"Well, that was when we were kids. This time I don't want to just jump your bones. I guess I want something more."

Rage looked puzzled, "More than getting my bones jumped? I didn't know there was more than that. What exactly have you got in mind? I mean, don't forget I'm still hospitalized, there may be some limits to what I'm capable of."

She laid back down and put her head on his chest. She said, "I guess I meant this. It was nice, wasn't it... just sleeping together."

"You may need to run this by me again. Sleeping together is more than sex? I guess I had that turned around all these years."

Alicia nodded, "Exactly. Me too."

Rage thought about the fact this was the first time he remembered waking up with a woman on his shoulder. He'd always found a way to slip out and avoid this whole intimacy thing. The only time he ever really stayed in bed after sex was when he passed out. In those situations, he always found a way upon rousing later, to slip out of bed and disappear unnoticed - even from his own bed. He'd never thought about it, and wasn't now, but he had consistently avoided any kind of intimacy for as long as he could remember.

As he was drifting off, he started wondering at how the warmth he had felt for the past few days was a feeling of intimacy. A lifetime of avoiding it, without ever really thinking about it, had rendered him incapable of understanding why it was he had been avoiding it. Right now, the warmth he felt throughout his body - and let's be serious here, his whole body - made him wonder if there wasn't maybe something to it. Here was a beautiful woman that wanted to be with him - just be with him. She wasn't after his money or drugs or really anything. He kind of wished she was after his body but had to assume that was why she had sought him out after all these years.

Just before dropping off, he asked, "Okay, I guess I understand the no sex part. But do hand jobs really count?"

Alicia patted his thigh, right next to where he did most of his important business and said, "I really never thought so. But I think I'll wait until you get clearance from the doctor."

Then, for the second time in his life, without the aid of drugs or alcohol, Rage intentionally went to sleep with a woman he hadn't just defiled in some way.

57

Everyone Comes up the Hill

It was getting dark as Pippi, Dora, and Alan headed back up the hill. There was no point in searching further. Alan and Pippi were both convinced Bruno wasn't coming back, but neither had it in them to talk about it. Dora wasn't talking either, but for different reasons.

Dora had been thinking about her old life for the last few days. She had pushed it out of her memory for years. It was the thing one said, but over the past couple of days, she realized she really had done it. Her life, the life she cherished, skipped right from childhood to Don Hardman. The almost thirty years with Emile were, for all intents and purposes, just a lost weekend.

After unexpectedly seeing her old house the other day, then, for just a second imagining she had seen Emile watching her in the woods, her mind had been diverted down some hallways she had made it a point to keep closed off for the past twenty years. He had been a dark man who had a way of sucking the joy out of anything around him. Once handsome and seemingly sophisticated, at least to the seventeen-year-old Dora, he became bitter, and that bitterness turned him mean. He had never laid a hand on her in anger, but she never really knew why. He clearly grew to despise her. She spent nearly thirty years of her life, bound to a man who thought less of her than he did any strange young girl on the street.

***

Maybe it was all those years of marriage that put them in sync, or maybe it was just an odd sort of coincidence, but at that very moment, Navarro was watching the little search party retreating up the hill and was doing exactly what Dora was accusing him of in her mind. He was looking past his wife of thirty years at the little girl walking with her. It was the girl from the other day, the one he'd seen with Hardman. He could smell her on the breeze. He tried to imagine what she might taste like.

He watched them from the darkened mouth of his cave, as the child, Dora and the unidentified man continued up the hill. Emboldened by a combination of the oncoming of twilight and the need to see his new prey, he got down on all sixes, and started up the hill after them. He went slowly, not meaning to take the girl yet; just wanting to get a better taste of her scent. She was walking too close to Dora for him to truly be able to revel in the girl's freshness. There was an overwhelming abundance of Dora's decay in the air.

He wondered at the girl. He decided the man they were with must be the child's father. It was clear from the way the man touched the child. It differed greatly from the way Navarro intended to touch her. He wanted to touch her...and so much more.

Bruno thrust out his neck and managed a guttural, growled version of "Pi... ppi." Navarro continued to scramble up the hill as Bruno managed to choke out, "Pi... ppi".

Navarro thought, "What an odd little name."

He closed the gap to about twenty feet and could hear when Pippi asked Dora, without a real trace of hope in her voice, "Let me know if you see Bruno. I'll call you later."

Dora said, "Of course I will, sweetheart. I'll talk to you in a little while."

Navarro thought, looking at the dog, *So you must be her missing dog. You must be Bruno.* Bruno looked at the ground and said, "Pi... ppi".

Dora went through the gate to her and Hardman's place, and Navarro followed the girl and her father to their gate. He crawled under some bushes about fifteen feet behind them and watched them enter their yard. He hoped that perhaps the girl would stay outside while the father went in. They closed the gate behind them, and he thought he was out of luck when the gate opened again. The girl stuck her head out, scanning the horizon, then pulled her head back, leaving the gate open just enough for a small dog to slip in.

Navarro waited and listened. And smelled. He explored the girl's backyard with the benefit of his pets. The chihuahua and Bruno were lost in their own world. Ever since Bruno had begun talking, the chihuahua had taken to licking his face. Navarro could feel her worry. This was clearly abhorrent behavior for canines, and the little hairless beast wondered what was happening to the object of her affections.

Even though the little ones weren't much help, the presence of the four coyotes gave Navarro the ability to mentally map out the space where Pippi was lingering. He could smell that she was alone. He could hear every step she took and crept from the bushes to the edge of the gate. Rather than move into the yard and risk the attention of the father, he would wait here and snatch the child when she stepped to the gate again. She was bound to do it, as he had a feeling she was about to hear the whimpering of her little dog.

Navarro glanced down at Bruno and saw the dog was eyeing him suspiciously. There was no denying for Navarro that they were linked. He could see that the dog knew what he was about to do, but he was working for the larger good, so went ahead and grabbed the dog around the throat and squeezed. The little dog, knowing the point of the exercise, refused to oblige and closed his eyes, refusing to give in to the pain and squeal.

The chihuahua bit Navarro's arm as savagely as a three pound dog was capable, but he smacked her with a free hand and bound her with tendrils. He pulled her closer to himself and she was completely absorbed into his fungus flesh. He could feel her struggling within his chest while he continued to squeeze Bruno's neck. He was careful not to kill the dog. He still felt a strong affection for the creature. He'd never had a dog before and could see now why so many people felt an attachment.

Bruno suppressed his natural inclination to cry out. He knew the beast that held him wanted to do bad things to Pippi. He didn't know what, and he didn't know why. He didn't even know how he knew they were bad. Truth be told, there is a pretty broad swath of gray in a dog's mind that separated good from bad and almost all behavior was either in the gray area or firmly in the good. Bad for a dog was the equivalent of evil in a human, something much rarer than most folks liked to think.

Bruno started to pass out, and Navarro could sense he might actually be killing him. He let go. And then he flicked the dog in the back of the head and for just a second, as Bruno was coming out of it, he yelped. The dog went instantly silent, alert, and listening to see if he had somehow participated in alerting Pippi and causing no telling what kind of trouble.

He heard Pippi cry out, "Dad, I think I heard Bruno." He could hear a rush of activity from beyond the gate.

Navarro heard it too, of course, and he readied himself for when she appeared. He had to be careful to not hurt her, as he needed her to last a long time. He knew he had to eventually bring her to his mother but wanted to keep the girl alive as long as possible. Before he brought her to mother, he wanted to enjoy the child and the healthier she was, the longer they could play.

***

Dora was getting worried. It was time for dinner and Don hadn't come home. In fact, she couldn't say when he had left. He had run a few errands early this morning, said something about picking up some more weed killer, though why he needed it she couldn't fathom. It wasn't that odd for Don to get caught up in some kind of project, but it wasn't like him to stay away this long.

She had checked his shed and each room of the house several times over the last hour and now was passed annoyed and moving solidly into being afraid. She poured herself a large vodka, sat down in Don's chair, and played back the day. Just before she nodded off, she put together that she had lost track of Don sometime in the morning, not too long after Pippi had first come by about her dog.

58

Fatty for the Save

Fatty was pacing in the kitchen when Tim arrived home. He thought it was about time. Although dogs rarely had what you would call a bad day, this day was the sort that a human might think of as such. As it was, all Fatty knew was that for some reason, not that reason was really in his arsenal, there weren't any other animals on the hill today.

Normally, on any other day, by now he would have chased a few cats and cavorted with any number of dogs for any number of reasons. As for the cats, it was pretty much a catch and release kind of arrangement. Early in his career he had learned humans took a dim view of dogs that played for keeps. This way, everyone was happy, and he never ran out of cats to chase. Not today, though.

Then there was the whole dog situation. Of course, he and Bruno had had a long running dispute over territory, but he also had several other relationships that usually had daily reinforcements. Sometimes, there was food to wrestle over and in others, there was a little humping and sniffing that helped keep the aforementioned boredom at bay. Today, no dogs.

Being a dog, his powers of observation were acute, but his ability to make assumptions based on his massive intake of intel was limited. As such, he hadn't yet considered that the lack of dogs, cats, and the less domesticated inhabitants of the hill were in any way related. He did, however, know that with Tim's arrival, at least he could mooch a few treats and getting a bowl of food was something that never got boring. He was always grateful when Tim came home first. He was far more likely to put out Fatty's bowl and was a much easier touch when it came to treat extraction.

Tim tossed Fatty a treat and went to fill the dog's bowl. Fatty took the hunk of jerky out to the backyard to eat it. Food always tasted better when there was no one around to snatch it.

He was halfway through his jerky, really appreciating it, thinking, as he did every time, this just might be the best thing he had ever eaten, when he heard the sound of his arch nemesis, Bruno, barking back behind the house. He took off like a streak, fearing Bruno might be about to piss on one of Fatty's favorite things.

Fatty turned the corner outside his gate and saw, not Bruno - not at first - but what looked like the stinky bone man that had had such a delicious leg the other day. Fatty thought it odd, but a good kind of odd, that the man had grown another leg already. The man had his back to Fatty, so he didn't slow down, knowing he could hit him at full speed and get another tasty leg—or better.

When Fatty had closed the gap to less than twenty feet, he saw the back of the bone man was growling at him. There were coyote faces staring at him, and the man turned around. Fatty, not one to second guess himself, kept coming, thinking that although this seemed to be an odd situation, aborting his mission was to admit defeat - something that required more advanced reasoning than he was capable of. The man was made of tasty bones, for goodness' sake. On top of that, he was far stinkier than when last they met. He reeked of rotting meat.

At three feet and closing, Fatty took to the air. He wasn't terribly athletic, but as he was built with roughly the same aerodynamic qualities as a cannonball, he usually found this particular maneuver to be quite effective.

It wasn't this time.

Navarro turned because he had seen the accursed dog bearing down on him. The fool dog thought he was a walking bone shop, but that was about to stop. He turned smoothly and swung his mace at the dog's face. He connected, but not as solidly as he had intended. Instead of smashing the dog's head, which had been Navarro's intent, he merely grazed Fatty's right shoulder.

As Navarro realized he would miss, he turned quickly and tried to catch the dog in mid-air with his scythe. He not only missed, but the quick change of balance, along with a sudden hitch in his accursed left leg, sent him sprawling forward, away from the gate. He landed on a patch of dead fungus and slid twenty feet down the steep hill that abutted the McNealy back yard.

Fatty had been airborne when he was hit, and the effect caused him to spin out of control, not that he had had much control to begin with, and he missed Navarro by a good four feet, rolling another six.

Fatty stood and felt a sharp pain in his shoulder. He found it odd, because he didn't usually feel that pain. Initially he let out a whimper and turned to run back to where he had been hit, then readied himself to jump down the hill and pursue the bone man.

Just as Fatty was reaching the gate, Pippi came out. "Oh Fatty. I thought you were Bruno." She stomped her foot in frustration.

Fatty stopped to watch the girl. He, of course, did not understand what she was talking about. In fact, he had no real understanding that when people barked, they were communicating at all. All he knew was, sometimes when people barked while looking at you—if they didn't seem particularly mad— they gave you treats. He waited to see if this was one of those situations.

***

Navarro saw the little girl and the dog. He was on all sixes in the shadows, not ten feet away. He was considering if it was wise to take on the dog while trying to capture the girl when the issue was decided for him. The girl's father came running to the gate, shouting, "Patty, is it him?"

Pippi looked both disgusted and disappointed as she said, "No. It was just Fatty."

Navarro wasn't going to risk capturing the girl now. The dog gave him pause, but the dog and the girl's father were probably too much for him, particularly if he was trying to carry off the girl without too much damage to her.

He quietly slid down the hill, thinking about the girl. Bruno looked at the spot where the chihuahua had been and wondered how she had gotten away.

He missed the dog and was afraid. He was afraid for himself but was also afraid for Pippi. Under normal circumstances, he wouldn't have been able to understand what was in store for the girl, or why it should be something to fear. But he was able to understand enough of the thoughts he was sharing with Navarro that he knew whatever they were going to do to Pippi was bad. It was very bad.

***

Pippi was petting Fatty and talking to him, trying to see if he knew anything about Bruno's whereabouts. He didn't, but it didn't matter. He could never have understood her nonsensical barking and would never have been able to explain to her what he knew if he had. Instead, he just wagged his tail and hoped for a reward for all his attention.

Neither Fatty, Pippi, or Alan heard the sound of Bruno's litany of "Pi-ppi" as Navarro skulked back to his cave.

59

What's up with Lisa

After the dog attacked Navarro, Lisa had done everything in her power to slow things down. She tried to keep her arms and legs—emphasis on the word "her"—from cooperating to the extent she could. She had tried to trip him, and to some degree had succeeded. After that, as he scrambled to regain control while sliding down the hill, she was able to keep her arms from helping out too much as he attempted to right himself.

Unfortunately, too much of her was becoming too much of him. She hadn't gone to her heaven place in what felt like years, and aside from the occasional, frightening and seemingly pointless trip back into Navarro's past, had been stuck here as part of the pile of crap that Navarro had become.

Her thoughts were becoming mingled with his, not to mention those of the animals and what seemed like thousands of other, smaller thoughts and voices. She could understand his logic sometimes. When she looked at Pippi, she knew the girl was in danger, but she also understood Navarro's reasoning. She knew the girl would probably suffer not just fear and humiliation, but actual physical torture before she was added to Navarro's list of kills. She knew that. But she also in some small recesses of the self that was still hers—although maybe not entirely hers—kind of wanted to watch. She was becoming afraid that if she couldn't escape this smelly bag of bones, she might begin to think that way forever.

She missed heaven and was becoming certain her existence inside Navarro could only be considered hell for her.

V

Wednesday

60

A Rude Awakening

The nurse, Leticia, ripped the sheet off the bed and cried out, "Oh, hell no. Not in my ward, you don't."

Rage opened his eyes to the sight of the nurse - the one that clearly had it in for him - pulling the sheets off his bed and, if he wasn't mistaken, taking a quick peek south to see if there might be a not so little something to see.

There was. Rage was only wearing a hospital gown, and he was still lying in bed with a woman who was by far the hottest non-professional he could remember sleeping with in this lifetime. For Christ's sake, he wasn't made of stone. *Not completely, at least.*

Leticia said, "Mr. Sutherland. We don't allow guests after visiting hours, and if we did, it wouldn't be the likes of this one here."

Alicia sat up and brushed the front of her clothes, making sure everything was in place. She peered up at the nurse. "Hey... What do you mean by the likes of this one here?"

Leticia glared at Alicia top to bottom, then up again. She didn't answer, she just said, "Um Hum."

She ignored Alicia and turned to Rage. "Mr. Sutherland, kindly ask your little friend here to go home or I will have the orderlies come and throw this little bitch out." She paused and then continued, "Onto the streets." Then turning toward Alicia, she asked, as though speaking to a child. "That's right. The streets. I think you may know something about the streets. Am I

277

right?"

Alicia was blinking. She wasn't offended by the thinly veiled reference to Alicia being a prostitute, as it wasn't veiled so thinly that she understood it. But she understood enough to know the fat nurse was being mean to her. This usually had one of two outcomes—sometimes both. First off, it hurt Alicia's feelings. She didn't understand why people were always mad at her. It was, she figured, one of life's great mysteries. The second thing that often followed her hurt feelings was her kicking the ass of the culprit. She couldn't teach them manners, but she could usually teach them not to fuck with her.

Alicia wasn't yet at the point where she usually was when she transitioned from victim to ass-kicking mentor before Rage got out of bed, still sporting some seriously ill-timed morning wood and said, "Better bring a fucking army then, bitch."

Leticia smiled at Rage, looking like someone who was just served a big plate of the only thing that could really satisfy them, and took a deep cleansing breath. She said, as calmly as if she were delivering grace, although with the slightest little tremor in her voice, "Well then, Mr. Sutherland, I'll make sure to bring an appropriately sized escort for your little... friend." With that, Leticia headed out of his room, presumably to fetch some muscle.

Alicia looked at Rage with mixed feelings. She felt in awe, and not just a little wet, due to the way Rage had stood up for her. She had also started to think that stupid nurse thought she was a pro. But, worst of all, she realized no matter how it was accomplished, she had to be leaving the hospital and she wasn't really feeling like saying goodbye to Rage right now.

She got out of bed and said, "Gee, Rage, I'm really sorry."

Rage said, "You're sorry? What the fuck for? She should be sorry."

"I guess I broke the rules by getting into your bed. And I wasn't supposed to stay so long."

Rage laughed, "You and me both. Let's get out of here before she comes back with the goon squad."

"Can you leave?"

"I'll tell you what. I hope you don't think I sound too much like a fag for saying this, but so far, the only healing I've had this whole time in this place

278

has been laying there with you."

She looked at Rage and shrugged. He did sound a little like a fag, but she'd been weird for him long enough that she could overlook it, as long as he didn't get all weepy on her. "It's cool."

He opened the window and looked down to make sure the ground was clear. It was still dark out. He had no shoes or other clothes as he'd been brought to the hospital naked. The ground looked to be covered with grass, all the way up to the building, so Rage saw no reason not to use the window for his escape. The hospital gown would have to do until he got home. He held out his hand to Alicia, and she took it and came to the window.

Rage lowered Alicia out the window, then jumped down next to her. He didn't feel any pain in his broken leg, not sure if the cast was working, or it had healed again. Before grabbing her by the hand and making a run for it, he pulled her close and kissed her. It had been many years since he'd kissed a woman for any other reason than to be polite before boning her. It felt kind of good. She kissed him back and they stood, just kissing for what seemed to Rage like an eternity but was probably less than a minute. As good as it felt to just kiss Alicia, his dick didn't get the message that this was a different kind of kissing situation and Alicia giggled thinking maybe he wasn't such a fag after all.

She took his hand and led him to her car. "Put that thing away, we've got to get out of here before that mean nurse comes back."

61

Navarro Tends to Hardman

Navarro slid down his hole and found that Hardman was awake. Hardman was bound to Mother spread eagle, and with his arms outstretched. He looked like something between Da Vinci's sketch of the human form and someone creating a snow angel. He was bound by long ropey tendrils and smaller ones had burrowed into his flesh. Thin red, gray and blue shoots draped from each visible orifice. Despite the horror that engulfed him, he was alert - and pissed.

He eyed Navarro as his wife's first husband, dead fucking thing that he was, approached him. "So, Emile, what's the plan?"

Navarro stared at Don Hardman and considered him as he did the chihuahua. This was food. The fact it was food that had taken what was his didn't matter. Perhaps that was because he didn't want Dora anyway. But mainly, it was because he was food. That was more important than anything else.

Well, almost anything else. This was also Hardman. Hardman who had destroyed millions of his brothers and sisters. Hardman who Navarro had believed for a time had killed his mother. Now his mother held him and would soon devour him. She was eating him even now. Navarro wanted to see him suffer for what he had done but knew that Mother didn't care about such things. She wasn't vindictive, she only sought to perpetuate life.

Hardman asked, "So, no plan? You just drop me here for this fucking mushroom to do your dirty work? You always were a goddamn pansy."

Navarro smacked Hardman in the ribs with his mace, breaking two and causing Hardman to scream out. Hardman coughed, happy to see no blood, and heard a thousand voices in his head scream in protest at the attack. Hardman tried to consider what it meant that there were voices in his head that seemed to come from a mass of fungus that held him captive. He couldn't be sure if he could trust his mental faculties. After one accepts that a reanimated corpse is a viable part of one's worldview, then nothing that follows is suspect or spectacular.

He glanced up at Navarro, realizing there was something much bigger going on here than a mere resurrection. He could feel his skin crawling and knew somehow what was burrowing into his flesh was starting to consume him. He didn't know if it had eaten Navarro, or what, but realized it was the fungus, not Navarro running things here. He gazed at Navarro with a mixture of contempt and pity, "So, no plan because you aren't in charge here, huh?"

Bruno stared at the lump on Navarro's chest that he was now sure contained his former mate. "Pi-ppi. Plan is Pi-ppi." Navarro laughed silently and nodded. When he saw the look of recognition and horror on Don's face, he laughed again, much harder. Only this time, Bruno barked a caricature of the evil laugh that Navarro aspired to.

As Navarro dropped to all sixes, he started crawling up the tunnel while Hardman yelled after him, "You leave that child alone. Goddamn it, Emile, I'll kill you if you hurt that child."

The absurdity of his idle threat was lost on Hardman, but not on Navarro. He smiled at the thought of Hardman wanting to kill him. Aside from the fact Hardman wasn't going to leave that cave, Navarro had been dead for the last twenty years and liked the idea that killing him was the worst thing Hardman could think of.

He did, however, consider he wouldn't be bringing the child down into mother's chamber. He wasn't afraid of Hardman and didn't care if his former neighbor knew what he was going to do to the child. After all, Hardman wouldn't live to tell. But he just knew Mother wouldn't understand that the girl wasn't for food. He would bring her plenty, but she would want more. She would want him to feed her the girl. Perhaps he would, once he'd had all the fun he could think of. He could find other girls once Pippi was used up, but it was too early for thinking that way. It was too early for him to even consider that there would be other girls. Right now, Pippi was the one thing he would be keeping from Mother. The girl was his. All else belonged to Mother.

62

Rage Does(n't) Alicia

Rage was feeling better by the moment. The farther he got from the hospital, the more sure he was that he was cured and there was hope for him still. Alicia was this smoking hot chick who just dropped into his lap. Well, not into his lap, not yet, but that part was just a matter of time. No, the thing here was, this was a girl who was already nuts about him. He couldn't really remember why, and he wasn't sure he wouldn't somehow piss her off. But he was really wanting to give this a try.

Alicia was driving, and Rage was riding shotgun, doing the navigating. Thing was, she remembered where he lived, from a few times that they had done stuff in his happy place. Come to think of it, that may have been how it got its name. All the way up the hill he'd had trouble keeping his eyes on the road and off her legs. Her skirt was short enough that had he been driving, they would have veered off the road less than a half mile from the hospital.

Walking into the kitchen, Tim started in on Rage, "What are you doing here?"

"Last I checked, I lived here, dude."

Tim looked at Alicia. She was nodding. Tim looked back at Rage, "But, you were supposed to be there for at least another day or two."

"And yet, here we stand." He turned to Alicia. "Come on, let's hit the happy place," he paused, smiled, "and then we can see if we can find the happy spot." He grabbed her by the hand, and they headed out to the backyard.

Tim followed, "Did you even bother to check yourself out of the hospital, or did you sneak off again?"

Rage waved him off. "You need to let this whole submitting to authority thing go. I mean, I was the customer there. You never heard the customer is always right?"

"It doesn't apply here."

Rage shook his head, "No? Last I checked, this was still America. That shit applies here."

Tim was about to ask if Dr. Patel had cleared him to leave when Rage stopped dead in his tracks. "What the fuck happened here? Where are they?"

Tim asked, "Where are who?"

Rage's voice dropped. He sounded like he'd just lost a friend. "My mushrooms. I left them right here."

Tim said, "I told you at the hospital. Hardman sprayed them. They're all gone."

Rage slowly spun around, looking for some sign of hope. Then he headed out to his happy place for a look down the hill. "Gone? All of them are gone?"

"Yeah, he sprayed all the way down in the wash."

All Rage could say was "Fuck!"

Alicia squeezed Rage's hand, "Don't worry, babe." She paused, waiting to see if calling Rage 'babe' would weird him out, but he just stared at her. But he didn't look like someone who had taken the whole don't worry advice seriously. She offered, "I know where there's more."

Rage looked at her suspiciously. He'd never seen these particular mushrooms before they appeared in the wash. He whispered, "Where?"

"I told you. I found them at the cemetery."

Rage smiled, and never having let go of her hand, led her right back through the house on the way back to where she parked.

Tim walked behind him the whole way, "Seriously? You almost got killed by those mushrooms and now you are going to find more?"

Rage said, "You just don't get it. That was because I wasn't being careful. Now I understand how to, you know, master them."

"Master them?"

"Yeah. Before I let them master me. But now, I got this." He looked at Alicia and squeezed her hand. "We got this."

When they exited the house, he led Alicia to his truck. She looked at the green, purple, and orange markings on the impractical homage to a sports vehicle. "Righteous ride."

Rage said, "No shit!" He hit the gas, setting his sights on the cross that marked the top of the biggest hill at Forest Lawn.

63

Dora Faces Her Fears

Dora started awake. It was dark in the house. Was it morning? She peered around and slowly came to the realization she had fallen asleep in Don's chair. She couldn't believe Don wouldn't have woken her up when he got home.

She stood slowly. Her head was pounding...too much vodka last night. She ambled to the bedroom. Don wasn't there. He hadn't come home last night. She spent a few minutes checking different rooms, making sure there was no sign of his having come and gone.

She went outside to the shed. It was still dark out. Last night she had noticed there was a mess on the floor where what looked like his weed sprayer had been smashed up pretty badly. Tools were jumbled up pretty good as well. It wasn't like Don to leave a mess, so she was pretty sure this wasn't his handiwork. This added to her worry.

Dora stood at the edge of the hill and called out his name several times. She listened for some response. She could hear the sound of her voice echoing down in the wash, but there was no other response. Don's car was in the garage. He wasn't in the house or in his shed. He must be down the hill. She called out once more and waited. There was no response, and she knew she would have to go down into the wash and find her husband. She only prayed he was okay, and not laying some place where he could hear her calling his name, too weak to call out for help.

Dora went into the house to change her shoes and get a flashlight. Her nerves and fears were starting to get the best of her. First, she had been afraid for Don, a fear that hadn't subsided, but was being muddled with what she had to assume now was fear for herself. She didn't want to be down in the wash alone. She feared Don was down at that damn house and now here she was about to go down there herself. She wasn't a superstitious old nit, nor was she a child. She knew there was nothing in the dark that couldn't get you in the light. But something had been bothering her for days. She guessed she had started to remember all those things that had made life not worth living and somehow had a feeling in her bones that they were back. And feelings like that could get to you a little more effectively in the dark.

Dora stopped in the shed again, this time to see if there might be something like a walking stick - or a weapon - she could hold on to as she descended into the wash. She found a hoe. Turned upside down, it could act as a walking stick. It wouldn't help much against the dark, but she could smack a coyote with it, and it might help calm her nerves having it to hold on to.

She flashed the light ahead of her as she started down into the wash. She called out Don's name as she went, waiting for a response, and when none came, she moved down another fifty feet and repeated.

It only took her about twenty minutes to work her way down past the cave and was just starting to make her way toward the house when she heard something creeping up behind her. She almost lost her footing, trying to shift her weight off the hoe and to use it as some kind of defensive weapon. Even as she thought the thought, she almost laughed at how ridiculous it sounded. She turned and realized sometimes there are worse things than sounding ridiculous.

There was no way in the time she had to think, to formulate an opinion as to what it was that was about to strike her. It had too many heads and appendages to get a real bead on what she was looking at. All she could say for sure was that at the center of it all, she saw the horribly disfigured face of Emile Navarro.

If Dora was the sort of person to use such language, this would have been the perfect time to say something like, 'Oh, shit.' Instead, she closed her eyes and attempted to pray. She only got as far as "Our Father who" when something very heavy hit her in the forehead and the next thing she knew, she didn't know anything at all.

64

Rage and Alicia Bury Something

At the cemetery, Alicia showed Rage where she had picked her mushrooms. They were thick little ones that were dark gray and covered with little red and blue flecks. It looked like they covered the whole hill where Rage's parents were buried.

He felt a moment's pride, just as though he had been a parent. He didn't know the ancestry of the mushrooms that had cropped up in his backyard, but he knew that of these. These were his very own. He filled his bag and then ate a handful. If not for him, this strain could very well have died out when old man Hardman had gone on his rampage.

Rage went to the place where his mother and father were buried. Alicia followed. It wasn't hard to find the graves; they were located in the spot on the hill where the mushrooms were the thickest. He stood over his mother's grave and held Alicia's hand. Proudly, he said, "I planted these mushrooms here myself. "I guess I planted them so you would come and save me."

Alicia nodded, "Cool."

He turned and stared at her. "Why did you come here, anyway?"

"I don't know. You don't remember that we used to come up here and get high?"

Rage nodded and lied, "I guess I do. I got high in a lot of places over the years."

"Me too. But this place, and your place, were my favorite places back when

I lived in Eagle Rock. I've been thinking about you a lot. I wanted to see you but wanted to get my shit together first. You know, get a job and get back in the flow of things here. I came here this morning just to get high but found the mushrooms and they just blew my mind."

Rage nodded, "You see the lights?"

She laughed, "Fuck yes. They are amazing... Red ones and blue ones. You see them too?"

"Yes."

"I thought they were just my imagination."

Rage said, "No, they're real. Watch this." Rage reached into his pants and pulled out a pen knife.

As he opened the knife, exposing a tiny, thin blade, and pointed it at a finger, Alicia held out a hand to stop him. "Hey, chill out, okay?"

He laughed. "No, just check this out." He stuck the knife into the edge of his left middle finger. Not hard, but hard enough that he was able to cause it to bleed when squeezed. He held it up so they could both see the blood. More to the point, he held it so Alicia could see the trail of blue light that flowed out of his finger and onto the ground.

***

Alicia gazed at the lights and found them mesmerizing. She took Rage's hand and held it up to the light, then close to her face, then up in the sunlight again. It was marvelous. What struck her about the blue light, though, was that it was leaving Rage and that somehow it was precious. Rage needed it. She needed it. The light had to be preserved and not wasted.

The beauty of the light was such that she felt her eyes welling. She rubbed Rages finger to get the light on her and rubbed it onto her arm. She could see the lights fading slowly, not sure whether they were going out or being absorbed into her. She hoped it was the latter. She held Rage's hand closer to her face and licked his wound. The blood was salty, but she could have sworn she could also taste the lights. She could feel them glowing in her mouth and as she swallowed them, could feel them running through her. She felt Rage flowing through her as she sucked on his finger, trying to get more out of him.

***

Before Rage was entirely sure how or why, Alicia was pulling Rage down onto the ground and kissing him on the neck and face, while taking his bleeding finger and using it to rub herself. As long as there were no other dudes involved, Rage wasn't one to shy away from any sexual encounter, no matter how strange. This was the weirdest way he'd ever been come on to but thought it would be rude to object. However, he did offer an alternative object for Alicia to focus on and she was engrossed enough at the moment that she was able to incorporate all of Rage's other body parts into her world.

For the next forty minutes, Rage and Alicia by turns, removed each other's clothes, ate at least a dozen or more mushrooms each and found ways to make lights come out of or go into every orifice either of them could find. They were both exhausted and invigorated. They were both locked away in their own heads and fully integrated with each other.

This would have gone on all day were it not for the security guard that came upon the two of them. He said, "Move it along, folks."

Rage said, "Hey, we're consenting adults, man. Just move along yourself."

"We have laws against public nudity."

Rage objected, "But this is private property. How can this be public?"

Alicia laid back and stared at the security guard, who looked away, trying to avoid staring at Alicia's body. "Yeah, how can this be public?"

"Well. First off, this isn't private property, it's a public space. But it's even more public because you can be seen from the street. That's why I'm here now. The guy at the liquor store called it in."

Rage peered down the hill and sure enough, could see a few people standing in front of the liquor store watching them. He waved, "Well, then. I guess we'll just crawl over to the bushes."

Alicia nodded and turned over to combat crawl to the bushes.

The guard watched her for a few seconds, distracted, before saying, "No. That won't do it. You two need to leave the premises."

Rage and Alicia stood to gather their things. The guard looked again at Alicia. He thought that she was a good-looking woman. Nice body, but she had blood smeared on her shoulders and breasts. There was also a pretty hefty smear of blood around her privates. He asked, "Ma'am, are you okay?"

Rage said, "Hell, man, she's much better than okay."

"Sir, I was speaking to the lady." He turned to Alicia and motioned toward the blood on her breasts. "Ma'am, are you all right? I couldn't help noticing the blood."

Alicia looked down, she said, "Blood?"

"Yes ma'am. On your... um... chest."

Alicia reacted strongly, "What? Are you looking at my tits? Is that what my tax dollars are going for?"

"Ma'am, I just want to make sure that this man hasn't forced his way with you."

She laughed, "Not to worry officer. There's a place for everything and I'm thinking I'm his place. I mean, he's my place?" She laughed again, peeking at Rage and then back again, "I mean, everything is fantastic."

Rage filled up his bag of mushrooms and grabbed his pants and shirt. He stood naked while Alicia slipped on her skirt, and then he bowed to his mother's headstone. "Mother, I'm not sure if you remember Alicia. Mother, Alicia. Alicia, Mother."

Alicia, still fumbling with her shirt, curtsied, "Pleased."

Rage said, "Come on, man. This place blows. I know a real happy spot where we can continue this little party." He turned to the guard and added, theatrically, "In private."

65

Dora and Hardman - Together at Last?

Dora woke up in the dark. She was being carried. She put her hand to her face and could feel blood on her forehead. Her eyes hadn't adjusted to the dark, so she couldn't see where she was or who was carrying her. But, since she went down into the wash to find Don, she had to assume he had found her instead. "Don, honey, where are we?"

There was no answer.

She didn't wonder. Don was seventy years old. Even as good a shape as he kept, he had no business carrying her back up the hill. "Don, put me down! There's no call to be such a hero."

There was still no answer.

She reached up to touch his face and instead of the square chin covered with his afternoon stubble, she touched something cold. Her body stiffened. She cried out, "Put me down!" and started to struggle to get free. She reached up and tried to scratch the face of her captor and found her fingers dug in deeper than she had expected, but came away wet and covered with muck.

She was about to reach up for another handful, thinking whatever the man had covered himself with, could only be so deep. She would keep digging until she hit flesh and blood. Before she could take a second shot at him, he dropped her. She fell farther than she would have expected, rolling and sliding down a long dirt tunnel and landing, maybe twenty seconds later, on a cool dirt floor.

She started to carefully test her arms and legs, checking for broken bones. She couldn't imagine that this was something her life had abruptly come to. She wondered if this was how crime victims felt, suddenly out of their routine and into something so foreign to them that they never saw the significance until it was too late. Just yesterday morning she and Don had been helping look for a lost dog, and now here she was, having been attacked and looking for broken bones? It just didn't make sense.

She heard Don's voice, "Dora, sweetheart. Are you okay?"

She cried out, "Don, is that you?"

"I'm here."

"Thank God for that."

He shook his head. "I don't know if there's cause for celebration just yet. Are you okay?"

She winced. "I don't think so. I think I broke my arm."

Her eyes were just starting to adjust to the light when she asked, "Don, I don't think I can sit up on my own, come help me."

"Sorry, honey, I don't think I can do that." When Don responded, she followed the sound of his voice and was just able to make out his face sticking out of a big pile of what looked like slime. He was looking at her and seemed to be nodding slowly.

"Jesus, Don, what the hell is that?"

"Well, let me see if I can explain it. If I understand the voices in my head, this is something that has no name. It thinks of itself like it was a God, but there are so many voices in it and so many names. Most of them call this 'Mother.'"

Dora blinked at Don. "Voices? In your head?"

He nodded. "I know, I know... crazy. But here we are. The voices are running through me. Not just through my head, but I can feel my whole body in some kind of..." He considered his next word, "communion with them."

Dora thought, *Great, I broke my arm falling down here, he must have landed on his head.* She said, "Okay, Don. Don't talk. I'm going to find a way to get us out of here."

He laughed, "I don't know if that's possible. From what I understand, this is the new center of civilization. All living things will be brought here." There was a look on Don's face that suggested he found this a little hard to buy into.

Dora forced herself up onto her good arm. The pain was almost enough to make her pass out. She managed to get to her feet and slowly took inventory. Only her left arm was out of commission, but the pain was pretty bad. She found that if she carefully shoved her left arm up under her sweatshirt, she could form something of a sling and the pain was bearable. She asked Don as she approached, "So, how did you get down here, anyway?"

In a completely matter-of-fact tone, he said, "It was Emile."

She stopped dead in her tracks and stared at Don. Don was staring back, and this time, the look on his face wasn't one of disbelief. He didn't look like he had just said something shocking. He looked as innocent as a child in a spelling bee, merely answering a question with a simple set of facts. His captor was Emile, E-M-I-L-E.

She said, "What do you mean, it was Emile?"

Don said, "Didn't he throw you down here too?"

She looked puzzled. She said, "I don't know who dropped me in that hole. I'll tell you what I do know, though. It wasn't a dead man."

Don laughed. "See there. I've learned so much in my time with Mother here, and I'll tell you one thing that makes the most sense. Deal with reality as it comes. That was a dead man, and it was, or once was, Emile Navarro. Accepting that one fact allows me the freedom to pursue others. Fighting that reality gets me nowhere and forces me to look for answers that aren't there."

Don looked off in space and wondered out loud, "Knowing that now, I wish I'd let you drag me off to church all those times you tried. Getting some answers, and considering the big questions answered, would have freed up so much of my anxieties."

Dora stared at Don and wondered at his anxieties. She'd never met a more grounded individual in her life. She needed to get him to a hospital now. "We'll talk about getting you to church later. Today we need to get you out of that mess."

She walked slowly, sore in every bone in her body. When she reached Don, she could see blood on his face. She wiped it away and thought about how much she loved this man. She started to peel away the slime, which turned out to be fungus, from around his neck. She could see that where she pulled back the fungus, his skin was rough and red, like the fungus had somehow permeated it.

She ran her hands along his bare shoulders, wiping away fungus and seeing that there were tendrils that had burrowed into his flesh. "You should probably leave those in place. I think they're keeping me alive."

She looked indignant "Don Hardman. I have no intention of leaving you down here to be eaten by a bunch of mushrooms." She said this as she felt the first tendrils starting to wrap around her legs. She stepped back and pulled them loose. She looked down at the fungus, just starting to get her mind around the fact it was somehow acting with purpose.

She ground her heels into a few tendrils, allowing herself to get back to Don and started peeling him loose again. As she did, she heard more Don in Don's voice than when he'd been completely engulfed in the fungus.

Once she had his upper arms cleared, he took over the task himself, pulling the tendrils out of and off of himself. He felt a loneliness come over him as he did so.

She asked, "So, did this thing get Pippi's dog?"

Don looked up at Dora, eyes wide, "Pippi! Emile is going to try to get her."

Dora said, "Stop it, stop talking about Emile. I thought when we got that crap off you, you'd come to your senses."

Before Don could respond, she got her confirmation from Bruno. She heard what could only be a dog's voice, coughing out the words, "Pi-ppi. That's...the... plan."

Dora turned and saw a monster. It had many heads and arms and spoke through the mouth of Pippi's poor little dog, Bruno. The creature was covered with fungus, meat, and fur. But at its core, in the center of the vile, smelly mess of rotting meat, fungus and fur, was unquestionably the corpse of Emile Navarro. Bruno growled out, "Hel-lo, Do-ra."

Dora was paralyzed with the shock of it all. She didn't even feel the long ropey tendrils that reached her from behind, winding round her and starting to pull her into the core. "Emile?"

She didn't expect his response. Bruno stared up at his new master's face and said, "Fuck you, Nav-ar-ro."

Dora looked away from Navarro and saw that both she and Don were being pulled into the core. She thought it odd that Don didn't look to mind it all that much. She tried to fight it but was too weak and with only one useful arm wasn't able to get away.

Navarro stopped his internal bickering long enough to come and make sure Don and Dora were held tight by the core. He watched as long tendrils began to weave the two into the core and smiled. Before he turned and dropped to all sixes to climb up the tunnel, Bruno managed to cough out a strained, "Good-Bye, Do-ra."

Dora was starting to feel the warmth of the Mother as Emile started crawling up the tunnel. She felt the many voices and many threads that made up the whole that she was becoming one with. She felt Don, and he felt her. She heard a dog in the distance, saying "Fuck you, Nav-ar-ro," but found it hard to care.

She tried to reach out and see if she could touch Don's hand. After a few tries, she realized that although physically, she couldn't, she could actually feel Don - inside. She could feel him like he was a part of her. She thought if this was how she was to die, she could hardly object. Don and Dora both nodded as she thought that this was as good as she'd ever felt.

66

Tim, Rage and Alicia Go Boom

When Rage and Alicia got back to Rage's place, they were feeling the love. She had reconnected with the love of her young life, and he had connected with someone in a way he never had. Normally if someone had suggested to Rage a connection could be made with a woman more than with just his dick, he would have suspected some kind of fag agenda. But that was before he had become reacquainted with Alicia, and more importantly for our tale, before he had eaten what he was beginning to think of as the "love mushrooms."

Both Alicia and Rage were flying high on said mushrooms. Although Rage had been being eaten alive by the fungus just two days earlier, once again, he was feeling the glow of warmth and togetherness they had instilled in him all week.

Even Tim couldn't kill the buzz when he asked, "So, you got more mushrooms, I take it?"

Rage smiled and held up his shopping bag that was at least half full, "These ought to tide us over for a while."

"Wow. So, you learned nothing from your experience in the hospital?"

"I learned two things. I hate hospitals, and I hate not being high."

Tim shook his head, "You hate hospitals worse than being eaten?"

Rage laughed and said, "Hey man, watch the language." He looked at Alicia and smiled, "There's a lady present."

Alicia smiled, a bit confused, while Tim ignored the aside. "You told me the doctor said the fungus was killing you."

Rage turned and said with a touch of anger in his voice, "Let it go, dude. The doctor also said he had no idea what they were dealing with. If they didn't know what it was, how could they know what *it* was doing. Same guy said I broke my leg three days ago." Rage stomped his foot to show all was well with his leg. "All I know is, I'm feeling like a new man."

Tim shook his head, not in disagreement, but in disgust.

Alicia asked, "The doctors said the mushrooms were deadly?"

Rage said, "Not the mushrooms. The fungus. Big difference."

Alicia squinted, trying to remember what she knew about fungus. Mainly it was stuff to do with personal hygiene. She shook her head. "What fungus?"

Tim helped Rage explain. "The fungus is the larger organism. Mushrooms are essentially the fruit, or the seeding component, if you will."

Alicia looked suspicious. "Fruit? Are you sure? That doesn't sound right."

Rage said, "He doesn't know what he's talking about." He turned to Tim and added, "As usual... too much studying and not enough living." He turned back to Alicia. "The mushrooms grow out of the fungus. They're like the fungus, but different."

Alicia nodded. Rage made the kind of sense she could understand. She asked, "So you ate some fungus, and it almost killed you?"

Rage shrugged, "That's what the doctor's said, anyway."

Tim said, "Rage didn't eat the fungus. The fungus was eating him. It was turning him into mushrooms if you ask me."

"Which. We. Didn't." He turned to Alicia. "Come on, let's go out to the happy place and see about continuing our little getting to know you session."

Tim said, "You two need to see a doctor if you've been eating those mushrooms again."

Rage turned to Tim and stepped close enough that Tim had to step back a bit. Gritting his teeth and speaking with a landlord's authority in his voice, "Listen here, tenant. It's time to learn the rules around here. This is my house. I own it and I rent a room to you."

Tim started to say, "Yes, but..." but didn't get it out.

Rage continued, "If you want to stay here, stop interfering with my life.

Got it?"

Tim said, "Interfering? So, by your definition, finding you being eaten alive and calling an ambulance is interfering with your life?"

Rage smiled. "So, now you're getting it. Think you can manage to live by my rules."

Tim shook his head, "I don't think so, no. If I find a man dying, I'm going to help. Call me what you want, but letting you kill yourself isn't something I'm capable of."

Rage said, "Well then, I guess you are going to have to move out."

Tim said, "I'm trying. There aren't any rooms right now."

Rage said, "Not my problem. Try harder. And in the meantime - keep the fuck out of my way."

Rage turned and immediately changing gears, took Alicia by the arm and led her back out to his happy place. Fatty was running around the area, acting weird. Everybody was trying to ruin his action tonight. Rage shooed the dog off.

He held up the bag of mushrooms for Alicia and said, "So, what do you say we keep this party going?"

She looked at the bag and then at Rage. "Did these really almost kill you?"

"Not to the best of my knowledge."

She said, "Well, what did happen then."

He said, "Really? You want to talk about that?"

She grabbed a mushroom and held it in her right hand. She took Rage's hand and led him to the bench that adorned his happy place. She sat down, tossed back the mushroom and motioned for him to sit down beside her. "Rage. I didn't just come here to jump your bones. We've got plenty of time for that. I want to know what happened to you."

"Well, you know how you feel right now, right?"

She giggled. "You mean, horny?"

He like the sound of that. "Yeah, well, hold that thought. But, I mean, the way the mushrooms make you feel. Kind of warm or something."

She nodded. "Yeah, it feels a little like when I was a kid."

"A kid?"

"Yeah, you know. Everything just takes care of itself when you are little. No rent. No job. Everyone tells you you did a good job, even when you didn't. And all kinds of people are patting your head and hugging you and stuff."

Rage nodded, "Yeah, I get it. No cares, just good shit."

She nodded too, "I feel that kind of warm. Like everything just makes sense."

"Exactly. So, my question is, if you feel like everything just makes sense, would you fear dying at a time like that? I mean, if you really felt like you did when you were a kid?"

She looked down at the wash. There were red and blue lights visible in patches all over the landscape. Beyond that, there were the lights of the city of Eagle Rock. The red and blue lights looked more alluring than the man-made ones that lined the streets below. "I guess I never thought about it. But..." and she paused.

"But what?"

"I don't know... I guess I just want more before I die."

"I'm not saying I wanted to die, just that I realized since taking these mushrooms that this isn't everything. There's more to life than just being here. And there's more beyond this."

"How do you know?"

He laughed. "How can you not. Don't you feel it in your bones right now?"

She shrugged, not sure.

"It's like I want more. I always have. I want more of what I love. But I understand now that there's so much more I can never feel. There are billions of people out there. I can never know them all. Half of them are chicks and I bet at least a few million are hot. I used to be bummed that I could never bone them all. But now, somehow, I know I don't need to."

Alicia frowned. "But do you want to?"

He smiled to himself, "Probably, yes. But that isn't what I'm saying. I'm saying there is so much more than I could ever do, and that I didn't really understand before, but that is the way it's supposed to be. There is abundance. More than enough for everyone. And there isn't enough time to explore it all."

"And that's good?"

"I guess it either means we are all losers or all winners. The mushrooms made me realize it was more like we were winners than losers. We just need to let go of being afraid of missing something. We could just go for it."

Alicia considered for a moment. "So how did you almost die."

Rage shook his head. "I didn't almost die."

She rolled her eyes. "Okay, how did you do whatever you did when they said you almost died?"

Rage thought for a moment. "I wanted to be a bigger part of it. I realized I was part of everything, and I wanted to really dive in and feel it all over me. So, I buried myself over there. I didn't think too much about it. I just did it." He pointed to the hole twenty feet away. "I guess that while I laid there, the fungus started to, I don't know, maybe merge with me?"

"Fuck."

He shook his head. "It wasn't so bad. I liked it. I could feel not just like I was part of everything, but that I was becoming little pieces of everything. I guess it made me feel bigger than anything I've ever felt."

"So, you felt part of something?"

"Hell, I felt part of everything. Or maybe connected to everything. You know what that's like?"

"I think I do. You know, I came looking for you because I've always felt some connection."

Rage felt a connection now but couldn't have picked Alicia out of a lineup two days ago. He just nodded.

Alicia continued, "Well, you know, I guess it is because you were my first. I mean, you were the first guy I ever did it with. I know it sounds weird, but in some cultures, that would have made us married for life, right?"

He laughed. "You said you were twelve. I think in some cultures they could have stoned us to death."

She shrugged. "Well, I'm not talking exactly about how cultures work. I'm talking about some connection I've always felt. I feel like somehow we completed some circuit or something today."

He nodded. "You don't feel like that was the mushrooms?"

She just stared back.

Rage continued, "The mushrooms are making us both feel in tune with everything. Why wouldn't they make us feel more in tune with each other?"

She glared at him and spoke a little more forcefully. "You don't really think that, do you? I didn't see you and Tim back there going at it like you were completely in tune with each other. You know this is different." She paused. "Don't you?"

He did. This was different. "Yes, I do. I'm not used to feeling this way about someone but know that I've been more in tune with everything since I started eating these things. How about if they are making me even more into you?"

She laughed and grabbed one out of the bag, holding it up to Rage's mouth. "Then I guess you better have a few more before I go down on you."

A few minutes later, looking down at the wash, Rage closed his eyes, overwhelmed by the abundance and the wonders in his world.

67

Navarro Nabs Pippi

Navarro carefully navigated the slope up the hill. He was heading for the house where he had acquired the little white dog. He was heading for the home of the little girl, the one the dog called Pippi.

After he entered the gate, he smelled a cat and moved carefully along the fence, trying to get as close to the house as possible, without stepping into a well-lit area. The cat was hiding behind a four-foot wall that separated the pool from the house. Navarro could smell it, his ears all stood up and given the advantage of a multitude of canine noses, he was able to smell in what could be described as 3D. The cat, thinking it was going to surprise the intruder by jumping onto its back as it passed, was only briefly surprised when it jumped into four waiting arms.

Navarro didn't dare toy with the cat. He needed silence. Although he was certain the advantage of four arms would constantly prove itself, his first realization was with how easy it was to grip the cat's body with two hands while ripping off its head with the other two. That cat merely had time to say, "Me," and the head was rolling down Navarro's gullet before it was able to spit out the "ow."

Blood gushed from the cat's neck as Navarro held it to his side, allowing fresh tendrils to bear its weight. It drenched his arms and chest before draining it on the cement.

Navarro advanced toward the house, keeping to the shadows, avoiding the lights. He could hear children talking beyond one of the windows on the right side of the house. It turned out not to be children, but a child. He had heard several voices laughing and talking, but as he approached the window, he saw she was alone, sitting and watching. He wondered at the fact a child of no more than eight or nine would have a computer in her room. Times had certainly changed. She asked the computer, "And so what did she say?"

A girl's voice came out of the computer, "She said that he liked me."

The girl squealed, "Tell me exactly. What were her exact words?"

"I told you; I don't know. Jenna said he told Heather, and she told me. All I know is he likes me."

Navarro remembered from a lifetime spent among the living that listening to children, and girl children in particular, could be a test of one's patience. However, this was the first human discourse he'd experienced in twenty years. Hearing the girl debate with her computer, the age old he loves me he loves me not scenario was music to his ears.

She was a beautiful child. She was clean and new. Her hair, in childish pigtails, fell over her shoulders. Her face was the picture of happiness and promise. Whatever idea she had of pain, disappointment or tragedy, though undoubtedly overly dramatic given her age, was of a scale so as to be complete nonsense to an adult. Jimmy doesn't like me. Heather is prettier. All tragic in a childish way. But, true pain, lasting regret, loss - real loss - not even yet blips on the horizon.

He watched the way she moved when she talked. She moved her arms and tossed her head, still discovering which mannerisms she would make her own. She was still forming, still taking this move from that celebrity, affirming that gesture that she had copied from some woman in her life. She was so alive and was thriving. He wished he could smell her through the glass. With his enhanced hearing, he was able to hear her fine. But, even with his now spectacular set of olfactory skills, he wasn't able to get a good bead on the girl's scent. He, of course, could smell that she had been outside recently. He smelled various human smells in the yard. It struck him that it was odd he had identified the smells as 'human' smells. It was as though he was identifying the smells and categorizing them as would the canines who actually did the smelling.

He roamed the yard, carefully staying near the darkened perimeter. He sensed there had been at least two, maybe three, adults in the yard earlier and that there was the faded scent of what he assumed to be the girl.

Coming back to the window, he finally realized the girl wasn't talking to her computer, but to a little friend who somehow was talking to her through the computer. What was wrong with kids today? Wouldn't it be nice if they were both here? Talking in person. Where he could see them both. Perhaps they could take a tea outside, where he could better take them in.

***

Lisa watched in horror as Navarro watched the child. She knew why men watched girls. The quiet ones that stared, rather than speak. They didn't quite make the connection that there was a person inside. They saw a thing. Perhaps a thing of beauty, or a thing to play with, but always with an odd detachment that kept the object of their obsession firmly in the thing category.

She kicked out with her left leg as she had when the dog had attacked. Navarro caught himself and steadied himself by putting out a hand and bracing himself against the side of the house.

She tried the same thing with her right leg, but didn't even cause it to budge, owing she thought to the fact it was only a partial leg.

The nonexistent fiber of her being screamed with rage, attempting to flail her arms and legs. In her mind she screamed, *Don't you hurt this child, you mother fucker.*

***

Among the voices that made up the new Navarro, he heard a now familiar one. This was the 'fuck you, Navarro' voice. He thought, *But, I'm not going to hurt this child.*

"Fuck you, you probably weren't going to hurt me either."

Navarro frowned at the voice in his head. "Are you...?" he paused. He wondered if this was the girl. He didn't know her name. He had always thought of her as just "the girl".

He heard himself thinking, *Hell yes, I'm 'the girl. I'm the girl you murdered.*

306

But I had a name. I was Lisa. Lisa Whitely.

Navarro wondered at the voice that had entered his stream of conscious. It occurred to him he must be going crazy.

"You're god damn right you're crazy. But you already were when you killed me." The voice paused before continuing its thought. "Mother Fucker!"

Navarro didn't consider entering into a conversation with himself, or the voice, or whatever. He looked at the girl in her room. She wasn't talking to her friend anymore. She was getting ready for bed. She took a magazine from her desk, tossed it on the bed, and then climbed into bed and began flipping through its pages. He obsessed over the girl as she was obsessing over the pre-teen marketing nonsense that filled her magazine. It was designed to lure her in, just as he assumed she had been designed somehow to lure him in.

He couldn't quite concentrate on this object of his—was it desire?—because throughout the whole time the girl was examining the magazine, and he was examining the girl, two alternating mantras kept running through his head. *Lisa Whitely* followed briefly by, *you Mother Fucker!*

Navarro's distractions almost lead to his undoing. Torn between leering at the child, wondering at the faint lingering of her aroma and trying to ignore the imaginary voice screaming in his head, he failed to take note when his new arms, Lisa's former arms, began beating him about the face. If Lisa had taken a different tack, if she had kept the flailing of her arms out of his line of vision, or of any of his lines of vision, she could have done some damage. Instead, he saw the fists flying at his face and was able to wrestle his newest arms to a standoff. Throughout it all, he found himself being mentally pelted by a string of expletives that in his day, young ladies weren't wont to use.

After struggling with himself for several minutes, Navarro finally found himself forced to tear off his new arms. Each time he had felt that they had been subdued, and he would let them go, they began pummeling him with a newfound rage and an even more offensive fight song. Now he stood, holding Lisa's now lifeless arms in his hands. The arms hung to the ground. He thought, *Fuck you, Lisa Whitely. You ruined my life for the last time.*

The sound of the bones popping was loud enough that the girl looked up from her magazine. She got out of bed and came to the window. Navarro jumped to the right, and hugged the side of the house, making sure he couldn't be seen. He stood as still as he could, wondering how it was that the memory of a dead girl had brought him to this.

The girl peered out her window, wondering what had made the sound. She opened the window so she could get a better look at the yard. She looked warily out into the darkened yard.

Navarro could smell her. He could really smell her. She was exquisite. He felt a weakness in his knees as he found himself transported back to another time. He found himself flying through the decades, momentarily feasting on the smells of Innocencia, wondering at the beauty of her young body and then just as amazed by the sights and smells of the girl, Lisa. With the combination of the memories, visceral though they usually were, but now combined with the smell of this child, Navarro could barely contain himself.

Lisa was screaming, *You raped that little girl and killed me! Stop this, you bastard* as Navarro was slowly turning his head to the right, trying to see the girl. He believed she may have only been a couple of feet away from him. He wanted a better look. And perhaps just to touch her. *Leave her alone,* as she began to try to trip him again, willing her legs to knock him down.

But, Navarro was in control now. All his imaginary juices were flowing, and he used the combination of four canine noses, nine functioning eyes and his two remaining arms to determine exactly where he was in relation to the girl, and then to act on that knowledge.

Navarro whirled around to his right and thrust his arms through the window. He grabbed the girl by her arms and pulled her outside. For a fraction of a second, the girl was too stunned to react.

***

The thing that grabbed her wasn't human, and she was just old enough to have finally accepted that that wasn't possible. But just barely, and that progress was lost in an instant. It had one eye and a gaping mouth. It was covered with some kind of slimy junk and there were dogs and things caught in it. And one of them, oh God, was Bruno. After a couple of seconds of shock, she was able to start screaming. The thing held its hand over her mouth and tried to muffle her screams. She bit down and took off one of its fingers. *Oh God, it tasted terrible.* The creature didn't react to the pain, but that did open a space through which she could be heard. She screamed again as the beast used its other hand to pick her up by her waist. As she screamed for dear life, the thing carried her into the woods. She knew her dad wasn't home, but truly believed one of the neighbors would hear.

***

Navarro carried the screaming child through the woods and down the hill. He held her face with his left hand and supported her weight with his right hand tightly around her waist. Even though he could feel nothing in his extremities, mentally his right hand was on fire, knowing how close it was to the child's private parts. Navarro was alternating between joy and terror as he loped the last fifty yards to his cave.

Lisa was screaming "NO!"

68

Pippi Wakes Up

Her name was Pippi. Of course, that was just what everyone called her. But after all, isn't that what makes it your name? If one looked at her birth certificate, they would see a listing for a baby girl named Patricia McNealy. But when she was little, back before the beginning of her memories, her mother had read her a book about Pippi Longstocking. Her mom said "Goodnight, Pippi" and after that, the name stuck. Her mom died not too long after that.

She knew everyone was named after someone and she had been named after a couple of someones. Her daddy's mother was named Patricia. She had died long, long ago when her dad was just about her age now. Which, by the way, was ten. Once Pippi had been old enough for her dad to show her a Pippi Longstocking movie, she decided her mother had named her after the strange little Swedish heroine. Given that she didn't have red hair, and only had a freckle or two, she didn't look much like her namesake, but she did like to wear her hair in pigtails and often donned long leggings that looked just like what Pippi would wear. She decided that was her thing.

That of course, wasn't what she was thinking now. She was too afraid to voice it, but she wondered if she would live the night. She wondered about all the stuff they taught at school and at Sunday school about strangers. She knew to avoid them and not to go with them. She knew it wasn't okay for them to touch her in certain places and was even old enough to know why.

They taught her how to avoid being taken, but not how to prepare for having been taken.

She knew from television that sometimes kids disappeared. But they only showed you where they were taken from, not where they were taken to. Until now, she hadn't thought about it. Now it was so horrible that she wasn't really handling it all that well, to be honest. She had closed her eyes when the monster man had brought her into the cave and had been wondering about Pippi Longstocking ever since. At first, she thought the other Pippi wouldn't allow herself to be treated like this. But then, she became kind of numb to what was happening to her and started wondering if maybe this year she would be allowed to use a red rinse on her hair. She could use some water-based paint to give herself better freckles. She would look just like Pippi.

She wondered if the monster man had left her alone. She couldn't feel him touching her anymore. Earlier he had torn off her nightclothes and laid her on the ground. At that point, too in shock to scream anymore, she had kept her eyes closed tight and thought about Pippi. She remembered what all kids instinctively believed when they were small - if you can't see the monster, the monster can't see you. So far, it seemed to be working.

It was so quiet. The longer she waited, the harder it was to picture what had really happened to her - in her mind. She did a quick inventory. A monster— yes, a monster—had pulled her out of her window. He had carried her into the woods and deposited her into a cave. He stripped her down to her panties and left her laying on the soft mossy floor of the cave. And once he had done that, he—or it—had apparently left her there. When she thought of it, it didn't sound plausible. It sounded like a bad dream. A really bad dream.

She decided to look, but just for a second. She opened her eyes to a squint. The monster was still there. He was studying her legs. At least that was what it looked like, until she noticed his head was looking at her legs, but there were more heads. And one of them, sticking out of his shoulder, was a dog. But it wasn't *a* dog. It was *her* dog. Bruno. And Bruno's head was sniffing the front of her panties.

She closed her eyes, thinking that it was a much worse dream than she

311

had remembered. She decided it was time to wake up. Ever since she was little, she had been able to get out of bad dreams the same way. Her father had taught her. All she had to do was pinch herself. Knowing this would all be over soon, she let out a calm, cleansing breath and pinched her left thigh.

It worked! She woke up. Not from the dream, but from the dreamlike trance that her survival instincts had placed her in. She was on the floor of a cave with a monster.

She screamed.

69

This Time Rage Means it

Rage was overwhelmed by the beauty in the world. He'd always appreciated the finer things: pizza, weed, hotties, video games. But now, here, he understood the beauty that surrounded him. The sky. The earth. Everything that lived, and it turns out, everything that died or was dying. Stretched out before him was a world of green things, dotted with the blue and red lights that somehow tied it all together and made the green possible.

At his side, tucked under his arm, head on his shoulder... the beautiful Alicia. And she apparently saw beauty in him. She seemed to purr, having also had a few too many mushrooms, she was lost in her own kumbaya moment. He hated to disturb her, but his mouth tasted like something had died in it and he needed to get up and get the two of them something to drink.

Rage carefully moved her head off his shoulder so he could rise. "Back in a minute with some brews."

She grunted.

He asked, "You okay?"

She grunted again. It was a fairly noncommittal sort of grunt.

"You want anything else?"

Without opening her eyes, Alicia managed a breathy "Fucking... beautiful."

Rage shrugged and headed back into the house.

Tim was still in the kitchen and turned to say something, but before he could speak, Rage held up his hand in a sort of "say anything and you die" kind of way. Tim shook his head and headed off to his room.

Rage went to the refrigerator, opened it, and rustled up an armful of liquid refreshments. Armed with six-packs of both beer and Mountain Dew, Rage headed back to his now even more happy, Happy Place.

Fatty was there, looking like a dog that wanted to play. Alicia looked more like someone who wanted to impersonate a statue. Fatty was jumping back and forth, barking and doing everything his peculiar little mind could come up with to engage his potential playmate. Alicia looked like she was trying to shoo away a fly, but in slow motion. With her eyes closed, she dreamily waved her arm in Fatty's general direction.

This was enough for Fatty to believe he'd properly engaged her, so he soldiered on, barking and nipping at her fingers.

Alicia waved her arm a little faster, and slurred, "Fuck off."

Fatty had the tiniest of human vocabularies, but he'd heard "Fuck off" enough to know it was a common way to ask him to ratchet things up. In agreement, he barked the canine equivalent of "Fuck off."

Rage and Alicia both winced at the buzz killing volume coming from Fatty's incessant barking. "Fuck, dude, lay off the lady."

Fatty responded by nipping at Alicia's toes. Alicia responded by pulling up her legs into a fetal position - never opening her eyes.

Rage dropped his six packs and tried to swat Fatty away from the newly found love of his life.

Fatty barked at the playful gestures Rage was throwing, signaling he was fully engaged. This was going great, so he ran in a circle around both Rage and the motionless Alicia, then turned and jumped over her.

Rage picked up a six-pack and pulled a beer loose, intent on beaning Fatty with it, when Fatty stopped cold. Fatty's ears shot up in that way a dog's do when they hear what only dogs can hear. In an instant, Fatty turned toward the wash and sped off, leaving Rage and Alicia in a cloud of kicked up dust.

Rage shrugged, popped the top on the beer he had been about to sacrifice, and handed it to the apparent love of his life. As she sat up to accept it, flashing him a sleepy smile, he spotted a mushroom peeking out from her hairline, plucked it, and popped it into his mouth.

He sat down next to her and dug in his pocket, pulling out a joint. He lit it and offered it to her. "Fatty?"

She laughed. "Sure, when you put it like that..."

They sat there passing the joint and silently enjoying just being. Once thoroughly baked, having also eaten a few more of the mushrooms that kept cropping up, they both quietly, without discussion, stripped down and crawled into Rage's previous burial spot. They pulled the earth over themselves, held each other's hands, and peacefully drifted off to sleep.

70

Navarro Speaks!

Navarro flinched at the sound of the girl screaming. It wasn't as though he had fooled himself into thinking she was enjoying this—yet. That girl Lisa was busy screaming into his mind's ear, forcing herself above the general din of voices that flowed through and around him. But still, it was hard for minds like Navarro's to ever understand how they were truly perceived. Even now, he thought his actions were normal, and objection to them was some form of general unfairness.

The screaming girl—Pippi, the live one—kicked him in his face with her flailing legs and got to her feet, scanning the room, searching for the exit. She had caught Navarro off guard and got to the mouth of the cave just as he got to his feet. She took off like a rabbit, the kind that screams as it runs, and Navarro headed after her. Lisa, in the meantime, did her part and tried to control Navarro's purloined legs, and to ensure he couldn't catch the girl.

Unfortunately for Pippi, she was running through the hillside in her bare feet. After stubbing her toes several times, she lost a little speed and when her foot came down on a broken beer bottle, she lost her footing, tripped, and went down.

Navarro, stumbling a bit because of his slightly uncooperative legs, was still able to close the gap before Pippi could right herself. Still screaming, she found herself lifted again by the monster. But this time, he held her tighter and a whole lot rougher.

Navarro was hurt. Not physically. In that realm he was near invincible—he felt no pain. But the girl had hurt him. He had somehow believed this was something she would eventually warm to. Who wouldn't want to be the object of someone's love and attention? Carrying her back to the cave, he carried her less like the embodiment of his lifetime's obsession, and more like a spoiled child, or another addition to his collection of nutritious guests.

The girl felt tiny little things rubbing her all over her body. She didn't know what to call them. They were like long skinny worms that were sticking out of the monster man's body. Some were holding her, while others seemed to be feeling her, testing her, running along her surface, looking for better grips. A group of the worms had wrapped themselves tightly around her neck and head and held her mouth tightly closed. The sounds of her attempted screams were muffled and were soon replaced by the sound of the girl gagging as she felt the worms work their way through Pippi's nose and then down the back of Pippi's throat.

Navarro held the girl close to him. He wanted to make this work. He needed to be near her, and she had to learn to accept it. At first, he held her against him, face to face, their bodies touching. He had wanted to weave her to him, so that he could smell her and see her. Maybe he could even kiss her when she was ready. But, after holding her this way for a moment, he noted that these were old thoughts, routed in his old self. His actual face had no sense of smell. Besides, with her face next to his face, it obscured his actual view of the girl. He wanted her framed better, and nearer a functioning nose.

Navarro held the girl torso to torso, stomach to stomach. He wrapped her legs around him and held them in place with tendrils as he turned her upper body to its left, so that although she faced his face, the side of her face was on his shoulder. He imagined it looked like some sort of ballroom dance pose. The smell of the girl's face, resting less than an inch from one of the coyote's noses, was intoxicating. For a moment, Navarro was lost in a dream. A wonderful dream where Innocencia was held in just such a position, her legs tightly around him, her scent overwhelming him as they lingered, waiting to make love.

Navarro's mind may have been occupied and lost over a half century away, but his body was still at work and functioned without his further instructions. Tendrils covered the girl's body. They wrapped her tightly, and just as they had with the other small animals he had captured, they slithered around her looking for and exploiting the openings they found. They entered each orifice they found, working their way into the child, deeper and deeper. Pippi was slowly being integrated into the new and improved Mr. Navarro. Now with actual fulfillment potential.

Pippi felt the worms crawling not just all over her, but inside her. They were wiggling around in her ears and nose. They were running down her throat, making it increasingly hard to swallow. She felt one wiggling up her butt and could feel them in her vagina. Worse than the feeling of the worms in her, and the visceral fear that they were somehow eating her, was the fact that she felt that somehow that the monster man was inside her too.

Navarro could feel the new vital presence joining him. It made his dream of Innocencia even more real. He stared down at the girl. He tried to smile at her. He wanted to kiss the little girl. He wanted to feel the sweet, unspoiled lips of the little girl. He willed the tendrils to part, not just allowing him to kiss the girl, but to enjoy the perfect beauty of her face, as yet unspoiled by age. She was breathtaking. Not that there was any breath to be found in the old zombie.

As he leaned down to kiss the child, Pippi opened her mouth and yelled, "Let go of her you mother fucking, cocksucker!"

Pippi's eyes were wide with shock. She had never in her life uttered such foul language and although this monster man was probably an appropriate target for such a nasty thing to say, she couldn't keep herself from blushing at the c word. Her mouth popped open again and screamed, "Let... Her... Go!"

Pippi laughed. Well... not Pippi, but Pippi's mouth did. And then it said, "Lisa, you little bitch. Is that you?"

"Leave her alone. Haven't you killed enough?"

Navarro's face moved with the proper expression, and it mouthed the words, but so did Pippi's and that was where the sound came from, "I didn't kill you. It was an accident."

"Hitting someone in the face with a brick somehow doesn't strike most people as an accident."

"But you made me do it. I just wanted..." Navarro's could never articulate what he wanted.

"You wanted to smell my pussy. I think that is what you were after there. Were you going to fuck me too?"

Pippi's eyes were wide at the conversation that was occurring in her mouth. Her face was glowing bright red, and she was trying to squirm free. She said, "Shut up, both of you. Please, let me go."

Pippi raised her voice and yelled, "Kick him, little girl. Kick him in the crotch and then run like hell."

Pippi tried, but she could barely budge.

Navarro smiled and said through Pippi, "No, I think that Innocencia and I are ready to truly be united." Then, he leaned forward and kissed her. He kissed her forcefully and he held her tight. Although he had no tongue, in his mind's eye, he was probing her mouth with his tongue, tasting every bit of the freshness he knew she possessed. It became so real to him he believed he could feel his tongue actually moving. More to the point, it was so real it actually felt like he had a tongue. He realized that for the first time since coming back to life, he could taste. It had been so long, and it took a few seconds to identify the flavor. He had believed he was tasting Innocencia's young, willing tongue, but that wasn't it. It turned out to be the taste of rotting mushrooms. He opened his eyes to the realization that he was using the girl's tongue to kiss himself. He couldn't be sure if it was his reaction or the girl's, but he suddenly felt the urge to vomit. It was a need that would have to go unheeded, as he couldn't really see the point, or the possibility.

Pippi started to say, "That was disgusting," but before she could spit it out, she lost control and began projectile vomiting onto Navarro's face.

71

Fatty Barges in

Fatty, having heard the sound of a girl screaming just moments before, heads down the hill and straight for the cave where he'd once hidden a wonderful stash of bones. He was overcome with the wonder of the olfactory extravaganza he had walked into. Rotting decay, dead and dying animals, bones and what was that, vomit? It was dog heaven. And looking up, there was that stupid bone man who had tried to hurt him. Wasn't that always the way? There was always something getting in the way of perfect dog happiness. At least the bone man had his back to Fatty. He crept up and bit his ankle, getting a mouthful of fungus. He spat it out and went for another bite when Navarro turned around.

A child that was attached to the bone man looked down, eyes wide and shouted, "Well, if it isn't my little friend, the bone thief. Come back for another snack?"

Fatty stood still, staring back and forth from the bone man and the child it held. He of course had no idea what the child had said - he was a dog for Christ's sake. But he knew the child. He had played with her and her friends. The look on her face didn't belong there. She looked like someone else. He barked, "Hey you, nice girl there. What the hell is wrong with you? Hey, do you have a ball or something we could play with?"

Of course, what Pippi heard was something along the lines of "woof woof... "

During the moments of Fatty's confusion and communication failures, Navarro was able to pick up a good-sized rock. It was plenty heavy enough to allow him, once he got a good opening, to bash in that god damn dog's skull. He realized his days of using animals to regain his senses was over. He would use this girl and then, when she was consumed, find more. They were a little harder to catch, but oh, they were going to be worth the trouble. He could use them as puppets to lure others. When he heard through their ears it wouldn't be muffled with the confusion brought on by dumb animals. When he smelled what they smelled, it wouldn't be polluted with some disembodied need to sniff out dog shit or other foul odors. He thought that maybe, just maybe, he could feel the rest of their bodies. He could explore them in ways as a human he couldn't have even dreamed of.

But first...the dog.

Pippi, who recognized the dog as she would any of the dogs in her neighborhood said, "Run Fatty, Run. Go get help."

None of that was in any way meaningful to Fatty, who neither understood human all that well or had ever seen an episode of Lassie. That said, the confusion in the cave, along with the distraction of the thousands of smells assailing Fatty did create the almost perfect opportunity for Navarro to rid himself of the dog forever.

Almost.

Navarro brought down one of his mighty bludgeons and hit Fatty, not in the head as intended, but in the shoulder, knocking Fatty across the cave and onto a rock outcropping.

Fatty stood with some difficulty, bleeding from his neck and shoulder. He glared at the bone man and took a few steps to get a feel for his injury. Something was wrong and for the first time realized the bone man wasn't as fun as he had always thought. Fatty limped to the mouth of the cave, turned, and shouted a series of scolds and swear words that only had meaning for dogs, then ran out of the cave, looking to find some love and sympathy from his people.

72

Not With My Dog!

Tim looked out the back window and could see the tops of Rage's and Alicia's heads sticking out of the hole where he'd recently found Rage. He thought, "Damn it, here we go again."

Heading out to the place where they lay, he saw that Rage had once again buried himself in his Happy Place, this time dragging his latest lady friend into the mix. Noting the spotty job they'd done burying themselves, it was pretty clear they were naked too.

"That's it. This has got to stop."

Thinking out loud, he muttered, "Time for a serious anti-fungal assault." He headed next door to raid Mr. Hardman's tool shed.

At the sound of the words "anti-fungal assault," Rage, his face obscured by dirt, opened his eyes. He looked toward where Tim had gone and began to climb out of his hole. Alicia stirred, but he patted her head and whispered, "Be right back." Using exaggerated ninja like stealth, the naked, heavily medicated Rage followed Tim at a safe distance.

As they moved through the trees to the edge of the wash, where they could cross properties out past the wall, Rage picked up a rock. He wasn't sure what he was going to do with it but was feeling a little too naked and vulnerable.

Up ahead, Tim entered Don's shed. While he was rummaging around, looking for Don's weed or fungus killing paraphernalia, Rage crept up and bolted the door.

Tim called out, "Hey!"

Rage leaned in close to the door and whispered, "You need to stay out of my shit."

"Open the door."

"Sorry man, that shit has sailed."

"Damn it, Rage, open the door."

As he walked away, Rage called over his shoulder, "My lady and I have a date with destiny, and you just need to cool your heels for a bit."

Walking around the wall, Rage could still hear the sound of Tim pounding on the shed door and yelling for Rage to come let him out. Rage muttered, "Yeah, fuck that."

As he was about to burrow in next to Alicia, Fatty came up out of the wash, hop-limping and covered in blood. Seeing Fatty's condition flipped Rage's mood from quasi-suicidal to full-on homicidal. He ran over to Fatty's side and tried to check his shoulder, but Fatty yelped and jumped away at Rage's touch.

Fatty hopped a few yards toward the wash, then stopped, turned, and looked over his shoulder in a way he hoped even Rage would understand.

Rage stared at him for a moment and Fatty jumped again, another foot toward the wash, without turning away from Rage.

After a few more of Fatty's feints, Rage nodded, then looked around where he stood until he saw the shovel he wished he'd found when he and Alicia had been burying themselves. He grabbed the shovel, turned to Fatty, nodded and said, "Come on boy, let's fuck some shit up!"

Fatty started hop-limping down into the wash with a newly energized Rage following behind him, armed with a rusty shovel.

73

Rage Crashes the Party

Fatty charged into the cave, barking a fair warning that trouble was on the way.

The multi-headed mass that was Navarro and the soon to be fully melded Pippi, turned its Pippi head toward the commotion. Pippi called out, "Fatty, you came back. Save me boy." Then she shook her head and scoffed. "Fatty? What kind of dog's name is Fatty?"

Rage stepped into the room in time to say, "My dog's kind of name."

Navarro and Pippi regarded the naked, filthy man standing in the mouth of the cave. Navarro could feel the child's reflexive recoiling at the sight of a naked man and felt for her. He turned a bit, so her back was to the man. He thought not only would he be protecting her delicate sensibilities from this obvious miscreant, but if things went south, she would be a good shield.

Rage said, "Hey, Mister Navarro?"

Navarro squinted. Pippi said, "You know me?"

Rage shrugged, "Well, yeah. You used to live next door when I was a kid. I mean, you look like shit and all. I'm guessing you're some kind of zombie now. But yeah, I recognize you and guess I knew you, too."

Navarro struggled to place the face. He really never paid all that much attention to little boys. They smelled nasty, and besides, he wasn't that kind of guy. Pippi looked at Rage quizzically. "You said next door. Are you Bob and Nancy's boy?"

Rage said, "That's right. Bob and Nancy Sutherland. I'm Rage. But back then you would have known me as Reggie, you sick old fuck."

Navarro eyed him and nodded slowly. "How are Bob and Nancy?"

Rage was momentarily struck by the oddity that he was conversing with this old zombie by way of the child he was carrying. But then again, Rage had spent a lifetime watching horror movies, playing video games, and getting stoned, so it was just a momentary oddity. Everything about it was easily incorporated into his world view. In fact, this just might be the type of situation he had been training for his whole life. He got the hang of it pretty quickly, considering. He said, "They're dead."

Navarro nodded and the little girl said, "Yes... There's a lot of that going around."

The child leaned its head back and screamed, "Kill this fucker. He's going to kill the child."

Once again, to a rational, linear thinker, this would have been a real mind twister. But, to Rage, it made a kind of poetic sense. Clearly there was a larger cast at play here than the naked eye revealed, but Rage realized almost immediately that among the multitude that may or may not be in the room right now, Mr. Navarro was clearly the asshole. Zombies usually were.

Rage said, "Mr. Navarro. I need you to put down the little girl."

Navarro found it freeing to be able to speak again. In life, he had found it increasingly bothersome to have to deal with polite chatter. The older he got, the more it seemed that every conversation that needed to be had already had happened. Past the age of forty, it was all just the same useless warmed-over drivel, masquerading as a reason to interact with others. He had found himself more and more retreating into his own quiet, hermit-like existence. If you had asked him thirty years ago how it would have been to be locked away somewhere without the ability to get dragged into conversation, he would have told you it sounded perfect. But after twenty years in the dirt without the ability to project his own thoughts and ideas, the ability to talk, even to this weird hippie boy, was just about the icing on his cake.

Navarro said, "Well, you see, Reggie, I don't think I can do that. You see, the girl's with me now." Then, he began to thrust his hips in a crude pantomime of humping. Without being able to control herself, Pippi threw her head back and laughed a maniacal little girl laugh.

Then, as if her head was on some kind of hinge, it turned at a strange, seemingly impossible angle and looked straight at Rage and she said, "Kill this mother fucking asshole. Bash his head in. You go high. I'll go low." Pippi turned her head back and looked Navarro in his eye and said "I've watched you kill me over and over for forty years now. I think I'm going to really enjoy this."

Rage watched as Mr. Navarro seemed to lose his footing. Really, his legs just seemed to give way. He fell to his knees and Rage didn't miss a beat. He stepped forward and swing his shovel into Navarro's head. He swung again, lower this time and could hear the sound of the bone's breaking in Navarro's neck. He swung again and knocked his head back, causing it to hang loosely behind him. It looked like it was held on by some strands of fungus. Rage then kicked twice at his shoulder and where his head was still attached.

As Rage waited for the now obviously defeated zombie to fall, these tendrils began to pull Navarro's head back into roughly the right spot, but at an odd angle. His shoulder began to reform where Rage had crushed it and the dog head—*shit was that a dog head?*—started licking the wound that Rage had formed. Pippi said, "You can't be serious. You want to kill me? I've been dead more years than this child was alive. Yes, little girl, that's right. You're mine now and the end of your miserable little life has come. But I offer you more than you could have dreamed of in your little mortal mind."

Navarro was slowly starting to stand now and Pippi screamed, "Stay down, you miserable old bastard." But Lisa wasn't able to control her legs anymore. Navarro was back in charge.

"That's right. It's no more my little pony and pretty little pink plastic crap for you, sweetheart. From now on, we'll have the whole world at our feet. We'll dine on the finest people and watch as civilizations crumble."

Pippi looked at Navarro's head, the way it tilted and the way that he didn't really look like he was in there anymore. Before he had looked like some big monster man, but now, he was like a bunch of slime covered bones, but like at a fun house where you knew there wasn't really anyone in it. You knew it was just controlled by someone in the ceiling pulling strings. She said, "Let me go. You aren't even real."

She smiled and shook her head, "Oh, we're real all right."

Rage yelled, "Who are you?" But he thought he knew.

"We are ... many. We are that is, and all that we will become."

Navarro's jaw hung loose where Rage had kicked it. The tendrils that hung from Navarro's face were pulling it into place while both Rage and Pippi were visualizing Navarro as a puppet.

Navarro and Pippi both turned to look at Rage as Pippi said, "You know me, boy. You, too, are one of my children and have chosen a new path. You've chosen to follow the light. To follow it home."

Rage asked, "The light? Home?" But he knew. The light he had seen for days had been calling him to this spot. It had helped him spot the fertile places where the fungus could grow. Or was growing. For God's sake, he was no fucking nerd scientist, but he was getting the picture.

He asked, "Why are you trying to eat the girl? Aren't you supposed to feast on the dead and rotting."

"All things die and all things rot. Then they all come to me."

"But you don't usually kill them, do you?"

Pippi whined, "But I'm not killing her. I just wanted to taste her..." Pippi swallowed, savoring. "So fresh." The tendrils that held her to Navarro pulled at her legs, causing her to shift her position, pulling her even tighter against him.

Pippi spoke, "This is not our way. The Navarro chose the human girl. But all things come to us in their end. There is no judgment."

A voice in Rage's head agreed. This was togetherness. The girl, too, was joining the community he was about to join. Of course, he was going willingly, whereas she was being taken as a captive.

Rage asked, "So, what the fuck are you?"

Pippi nodded, "I am everything. We are everything. All voices are present, and we are together. I am the mother."

Pippi then added, "Bullshit. They aren't everything. There's more. Much more. I've been there many times."

Rage asked, "Where's there?"

Pippi said, "Everywhere and every time. And someplace else... but never with her."

Both Pippi and Navarro stared into Rage's face, "Boy, you know that's not true. You've been with us. You know the truth."

Rage had to agree. He'd been feeling the love and knew the fungus was where he was bound. It was a fresh start. A do over and the next phase of his becoming. He was ready and didn't see any reason to fight it anymore. It was the voice of reason. He dropped his shovel and stepped forward to embrace his path.

Pippi turned to Rage and yelled, "Jesus, you fucking loser. Don't you see what's happening here?"

Fatty ran-hopped around Rage, barking his head off.

Rage said, "Oh yes, I see it." He closed his eyes and smiled, "And it's beautiful."

Rage put his arms around Navarro and the child. He held them tight and felt tendrils begin to embrace him, wrapping around his legs and arms, beginning to enter him.

74

Tim Gets His Axe On

Tim had grown horse yelling for Rage. He was pretty sure Rage wasn't coming back. There was just enough light in the shed for him to make out the tools lining the wall. As he saw the two-headed axe leaning against the wall just a foot from the door, he smiled. Although it seemed an odd choice for a suburban tool shed, on this day it seemed the perfect find. He thought, "If you are going to be locked in a shed, a tool shed is the one to choose."

Never having actually swung an axe before, Tim discovered the weight of the head pretty much made up for his inexperience. It only took three swings before the door unhinged, collapsed, and let in a blinding light.

Standing in the open doorway, Tim scanned the shed. Sitting on a workbench, nestled among the various rusting bug sprays and rotting bags of fertilizer, he spotted a half-gallon jug of a very popular weed killer. It had a spray nozzle attached, and Tim checked the label to ensure it would take out fungus. He was going to make sure Rage's little happy place was cleared of its newly discovered fairy ring, and then he was going to take both his asshole roommate and his date to the hospital.

He was surprised to find Rage's little homemade grave half empty. Alicia was still asleep, and it occurred to him he didn't know her well enough to wake her with a poison shower. He was about to politely tap her shoulder with his axe handle when he heard the commotion. It had started with some muffled shouting down in the wash but was punctuated by some serious arguments coming from Fatty.

Looking down toward the wash, he caught sight of what looked to be a trail of blood, and briefly wondering if he had just heard someone shout "fucking loser." It sounded to him like someone perfectly describing Rage. He tightened up his grip on both the axe and jug of weed killer and headed down the path.

75

Navarro Takes the Hit

Rage could feel the wonder of it all. Voices swirled through him, and the fungus was encircling him. He had never felt so alive, so connected. The girl broke into his thoughts. "Save me."

He looked at her. She was crying. She asked again, "Please, Rage, save me. I don't want to die."

He shrugged, smiled, and said, "We all die, honey. It's gonna be okay."

She shook her head and said, "I know that we all die. But I'm not ready. I'm just a little girl."

He heard his dad screaming in his head, "Reggie, son, for Christ's sake, save the girl."

Rage had always been a loner. His parents had always wanted him to go out and make friends. He had a few friends, just not the kind his parents wanted for him. They didn't play ball or go to the mall together. They skateboarded, got high, and looked for excitement. And they played video games. Now he was going to join something bigger than himself, and even now, here was his dad, bitching at him.

He glanced down. He was being swallowed up into the mass that was Mr. Navarro and the child. And something suddenly hit him. He may not have learned much all those years playing video games, but one thing he had learned was this: if you are picking sides, don't go with the virgin-eating zombie. They were usually the bad guys.

Rage let go of Mr. Navarro and the girl, and pushed himself away, falling down. He had tendrils wrapped all around his lower half. He started ripping at them with both hands. He pulled away what had been winding up his ass and encircling his junk and stood.

As Rage stood and kicked Navarro, he felt the fungus in his body start to cramp up. He felt his strength starting to fade as he reached down and grabbed the girl by her waist. He pulled at her with all his might, while voices in his head screamed at him both to stop and listen to reason and to cheer him on.

The girl was screaming too.

Rage wasn't sure he was doing the right thing and stopped pulling on her as she screamed, "Stop it, you're killing me!"

He looked down to make sure he wasn't really hurting her, when she punched him in the face and screamed, "Let her go, she's ours now." The girl, her extremities now freed from the tendrils that had bound her to Navarro, kicked out with all her might and connected with Rage's unprotected balls. He crumpled over as she jumped onto Navarro, wrapping herself around him.

As the girl was being pulled into a tighter union with Navarro, she screamed, "Please help me, Rage, Please."

Rage was sure he would be pissing blood for a week if he lived that long. He stood, holding his wounded scrotum while watching the girl being sucked into the pile of Mr. Navarro's bones and flesh. He let go of his junk and reached for Pippi, hugging her tightly when he heard his roommate's voice behind him.

"What in the fuck!?"

Rage turned to look as Tim dropped the jug of weed killer and came running into the room, axe handle coming up, ready to swing. Rage yelled, "Don't hit the girl."

Tim said, "I'm not gonna hit the girl, I'm just gonna hit you, you fucking pervert."

Rage was able to jump out of the way of the axe as it swung by where his head had been a half second before.

Tim readied himself for a second swing when he heard the girl scream, "Don't hurt him!" He looked at the naked little girl. He knew that sometimes molestation victims tried to protect their molesters. He couldn't believe all this time he had been living with a child molester. He turned to make sure Rage wouldn't get near the girl again.

Rage stood where Tim had entered the cave, holding the weed killer jug in his left hand and the spray nozzle in his right. He said, "Stand back, Bro. This isn't for you."

Perhaps it was because no matter how big a fuck-up your roommate is, thirty seconds is too short a time span to completely wrap your head around something as vile as them being a child molester. And of course, there was the slimy thing wrapped around the girl. Tim stepped aside.

Rage stepped up to the mass of fungus, fur, meat, and bones that clung to the child. He said, "Close your eyes, sweetheart."

Pippi closed her eyes and Rage began to spray Mr. Navarro.

Tim shifted his gaze back and forth between Rage, the girl, and the—what the fuck was that thing—zombie? Having been so absorbed by his first vision of a naked Rage and the girl, he'd entirely missed the main attraction. Now his mind was starting to seize up.

During the ten seconds or so it took for Mr. Navarro to melt down to bone, the girl stood up and turned to address Rage. "Please spare us. The Navarro is gone from us. Leave us, we mean you no harm."

Rage shook his head. "Sorry bitch. Once you've tasted the forbidden fruit, you can't go back."

Rage sprayed down the room and then unscrewed the top of the weed killer jug. He looked down at it, took a deep breath, and took a drink.

Tim ran up to him, "Jesus, man, that stuff is poison."

Rage coughed and said, "Yeah, but they always tell you shit is worse than it is. I'm sure this is what they gave me at the hospital, just without all the fancy prices."

Rage turned to the little girl. She looked dazed. He handed her the jug and said, "Take a little drink. Not too much or it'll make you puke."

She did as she was told. Then she coughed a bit and sat and started crying.

Rage took the axe from Tim and started methodically smashing Mr. Navarro's bones into dust. Fatty, of course, squirreled away a few for later.

VI

Thursday

76

Aftermath - Epilogue Sounds Too ... You Know

Rage and Pippi sat outside of the cave, watching the stars which were just starting to come out. They were still naked, but they couldn't have cared less. Anyway, it would be remedied soon enough, as Tim had gone up the hill to get Rage some clothes and a blanket and an oversized t-shirt for Pippi.

Rage could feel the emptiness in him as the weed killer had done its work and removed the fungus from his system. He knew he had done the right thing, killing Mr. Navarro and freeing the child, but he felt the loneliness overtaking him again.

Pippi put her arm around him and said, "Thank you for saving me."

He said, "I guess it was nothing."

She said, "No Rage, it wasn't nothing. I know just how you felt. I know what you think you gave up. You're my hero."

Rage blushed. He didn't feel like a hero but felt a rush of warmth at the idea that to this little girl he had made a difference. He'd made very few positive impressions in his life. He thought about Alicia up the hill, still melting into the fungus, and knew he was about to bum her out too. Somehow, thinking about Alicia gave him another hit of warmth. He hoped they could still connect without the mushrooms. They had to face life without the hard stuff.

From here on out, it was just Mountain Dew, beer and weed.

***

For the last few years, the scenes of her life that Lisa relived reduced in number. There were hard lessons she had to learn over and over again. There were pleasures, to be sure, and she had felt that even in her toughest sessions, there were blessings.

Except for one. Her murder. She had found some peace in some details, but she had never been able to make sense of Navarro. He was evil. He had killed her. And there had been no reason for it. He hadn't raped her. He hadn't robbed her. He hadn't even meant to do anything to her. He had wanted to smell her, and it just made no fucking sense. She hated him and saw no point in any of it. Reliving the scene made a kind of sense to her, but why she kept reliving it made no sense to her. There was no new insight to be gained.

Emile Navarro hadn't just come into being one afternoon in 1969 for the purpose of brutally killing Lisa. There was more to him than she would ever understand. He hadn't chosen to be what he was. It had been the result of God only knew what. In fact, those who had made him the way he was were also the result of countless other unknowable forces.

Hating Navarro wasn't helping her. It wasn't hurting him. And it was holding her here.

Lisa forgave Mr. Navarro... and was gone.

***

Mr. Navarro waited quietly. He had all the time in the world and couldn't imagine how he would fill it. First off, he wanted to understand what had gone wrong. Was there something he could have done differently? He would use this time to wonder and question himself.

He tried to move something... anything. He was in pieces all over the floor of his cave. Nothing would move. He thought about that sweet smelling young girl. She had been his undoing. Why was it always the girls that messed things up for him? What was it about them that both made life worth living, yet made it so painful and filled him with regret?

That damn dog with the stupid name ate a couple more of his bones when that awful boy destroyed him. He couldn't sense their presence, so assumed that whatever it was that held him here was specific to some particular set of bones. He didn't know how long it would take for that particular bone, or set of bones, to decompose, or for that matter, if it would matter that they did. All he knew was, the twenty years he had already done were going to look like a cake walk in a few hundred years.

He remembered the smell of the girl in his mind's eye and wished he could forget.

Made in United States
Orlando, FL
10 September 2024

51369664R10191